Rosie GOODWIN

The Winter Promise

ZAFFRE

First published in the UK in 2020
This paperback edition published in 2021 by
ZAFFRE
An imprint of Bonnier Books UK
80–81 Wimpole St, London W1G 9RE
Owned by Bonnier Books
Sveavägen 56, Stockholm, Sweden

A CIP catalogue record for this book is
available from the British Library.

ISBN: 978–1–83877–299–4

Also available as an ebook

1 3 5 7 9 10 8 6 4 2

Typeset by IDSUK (Data Connection) Ltd
Printed and bound in Great Britain by Clays Ltd, Elcograf S.p.A.

Zaffre is an imprint of Bonnier Books UK
www.bonnierbooks.co.uk

Y035860

The Winter

Rosie Goodwin is a *Sunday Times* bestselling author, and the first writer in the world to be allowed to follow three of Catherine Cookson's trilogies with her own sequels. Having worked in the social services sector for many years, then fostered a number of children, she is now a full-time novelist. She is one of the top 50 most borrowed authors from UK libraries. Rosie lives in Nuneaton, the setting for many of her books, with her husband and their beloved dogs. *The Winter Promise* is her thirty-fifth published novel.

Also by Rosie Goodwin

The Bad Apple
No One's Girl
Dancing Till Midnight
Tilly Trotter's Legacy
Moonlight and Ashes
The Mallen Secret
Forsaken
The Sand Dancer
Yesterday's Shadows
The Boy from Nowhere
A Rose Among Thorns
The Lost Soul
The Ribbon Weaver
A Band of Steel
Whispers
The Misfit
The Empty Cradle
Home Front Girls
A Mother's Shame
The Soldier's Daughter
The Mill Girl
The Maid's Courage

The Claire McMullen Series
Our Little Secret
Crying Shame

This book is for Charlotte Bethany Yates, my precious granddaughter, to mark the occasion of her 18th birthday. I am so proud of you and love you millions!

Chapter One

'*Please*, Opal . . . can we stop now? Me feet are hurtin' an' me tummy aches.'

'Not yet, sweetheart, we have to find somewhere to stay first before it gets properly dark.'

Opal Sharp stared down at Susie, her six-year-old sister and gave her an encouraging smile as she shifted the weight of her two-year-old brother, Jack, on her hip. He was fast asleep, although how he managed it she had no idea. She had wrapped him tightly in her shawl, then tied it about her waist – but despite the bitter cold she could feel the burning heat of him against her chest, and she was gravely concerned.

He obviously had the fever that had taken their father just days before, and she was all too aware that he shouldn't be out in the bad weather – but she had had no choice in the matter. The cottage they had lived in was tied to the farm that her father had worked for, and when he died, the farmer had turned up on the day of the funeral and told her they must all be out by late afternoon.

Left with no alternative, Opal had instructed Charlie to load whatever he could of their possessions on to the hand-cart, and now they were in search of somewhere to shelter from the storm. The snow was coming down thick and fast, getting deeper underfoot by the minute, and behind her she could hear fifteen-year-old Charlie grunting softly with exertion as he yanked at the handles of the small wooden cart, piled with bags and bedding. The rest of their possessions had been left with a kindly neighbour until they found somewhere to stay.

'I'd have you all 'ere in a sigh,' Mrs Kitely had told them sympathetically. 'But I daren't upset Farmer Gold, else my Stan might be out of a job an' all.'

'We – have – to – find – somewhere soon,' Charlie gasped. 'I don't know how much further I can pull this thing.'

'We'll find somewhere, you'll see,' Opal answered, with a confidence she was far from feeling.

They had already tramped for miles: first down the old Roman Road, then through the village of Hartshill. They had then slid and slithered their way down Bucks Hill, and now they were on the ground known to the locals as Rapper's Hole. It was nothing more than a wasteland of fields with a scattering of huts and dilapidated cottages here and there, but Opal could think of nowhere else they could go. Even a run-down cottage would be some shelter from the cold – if they could only find one.

They trudged on, getting more dispirited by the minute, but at last a building loomed up out of the snow ahead of them and, dropping the handles of the cart, Charlie rushed towards it. It appeared to be a very old derelict cottage.

'It's empty,' he shouted excitedly. 'Perhaps we could rest here for the night, Opal?'

As she approached, she saw that there was a large hole in the roof on one side of the building. It was surrounded by a picket fence from which an old gate hung on a single hinge. The tiny, leaded windows – or what remained of them – were black and bleak-looking and it seemed barely habitable. But then she supposed Charlie was right – any port in a storm would be welcome at that moment.

As Susie raced ahead, Opal followed as fast as she could. On entering, she found herself in what she presumed must once have been a small kitchen-cum-sitting room, although it was hard to see in the all-enveloping gloom. The roof in this room seemed to be intact, so, making a quick decision, she turned to Charlie. 'Go and grab the cart. We'll light some candles and try to get a fire going.'

He was gone before the words had left her mouth and, soon, she heard him grunting as he yanked the cart down the small, overgrown path. Placing Jack in Susie's arms, she located the candles and matches and managed to light one; they looked around. There were odd bits of broken furniture lying about, so at least they would have some dry wood for the fire. A small inglenook fireplace was set into one wall and, after scraping out the dead ashes with his hands, Charlie began to break the wood into pieces and set them into the fire basket. Presently he had it alight and now, with the candle burning and the faint glow from the fire, they could better see the room. A grimy deep stone sink stood against one wall and low beams framed the ceiling, but at least this room was fairly dry. The floor was littered with dirt and, from the terrible smell that hung in the air, Opal suspected animals had found refuge here. Her heart sank; she couldn't believe how quickly their lives had changed, and they were now reduced to sleeping here – but she couldn't think about that now.

Pushing her worries aside, she searched through the cart and pulled out the blankets she had packed, shaking the snow from them. Little Susie was struggling to keep her eyes open and Opal laid some of the blankets on the floor in front of the fire.

'Take the kettle and fill it with snow. I'll make us a brew of tea and at least it will warm us,' she instructed Charlie.

While Charlie was doing that, Opal settled Susie and Jack on the blankets and blocked up the broken panes in the window with rags and anything that came to hand. Soon the kettle was heating up over the fire, and Opal rooted in the cart for the half a loaf she had brought with them. Tearing chunks off it, she handed a piece each to Jack and Susie. But while Susie hungrily began to gnaw on hers, Jack turned his head away.

'He really needs to see a doctor,' Charlie said worriedly, noting the beads of sweat on his forehead that stood out like jewels in the red glow of the flames.

Opal snorted. 'I don't even know how we're going to *eat* tomorrow, let alone pay for a doctor's visit!' she snapped, but was instantly repentant. 'Sorry, Charlie, I'm just tired,' she explained guiltily.

'It's all right.' He patted her arm awkwardly and fell silent as she poured the now-boiling water into an old brown tea-pot and set it on the hearth to mash. She found the mismatched cups and poured them their tea and soon Susie was snoring softly.

Opal almost envied her. She seemed to have no idea what a terrible position they were in. It was hard to believe that only a few short months before they had been a close-knit, happy family. Admittedly, her mother had suffered from ill health for some time, so Opal had had to give up her job in the little village shop to help at home, but even then they had been comfortable with the wages that her father and Charlie earned on the farm.

Then their hearts had all broken when their mother had died giving birth to a stillborn baby girl, and just nine weeks later their world collapsed when their father was suddenly struck down with the fever, and soon followed their ma. Now here they were, with no home, no parents, no money and no prospects.

'What are we goin' to do, Opal?' Charlie's face was fearful. Although he was only a year younger than his sister, he usually depended on her to make the decisions.

'Whatever we have to do to survive,' she answered, although she dreaded what might be ahead.

'I think we may well have to put the little two into the workhouse. At least Jack can see a doctor there, and they'll both be fed,' he said tentatively.

Opal was so horrified that she almost dropped her cup and slopped hot tea over her leg. 'Ouch! *Over my dead body*!'

'Well, have you got a *better* idea?' Tears stung at the back of his eyes as he pictured the cold grim façade of the Union Workhouse up on the Bullring, but he pushed back his mop of thick, curly brown hair and blinked them away. Just the mention of the place could strike terror into the hardest of hearts, but what choice did they have? At least, if he knew the little ones were being looked after, he and Opal could find work and somewhere to live and hopefully they could get them back out of the place before too long. As she miserably shook her head, his voice gentled. 'It would only be until we could find somewhere decent to live and have enough money coming in to feed them.'

'I know, but I can't bear to think of them in that place, or of us separated. We're the only family they've got now; we need to stick together.'

She hung her head despondently as she stared at her two younger siblings. With their thick, black hair and their pale skin, they looked like two little peas in a pod. They all did, if it came to that, as they took after their late mother in looks. She could hear her father even now laughing and teasing that it wasn't fair that not one of his children had taken after him. As the painful memories of happier times rushed back, she rose and went to stuff an old sack beneath the door to try and stop the wicked draught that was whistling beneath it.

'Let's try an' get some sleep, eh?' Charlie suggested, seeing that Opal was almost at the end of her tether. 'Jack might be a lot better in the morning an' things will look brighter. An' at least we have somewhere dry to sleep.'

She managed to raise a weak smile, but as she curled up beneath the thin blanket she wasn't so sure, and when she finally fell into an exhausted sleep there were tears on her cheeks.

Chapter Two

Early the next morning, Opal woke to an eerie, grey silence, and as she stared towards the window, all she could see was the snow piled high on the ledge. The fire was almost out and it was bitterly cold again, so she hastily broke up what was left of an old chair and threw it on to the fire. Charlie stretched and yawned and, pulling himself on to his elbow, asked, 'What time is it?'

Opal shrugged. 'I don't know. We took the mantel clock to the pawnbroker's last week, if you remember?' She could have added, 'Along with everything else decent we owned,' but thought better of it – although she had managed to keep her mother's wedding ring, which she wore on a string around her neck. She put her hand over it now, to reassure herself it was still there.

'Ah, yes.' He sighed and, pushing his blanket aside, rose and lifted the kettle. 'I'll go and get some more snow. At least we can have a hot drink.'

They had no sugar or milk, but they'd grown used to drinking their tea without over the last weeks.

After slipping his boots on, Charlie attempted to open the door and was almost knocked over by the drift that had piled up against it during the night as it spilled into the room.

'Cor blimey,' he breathed. 'Would yer just look at that!' As far as his eye could see was nothing but a vast, eerily silent white wilderness. He suddenly felt as if they might be the only people left in the world. Even the birds weren't singing, and the snow was still coming down like a thick white blanket. Hastily, he stooped and filled the kettle then, kicking what he could of the snow back out of the door, he quickly closed it again.

Susie stirred at that moment and when she looked towards the window she clapped her hands with delight. 'Ooh, look at the snow,' she chirped. 'Will I be able to go out on me sledge, Opal?'

Opal smiled indulgently as she smoothed the fall of black curls from the little girl's face. Suddenly she felt old; not so long ago, she would have been excited to see the snow, too. Now she could only see the problems it would bring.

'Your sledge is back at Mrs Kitely's, love,' she explained and Susie pouted. But then she began to cough, and Opal quickly felt her forehead. It was hot and Opal's heart sank. It looked as if Susie was about to come down with the fever, too.

Charlie also looked concerned as he saw the unnatural flush in his little sister's cheeks, but he said nothing as he wedged the kettle into the heart of the fire.

'Right now, let's see what we've got for breakfast,' Opal said in a falsely bright voice, as she rummaged in the small food bag in the cart. 'Ah, we have some oats here, look, that should fill us up.' They had no milk so she would have to boil them in water and they would be fairly tasteless – but she supposed it was better than nothing.

'I'm not hungry.' As Susie burrowed down beneath her blanket again, Charlie and Opal exchanged a worried glance.

Opal boiled the remainder of the oats and somehow, she and Charlie washed them down with tea; but Susie refused them and Opal decided it was best to let Jack sleep.

'We're going to have to get some food in,' Opal muttered, glancing worriedly at the blizzard beyond the window. 'Though goodness knows how we're going to get through this lot. The nearest store to here is in Stockingford.'

'I know where it is,' Charlie assured her. 'And don't worry, I'll get through. But do we have any money left for food? And where are we going to stay tonight?'

'It looks like we'll have to stay here,' Opal responded. 'I can give the room a clean and at least it's dry. And yes, I do have a little left from the money we got at the pawnbroker's, but not much.'

As she rummaged in the pocket of her dress and withdrew a few pennies, Charlie sighed. 'We're not going to get much with that,' he commented glumly.

'We'll just get basics: some flour, a twist of tea and a pat of butter. I can bake some bread then. There's a small oven in the side of the inglenook, look, though I dread to think what state it will be in. But never mind, I can soon scrub it out while you're gone. I'll have a look round the other rooms as well and see if there's anything we can use to make ourselves a little more comfortable. It looks like we're going to be stuck here at least until the snow goes.'

Charlie pulled his boots on and wrapped up as warmly as he could. Then, with a nod at his sister, he set off.

The two smaller children were snoring softly so, now that it was light, Opal decided to see what state the rest of the rooms were in. A door was set into the wall at the side of the fireplace and on opening it she found herself in what had clearly once been a bedroom. It was so cold in there that it almost took her breath away, so she quickly stepped inside, shutting the door behind her to keep what warmth she could in the kitchen, clutching her shawl more tightly about her. There was a yawning hole in the roof and a pile of snow was heaped in the centre of the room. Against one wall was an old iron-framed bed with what remained of a straw mattress on it, and against another wall was a chest of drawers with one drawer missing.

Well, there's no way we can use this room until the roof has been repaired, she thought despondently, kicking at what appeared to be the remains of a wooden chair. At least the wood could be used to keep the fire burning, though. She quickly stooped to gather it up and carried it back to the kitchen, before cautiously starting up a staircase, which was little more than a ladder, that led to the upper storey.

She found herself in a small, surprisingly dry room with yet another old bed standing against one wall. The roof sloped and she could only stand up in the centre of the room, but even so, she could see that without too much work it could become usable.

She went back down the stairs as quietly as she could so as not to wake the children, and opened the last door to the other side of the fireplace. She found herself in what had clearly once been used as a small sitting room. An old sideboard, thick with dirt and grime, stood beneath the window, but a quick glance around showed that the rest of the furniture was broken and probably beyond repair, apart from a solid-looking oak table that took pride of place in the centre of the room.

With a sigh, Opal made her way back into the kitchen and began to remove some of the cleaning things she had loaded into the cart, deciding that she could clean the kitchen up at least. Next, she filled the kettle with more snow and, after heating it on the fire, she poured the water into a bucket and attacked the floor with a broom, causing dust to fly everywhere. She was pleased to find that, although filthy, there were old quarry tiles on the floor – many of the cottages thereabouts only had earth floors – and after scrubbing them, they began to look quite nice. Once that was done, she started on the windows and, now that all the rubbish was piled at the side of the inglenook ready to be burned, the room began to look much better and her spirits began to lift a little.

Charlie looked about in amazement when he returned almost two hours later and a smile formed at the corners of his mouth.

'Blimey, sis, someone's been busy,' he said approvingly, stamping the snow from his boots.

'There's a room upstairs under the eaves and another one through that door there that are quite dry,' she informed him, as she took the basket containing the shopping from him. 'Although that room through there can't be used till the roof is repaired. But for now, come and sit by the fire and get those wet clothes off; you look frozen through and you'll be ill next if you don't do as you're told.'

Charlie's teeth were chattering and his hands and feet were blue as Opal searched through the cart for a change of clothes for him. Once she'd found them, he turned his back and quickly scrambled into them, then made for the fire, glancing anxiously towards the two little ones. 'So, how are they this morning?'

Opal shrugged helplessly. 'Jack hasn't even woken up and Susie doesn't seem well either, but there's not much we can do apart from try to keep them warm for now.'

He sighed and took a good look around the room. 'Aw well, it looks like we could be here for a while in that case,' he commented. 'But it won't be so bad when I fetch our things from Mrs Kitely's.'

Opal snorted as she glanced at the storm that was raging outside. 'And how are you going to do that in this weather? You'd never be able to drag the cart through this.'

She began to knead the flour and yeast to make some bread on the recently scrubbed wooden draining board that was attached to the sink. Once it was ready, she wet a cloth to throw over the dough and put it on to the hearth to prove. She'd discovered a pump over the sink that she assumed must lead to a well outside. At first, the water it yielded had been brown and rusty-looking, but now it was crystal clear, so she no longer had to rely on melting snow for their water supply, which was one blessing. She had also found the precious jar of home-made strawberry jam that she had made in the summer so they were assured of eating for today at least.

Susie stirred at that moment and raising herself up on to one elbow she croaked, 'Me throat is sore, Opal.'

It was so unlike the placid child to complain that Opal was instantly concerned. 'I'll make you a nice warm cup of tea; that'll help it,' she soothed, pushing the kettle into the heart of the fire again. Jack was stirring too, but one glance into his sunken eyes made Opal's heart sink. His cheeks were rosy red and his clothes were plastered to his thin frame with sweat. Charlie had also noticed and he chewed on his lip worriedly.

'He's burning up. What can we do for him?'

'Get me a bowl of cool water, I'll try sponging him down,' Opal answered and he shot away to do as he was asked. For the next few hours they took turns dripping water into the children's mouths and sponging their feverish brows, but as the afternoon began to darken it was clear that their efforts had been in vain. Opal herself was feeling unwell by then and although she didn't mention it, Charlie had noticed the tell-tale flush in her cheeks.

'Why don't you lie down and have a rest?' he suggested kindly. 'I can see to the children.'

He grew even more concerned when Opal agreed. Usually she would have just kept going, so he knew she must be feeling ill. Curling up on the blankets next to the children, she drew herself into a ball and slipped into an exhausted sleep.

Charlie divided his attention between the two children, trying hard to swallow the knot of fear in his throat. What would he do if anything should happen to Opal? How would he cope? She had kept the family together ever since his father had died and somehow they had all come to rely on her. He tried not to look too far ahead; the future looked bleak at present and it was just too frightening. He knew he should be out looking for work, any work that brought a little money in, but how could he leave his family when they were all so ill?

Eventually, as Opal tossed and turned restlessly he lit the candles and tried to tempt the children with some of the fresh bread his sister had baked, but they both turned their heads away, and now he was so worried that even he had no appetite anymore.

The snow continued to fall, and all he could hear was the spitting of the wood on the fire and the whimpers of the children. He had no way of knowing what time it was, but after what seemed like a lifetime, Opal stirred and painfully dragged herself up on to one elbow.

'How are you feeling now?' Even as the words left his lips he realised how inadequate they were. Any fool could see that his sister was very poorly indeed. Beads of sweat were dripping into her eyes and yet she was shivering uncontrollably.

Rising hastily, he fetched her a cup of water but, after gulping at it greedily, she leaned over and vomited it back on to the floor.

'I . . . I'm sorry,' she croaked. 'But I . . . I'm not feeling so good. Can you manage if I go back to sleep?'

'Of course I can,' he assured her, but inside he was quaking. Suddenly, he had to accept that he could well be about to lose the rest of his family, and it was a terrifying thought.

The night that followed was one of the longest Charlie had ever known as he ran amongst the invalids, offering cool drinks and whatever comfort he could. And when another eerie grey morning finally dawned, Charlie knew what he had to do; it was not going to be easy and he doubted that Opal would ever forgive him.

If she recovered, that was.

Chapter Three

With a heavy heart, Charlie laid a blanket in the bottom of the little wooden cart, then gently lifted first Jack and then Susie into it. They stirred before snuggling together, and he covered them with yet more blankets and made them as comfortable as he could. There was no way he could carry both of them, so the cart was the only option, and in the thick snow even that would not be easy. Even so, he knew that he had no choice. Both of them were seriously ill and there was a good chance they would die if they didn't get the medical attention they both so desperately needed.

Next, he pulled his outdoor clothes on and, glancing towards his older sister, who was still curled into a ball, he whispered, 'Forgive me, Opal. I don't know what else to do.'

He opened the door, dragged the cart outside, and struggled away into the swirling snow.

'Ah, you're awake at last!' Charlie sighed with relief as Opal opened her eyes and blinked up at him. He had sat beside her, sponging her brow and wetting her lips all night and now he was so tired he felt as if he could have slept for a month.

'Wh-what time is it?' she asked hoarsely.

He grinned. 'Well, I'm not sure what time it is but it's two days since the last time you asked,' he told her.

Confused, she frowned. '*What?* I've been lying here for two days?'

He nodded as she took the cup of water he was holding out to her. She took a long drink and he was relieved to see that she kept it down this time. And then, what he had been dreading happened – she looked towards the fireside and asked, 'But where are the children?'

He gulped. 'They weren't getting any better,' he told her defensively. 'So I did what I had to do . . . I admitted them into the workhouse two days ago.'

'*You did what?*' She gaped at him in disbelief, her lovely brown eyes huge in her pale face. 'But *why*, Charlie? How *could* you?'

He stuck his chin out stubbornly. 'What *else* could I have done? I was afraid they were going to die and I was at my wits' end. I told you we might have to resort to that. It was the only place I could think of where they could at least get seen by a doctor and be looked after.'

'But I never dreamed it would come to that. I need to go to them . . . they'll be so frightened.' She gasped as she struggled to sit up, but she was so weak that she soon dropped back on to the blanket.

'Just lie still,' Charlie told her, gently taking control again. 'As soon as you're feeling better, we'll see what we can do about getting them out of there, but for now you need to get your strength back.'

He moved to the table and sawed off a wedge of the bread she had baked a few days ago. It was slightly stale but better than nothing and, seeing the sense in what he said, Opal tried to chew on it. She didn't feel hungry at all and the bread tasted like sawdust, but she forced herself to swallow it, knowing she needed to get her strength up – not just for herself but to get the children back.

Charlie nodded approvingly and moved to place another log on the fire.

'Where did those come from?' she asked, pointing at the pile of kindling by the fire. She could see that they had used all the old broken bits of wood that had been scattered about the floor when they first arrived.

Charlie smiled. 'Ah well, we dropped lucky there. I went to have a root about outside and found a log store almost full. How lucky was that, eh? Whoever lived here last must have left them behind and there's enough to keep us going for quite a while, so we have water and warmth at least. Now that you're awake again, I'm goin' to take the cart an' fetch some of our stuff from Mrs Kitely's an' all. If I fetch our mattresses, we can put 'em on the beds you found and at least sleep a bit more comfortably. I'll bring a couple of chairs as well, an' we can use that table in there if we carry it through. It only needs a good scrub. I was going to do it but I've been too busy looking after you.'

Opal was still heartbroken at the thought of the little ones being in the formidable workhouse, but deep down she understood why Charlie had done it and now all she cared about was being able to get them out of there again.

'You'll never be able to drag the cart through that lot,' she told him, glancing at the snow through the window.

'Of course I will.' He was already dragging his boots and outdoor clothes on. 'I'll just bring back what I can for now. But will you be all right on your own while I'm gone?'

She nodded wearily. She still felt as weak as a kitten, but was much better than she had been. 'I shall be fine. But mind how you go.'

Charlie dragged the cart to the door and was soon lost to sight, so she turned on her side and sank into sleep again.

The next time she woke, she found that not only was Charlie back but that he had been very busy indeed. He had dragged the table from the next room into the kitchen and two of her mother's sturdy, ladder-back chairs now stood at either end of it. He had also brought in the iron-framed beds and laid their mattresses on them to one side of the fire and in the flickering candlelight, the room looked almost cosy.

'Mrs Kitely sent us a pan o' stew for our tea,' he informed her gleefully, pointing to a pot that was simmering on the fire. 'An' she's getting her Stan to bring the rest of our stuff on the horse an' cart tomorrow. We can really start to make this place into a proper home then, an' when you're better an' we've both got a job, we can get the children back. We might even manage it in time for Christmas. I mean, I know this place ain't ideal but it's better than nowt for now, an' at least we're warm an' dry.'

Opal managed to raise a weak smile, although her heart was breaking as she thought of Jack and Susie. They must be so afraid surrounded by strangers in such a forbidding place, but there was nothing she could do about it for now;

she knew Charlie had only resorted to such desperate measures because he was worried about them.

Charlie filled a bowl with the stew and carried it to the table, saying, 'Come on, sis, if you want to get your strength back, you have to eat. Dip some bread in it – then we might be able to make the stew stretch to two days. I'll help you to the table, then when you're ready we'll get you into a proper bed.'

When Opal tried to rise, the room swam about her. She felt as if the floor was rising up to meet her and she had to cling to her brother. She knew that every day she lay about would be another day she would be forced to be away from Jack and Susie. Even so, it was an effort even to lift her spoon; but with Charlie's encouragement she managed to swallow a few mouthfuls and found, surprisingly, that she did feel a little better with something in her stomach.

'Right, it's into bed with you,' Charlie said bossily when he could see that she was struggling, and she went willingly. It was nice to be lying on her own mattress again and she was soon fast asleep once more.

Charlie stared at her approvingly. He felt that she had turned a corner and for now, sleep was the best medicine she could have – but knowing her as he did, he had no doubt she would soon be up and about again.

As promised, Mr Kitely arrived mid-morning the following day with the rest of their possessions on the back of his cart.

'Had a right old game gettin' here, I did,' he told Charlie when he hurried out to meet him. 'I didn't think the old mare were goin' to make it across the fields in all this, but here we are.'

He jumped down from the wooden seat at the front of the cart. He was surprisingly lithe for a man of his size; Mr Kitely was well over six foot tall and almost as broad as he was high, with a ruddy complexion and a thick thatch of silver-grey hair, which was now covered in a cap. Thankfully it had stopped snowing, and the fields around them sparkled like shattered glass in the weak winter sun.

Taking off his cap, he scratched his head as he surveyed the old cottage. 'By 'eck, lad, looks like you've got your work cut out if you're plannin' to stay 'ere,' he commented, gazing at the gaping hole in the roof. 'Could yer not find somewhere a bit better?'

'Aye, I could if I paid the rent wi' brass buttons,' Charlie answered wryly. 'But it's not as bad as it looks. There's only that one room with a hole in the roof an' now we've got our stuff we'll be a lot more comfortable.'

'If you say so.' Stan Kitely thought otherwise, but wisely kept his opinion to himself as he and Charlie began to unload the cart. As far as he was concerned, it was a crying shame that the Sharps had come to this. Both their parents had been good, hard-working, God-fearing people, and to see their children in such a plight almost broke his heart.

'The missus sent another pan o' stew an' some fresh bread,' he remembered, once the cart was unloaded. He lifted a basket from beneath the seat and handed it over. 'An' 'ere . . . it ain't much but happen it'll get you a bit o' food in till yer get some work.' He pressed a shiny silver shilling into Charlie's hand and the lad felt himself flushing. He wanted to refuse it – he still had his pride after all – but there was Opal to think about as well, and he could buy a fair bit of food with a bob.

'Th-thanks, Mr Kitely, I appreciate it,' he stammered. 'But can we consider it a loan? Just till we get back on us feet, like.'

'If that's what yer like, son.' The kindly man slapped him on the shoulder. 'But I'd best be off now, afore it starts snowin' again.' Even in the short time he had been there, the sun had disappeared and the sky was low and grey again. 'Take care o' yourselves an' keep in touch.' He touched his cap and geed the horse up. 'Ta-ra fer now.'

'Ta-ra . . . an' thanks again,' Charlie shouted, as the old horse dragged the cart back the way it had come. He stood there for a time, staring down at the money in his hand and wondering how they had come to this, before turning and wearily making his way back inside the little tumbledown cottage.

Three days later, Opal was feeling strong enough to get out of bed again, although she still tired very easily and had to take her time. Even so, she managed to hang some curtains at the small window and set out the rest of their furniture – not that there was much, just a small dresser, their beds and two fireside chairs. The effort had taken it out of her small frame, and as her brother looked at her, his heart was heavy as he realised that, although she had taken on responsibility for them all, she was little more than a child herself.

'It's lookin' more like home now, ain't it?' Charlie said, hoping to lift her spirits, but she merely nodded.

Her head was still full of thoughts of Susie and Jack and she felt frustrated that she still didn't feel strong enough to go and see them at least.

Now that Opal was up and about again, Charlie had spent most of the last couple of days going out to search for work. One big house near the town centre had paid him to clear the snow from their drive, which, added to the money Mr Kitely had given him, would provide them with enough money to eat for the next few days, but as yet he'd found nothing full-time and he was growing increasingly frustrated.

'I don't know why the farmer couldn't have kept me on,' he grumbled to Opal.

'It was probably because if he had he would have had to let us stay in the cottage,' she responded bitterly.

He nodded glumly. He'd worked on the farm with his father since leaving school and wasn't skilled at any other work, which limited his chances of finding another job.

Christmas was now just three days away, and Opal was eager to have the children home, although it was looking increasingly unlikely that they would be able to.

'I wonder how they are,' she fretted, as they sat either side of the fire that night.

Charlie quickly averted his gaze. He had been very careful to tell her as little as possible about how he had been treated when he delivered the children to the workhouse.

Miss Frost, the matron, had been a cold, hard woman who had stared at him as if he was so much muck on the bottom of her shoe, but he hadn't dared to tell Opal that. Tall and well made, she had steel-grey eyes that seemed to be able to see into his very soul, and grey hair that she wore in a tight bun in the nape of her neck. This, added to the plain, grey dress and the heavy chatelaine she wore about her waist, made her a formidable sight.

Once he had carried the children inside, she had looked at them with disdain.

'Well, I don't hold out much hope of *him* surviving,' she had said as she stared at Jack.

Charlie had felt tempted to bring the children straight back home again, but he knew that this was the only chance of them seeing a doctor, so he had held his tongue.

'And you do realise that they will have to be admitted as orphans, don't you?' she had added, as she wrote their names into a large ledger.

'But they've still got me an' their sister,' Charlie had pointed out. 'An' this is only till we can find somewhere for them to live – then we'll fetch them out again.'

Miss Frost had snorted with disgust. 'Huh! If only I had a shilling for every time I've heard that when children have been abandoned here!'

'But it's *true*!' Charlie had had to control his temper by this time. 'And we're *not* abandoning them!'

Miss Frost had completely ignored him as she slammed the ledger shut and beckoned two of the staff to take the children away. 'What I'm telling you is that because the children's parents are deceased and you and your sister are not of age, they will be under the workhouse's jurisdiction. Do you understand what that means?'

Charlie had wet his lips and shook his head, as he shuffled from foot to foot.

'It means that myself and the master, Mr Pinnegar, will take on parental responsibility for them for the foreseeable future.'

Charlie hadn't liked the sound of that at all, but seeing no other choice he had nodded miserably and left with a sick feeling in the pit of his stomach.

'So . . . Charlie, are you listening to me? I asked when we might be able to go and see them. They're bound to have visiting days?'

Opal's voice brought his thoughts sharply back to the present. 'Oh, sorry,' he muttered. 'Er . . . we can go on Sunday between two o'clock and four if you're well enough.'

'I shall be,' she said determinedly. 'Even if I have to crawl there!'

And Charlie had no doubt that she would do just that if need be.

Chapter Four

The following Sunday, as they reached the top of Church Road, Opal had to stop to catch her breath. Thankfully the snow had stopped falling the day before, but it was still bitterly cold and the ground was covered in slush and was treacherously slippery.

'I . . . I shall be all right in a minute if I just have a little rest,' she gasped.

Charlie frowned. She was still nowhere near well enough to be out and about, as far as he was concerned, but Opal could be as stubborn as a mule when she set her mind to something and nothing could have stopped her going to see Susie and Jack.

He waited patiently until she felt able to move on again and tucked her arm through his. 'Lean on me,' he encouraged, and she was only too glad to do as she was told. They still had quite a distance to go, right along Arbury Road and then along Heath End Road before they reached the Bullring, and he wondered if she was going to manage it.

Because Opal still wasn't strong and the weather conditions were so atrocious, the journey took them at least twice as long as it should have but at last the grey, forbidding walls of the workhouse loomed ahead. They were a little early, but already a line of people who had gone to visit the inmates was snaking along the lane. Charlie and Opal joined the back of the queue and Opal's heart began to beat faster at the thought of seeing the children again.

At last the door creaked open and people began to file inside. A staff member stood to one side asking each person who they had come to see, and when it came to their turn Opal told her, 'Susie and Jack Sharp.'

The woman frowned as she stared down at the list of names in the book she was holding. She then asked them to step to one side.

Opal glanced at Charlie in alarm, every instinct she had telling her that something was wrong.

Eventually, the last of the visitors was admitted and the woman told them, 'I'll just go and see if I can find Miss Frost; would you wait there?'

'Something is wrong, I can feel it,' Opal hissed at Charlie as they waited anxiously.

At last they saw the woman coming back and she told them primly, 'If you'll come this way, Miss Frost will see you in her office.'

They followed her along corridors painted a drab brown, and Opal couldn't help but notice that it was almost as cold inside as it was out.

'Here we are.' The woman stopped so abruptly that Charlie almost walked into the back of her. She tapped on the door and, when a voice bade them to enter, she stood aside and ushered them into the room.

Charlie was instantly confronted with the woman who had admitted the children and she glared at him. 'Yes? What is it you want?'

Charlie drew himself up to his full height as Opal clung fearfully to his arm. 'We've come to see our brother an' sister. I brought them here a few days ago.'

'Names?' she barked as if she had never seen him before.

'Jack and Susie Sharp.'

She ran her finger down a list of names on the desk in front of her. 'Ah yes, here we are, although I'm afraid you have had a wasted journey.'

'What do you mean?' The colour had drained from Charlie's face and Opal looked as if she was about to faint.

'Jack Sharp died the day after being admitted here,' she told him coldly.

'*What!*' Charlie clung to the back of a chair; the shock of her bald statement made him feel as if he might faint.

Beside him, Opal let out a low groan of distress, putting her hand to her mouth as she tried to hold back the nausea. How could her little brother be dead? He had been so full of life just a few weeks before; how was it possible that his little life had been snuffed out so soon?

'B-but there must be some mistake . . . Jack *can't* be dead!' Opal stammered.

'I assure you he is.' Miss Frost's eyes were as icy as the ground outside. 'An undertaker took his body away the same day he died and he will have been buried in a pauper's grave by now.'

Opal felt as if Miss Frost had stabbed her straight through the heart, and the pain was so intense, she wasn't sure she'd ever recover. With her mother so sick, Jack had become *her* responsibility, and she'd shouldered it gladly. It had been up to her to keep him safe and she'd failed.

An image rose in her mind of Jack, just a year ago, when he had taken his first steps; she could hear his gurgling cry of delight and picture his small face – his eyes sparkling and his black hair tousled around his rosy cheeks – as he wobbled towards her. She had caught him up in her arms, kissing him over and over as she twirled him around, his plump arms clasped tight around her neck, his squeals of delight making her ears ring. And now the thought of him lying cold and alone in an umarked grave nearly sent her to her knees.

'And what about our Susie?' Charlie demanded, realising that Opal was incapable of speech.

'It is my job to do what I feel is in the best interests of the children, so when a good family showed interest in her I rehomed her with them.'

'You *wicked* cow!' Charlie spat, angry colour flaring in his cheeks. 'I *told* you clearly we would be coming back for them. Tell me where she is *right* now!'

The woman grinned – a cold, hard grin that could strike terror into the hearts of the children in her care. 'I am not at liberty to divulge the name of adopters, but you can rest assured that she will have a very good life. And now, if that is all, I must wish you good day.'

For a few seconds brother and sister stood rooted to the spot, too shocked to say a word. But then Charlie stepped towards the desk, his fists clenched and his face twisted with fury. 'No! That is *not* all! Tell us where she is, or . . . or—' Words failed him, and he had to take a deep breath to stop himself leaning over the desk and shaking the woman until her teeth rattled.

Sensing this, Miss Frost narrowed her eyes at him. 'Or what?' Her eyes dropped to his fists, then she looked back up at him. 'I suggest you leave immediately, and if you don't I will have to call the constable. Perhaps a few days in a cell will calm you down.'

Charlie felt a tug on his jacket and he looked around at Opal; her face was deathly pale as she shook her head at him.

She needed to gather her strength and then she would be back. She would find out where her sister was if it was the last thing she did.

Miss Frost, meanwhile, merely nodded towards the door. 'I thought as much. Now kindly leave and don't come back.'

Then picking up her pen, she started to write in a ledger on the desk in front of her, as though the grief-stricken boy and girl standing in front of her had ceased to exist. And for her, they had.

Opal pulled on Charlie's hand, and, shoulders sagging with defeat, they staggered from the room.

Once in the corridor, Opal began to cry: great gulping sobs that tore at Charlie's heart. He had truly thought he was doing the right thing when he had brought the children there and now look what had happened. He didn't know how he was going to live with himself.

'Dear God . . . I'm *so* sorry, Opal.' He reached out to her as she leaned heavily against the wall, but she slapped his hand away.

'*Why* did you bring them to this godforsaken place?' she said in a choked voice. 'Jack is dead and now we'll never see Susie again.'

'B-but I thought I was doin' what was best for 'em. I didn't know what else to do.'

Taking her arm, he led her towards the door. There seemed no point in remaining now, and with a heart heavy with grief and guilt, he half carried and half dragged his sister back to the little derelict cottage.

'Just look what we've come to,' Opal said dully when the cottage came into sight. It was hard to accept that she and Charlie were all that was left of their family now and that they had been reduced to living in such a place.

'Come the spring I can repair the hole in the roof and start to make it more habitable,' Charlie told her, but she shook her head.

'And what will we use to pay for the improvements, eh? Brass buttons?' Her voice held no hope and once again guilt sliced through Charlie like a knife.

She shrugged off his arm and staggered towards the door. Once inside, she went to the blankets that the younger children had lain on and raised them to her nose. She could still smell them, and the tears started afresh as Charlie looked on helplessly.

For the rest of that day and night, she lay curled up, refusing food or drink – not that they had much – and Charlie grew increasingly concerned. He had never known Opal to be like this. In the past, she had taken whatever life threw at her in her stride, but now it was as if her spirit had been broken and she had lost the will to live.

He vowed then that he would do whatever it took to make it up to her; he had let all his siblings down so badly, and all that was left for him now was to do everything in his power to make sure Opal was safe and to find Susie.

With this in mind, early the next morning he set off for the town, determined to find work – any work – that would earn enough to get them some food. It was Christmas Eve, and as he thought of Christmases past, a lump swelled in his throat. Those happy times could never come again and now it was up to him to ensure that he and Opal at least had something to eat. The realisation made him hurry his steps. There was bound to be a market on; perhaps a stallholder would employ him for the day?

Opal meanwhile lay staring into the flickering flames of the fire, steeped in misery. The time spent out in the cold the day before had made her chest tight again and she could never remember feeling so ill. Sweet memories of Jack and Susie went round and round in her head and the pain in her heart was unbearable as she thought of them. Where was Susie now? And where was little Jack buried? There were no answers to either of the questions, and so she just lay there, wishing that she could die too.

When Charlie reached the market, it was teeming with shoppers crowding around the stalls, all preparing for Christmas Day. The atmosphere was light and it seemed as if everyone was smiling – everyone but Charlie, that was. For a short

32

while he surveyed the scene, feeling out of place amongst the cheerful crowds, and wondering where he should ask first.

He decided on the fruit and vegetable stall. As he approached, the stallholder – a short, thin man wearing fingerless gloves, his nose pink with cold – was shouting out his wares as he cheerfully tossed potatoes into a basket being held out to him by one of the women crowding in front of him. Gathering his courage, Charlie tapped the man on the arm. Annoyed at the interruption, the stall-holder looked round impatiently, and before Charlie could say a word, he frowned and shook his head. Undeterred, Charlie moved on to the next stall, a cart piled with second-hand clothes that were being pawed through by a gaggle of women wearing shawls over their heads. Once again he was turned away. Despite his disappointment, he kept going, but most of the market folk had already taken on someone to help with the Christmas rush and Charlie's spirits sank even further.

Eventually he stood dejectedly against a wall, watching as people bustled past, swaddled up against the cold in thick coats and hats, baskets over their arms full of paper-wrapped parcels. The smells issuing from the stalls selling hot peas and faggots or jacket potatoes were enticing, and his stomach began to rumble with hunger as he realised that neither he nor Opal had eaten that day.

If he didn't find work soon, he might have to admit himself and Opal into the workhouse, too, but he knew she would rather die than end up in there, and his sense of desperation grew.

But he couldn't give up now. So, pushing himself away from the wall, he shuffled on.

'Any work going?' he asked a red-faced, portly stallholder.

The man shook his head as he finished serving a customer and turned to the next. 'Sorry, son. The missus 'ere is 'elping out today.'

Charlie's shoulders sagged as he turned to make his way through the crush of people around him – and it was then that he spotted a very well-dressed, elderly gentleman in front of him, clad in a smart top hat and a coat that looked as if it had cost more than Charlie could earn in a year.

And out of the pocket of the coat was sticking a finely tooled leather wallet.

Charlie licked his lips and gulped. The man looked wealthy, and there was no doubt a lot of money in that wallet. He had never stolen anything in his life before, apart from eating a few of the strawberries he had picked for the farmer – but then, he told himself, he had never been this desperate before, and the money wasn't really for him, was it? It was for Opal. Somehow, he had to make it up to her for taking the children to the workhouse, but how could he buy her food if they had no money?

Without even realising he'd decided to do it, his hand snaked out as if of its own volition and suddenly the wallet was in his hand. He felt as if all eyes were on him as guilt coursed through him, but a quick glance around assured him that no one was paying him any attention, so he melted into the crowd, with the wallet seeming to burn his hand. Once he was a good distance from the man, he stole into a narrow alley and with shaking hands he opened the wallet and gasped.

There were two crisp, white pound notes in there, as well as a small amount of change. Suddenly his legs felt as if they had turned to jelly as he realised what he'd done. Opal would never forgive him if she ever found out, and had his father been alive, although he had been a mild-mannered man, he would have skelped his backside with a belt, for sure. Just for a moment he felt like throwing the wallet away, but then common sense took over and he knew that this was the only way he and Opal were going to survive – until he could get a job, at least. Stuffing the money into his pocket, he threw the wallet down and stepped back out into the marketplace, and gasped as he saw the man whose wallet he had taken talking to a policeman. Shame and guilt washed through him, but he raised his chin and marched into the butchers'.

'I'll have that cockerel hanging in the window, please. Oh, and I'll take some of them sausages an' all.'

'Right, y'are, son.' The plump butcher hooked the bird down and after throwing some sausages in with it he wrapped them up in brown paper and plonked them on the counter. Next stop was the fruit and vegetable stall, and then it was on to the baker.

An hour later, Charlie set off for his temporary home with a sack bursting with goodies slung across his shoulders. He had even bought Opal a very pretty warm woollen shawl for Christmas. All he had to do now was pray she would never find out how he had come across the money to pay for it.

When he arrived home, Opal was still lying curled up in the same position he had left her in. She barely glanced at him as he entered, but as she watched him unpacking all the food on to the table she slowly pulled herself into a sitting position.

'What's all this?' She stared at the food incredulously.

'I've been working here, there and everywhere and everyone was in a generous mood with it being Christmas so they paid me partly with food and partly with money. I did some deliveries for the baker an' the butcher an' all, then bought everything else with me wages.' All the time he was talking he kept his eyes downcast, for he was too ashamed to look at her.

Opal pulled herself to her feet and tottered unsteadily to the table. 'Why, this cockerel is enormous,' she commented wide-eyed, her stomach rumbling at the sight of it. 'There'll be enough on that to make stews for the rest of the week after I've cooked it.'

'Aye, that's what I thought.' Charlie gave her a nervous grin. 'An' look, I've got swede, carrots, onions, turnips an' potatoes, an' all. I even bought you a bit o' fruit. Some apples an' oranges, look. Didn't our mam always say how good fruit was for you?'

Opal gaped. She couldn't even remember when she had last tasted an orange, and the sight of them made her suddenly feel hungry.

Charlie, meanwhile, was still unpacking the bag. 'I've got flour and yeast, an' some oats. Oh, an' there's a twist of tea and a pat o' butter here as well. I even got some oil for the lamp an' some candles.'

Opal shook her head incredulously. 'I don't even know how you've managed to carry it all, let alone earn enough to buy it.'

Charlie quickly turned his head to hide the guilty flush that rose in his cheeks as he pictured the posh gentleman he had stolen from. But then, he was probably so rich that he wouldn't even miss it, he tried to convince himself. It wasn't as if he had stolen from someone who was in the same position as he and Opal, after all. The thought made him feel a little better and, dragging a chair up to the table, he began to peel some vegetables and potatoes. He would fry some sausages with them when they were cooked and, with decent food inside her, Opal would be well again in no time, surely.

Chapter Five

On Christmas morning Charlie plucked the cockerel while Opal prepared the vegetables – but despite the feast ahead of them, they were both still miserable.

'Oh, I almost forgot. I got you a present,' Charlie said when the vegetables were simmering in a pot on the fire. They had no oven, so he had chopped the cockerel into pieces and that was simmering in a pot next to the vegetables. He hurried away to fetch her shawl, and when he presented her with it, her mouth dropped open.

'Why, Charlie, it's *beautiful*,' she gasped, as she placed it about her shoulders. 'But it must have cost a fortune.'

She was peering at him suspiciously again and he felt his cheeks grow hot.

'I told you, everyone was in a generous mood and it didn't cost as much as you might think.'

'Well I'm afraid I haven't got you anything.' She reached out and tenderly squeezed his hand as she told him softly, 'I'm sorry I blamed you for taking the children to the workhouse, Charlie. I know you only did what you thought was best for them.'

He shrugged. 'That's all right. I just want to see you get better. You're all I've got left now.'

Yet even as the words left his lips, he saw her glance towards the blankets that the children had slept on and he knew she might never get over their loss, especially so soon after losing their parents. She didn't even seem like Opal anymore. All the sparkle had gone out of her and her eyes looked dull and haunted. Even so, for each other's sakes, they made the best of the day and if either of their minds were on loved ones who were no longer with them, neither of them mentioned it.

January passed in a blur of snow and rain. Charlie went off regularly to look for work. The money he had stolen wouldn't last forever, but come hell or high water he was determined to keep a roof over his sister's head, albeit a very humble one.

While Charlie searched desperately for work, Opal had started to stand for hours outside the workhouse, questioning every member of staff who left the building about Susie and where she had gone. So far she'd had no success, but still she persisted, unable to accept the fact that she might never see her little sister again. She had lost a serious amount of weight, despite their feast at Christmas, and there were dark circles beneath her eyes. It broke his heart to see her shivering outside the walls, her shawl clutched around her thin frame, and though at first he tried to stop her, eventually he had accepted that this was her way of grieving, so he left her to it.

February blew in with driving rain and harsh winds that rattled the window panes but now that the snow was gone

Charlie managed to retrieve quite a few of the tiles that had blown off the roof and into the long grass in the garden, and had made a start on fixing the roof; he had also boarded up the broken window panes.

'I shall have this place lookin' a treat come the spring,' he told Opal optimistically, but she merely nodded, not really bothered what he did to the place.

Finally, March arrived and slowly the ground started to come back to life after the long hard winter. Daffodils and crocuses sprang up amongst the weeds and primroses peeped from beneath the hedgerows.

Charlie still spent a large portion of each day looking for work, but it seemed fruitless. As the weeks wore on, he grew more and more desperate. The money he had stolen was gone now, apart from a few pennies, and the threat of them both having to enter the workhouse was looming like a great black cloud, keeping him awake at night as he fretted about it. He was also growing increasingly concerned about Opal, who, when she wasn't standing outside the workhouse asking for news of their sister, spent most of her time curled up on her bed.

It was with these worries in mind that he set off one windy day to the town centre. It was market day and as always the place was a bustle of activity. For a time, he strolled amongst the beasts in their pens in the cattle market, before stopping at each stall he came to to ask if there was any work going.

'I'll do anything,' he told the stallholders, but their answer was always the same, and as he fingered the few sparse pennies he had left in his pocket, his spirits sank.

The money he had left was scarcely enough to buy them food for more than another couple of days at the most, especially as, now that the little bread oven had stopped working, Opal couldn't even bake their bread anymore; she was too steeped in misery to care anyway, and he was having to buy that from the baker.

What would become of them? He stared gloomily down at the ground and for a moment he was so despondent that he didn't even see the fine leather wallet lying at his feet. His first instinct was to snatch it up and run like the wind, but then his conscience took over. It had clearly fallen from the pocket of a well-dressed gentleman who was perusing the goods on the stall and Charlie was still feeling guilty about the last wallet he had stolen. He would have to return it to its owner before someone else stole it. He stooped to grab it but as he made to stand up someone caught him by the back of the collar and almost lifted his feet from the ground.

'Here, let go o' me,' he protested loudly, as the well-dressed man directly in front of him turned to glare at him. At the same time his stomach sank as he saw that it was a constable who had hold of him.

'Is this your wallet, sir?' The constable snatched the wallet from Charlie's hand and the gentleman nodded.

'It is indeed, constable. Well done. No doubt this little thief would have made off with it had you not seen him with it.'

'But it was lyin' on the ground,' Charlie protested loudly. 'All I was doin' was pickin' it up to hand it back to you!'

'Picking my pocket more likely.' The man's eyes reminded Charlie of those of the dead fish he had just seen lying on a slab in the fishmongers'.

The constable handed the wallet back to the man, keeping a firm grip on Charlie. 'Don't worry, sir, I'll see as this little mongrel gets locked up good an' proper. Then when the rest o' the magistrates visit next week he'll be up afore you all.'

Charlie's gut twisted. *Magistrate!* Now he really was in trouble, but the irony of the situation was that this time he was innocent.

'It dropped out of his pocket, I tell you,' he protested, as the constable began to haul him towards the police station. 'I was just goin' to give it him back.'

'Aye, o' course you was, son,' the constable replied cynically. 'That's what they all say. It's just a shame fer you that yer chose to steal from Mr King. He's one o' the magistrates an' he don't take kindly to thieves. I reckon it'll be a long time till you get a chance to steal again.'

Charlie's heart was beating like a drum and his cheeks were burning with humiliation and frustration as he noted people stopping to gawp at him. Soon he stopped struggling – the constable was clearly as strong as a horse – and eventually the police station loomed ahead of them.

The policeman hauled him inside and once they reached the desk he told the sergeant there, 'Caught this young 'un red-handed trying to steal Magistrate King's wallet. I'll stick him in the cells, shall I, till the magistrates visit next?'

The sergeant nodded. 'Aye, you do that, Sid.' Then, turning his attention to Charlie he told him, 'I wouldn't want to be in your shoes, lad, not for all the tea in China, an' that's a fact. Magistrate King's been known to send men to prison for stealing a loaf of bread, let alone his wallet. But anyway, we'd best take some details.' He paused to lick the end of a pencil then barked, 'Name?'

Charlie's shoulders sagged. 'Charlie Sharp.'

'Address?'

'Rapper's Hole.'

The sergeant frowned. 'Rapper's Hole? But I thought all the dwellings left standin' there were derelict.'

Charlie flushed. 'They are, but me an' me sister had nowhere to go when we were turned out of our cottage when me mam an' dad died, so we ended up there. We had me little bother an' sister with us as well, but they were both poorly an' we couldn't afford to get a doctor to them so we put them in the workhouse just before Christmas. It was supposed to be just till we could get them back, but when we went to visit me little brother had died an' they'd let some couple take me little sister.'

The sergeant's face softened somewhat. Poor lad, it sounded as if he'd had a rough time of it, and he was only about the same age as his own son. Of course, that didn't excuse what he'd tried to do, but he supposed sometimes desperate times called for desperate measures.

'And just where is this cottage?' the sergeant asked. 'I dare say we could get word to your sister, else she'll think you've deserted her.'

'It's off Haunchwood Road, quite close to a small copse,' Charlie muttered dispiritedly. He dreaded to think what Opal would say when she heard what had happened but there wasn't much he could do about it now. The worst thing was knowing that although he hadn't intended to steal the wallet today, he had been guilty of theft before

Christmas, so he supposed he was due what was coming to him.

'Right, get him down to the cells, constable,' the sergeant ordered. Then, addressing Charlie, he told him in a gentler voice, 'We'll bring you some dinner down presently.'

'How long do you think I'll be here?' Charlie asked.

The policeman shrugged. 'The magistrates are due in the town sometime next week and you'll appear before them then.'

Charlie allowed himself to be led away down some steep, well-worn stone steps where he saw a row of cells in what appeared to be a large basement. Two of them were occupied – one by a drunk who was singing loudly – but the sergeant led him to one in a far corner, telling him, 'I'll put you in here. Fred Tollet is in that one and he's drunk as a skunk.'

Charlie glanced around at what was to be his home for the next week. The cell was tiny with a bucket in one corner and a wooden bed with a straw mattress covered by a thin grey blanket standing against one wall. The walls were bare brick and damp with one tiny window set high up and it was so cold that his breath hung on the air. Charlie had to fight the urge to cry as the cell door slammed shut and was securely locked. His spirits were at a very low ebb as he thought of Opal. He had let her down yet again, and he would never forgive himself for that.

Later that afternoon, the sergeant who had arrested Charlie picked his way across Rapper's Hole until he spotted a cottage in the shelter of a small copse. *This must be it*, he thought, as he walked down the weed-strewn path that led to the front door. He rapped on it and soon it was opened a fraction and a pair of frightened brown eyes stared out at him.

Opal's heart sank as she saw the policeman standing there and she wrapped her shawl more tightly about her.

'Y-yes?'

'Are you Miss Opal Sharp?' When she nodded the policeman removed his helmet. 'Then might I have a word with you, miss? It's concerning your brother, Charlie.'

He saw the fear flare in her eyes as she held the door wider for him to step inside. He glanced about and was surprised at what he saw. Although basic, the room was spotlessly clean, as was the young lass standing in front of him. 'I'm afraid I have bad news,' he told her as gently as he could. As he explained what had happened, her head wagged from side to side and her hand flew to her mouth.

'N-no, there must be some mistake,' she cried tearfully. 'Charlie would *never* steal!'

And yet even as the words left her lips, she was remembering the money he had come home with before Christmas.

The constable looked uncomfortable as he shuffled from foot to foot.

'The worst of it is it was Mr King the magistrate's wallet I caught him with,' he told her. 'And as you probably know, he's not a man to be messed with.'

Opal stood as if turned to stone; she had led a sheltered life until the death of her parents but even she had heard of how strict Magistrate King was. It felt as if her whole world was collapsing around her yet again. First she had lost her parents, then Jack and Susie, and now Charlie!

'When will he be tried?' she eventually managed to ask in a small voice.

'Sometime next week. And now if you'll excuse me, miss, I really should be going . . . I'm sorry to be the bearer of such bad news.'

With that, the sergeant replaced his helmet and left, leaving Opal to stare sightlessly after him.

The next morning, bright and early, she was at the police station. 'May I see my brother, please?' she asked the constable on the desk. 'His name is Charlie Sharp.'

'Ah, the young chap that was arrested yesterday.' He eyed the girl thoughtfully. Her clothes were little more than rags, although they were clean, and she was as thin as a rake, with deep dark circles beneath her eyes. But even so, it was clear that sometime in the near future, she was going to blossom into a beauty. 'By rights I'm not supposed to allow him any visitors till he's been up before the magistrates,' he told her. 'But seeing as you've come a good way, I'll allow you ten minutes. How would that be?'

She gave him a grateful smile, which totally transformed her pale face, as he called a constable from the next room.

'Take this young lady down to see Charlie Sharp,' he instructed him. 'But no more than ten minutes, mind.'

The young constable led her towards the cells and she followed meekly, her heart in her mouth. Charlie was sitting dejectedly on his bed, his head bowed, and when he looked up and saw her he flushed guiltily.

'I wasn't going to steal it, Opal – the wallet, I mean. It was on the floor and I was going to return it, I swear,' he told her in a choked voice.

'Well, it's done now, isn't it?' she answered dully.

'Perhaps if you were to go an' see Mr King he'd listen to you,' Charlie said desperately, as he gripped her cold hands through the bars of the cell.

'I suppose I could try . . .' Opal didn't see that it would do much good but she had to do *something*. 'Perhaps the sergeant would give me his address? But how are you? Are they feeding you?'

'Of course, but it's you I'm more worried about,' Charlie told her truthfully. Feeling in his pocket he removed the few pennies he had left and pressed them into her hand. 'It's not much but it should feed you for a couple of days . . .' His voice trailed away and tears pricked at the back of his eyes. He had never felt so useless in his life.

'Don't worry about me.' She squeezed his cold fingers as footsteps sounded on the concrete floor behind her and the young constable appeared again.

'Sorry, miss, but your time is up.'

Charlie clung to her hand for a moment longer, and Opal felt as if her heart was going to break in two, but then, taking a deep breath, she drew herself upright.

She was the only one who might be able to help Charlie now and that's just what she intended to do!

Chapter Six

As Opal stood at the end of the path leading to the smart house in Swan Lane, her heart sank. This was the home of Mr King, the magistrate who Charlie was accused of stealing from. The sergeant had taken a lot of persuading before he finally gave her his address because, as he had pointed out, it was highly unethical. Even so, Opal was hoping to play on the man's sympathy – if he had any, that was. Her hopes weren't particularly high, as she had heard what a harsh man he could be, but what other choice did she have?

The house was magnificent: three storeys high with windows that shone in the weak March sunshine. They were covered in snow-white lace curtains and the door was painted a bright, cherry red with a rather splendid brass door knocker in the shape of a lion's head. The walls were of huge, gleaming white stone. A far cry from the hovel she and Charlie were having to live in, she thought, and she wouldn't have minded betting that just one room in this place would be almost as big as the whole of the cottage put together. For a moment, her courage wavered. The man would no doubt send her off with a flea in her ear if what she'd heard about him was correct, but then who else would plead Charlie's case for him if she didn't?

She was very conscious of her old, worn clothes and down-at-heel-boots; but suddenly she felt her mother's presence, and she remembered her saying, 'Just remember, my love, you're a chip off the old block; you can do whatever you set your mind to.'

Pulling herself up to her full height, she smoothed her drab skirt, took a deep breath and ventured up the path. A tub of daffodils, their bright yellow trumpets opening to the sun, stood at the side of the door and she found herself staring at them as she lifted her hand to the knocker. She could hear the sound it made echo inside the house, and soon she heard footsteps approaching the door. It was opened by a lady in a plain, light-grey bombazine gown trimmed with black braid. She wore a chatelaine about her waist from which numerous keys dangled, and her dark hair was twisted into an elegant knot on the back of her head.

Opal felt the woman's eyes travel down her before she asked politely, 'May I help you?'

Opal gulped. 'Er . . . yes . . . please. I was wondering if it would be possible to have a word to Mr King?'

The woman's eyebrows rose. 'Do you have an appointment to see him?'

Opal shook her head, as tears sprang to her eyes. 'No . . . but if he would just be kind enough to give me a few moments of his time, I would be very grateful. It's about my brother and quite urgent.'

The woman's face was suspicious as she saw the tears shining in the girl's eyes. For a moment she stood quietly, deep in thought. Finally, she seemed to come to a decision as she said, 'Very well. Go around to the servants' entrance at the back of the house and tell Cook Mrs Wood sent you. Then I shall go and see if Mr King will see you. But I can make no promise he will, mind!'

'Thank you, ma'am.'

Straightaway, Opal took the path that led around to the back of the house and found herself in a large yard. There was a stable block to one side of it and two beautiful black stallions watched her progress from above the half doors of their stalls. To the side of the stables was a gate that led into what appeared to be an orchard where a young, heavily pregnant woman was busily pegging washing to a line that stretched from one side of the yard to the other.

She smiled at Opal. 'You come after the job, have you?' she asked cheerfully, and Opal was confused.

'Er . . . no, I was hoping to see Mr King, actually. The lady who answered the door sent me round here.'

'Ah, that'll be Mrs Wood, the housekeeper.' The girl pegged the last item to the line then, lifting the laundry basket, she perched it on her hip and pointed to a door. 'That's the kitchen there.'

Opal gave her a grateful smile and tentatively tapped on the door.

'Come in,' a voice shouted and she slowly opened the door and stepped into a kitchen that almost took her breath away. It was absolutely enormous, and the delicious smells of roasting pork made Opal's empty stomach rumble.

A plump, rosy-cheeked woman in a voluminous white apron was basting a large joint on top of a huge range and she looked at Opal enquiringly.

'Come for the job have you, luvvie?' she asked, much as the girl she had seen outside had.

'No, I've come to see Mr King, but the housekeeper told me to wait in here with you while she asks if he'll see me.'

As Opal twisted her hands together, the cook smiled as she popped the joint back into the oven and wiped her hands. 'Then sit yourself down at the table,' she said kindly. 'I reckon there's some tea left in the pot, if you fancy, though it might be a bit stewed be now.'

Before Opal could answer, the cook crossed to the table that took up the centre of the room and began to pour tea from a large, brown teapot into a cup before pushing it towards Opal.

She perched self-consciously on the edge of one of the ladder-backed chairs situated around the table and took a sip. The tea was lukewarm but of a far better quality than she was used to, and it tasted like nectar.

The cook eyed her curiously. The poor girl wasn't as far through as a lamppost and didn't look at all well, but she was polite and clean and she was certainly pretty enough.

'Mr King expectin' you, is he?' she asked curiously.

Opal shook her head. 'No but—'

She stopped speaking abruptly as Mrs Wood appeared through a green baize door and told her, 'The master says he will spare you two minutes Miss—? Sorry, I forgot to ask your name.'

'It's Sharp . . . Opal Sharp.' Opal rose so abruptly that she almost overturned the cup in front of her and glanced apologetically at the cook as a small amount of tea splashed onto the tabletop.

'Don't worry, I'll mop that up,' the woman told her good-naturedly, inclining her head as Opal headed towards the housekeeper.

She followed the woman into a hallway, the like of which she had never seen before. There were black-and-white patterned tiles buffed to a high shine on the floor and the walls were covered in elaborate velvet-flocked wallpaper and adorned with beautiful gilt-framed pictures and mirrors. In the centre of the hall was a sweeping staircase that led up to a galleried landing, and Opal felt as if she had stepped into one of the pages of the magazines her mother used to buy occasionally as a treat. It was like another world, and she was so busy admiring it that she almost walked into the back of Mrs Wood when she stopped in front of one of the many doors that led off it.

'The master is in here, but do remember he is very busy,' the woman warned her. Then, opening the door, she ushered her inside.

Opal found herself in yet another large room, this one dominated by a long mahogany desk where a man was seated in a huge green leather chair, writing. Behind him, bookshelves reached from floor to ceiling, but she barely glanced at them, so focused was she on the man who held her brother's fate in his hands.

After a few moments he glanced up, his expression stern, but as he looked her over, it softened. The girl was shabbily dressed but she was young and pretty with all the signs of turning into a great beauty.

'So, my dear, how may I help you?' He hurriedly rose and, coming around the desk, he pulled out a chair for her.

Opal licked her dry lips as she eyed him cautiously. He wasn't as old as she'd expected; he looked to be in his mid-to-late thirties and was quite portly with fair hair touched with grey and deep-grey eyes. She supposed that he might have been quite good-looking at one time but good living had added pounds to his frame and his stomach strained against the buttons on his brightly coloured waistcoat.

'I . . . I came to see you about my brother . . .' Her voice came out as a croak and he frowned.

'Your brother? Do I know him?'

'Well . . . not exactly. His name is Charlie Sharp and he has been arrested for trying to steal your wallet. But he *wasn't*, I assure you; he saw it on the ground and swears he was going to give it to you but the constable saw him lift it and thought he was going to make off with it!'

The words had come tumbling out and now she stared at him, waiting anxiously for his reaction.

The smile instantly slid from his face as he stroked his whiskery double chin. Normally he would have given any-one short shrift for invading his home, but there was some-thing very appealing about this young lady and he wondered if he might not use the situation to his advantage. She was a very tasty little piece, after all.

'I see . . . and what exactly do you expect me to do about it?' he said, getting up from behind the desk and walking towards her.

'I . . . I thought perhaps you could visit the police station and tell the police you don't wish to press charges?'

He heard the note of desperation in her voice and forced a sympathetic smile. 'I'm afraid it's gone too far for that, my dear. His name is already down to come before the magistrates when they visit the town next week.' To her shock and horror his hand suddenly snaked out and gently stroked her soft cheek. 'But . . . were you to be *nice* to me, I'm sure I could put in a good word for him and lessen his sentence . . .'

She stared at him uncomprehending for a moment and then, as the meaning of what he was saying sank in, she jumped away from him, her cheeks blazing. Although Opal had led a sheltered life in many ways, her mother had explained what being loose with her favours with a man before marriage could result in and she didn't want to end up like Meg Blower who had lived in the end cottage in Fenny Drayton with a host of kids all by different fathers.

'I'm sorry, sir.' Her face was red with indignation. 'But I'm not *that* sort of girl!'

Henry King regarded her for a moment, wondering whether he should send her on her way. But . . . there really was something about her that intrigued him. Her curly black hair shone like silk, her eyes reminded him of warm toffee and her skin was like peaches and cream.

'You misunderstand me,' he said, hoping to placate her. 'What I meant was . . .' He paused as he tried to come up with a plausible excuse, and then it came to him. 'What

I meant to say was our laundry maid will be leaving any day now to have her baby and I'm looking for someone to replace her. It would be very kind of you if you'd agree to come and take her place. Finding honest, reliable help is so difficult these days.'

'Oh . . .' Opal felt foolish for thinking the worst of him and she supposed that she *did* need a job . . . But then what would happen if Charlie were to be released? She didn't want to leave him to fend for himself in the cottage.

'Sorry, sir,' she said quietly with her head held high. 'Will your laundry maid be leaving before my brother goes before the magistrates?'

Seeing the way her mind was working, he shook his head. 'I doubt it, and I understand that you'll want to know what's going to happen to him before you commit yourself. Will you consider the offer at the end of next week? Mrs Wood will explain what hours you would be expected to work and what your wages would be, and of course you would live in the servants' quarters. In the meantime, if you would be so kind as to tell me where you are living, I will ensure that you are informed of when your brother is to appear before the magistrates.'

'Thank you, sir . . . and you *will* try to help him?'

He inclined his head. 'Of course.'

'You promise, sir?'

When he nodded again, Opal told him what he wished to know. When she considered the cold, draughty cottage where she was living now, the job offer sounded like the answer to a prayer, but only if Charlie were to be sent down, which she prayed he wouldn't be.

'Thank you, sir.' She edged towards the door, feeling uncomfortable in his presence. 'Goodbye for now, sir.' She dipped her knee respectfully and left the room as swiftly as she could, while Mr King stared after her, a thoughtful expression on his face.

Chapter Seven

'Now come along, Suzanne, your mama will not be pleased with you if you don't take your medicine.'

The child stared up at the nanny resentfully. 'My name *ain't* Suzanne, it's Susie,' she declared defiantly. 'An' she *ain't* my mama. My mam is dead!'

'That is quite enough of that sort of common talk,' the nurse said strictly. 'And it's *isn't*, not *ain't*!'

Susie stared stubbornly back at her. The woman was tall and thin with sharp features that reminded the child of the ferret one of their neighbours back in Fenny Drayton had once had. It had been a vicious little thing, just like the woman in front of her. She was dressed in a long black dress over which she wore a white apron, and on her head was a mob cap trimmed with lace.

The first few weeks in her new home had passed Susie by in a blur. She had been too poorly to know where she was, or even to care for that matter, but now she was well on the road to recovery and she just wanted to go home to Charlie and Opal and Jack. *They* were her family, not the woman who talked posh and who had told her that from now on she was to call her *Mamarr*! Mothers were called Mam, as far as she was concerned. And the woman was *not* her mam.

She was still not allowed out of bed except to use the toilet because the woman insisted that she still wasn't strong enough, and four times a day the nanny, Agatha Deverell, made her take two spoonfuls of the vilest medicine she had ever tasted. At first, she had been too weak to resist, but now as Agatha hovered over her with the first spoonful in her hand, Susie raised her hand and knocked it away. It splashed all over her lovely clean apron and Agatha's lips compressed into an angry straight line.

'*Now* look what you've done!' she scolded. 'I shall have to go and change and you can be sure I shall tell your mama how naughty you have been when she comes up to say goodnight.'

Susie shrugged, not much caring, and watched the nurse stamp away to the door that led into her own room, which adjoined the nursery. Once she was gone, Susie slid out of bed and crossed to the window to peer through it, but all she could see were rooftops and the street below, which looked a very long way down. There was lots of traffic and everything looked so strange to her that she knew she must be a very long way away from home. She had heard Agatha say something about a place – Mifair or Mayfair, or something like that, but she had no idea where it might be. She was still standing there when Agatha reappeared and tutted.

'Get back into bed immediately,' she ordered, just as the door opened and a woman appeared.

'Oh Suzanne, *my darling*, whatever are you doing out of bed?'

She was dressed in a beautiful gown of pale-lilac silk, heavily trimmed with white lace. Around her throat and dangling from her ears were jewels that almost matched the colour of her dress. Her silver-blonde hair was arranged high on her head in soft curls and she smelled of flowers. 'Come along.' She placed her arm about the little girl and gently but firmly led her back to the bed. 'Daddy and I are going to the opera this evening,' she informed her, as she tucked the blankets about the girl's small frame. 'And tomorrow I shall tell you all about it. Don't forget, dear Dr Willis is calling to see you again tomorrow, and he said if you had been very good he might let you get up for a little while. That will be nice, won't it?'

Susie folded her arms and glared at the woman. 'I want to go *home*!' she stated and, as if by magic, the woman hastily produced a tiny scrap of lace handkerchief from the bosom of her dress and dabbed at her eyes.

'Oh, *please* don't say things like that, sweetheart,' she implored. 'You'll make poor mama cry.'

'You *ain't* my mama,' Susie declared stubbornly. 'And I wanna go *home*!'

Seeing that her young mistress was getting distressed, Agatha took control of the situation. 'You just get off and have a good evening, ma'am,' she urged. 'Suzanne will be quite all right here with me and I'm sure she'll be in a better mood in the morning when she's had a good night's rest.'

'Yes . . . I'm sure you're right, Nanny. Goodnight. Good-night, Suzanne.'

The mistress swept from the room in a rustle of silk skirts and, when she was gone, Agatha glared at the child. Little devil, going and upsetting the poor young woman like that!

She should be grateful that a lovely couple like the Darby-Joneses had adopted her, though why they couldn't have chosen a younger child or a baby she'd never know. The little brat had been hanging on to life by the skin of her teeth when they'd first arrived home with her and for a while it had been touch and go. But thanks to careful nursing, she was on the mend now and when she was completely well again, Agatha was determined to knock some sense into her. In her time as a nanny, she had cared for much worse-behaved children than Suzanne but she'd tamed them all in the end. 'Spare the rod and spoil the child' was her motto, but of course she didn't dare risk bruising her while the doctor was still visiting her.

Once more, she picked up the medicine. '*Now*,' she said sternly. 'There are two ways you can take this. One I shall hold you down and tip it down your throat or two, you can take it nicely. Which is it to be?'

Knowing that the woman would do exactly as she threatened, Susie meekly opened her mouth and swallowed the foul-tasting liquid, gagging as it slid down her throat.

'That's better,' Agatha said approvingly, with a wicked gleam in her eye. 'Now, I'm going downstairs to have a cup of tea with Cook and when I come back I want to find you fast asleep. Is that quite clear?'

Susie nodded, and once the nanny had left the room she turned her face into the pillow and sobbed. She missed her family and, somehow, someday she would run away and find them again, she promised herself.

The doctor arrived mid-morning the next day and, to Susie's delight, he told the woman who called herself Mama that he considered she was now well enough to get up for a few hours.

Alicia Darby-Jones clapped her hands with delight, just as a small child might have done, and flew across to the wardrobe that housed all the new clothes she had bought for Susie.

'What would you like to wear, darling?' She withdrew a very pretty dress with a lace-trimmed pinafore and held it up for Susie's inspection, but when Susie made no comment she delved into the wardrobe again, dragging out a royal-blue velvet one. 'Hm, this one might be a little too warm,' she mused.

And so it went on, until at last she had made her choice.

'Nanny, can you see that she is dressed and looking her best?' She handed the woman two lengths of blue ribbon to match the dress she had chosen for Susie to wear. 'These are for her hair,' she instructed Agatha. 'I shall send the butler up to carry her downstairs when she's ready. Miss Timson and Lady Arcourt will be here any minute to take morning coffee with me and I can hardly wait to show my little gem off to them. I'm sure after all this time of her being ill that they are thinking I don't really have a little girl of my very own at last.'

Susie scowled at her as the nanny bobbed her knee. 'Of course, ma'am. I'll ring the bell when she's ready to come down.'

Alicia leaned towards Susie to give her a kiss but Susie turned her face away and with a sigh the woman swished from the room.

'Right, we'd best do as your mama says.' Nanny whipped the blankets and sheets back but Susie continued to lie there. 'Did you hear me?'

Susie found herself focusing on the hairs that were sprouting from the nanny's chin and then suddenly she felt a stinging slap on the leg and she started.

'*That's* what you'll get if you disobey me or ignore me from now on,' the woman told her, her eyes glinting with malice. 'You're better now, so it's time for you to start learning some manners.'

Tears started to fill Susie's eyes, but she held them back. The smack had really hurt but she wouldn't give the woman the satisfaction of seeing her cry. She slowly climbed from the bed and stood impassively as the woman dressed her. There were so many layers: a warm liberty bodice, bloomers, woollen stockings, layers of petticoats and finally the dress. She then pushed her feet into a dainty little pair of button-up leather boots. They were slightly large for her, but they were by far the best she had ever worn and she couldn't help but admire them as the woman none too gently attacked her long, curly hair with a wooden hairbrush.

'Well, I have to say you at least *look* the part of a little lady,' Nanny remarked. 'Let's just hope you don't have to open your mouth or you'll let yourself down. But I'll tell you now, if I hear that you've been rude or not minded your manners, you'll get another slap when you come back up here and it will be harder next time. Do you understand?'

Susie nodded meekly as Nanny crossed to pull the bell rope at the side of the fire. Soon, they heard the sound of the butler's footsteps on the stairs.

'Here she is, Mr Peters, all ready to be shown off,' Nanny told him.

Mr Peters inclined his head and swept Susie into his arms. Then, without uttering so much as a single word, he walked out of the room and carried her down the stairs, although she really couldn't see why it was necessary. She would have been quite capable of walking. However, she didn't dare complain. Her leg was still stinging from the sharp slap Nanny had given her and she didn't fancy another one if she could avoid it. As they descended the stairs her eyes grew rounder as she stared at the luxurious surroundings. This house was like the castle in a fairy-story book about a princess that her real mam had read to her.

As soon as they reached the hallway, Alicia came racing out of a doorway. 'Oh, *do* bring her in here, Peters. My visitors are *so* looking forward to meeting her.'

'Certainly, ma'am.' The man followed her into what Susie was later to discover was the drawing room and gently sat her down on a big wing chair to one side of the fireplace, before bowing and backing from the room. Opposite the chair, on a little red velvet sofa with spindly gold legs, sat two elderly ladies staring at her.

'Suzanne, sweetheart. Say hello to Miss Timson and Lady Arcourt; they've been so looking forward to meeting you.'

Susie thought of refusing but she remembered the nanny waiting for her upstairs so she muttered, 'Hello.'

The older of the two women, who was wearing the biggest hat Susie had ever seen, peered at her through a pair of pince-nez spectacles.

'She's a pretty little thing, I'll give you that, Alicia,' she said. 'And I do so admire you for giving a home to such a poor little waif. I just hope she shows you the gratitude you deserve.'

Despite Nanny's threat, Susie glared at her, but Alicia appeared not to notice.

'Oh, Matthew and I feel that *we* are the lucky ones to have found her,' she trilled. 'When we visited the workhouse and I saw her I just knew instantly that she was the one for us.'

Lady Arcourt frowned before asking, 'What were you doing in Nuneaton anyway? Surely you could have chosen a child from a nice orphanage closer to home?'

'Matthew had to go there on business, and we stayed with friends,' Alicia explained. 'So just on a whim I decided to visit the workhouse. I was told by the lady of the house where we were staying that a number of the children there had been rehomed so I just went on the off-chance really, and there she was. Of course, she was very, very poorly and we weren't even sure she would survive, but I knew somehow that I had to take that chance. I truly believe it was fate that took me to the workhouse door that day. If I hadn't gone, she might not have survived, so really it was lucky for both of us.'

She reached out and tenderly stroked Susie's cheek and the child was forced to admit to herself that she was very kind. But even so she yearned to be back with her family and she decided she would tell the kind lady so as soon as the visitors had left.

Just then, a maid in a starched white cap and a pretty white apron wheeled a tea trolley in and Susie's eyes grew round. The teapot looked as if it was made of solid silver and the tiny china cups and saucers, which were decorated with tiny roses, were so delicate that Susie could almost see right through them. There was also a three-tier stand filled with tiny pastries and cakes and suddenly Susie felt hungry for the first time since she had become ill.

'Shall I pour for you, ma'am?' the young maid enquired, as Alicia watched Susie eyeing the cakes with a twinkle in her eye.

'Yes please, Millie. And you could perhaps pour some milk for Miss Suzanne and give her a plate so that she might help herself to some cakes.'

This was a far cry from the rather bland diet Nanny had kept her on up in the nursery and Susie made the most of it, much to the disgust of the visitors.

'Really, Alicia, my dear, I'm not at all sure that the child should be eating so many sweet things. It's so bad for her teeth,' Miss Timson pointed out primly.

Alicia merely laughed. 'Oh, I'm sure a few treats now and then won't hurt.'

The older woman sniffed her disapproval. 'Then on your own head be it. Personally, I think you should start as you mean to go on. Children pick up bad habits so quickly and you are very new to parenting.'

'I'm quite aware of that,' Alicia answered with a smile at Susie. 'But I'm sure that we're going to do very well with each other.'

Susie gave a cautious smile in return. Perhaps it wouldn't be so bad living here after all? Just until she could go back to her family, that was.

Chapter Eight

Long after Opal had left, Henry King strode up and down the room, stroking his chin thoughtfully. He had lost his wife some two years ago in childbirth. The child, a boy, had also died, and with him Henry's hopes of ever becoming a father. Since then, Henry had paid for his pleasure when he felt the need to, despite the fact that widows had flocked to him like bees to honey. None of them had ever held the least appeal for him, though. Henry was a wealthy, well-respected member of the community and he knew that most of them only wanted him for his money and the respect that would be their due as his wife.

But there was something about the young girl who had come pleading for her brother that had touched a chord in him. Admittedly she was little more than a child at present and many years his junior, but that was how he liked them, and he could sense that within a few years she would blossom into a beauty. She was clearly very poor, too, but her hair had shone and, though her clothes were shabby, they were clean and as respectable as she had been able to make them.

He found himself picturing her in a fine gown with her hair stylishly dressed, and for the first time in many a long day he wondered what it would be like to be married again. His first wife, Marianne, had come from a very respectable family, but within months of his marriage he had realised that they had little in common. All Marianne could talk about was the latest fashions or who had called for afternoon tea and Henry had soon tired of her. But Opal . . . despite the fact that she had come to plead her brother's case, there had been a proud lift to her chin and an intelligent gleam in her eye that had appealed to him.

He could imagine her small firm breasts and her satin skin under his touch, and he shook his head as if to rid it of thoughts of her. It was ridiculous to even consider wedding her; she probably couldn't even read and write, and what would people say when it became known that he was consorting with a young woman of her class?

Crossing to the bell pull at the side of the fireplace, he yanked on it. When Mrs Wood appeared in the doorway, he barked, 'Tea if you please.'

'Certainly, Mr King.'

She backed out of the room and hurried away to the kitchen to place his order, wondering what the young woman who had just left might have said to him to put him in such a bad mood.

Opal meanwhile was trudging towards the cottage with a heavy heart. Mr King had told her that Charlie's case would be heard within the week, but at the moment a week seemed like a lifetime. Removing the money Charlie had given her from her pocket, she stared down at the few coins. If she was very careful she might just about be able to feed herself for a week, but once that was gone she would either have to find a job or admit herself to the workhouse. After what had happened to Jack and Susie there she shuddered at the thought, and waves of grief washed over her – but, once again, she straightened her back. She wasn't beaten yet, not by a long shot! She must try to believe that Charlie would walk free and then together they would try to build some sort of a life for themselves. Holding tight to that thought, she moved on.

Six days later, as Opal was placing some of the wood she had collected from the nearby copse on the fire, she heard the sound of a horse approaching. Standing up, she smoothed her drab skirt and crossed to the window, just in time to see Magistrate King climbing down from the saddle. She was shocked to see him there. What on earth could he want? Hastily she smoothed her hair and when he knocked on the door, she straightened her back and went to answer it.

'Mr King, do come in,' she said, for all the world as if she was inviting him into a stately home. She might be poor, but she still had her pride.

'Thank you, my dear.' He removed his hat and stepped past her, then paused to take in the surroundings.

The room was little more than a hovel and yet he noted that it was as clean as anyone could possibly make it. The floor was swept and the table in the centre of the room had been scrubbed until the wood was almost white. The bed that stood against one wall was neatly made too, and faded curtains hung at the window. The place was disgusting, but she clearly did her best, which made her even more attractive in his eyes.

'I came to tell you that your brother will be appearing before myself and the other magistrates tomorrow morning at eleven o'clock,' he informed her.

Opal clasped her hands together so that he wouldn't see how they had begun to shake. 'I see,' she said eventually. 'Thank you for informing me.'

He smiled. 'I did tell you I would, and I always keep my promises.'

At that moment the kettle began to hiss on the fire and Opal blushed. She had been about to make some tea and it seemed rude not to offer him a cup when he had come all this way.

'I, er, was just about to make some tea. Would you like a cup?'

'Oh, yes please.'

She nodded towards one of the chairs at the side of the table and busied herself preparing the teapot and cups and saucers.

Eventually, when she had filled his cup with the last of her tea, she dared to ask, 'So, what do you think will happen to Charlie?'

He took a long swig of his drink and instantly regretted it. This tea tasted nothing like the expensive brand he was used to, although he would not say that to her as he didn't want to upset her.

'I have already had a word with my fellow magistrates,' he told her solemnly. 'And I have told them that I have no wish to press charges.'

Her face lit up, and once again he was struck by how pretty she was. 'Oh, thank you, sir, thank you, I—'

He held up his hand to stop her flow of words. 'Unfortunately, because the case has already been put forward, it will have to be heard,' he explained. 'But I have every hope that now the other magistrates are aware that I don't wish to proceed with the charges they will be lenient with the sentencing. At this stage it is all I can do.'

'Oh . . . I see.' The lovely smile was gone again and she gulped to hide her disappointment. She had hoped that if he dropped the charges, Charlie would be released – but clearly this wasn't going to happen now.

He smiled kindly at her and she began to wonder if she might have misjudged him. He had done his best, after all.

'Well . . . thank you for that,' she said quietly as she lifted her cup and took a dainty sip from it. 'I did try to see Charlie again when I called into the police station yesterday, but they wouldn't allow me to.' A thought occurred to her then and she asked hopefully, 'I don't suppose you would be allowed to see him, would you? Or at least deliver a note to him?'

'A note?' He looked vaguely surprised.

'From me. Just to tell him that I will be there tomorrow to offer my support.'

'Oh . . . so you can write then?'

Her chin came up as she looked at him indignantly. 'Of *course* I can write. Our parents were very keen for us to have an education and we all attended the local school until we were each of an age to begin work.'

Hiding his surprise, he smiled. 'In that case I shall be delighted to do that for you, my dear.'

She rose and crossed to the dresser, returning with a small, shabby writing case that contained a quantity of cheap paper and envelopes, a nib pen, a small bottle of ink and a blotting pad. After dipping the pen in the ink she wrote:

My dear Charlie,
    Rest assured I am convinced of your innocence and shall be there tomorrow to hopefully see you released a free man. Then perhaps we can put this whole sorry incident behind us and concentrate on finding Susie.
    With much love,
    Your sister, Opal

Henry King remained silent, noting the tidiness of her handwriting. She placed the note in an envelope and, after addressing it to Charlie, she handed it to him with a grateful smile.

'Thank you, sir,' she told him, as he tucked it into the top pocket of his smart overcoat. 'I am most grateful for your help.'

Taking this as his cue to leave, he rose reluctantly – for he could quite happily have sat there all day watching her, despite the shabby surroundings. 'You are most welcome, my dear,' he assured her. Then, placing his hat back on, he strode across the small room to the door where he paused to say, 'Until tomorrow then? Let us hope for a good outcome for your brother.'

She inclined her head and watched as he rode away, feeling almost light-headed with relief; at last it looked as if there was something to hope for again.

After returning his horse to the groom in the stables at the back of his house in Swan Lane, Henry King walked the short distance into town. He called into the police station with instructions to deliver Opal's note to her brother, then made his way to the Bull Inn in the marketplace where the visiting magistrates were staying. An idea had occurred to him and now, after seeing Opal again, he was keen to set it in motion.

'Ah, James,' he greeted a portly gentleman with a handle-bar moustache and a ruddy complexion who was sitting at a table enjoying a jug of ale. 'You're just the person I was hoping to see.'

'Come and join me, Henry,' the man said, raising his hand for the landlord to bring more ale. 'What can I do for you?'

'Actually, it's quite a delicate matter.' Henry removed his hat and joined him at the table. 'The thing is, you will be sentencing a young man tomorrow at the court. His name is Charlie Sharp; the young devil tried to steal my wallet in the marketplace some days ago. Caught red-handed he was, and of course he denies it. But the thing is, because it was my wallet that he tried to steal, I would rather it be you that passed sentence. What I want to ask you is . . . could you see to it that he goes a long way away . . . for a long time?'

He fumbled in his wallet and discreetly pushed a crisp bank note across the table; it was quickly pocketed by the other man, who winked and tapped the side of his nose. 'You just leave it with me, Henry.' He grinned, and as the landlord approached with two more jugs brimming with ale, they went on to talk of other things.

The next day, Opal rose early. After washing herself from top to toe as she did every morning, she dressed in her Sunday best skirt and blouse. After brushing her hair until it shone, she tied it into a thick plait that hung down her back. Finally, she wrapped the shawl that Charlie had bought her for Christmas about her shoulders and set off in the chilly morning for the town.

She arrived at the courthouse early, and after taking a seat was forced to sit through several other prisoners' cases before at last Charlie was led into the room. The breath caught in her throat as she saw that his hands were chained. He looked pale and thin, but he managed a smile when he saw her, which brought tears springing to her eyes.

She trained her eyes on Magistrate King, but he behaved very professionally and avoided looking at her as Charlie's case was read out. The magistrates then adjourned to another room to consider the verdict, and when they returned the large gentleman with the big moustache sitting beside Henry King stared at Charlie solemnly.

'Stealing is a heinous offence,' he stated gravely. 'And although my colleague Magistrate King has declined to press charges, I feel that this cannot go unpunished. There have been too many cases of theft in this town over the last few months and so, Charlie Sharp, I intend to make an example of you. You shall be taken from here and placed on a ship and transported to the penal colony in New South Wales in Australia, where you will serve seven years hard labour. When you have served your sentence, you will be free to either return to England or make a new life for yourself there.'

Charlie's mouth fell open with shock, and a ripple ran through the court as Opal leaped to her feet.

'*No!*' she shouted, as tears spilled down her cheeks. But already two burly policemen were leading Charlie away, so lifting her skirts she ran from the room and down to the prison cart that had brought him there from the jail.

'I'm so sorry, Opal,' Charlie said brokenly when he appeared, flanked on either side by the officers. They instantly began to haul him into the back of the cart. 'Just take care of yourself now . . . and remember, it's not forever . . . I'll be back one day . . . *I promise!*'

'*No, no,*' she cried in deep distress, but already they were urging the horses on and she could only watch helplessly as the cart containing her brother was driven away.

Chapter Nine

Opal had no idea how long she stood there with tears streaming down her cold cheeks, but eventually a gentle hand on her arm made her glance up into the eyes of Magistrate King.

'I'm so sorry, my dear,' he said sorrowfully. 'I didn't press charges, as you heard, but I'm afraid that my colleagues felt the crime could not go unpunished.'

'I-it's . . . not your . . . f-fault,' she sobbed. 'You did what you could for him and I . . . . I am grateful for that. G-goodness knows how long they might have given him if you had decided to press charges.' Something occurred to her then and, looking up at him, she gabbled hopefully, 'Will I be allowed to see him before he goes?'

He shook his head, his expression solemn. 'I am afraid not. He will already be on his way to a prison close to the ship where he will be held until it sails,' he told her, and the sobs started again. Her whole world had fallen apart in such a short space of time that she could hardly take it in.

'Look, why don't you let me take you home?' he offered sympathetically. 'My carriage will be here any minute and it's no trouble, I assure you.'

Opal's initial reaction was to refuse the offer. But then she supposed that what had happened wasn't really his fault. He had tried to help by not pressing charges against Charlie, after all.

'Very well,' she said dully, as a smart carriage pulled by two matching black stallions drew to a halt beside them.

'Here we are then; in you go.' He helped her up the step, and she sank back miserably against the smart leather seats as he placed a thick travelling rug across her knees. Soon the carriage was rattling across the cobblestones. Opal had never been in a carriage before, but today she was so bereft that she barely even noticed the luxurious interior as she thought of Charlie's fate. Magistrate King's voice suddenly brought her thoughts back to the present.

'. . . I was saying, my dear . . .'

'Oh . . . sorry, I was miles away.'

'I've been thinking that I might just have a proposition to put to you that could be beneficial to us both.'

She raised an eyebrow. 'If you're referring to the job as a laundry maid that you offered me, I would be happy to accept it.' She really had no choice; it was that or the workhouse.

He shook his head. 'Actually, I have realised that you would be quite unsuited to such a position. You are far too intelligent to be wasted washing dirty laundry. However, I do have another idea that might appeal to you more.'

'Oh?' Opal found that she was interested despite herself – unless he was going to suggest something improper, in which case she had resigned herself to entering the workhouse.

'The thing is,' he went on, choosing his words carefully. 'My mother is becoming rather frail and is not able to get out and about as much as she used to. She has a rather splendid house on the outskirts of town in Red Deeps. She has servants, of course, but although her body is frail, her mind is still very alert, so I have been thinking of employing a companion for her, someone who could read to her and listen to her. I know she enjoys the company of young people. In fact, it is one of my biggest regrets that my late wife and I were never able to give her any grandchildren. Do you think this is a position that you might consider?'

Opal was so shocked that she could only stare at him open-mouthed for a moment. And then she glanced down at her shabby clothes and gave a wry grin. 'I hardly think that I am the class of person your mother would want around her,' she quietly pointed out.

He shook his head. Could she have known it, he was very aware of her past. He had made sure of that.

'I am quite sure that you could hold your own in any company,' he assured her. 'And you would, of course, be supplied with suitable clothes. It would also be a live-in position, so you would be safe and earning a salary. What do you think of the idea?'

Shocked, Opal shook her head. 'I . . . don't quite know what to think,' she admitted. 'I shall have to consider it.'

'Of course.' He gave her a gracious smile, and for the rest of the journey she sat staring from the window, thinking on all that had happened and his proposition. Eventually, the horses drew to a halt, and when the driver opened the door he told Mr King, 'I'm afraid the horses can't go any further, sir. The carriage would never go over that field.'

'It's all right,' Opal said hastily, casting the blanket aside and rising. 'The cottage isn't far from here. Thank you.'

'Would you like me to escort you the rest of the way?' Henry asked solicitously.

She shook her head. 'No, thank you, sir. I prefer to go the rest of the way on my own.'

'Very well – but you will think on what I suggested?'

When she nodded, he smiled with satisfaction. 'Good. Then I will wish you good day, my dear. You know where to find me should you wish to take me up on my offer.'

With another nod she got out of the carriage, and stood for some time watching it disappear into the distance. Then, wearily, she turned and made her way back to the empty cottage.

The carriage had gone only a short distance when it came to a row of tumbledown terraced houses and Henry shouted to the driver, 'Stop here, Brown!'

Once Henry was out on the lane, the driver enquired, 'Shall I wait for you, sir?'

'No, I shall make my own way home from here, drive on,' Henry told the driver, and as the carriage pulled away, he hurried towards one of the houses. It paid to have criminal friends sometimes, even if he was a magistrate, and right now he had a little job that he wanted doing.

The fire was out when Opal reached the cottage. It looked cold and bleak and, without Charlie, very empty. Dropping on to the nearest chair, she buried her face in her hands and sobbed broken-heartedly.

Eventually, as darkness was falling, she roused herself enough to light the fire and get out the small amount of bread she had left, which she smeared with dripping. She had no appetite whatsoever, but she knew she must stay strong if she was to find a job and keep herself. It looked like it would be many years until Charlie returned, and somehow she would have to survive.

Already she had decided not to take up Magistrate King's job offer. Jobs like that were not for the likes of simple working-class people like her. People might say she was trying to get above her station, and she was secretly afraid that if she wasn't satisfactory she might find herself out on her ear, which meant she would have to find some other means of keeping herself. She was prepared to do anything – washing, ironing, cleaning – but she also knew that even jobs like that were hard to come by.

She boiled the kettle, only to find that she had used the last of the tea leaves, so her meagre meal was washed down with water. As she began to prepare for bed, she became aware of a noise outside – but before she could ˙ ᵗᵒ the window to check what it was, the curtains sud- ˙ ᵃˢ the glass imploded and scattered across

she stared down at a large rock, as a voice f, yer rotten scum. We don't want the likes ds an' their kin around 'ere!'

Flying across to the door, she shot the bolt and pressed her back against it, her heart thudding wildly. It sounded like there were two or three people at least out there, and she knew that if they managed to break in she would stand no chance against them. Hurrying to the fireplace, she picked up the poker and shouted, 'Go away and leave me alone. We've done no one any harm!' They were brave words, but inside she was quaking with terror. And then the other window smashed, the glass scattering into the room, and she screamed again as she stood there helpless.

'That'll show yer what we think o' thieves,' the voice shouted again. 'An' we'll be back, so be warned!'

Slowly, the voices receded into the distance. Opal stood for a while, staring wide-eyed at the door as the wind whistled through the broken windows. When she was sure they had gone, she stuffed the tiny broken leaded panes with anything she could put her hand on to try and stop the draughts.

Eventually, she huddled down fully clothed on the bed, shaking with fear; she had never felt more alone and her ears strained for the sound of the men coming back, until at last she dropped into an exhausted sleep.

The next morning, Opal set off bright and early to try and find a job. Even the cottage didn't feel safe anymore, and she was glad to get away from it. But even though she tried every shop and house that she came to, there was no work to be found. Eventually, she came to the pawnbroker and, with tears in her eyes, she stared into the grimy window. The only thing of worth she had left now was her mother's th wedding band. She had worn it about her neck on a piece of string since the day her mother died and it was her most cherished possession – but common sense told her that she had to eat.

She pushed open the door and looked around. The interior of the shop was a hotchpotch of goods and each surface was piled high with everything from clothes to household goods. Behind the counter stood a small man, who appeared to be almost as far around as he was high. She gave a wry smile; he certainly didn't know what it was like to go hungry by the looks of him. Opal fingered the ring regretfully.

'So, what can I be doin' fer you this cold an' frosty mornin'?' the man enquired, peering at her through a pair of gold prince-nez spectacles that were perched on the end of his nose.

'I, er, was wondering how much you would give me for this. It was my mother's,' Opal told him, as she untied the string and slipped the ring from it.

He took it from her and, after examining it through an eyeglass, he snorted. 'Huh! These are ten a penny,' he told her. 'I can give yer a shillin' fer it.'

'A *shilling*! Is that all?' Opal gasped in horror.

He shrugged. 'Take it or leave it, dearie! Makes no differ-
~e to me. I've a drawer full of 'em.'

natched it back and with her head held high she
shop. *I'd rather starve than let it go for that*,

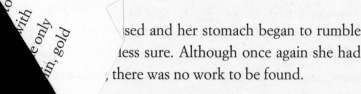

sed and her stomach began to rumble
less sure. Although once again she had
, there was no work to be found.

Finally, she went to the crowded marketplace, and found a shop doorway where she could shelter until the light began to fade and the stallholders began to pack up their wares. She had noticed that they threw away any damaged or bruised fruit and vegetables beneath the stalls and soon she was nipping between them, snatching up anything she could find that was edible. Then, with her last penny, she bought a day-old loaf that the baker let her have for half the price of a fresh one, before beginning the long walk home.

Once outside the cottage, she glanced nervously about to ensure she was alone before entering quickly. It was cold and draughty, so she lit the fire before sorting through her pockets to see what she had managed to collect. There was a bruised turnip, two misshapen potatoes and a winter cabbage – the leaves of which were turning brown – as well as a very squashed apple.

She quickly peeled and chopped the vegetables, poured water from the kettle into the pan and boiled them in a saucepan over the fire. The meal would be bland, but she was so hungry that she would have eaten anything. She went to fill the kettle at the pump over the sink and was surprised when no water trickled out of it. After venturing outside, she discovered that someone had yanked the pipe out of the wall and broken it beyond repair, and she felt her stomach clench with fear. It must have been done by the people who had broken the windows the night before, she thought, her heart hammering as she peered nervously into the darkness, listening for any sound, terrified the men would return. After standing shivering for a few moments, she went back in and bolted the door behind her.

When the vegetables were cooked she ate them, her eyes trained fearfully on the door. With her meal finished, she blew out the candle and climbed into bed, but sleep wouldn't come as she lay straining her ears for any sound outside the cottage.

It wasn't long before she heard a commotion again. Nerves stretched to breaking point, she hurried to the fireplace and lifted the poker in her shaking hands.

'Still 'ere are yer, scum?' a threatening voice shouted, as whoever it was began to pound on the door.

'*G-go away!*' she shrieked as panic took hold of her. 'I've done you no harm!'

'We don't want the likes o' you an' yer thievin' brother round 'ere,' the voice shot back. 'Just make sure as you ain't 'ere tomorrow when we come back, else it'll be the worse fer you! This is yer last warnin'!'

There was silence then, but it was a long time before Opal dared to return to her bed, and dawn was breaking before she finally fell into a troubled doze.

She was eating the rest of the boiled vegetables early the next morning when a horse's hooves sounded on the grass outside; instantly she was on her guard again as she lifted the poker and faced the door. Seconds later, someone knocked on it and she held her breath for a moment before shouting, 'Go away and leave me alone . . . do you hear me?'

'Miss Sharp . . . Opal, it's me, Henry King. Are you all right in there?'

Relief ran through her as she hurriedly fumbled with the lock on the door and, without stopping to think, she threw herself into his arms.

'My dear girl, whatever is the matter?' he asked solicitously as he savoured the feel of her warm flesh against his.

'P-people have been coming . . . at night,' she told him through her tears. 'Th-they broke the windows and told me I wasn't wanted around here.'

'Goodness me. Now come and sit down for a moment – you're all of a shake. Never fear, you are quite safe while I'm here.'

Opal did as she was told as she falteringly told him about the unwelcome visitors.

He stared at her sympathetically, his face a mask of concern. 'It sounds to me like it really isn't safe for you to be here,' he told her gently. 'Won't you at least agree to come and meet my mother? I'm sure you would be much safer living with her.'

Opal thought on his words for a few minutes, before nodding her head miserably. With no prospect of work here and no safety, it really did appear that there was no option open to her now except the workhouse; and after what had happened to Susie and Jack, as well as seeing the poor, wretched people who lived there when she'd stood outside its forbidding walls for all those weeks, she had no wish to go there.

'Very well,' she answered dully, staring at the floor and so not noticing the gleam that momentarily lit his eyes.

'Excellent. I shall go immediately and return with the carriage. There's no time like the present and you clearly aren't safe here. As soon as I am gone I want you to lock the door behind me and don't open it again until I come back. And don't worry, if you don't like my mother, you will be under no obligation to take the post.' He got up and strode towards the door.

'Th-thank you.' She sniffed, wondering why he was being so good to her.

He was back within the hour, by which time Opal had made herself look as presentable as she could.

'The carriage is down the lane waiting for us,' he explained, offering her his arm. Realising that she had no choice, Opal took it, relieved to be leaving this place, but feeling unaccountably nervous. After everything that had happened to her family over the past few months, she no longer believed that life could have any good in store for her.

Chapter Ten

'You look as if you're frozen through, my dear,' Henry said worriedly once they were settled in the carriage. 'And have you eaten today?'

'A little,' she told him in a small voice.

He tutted. 'As soon as we get to my mother's, you must go to her cook and get a good meal inside you,' he insisted. With a little grin he went on, 'And don't be put off by my mother's attitude. She can appear quite frosty until you get to know her, but she has a kind heart. Although she doesn't suffer fools gladly, which is why I feel that you and she might get on.'

Opal stared miserably from the window as the fine carriage rattled along. It was a bitterly cold, rainy day and her feet were so frozen that she had lost all feeling in them. Eventually, they turned into two high gates on the hill overlooking Griff Hollows.

'This is Hollow's House, my mother's residence,' he informed her, as he saw the look of surprise on her face. She clearly hadn't expected anything quite as grand as this. The drive was long and tree-lined, and when the house came into view, her eyes stretched wide. It was almost a mansion, with a turreted roof and numerous windows overlooking the sweeping drive. There were three steep steps leading up to two stout oak-studded doors and the walls were covered in climbing ivy.

'It's very big,' she squeaked.

He laughed. 'Nothing but the best for my mother. My father was a very wealthy man, and when he died he left her very well provided for. This is where I was brought up and I can remember them hosting some wonderful balls and parties here.'

The carriage drew up in front of the steps, and Henry climbed down and offered his hand as she cautiously followed him, feeling a little like a fish out of water.

'Come along, my dear. And don't look so frightened; she doesn't bite,' he encouraged.

He yanked on a bell to the side of the door and it was opened by a small maid in a navy dress over which she wore a cap and apron trimmed with *broderie anglaise.*

'Good morning, sir,' she greeted Henry, bobbing her knee and glancing curiously at Opal. 'The mistress is in the day room.'

'Excellent. I shall go to see her immediately. Meanwhile, Nancy, would you take my guest through to Cook and ask her to rustle her up some breakfast?'

'Of course, sir.' The maid gave a little curtsey again and, after an encouraging nod from Henry, Opal followed her along the enormous hallway. She had thought Henry's house was grand but it was nothing compared to this one, and once again she wondered how she could possibly fit in here.

'So who's this then?' a plump, rosy-faced woman asked with a frown when Nancy led her into the biggest kitchen Opal had ever seen.

'Mr King told me to bring her through, Cook, and said I was to tell you to give her some breakfast.'

'Did he now? Well, I reckon I can manage that. There's some sausage an' bacon left. And I could fry you an egg an' all. How does that sound, me dear?' Her voice had softened now and Opal felt herself relax a little.

'It sounds lovely . . . thank you,' she answered shyly as the warmth of the room wrapped around her like a cloak.

'Well, sit yourself down at the table while I get it ready,' the cook ordered bossily. 'An' you, Nancy, pour the young lady a cup o' tea. I just made a fresh pot an' it'll be mashed now.'

While the cook set about loading a plate with food, Nancy did as she was told, eyeing Opal curiously. 'So are you a friend o' Mr King's then?'

Opal flushed, not sure how to answer, but luckily she didn't have to because the cook snapped, 'Mind your own business, me girl! Why the young lady is 'ere is no concern of yours.'

'Sorry, Cook.' The girl gave Opal a cheeky grin and spooned sugar into her tea while the older woman placed a large plate of food in front of her.

Opal stared down at it. She had almost forgotten what bacon and sausage looked like and yet suddenly she was so nervous that she wasn't at all sure she was going to be able to eat it.

'Come on, now,' the woman ordered, but her voice was kindly. 'I hate to see good food go to waste, so get it down you.'

Opal did as she was told and once she had started her appetite came back with a vengeance and within minutes she had cleared her plate.

'Thank you, that was delicious.'

The cook eyed her curiously. If the state of the girl's shabby clothes were anything to go by, the poor lass had fallen on hard times and yet her manners were impeccable and she was clearly clean.

I wonder what the master wants with her, she thought. He was hardly known for his good deeds; in fact, there were many in the town that hated him. But then she supposed all would be revealed in good time.

Opal drank her tea, savouring every mouthful. It was a long time since she had been able to afford sugar. She had barely had time to drain the cup when Henry appeared in the doorway to ask, 'Are you ready to meet Mother now, Miss Sharp?'

'Er . . . yes.' Opal rose hastily and, after smiling her thanks to the cook, she followed him from the room with her heart pounding, as Cook and Nancy looked on without uttering a word.

'Now remember what I told you,' he said, when he paused at the door that she discovered led into the day room. 'Mother's bark is much worse than her bite, so don't let her intimidate you.'

When he pushed the door open Opal found herself in an elegantly furnished room, with long, green velvet drapes hanging at the two enormous sash-cord windows and a cheery fire glowing in the grate of an ornate marble fire-place. Her eyes were drawn to a large wing chair to one side of it, where a painfully thin, stern-faced woman sat staring suspiciously at her. She was dressed in a plain black bombazine gown, trimmed with black satin braid, and her steel-grey hair was coiled into two plaits pinned to either side of her head. About her neck hung a double strand of perfectly matched pearls, and diamond rings sparkled on her fingers. Her gnarled hands were resting on an ebony-topped walking cane, and a pair of gold spectacles were perched on the end of her nose. She peered at Opal over the top of them.

'Well, come in then,' she barked. 'What's wrong with you, girl? Has the cat got your tongue?'

Opal straightened her back, glared at her, and approached the chair.

The woman eyed her up and down. 'Mm, you're not very old are you?'

'I shall be seventeen next month,' Opal told her, lifting her chin.

'Seventeen, eh?' The woman chuckled. 'Barely out of binders. So what makes you think you could be company for me?'

'It was actually your son's suggestion, not mine!' Opal answered heatedly.

A small smile appeared at the corners of the woman's mouth. 'Well, you've got spirit at least,' she commented approvingly and, before Opal could respond, she went on, 'Can you read?'

'Of course I can read! My parents made sure of it,' Opal said indignantly. She was beginning to think this hadn't been such a good idea after all, but the woman hadn't done with her questions yet.

'And what do you like to read?'

'Some of my favourites are *Jane Eyre* and *Wuthering Heights*.'

'All right, all right, you've made your point,' the woman cut her off rudely. 'But where do you get your hands on such books?'

It was obvious that Opal could never have afforded to buy them.

'My mother and I used to go to the free reading rooms whenever we could and my father would read the books to us of an evening.'

'You'll be telling me next that you can speak French,' the woman said sarcastically.

Opal flushed as she retorted, 'I can't, actually, but I'd like to!'

Suddenly, the woman threw her head back and laughed. 'You were right,' she told her son. 'She *is* bright and I think I might actually enjoy getting her ready for genteel society – although I can see there's a lot of work to be done.'

Opal opened her mouth to object, but before she could get a word in the woman asked, 'Are you trustworthy? My son informs me that your brother is a thief.'

'He is *not*! He was merely seen picking up the wallet your son had dropped. He was going to return it to him!'

'Hm ... Well, here's what you would be expected to do – should I decide to employ you. You would be responsible for helping me to dress, undress and bathe, and it would also be your responsibility to make sure that all my clothes are kept in good order – laundered and suchlike. Not that I would expect you to wash them yourself; we have a woman come in twice a week to do the laundry. You would read to me when I wished you to and would also accompany me should I wish to visit someone. When I am entertaining you will pour the tea and hand around the refreshments – but you will stay quiet unless spoken to. In other words, you would be my lady's maid, or companion, as they term the post nowadays. My last one, Emily, retired some months ago and since then I've been at the mercy of my young maid, Nancy. She's a very good maid, admittedly, but she leaves a lot to be desired in this role.

'So, I'll tell you what I'm prepared to do: I'll give you a month's trial and we'll see how we get on. You'll live in and be at my beck and call, although I will allow you every Sunday afternoon off. Should you stay, your wages will be paid quarterly and you will earn twelve pounds a year. I shall have to have some new clothes made for you as well, but I will pay for them.' She peered at the ones Opal was wearing with an expression of distaste. 'I can't have you being seen in those rags when we go out. So, what do you say to that?'

Opal was inclined to tell the pompous little woman that she'd had a change of heart and didn't want the job after all. But then, as she thought of the lonely nights at the cottage and her smashed windows, she had second thoughts. Charlie would be gone for seven years – it wasn't forever and if she could only work until then, saving every penny she earned and using her Sundays to try and find Susie, it would give them a new beginning, surely.

'I'll accept your offer,' she told the woman.

Mrs King nodded. 'Good; you can start tomorrow. Now go and wait in the kitchen while I have a word with my son.'

Opal turned and left the room without another word, and the old woman grinned as she noted that she hadn't even dipped her knee. Yes, the girl certainly had spirit, there was no doubt about it.

Once the door had shut behind Opal, she turned her attention back to her son. 'Now you,' she said, 'just why have you become the good Samaritan all of a sudden?'

Henry grinned as he took a seat in the chair opposite, and held his feet out to the fire. 'Like you, I saw promise in her and thought she deserved a chance to better herself.'

'Huh! Stuff and nonsense!' she snorted. 'I happen to know that you have a position vacant in your own house for a laundry maid, so why didn't you offer her that?' Before he could answer she rushed on, 'It's because you could hardly go and marry a laundry maid, could you? What you forget, son, is that I know you inside out! She's a pretty little thing, isn't she? And with that lovely black hair and those deep, dark eyes, I've no doubt she'll be a beauty in a couple of years. You've not worried before about me not having a companion since Emily left, so why suddenly now, I wonder? I think what you actually want me to do is prepare young Opal to become your second wife. Would I be right?'

Henry had the good grace to flush, as he studiously avoided her eyes and stared into the fire. His mother had always been able to read him like a book.

'Well . . . she is a very attractive young woman,' he admitted cautiously.

Mrs King chortled with laughter. 'Quite. I knew I was right, and in a couple more years, when I have taught her all the social graces, she'll be ripe for the plucking, won't she?' She leaned heavily on her stick and narrowing her eyes, asked, 'But what if she doesn't *wish* to become the second Mrs King? You are over double her age.'

'So?' Deeply embarrassed, he glared at her. 'I can be charming when I want to be, you know. I have a lot to offer a wife! And age shouldn't come into it. The fact is, she's the first woman I've been attracted to since Marianne died and . . . well, she's young enough to bear me some children. You'd like that, wouldn't you? Some grandchildren, I mean?'

Winifred King sighed. Henry had been a difficult child and he had grown into a difficult man, as his first wife had soon discovered. But still, she could see no harm in giving Opal the job. She seemed to be a sensible young woman and, although she was too proud to admit it, there had been times since Emily had retired when she had felt acutely lonely. It would be nice to have a young companion for a change, and if in time Opal showed no inclination to wed her son, then he would just have to live with the fact.

'Let's just see how things go,' she said, picking up the tiny silver bell on the small table to the side of her; if she wasn't very much mistaken, it was time for her morning coffee.

Soon after, Henry King took Opal back to her cottage to pack her things and, once he had left, she glanced around at her meagre possessions regretfully. There wasn't much, but what there was had been her mother's pride and joy. There was no way she could afford to have the things stored, so she decided that rather than leave it there to rot she would go and see their old neighbour in Fenny Drayton to see if she could make use of it.

It meant a long walk, and before she had gone far, the drizzling rain had soaked through to her skin, but nonetheless she hurried on.

'Ah, luvvie, we heard about what happened to Charlie an' we've been worried sick about you,' Mrs Kitely greeted her, as she ushered her into her warm kitchen and handed her an old piece of towelling to rub her hair. 'Come an' sit by the fire an' I'll make you a brew. You look perished through.'

Gratefully, Opal did as she was told, and soon she had a steaming cup of tea in her hands. She told the kindly woman all that happened since Charlie had been imprisoned and about Henry King's offer of a job.

Mrs Kitely frowned. 'Well, I have to say it sounds rather out o' character fer that one to be 'elping anyone,' she commented. 'But then this job offer does sound like a grand opportunity fer you.'

'I don't have much choice but to accept it,' Opal answered miserably. 'I'm too afraid to stay in the cottage alone at night now. At least there I'll be safe.'

Mrs Kitely stretched her work-worn hand out to squeeze Opal's. 'Aye, you will, pet – an' think of all the money you'll be able to save till Charlie comes home. We all believe he were innocent an' yer poor mam an' dad must be turnin' in their graves at what's happened to him, God bless 'em. But things'll come right in the end, you'll see. And God willin' you might even be able to trace young Susie, given time.'

'I hope so,' Opal muttered. 'It's bad enough that we lost little Jack. It feels as if the whole family has been ripped apart.' And bowing her head, she gave way to a torrent of tears that threatened to choke her as the woman looked helplessly on.

'Anyway, the reason I came,' Opal eventually told her, when she had managed to pull herself together a little, 'was that I wondered if you would like what's left of our furniture? I can't take it with me to Hollow's House and it will just rot if I leave it in the cottage. Mam wouldn't have wanted that and I know she would have liked you to have it.'

'In that case, I'll get me old man to pick it up wi' the horse an' cart first thing in the mornin',' Mrs Kitely told her. 'An' if there's anythin' as I can't house I'll make sure it goes to someone as can. How's that, eh?'

Opal gave her a tearful smile. Her wet clothes were steaming in the heat from the fire now, but she knew that she must get back to the cottage and begin her packing.

Mrs Kitely, however, had other ideas. 'You're goin' nowhere till you've got a good meal inside you,' she told her, in a voice that brooked no argument. 'I've a big pan o' stew an' dumplin's cookin' on the range, so sit where you are till it's ready. That's an order.'

So Opal sat back and closed her eyes. It was nice to feel cared for, even if only for a little while.

Chapter Eleven

Luckily, the rain had stopped by the time Opal set off back to the cottage early that afternoon – but as she approached she saw at a glance that yet more damage had been done to it. The door was hanging off its hinges and someone had climbed up and smashed even more holes into the roof, exposing the small kitchen to the elements. Shattered roof tiles and her mother's precious mismatched china were scattered about the floor, and the curtains had been ripped down from the windows. This was supposed to have been the last day and night she would spend there, but now she knew she must leave immediately. Whoever was out to get her meant her harm and she couldn't risk staying there for another minute longer.

With a heavy heart, she fetched a pillowslip from the bed and folded the few clothes she had into it. There wasn't much: odd bits of underwear, a nightdress, her Sunday-best skirt and blouse. She consoled herself that at least it wouldn't be heavy to carry, and Mr Kitely would be coming early the next day to salvage anything that was worth keeping. With a sigh, she ran her hands across her mother's dresser. Her father had made it for her shortly after they were married, and it had always been one of her mother's most prized possessions.

Then, picking up the pillowslip, she took one last glance around the room. Tears came to her eyes again as she pictured Jack, Susie and Charlie there. *I have no one now*, she thought, clutching her mother's precious wedding ring; she had never felt more alone.

It was only when she set off with the pillowslip over her shoulder that she realised she had nowhere to go. Mr King had promised to fetch her the next morning. He would wonder where she was if he arrived and found that she wasn't there. Her mind raced as she set off up Haunchwood Road. She would have to visit his house and explain what had happened.

When she arrived, the door was opened by Mrs Wood, the housekeeper she had met on her previous visit, and when she saw Opal standing there on the doorstep she raised an eyebrow and looked less than pleased to see her.

'Hello again. Was it Mr King you were wishing to see?'

Opal nodded, her face a picture of pure misery. 'If you please.'

'Well, you should really make an appointment. He only just got in and he's in his study, I believe. You'd better come in while I go and see if he will see you.'

Once again, Opal found herself in the elegant hallway, although it didn't look quite so impressive now she had seen the one at Hollow's House.

'He'll see you now, if you come this way,' Mrs Wood announced primly when she returned, and she led Opal down the hallway.

'He's in there,' Mrs Wood said pompously, pointing to a door, and with that she turned about and hurried away as Opal nervously raised her hand and tapped on it.

'Come in!'

Opal stepped into a room where a fire was roaring in the grate, and saw Mr King sitting at a huge mahogany, leather-topped desk.

'Ah, Opal, what can I do for you?' His tone was pleasant. 'I thought we had agreed that you would start in my mother's employ tomorrow?'

'W-we did, sir,' she stuttered. 'But I went to see an old neighbour of ours this morning and when I returned some-one had ransacked the cottage and—' Her voice broke and she began to cry.

Instantly he came round the desk, patting her arm kindly. 'Why how *terrible*. You did right leaving there immedi-ately,' he said, concealing a smile. The petty criminals he had employed to terrify her had clearly done a good job and he would try to remember to slip them a little bonus the next time he needed to call on their services.

'I . . . I only came to tell you because you had said you would fetch me in the morning and you would have won-dered where I was if I wasn't there,' she gulped.

'Quite,' he agreed. 'But where are you planning on staying tonight?'

Opal hadn't thought that far ahead, and shrugged.

'In that case, I think I should take you to my mother's. I'm sure she won't mind you being there a day early and it will give you a little time to rest before you start your new post. I'm certainly not going to leave you with nowhere to go.'

'Y-you're very kind.'

'Not at all, my dear. You just sit there and rest while I ask my groom to prepare the coach. I'll get Mrs Wood to bring you a nice hot drink while you're waiting.'

Opal sat there, listening to the ticking of a large grand-father clock until Mrs Wood entered the room and slammed a tray down on the desk in front of her.

'Your tea,' she said, her voice heavy with disapproval as she looked pointedly at Opal's shabby attire.

She had been shocked when Henry had told her that his mother would be employing the girl as her compan-ion. Personally, from what she had seen of her, Mrs Wood thought she would have been far more suited to the post of laundry maid. *So why is he taking such an interest in her?* she wondered. But then, the girl *was* pretty! Could it be that Henry had designs on her? Mrs Wood had served Henry King faithfully for more years than she cared to remember, in more ways than one – even more so since the death of his wife – and she had hoped that eventually it might be she who became the second Mrs King. She was clearly much more suited to the role than this little slum girl.

But if that was what Henry King wanted with the girl, Blanche Wood supposed that it was better the girl went to Henry's mother than stay here. At least there it would not be so easy for him to visit her room during the night, as he sometimes did her own. She could think of no other rea-son why he was being so kind. She knew better than most that Henry King was not a generous man by nature, so why else this sudden interest in a girl who was way below him in

102

class? With a last disdainful look at the girl, she flounced out of the room.

Shortly after, Opal once again found herself in Henry's carriage as it rattled its way to his mother's house. She supposed she should be feeling excited at the prospect of her new job, but all she could feel was despair because nothing could ever replace the family that had been so cruelly snatched away from her.

Eventually they turned into the drive of Hollow's House again. Never in her wildest dreams had Opal ever imagined she would live in such a place, even as a servant.

'Here we are then,' Henry said jovially. 'I've no doubt you'll settle in in no time and I shall look forward to you telling me how you are getting on when I visit my mother.'

Feeling guilty that she didn't feel more enthusiastic about the opportunity he had given her, Opal managed a weak smile as he helped her down from the carriage. Instead of telling her to go round to the servants' entrance, Henry led her into the hallway through the front door.

'Wait here a moment, m'dear,' Henry said, as he handed his hat to a maid. 'I'll just go and inform my mother of what's happened and then you can get settled in. I've no doubt Belle here will already have your room ready for you.'

The young maid blushed and dropped a curtsey, hardly able to believe the change in Mr King. He was usually very rude to her and the rest of the servants, but today he seemed quite jovial.

While Opal waited, she and the young maid eyed each other curiously.

'I'm Belle,' the girl ventured eventually.

'I'm Opal Sharp, but please call me Opal.'

'Well, I'd be happy to, but I doubt the mistress will allow me to address you by your first name,' the girl whispered. 'She's a stickler for everything being just so, but just between you and me she isn't as hard as she makes out.'

'Have you worked here long?' Opal asked.

'Since I was fourteen,' Belle confided. 'So that's over two years now.'

Opal smiled. She had the feeling that they were going to get along, but she had no time to say more because Henry reappeared at that moment.

'Take Miss Sharp up to the room adjoining the mistress's, Belle,' he ordered. Then, turning back to Opal, he informed her, 'My mother says she has had a variety of gowns laid out on your bed for you. They are only some of the ones that have belonged to various other maids but she says they will suit until she can get you some new ones made. If they don't fit then I am afraid you will have to alter them as best you can. I'm sure young Belle here will help. My mother tells me she is quite a dab hand when it comes to sewing. But now I must be off – duty calls. Goodbye for now, my dear.'

Belle hurried to fetch his hat for him and once he had put it on, he gave a little bow and left.

'Phew, I don't know why but he allus makes me nervous,' Belle confided. 'But come on, I'll show you to yer room. I got it ready for yer meself this mornin', though I'm afraid the fire in there ain't been lit yet cos we weren't expectin' yer till tomorrow. Still, it's all laid ready so I'll only have to put a match to it.'

'I could quite easily do it myself,' Opal told her, feeling embarrassed. She wasn't used to being waited on and had always had to do things like that for herself.

Opal followed her up the rather splendid sweeping staircase, admiring the numerous gilt-framed portraits and landscapes they passed. It was like entering another world after what she had been used to, and once again she wondered if she was overreaching herself; Mrs King was clearly a very wealthy woman. At the top of the stairs, Belle led her down a long corridor; Opal's feet sank into the deep-pile carpet as she stared around at the fancy, spindly-legged chairs and ornate tables that were positioned along the walls.

Finally, Belle stopped outside a door. 'This will be your room, miss.'

'Oh please, call me Opal!'

Belle smiled. 'I might risk it when I'm on my own but as I said, I wouldn't dare do that in front of the mistress. She's already instructed all the staff to address you as Miss Sharp. As her companion you're above us in rank, see?'

Opal didn't see at all, but she said nothing as she followed the girl into a bedroom that almost took her breath away.

'Th-this can't be *my* room!' she gasped.

'It is, an' that door there leads into the mistress's room. Her last companion slept in 'ere so she were close at 'and should the mistress need anythin'.'

Belle hurried to the grate and struck a match to the fire, giving Opal the chance to have a good look around. There was a tall wardrobe made of rosewood, polished to such a shine that she could see her face in it, and beside it was a matching chest of drawers. In the deep bay window was a small desk and chair, next to which was a very handsome marble-topped washstand with a pretty china jug and bowl standing on it. On the floor, another luxurious carpet stretched almost wall to wall. But the centrepiece of the room was a beautiful four-poster bed. The velvet drapes around it exactly matched the heavy blue curtains hanging at the windows that gave a glorious view over the well-maintained grounds.

'Why . . . it's just *beautiful*!' she gasped.

Belle grinned. 'It is, ain't it,' she agreed enviously. 'An' a damn sight warmer than my room up in the attics. I don't mind tellin' you up there it's freezin' cold in winter an' stiflin' hot in summer. Still, I suppose I shouldn't complain, really. At least Mrs King keeps a good table an' none of us ever goes 'ungry. But let's look at these clothes now, eh? I dare say the mistress will expect you to dine with her tonight so she'll want yer lookin' respectable. No offence intended,' she added hastily, as she glanced at Opal's well-worn clothes.

Side by side they approached the garments laid out on the bed and, for the first time since arriving, Opal smiled. Used servants' dresses they may have been, but they were far better than anything she had ever owned and she could barely wait to try them on.

'This one might fit yer,' Belle told her, holding up a navy-blue muslin gown. It was very plain but beautifully made with not a single darn in it – a first for Opal. 'Come on, try it on an' if it don't fit I might have time to alter it for you before you go into dinner this evenin'.'

Opal obediently stripped down to her plain cotton chemise and Belle lowered the dress over her head and started to do up the tiny pearl buttons that ran all up the front of it from the waist. It was long-sleeved and high-necked and designed for an older lady, but Opal felt wonderful in it and gave a little twirl. The top half was actually quite a good fit, although it was fractionally too long.

''Ere, put some o' these petticoats on underneath it; that'll lift it a bit,' Belle suggested.

She was right, and as Opal turned to look in the long cheval mirror, she hardly recognised herself.

'I reckon this belonged to the mistress's last companion,' Belle told her. 'I can remember her wearin' it. She was a lot older than you, but to be honest it still suits yer. With your looks, anything would.'

Opal stared at herself in the mirror, barely able to drag her eyes away from the image. The material was so soft and she suddenly felt very grand.

'Now, let's see if any o' these shoes I sorted from the boot room will fit yer. No disrespect but them old boots yer wearin' are almost droppin' off yer feet.'

Belle began to search through a pile of shoes and dainty leather boots. ''Ere, try these,' she urged and Opal was only too happy to oblige. Perhaps it wasn't going to be as bad living here as she had thought. Unfortunately, the shoes were far too big and flapped about on her feet, but eventually they found a pair of soft leather ones that fit as if they had been made for her.

'They were the mistress's,' Belle said as she sat back on her heels to admire them. 'An' they certainly look a deal better than the ones yer were wearin'.'

There was a tap at the door and a woman in a grey dress appeared. 'Ah, here you are, Belle. Cook is asking for you, so you may go about your duties now if Miss Sharp has no further need of you.' The woman looked at Opal. 'Welcome to Hollow's House, Miss Sharp. I am Mrs Deep, the house-keeper, and the mistress requests that you join her in the dining room for dinner promptly at six o'clock; I shall send Belle to show you the way. In the meantime, I shall leave you to settle in.'

Both she and Belle left then and, once alone, Opal smiled as she looked ruefully at the pillowcase containing all her worldly possessions. It wouldn't take long to put those away. In fact, there were more clothes piled on the bed than she had ever owned in the whole of her life.

Crossing to the wardrobe, she took out some hangers and began to put everything neatly away. Once she had finished, she decided to try the bed out and was delighted to find that she had a feather mattress. She climbed up on to it and lay down – but no sooner had her head hit the pil-low than the many sleepless nights she had had caught up with her, and within minutes she was fast asleep.

'Miss Sharp!'

A knocking on the door brought her springing awake sometime later and she was shocked when she opened her eyes to find that it was dark.

The door inched open, and Belle appeared. 'It's quarter to six, miss. An' the mistress is a stickler for people bein' on time. Do yer want me to show yer the way to the dining room?' Belle hustled in and lit the oil lamp.

'Oh, yes please. I'll just give my hair a quick tidy up, if you don't mind.'

Opening a drawer she took out her hairbrush and quickly dragged it through her hair before fastening it at the nape of her neck with a scrap of ribbon. Then after pinching her cheeks to bring a little colour into them she turned to Belle and asked, 'Will I do?'

Belle smiled and nodded, and with Opal close behind her she led the way downstairs.

'It's that door there,' Belle told her, pointing. 'Make sure yer knock before goin' in,' she said, as she left to fetch the first course.

Opal drew herself up to her full height, tapped on the door and entered to find Mrs King already seated at the head of an enormous mahogany table. It was set at one end for two, and the woman gestured to the seat next to her. As Opal sat down, she stared perplexed at the vast amount of cutlery laid out.

Mrs King smiled. 'Lesson one. Table manners. When dining, one starts with the cutlery on the outside and works in like so.' She demonstrated what she meant and Opal nodded. 'Your soup and dessert spoons will always be positioned here.' Mrs King demonstrated and again Opal nodded. Having only ever used a knife, fork and spoon, she was finding it all rather confusing. *Why did one person need this amount of cutlery, anyway?* she wondered. Fancy making all that unnecessary washing up!

Minutes later Belle appeared, carrying a large tureen full of soup that she placed carefully in the centre of the table between them, before serving them both using a silver ladle that gleamed in the light of the candelabra. It was all very grand and again Opal felt sadly out of place.

'You hold your soup spoon like so and push the spoon away from you in the dish to get it on to the spoon, and of course you must *never*, ever slurp it. It is so common! Just take dainty little sips.' Mrs King demonstrated and, after checking that she had picked up the right spoon, Opal followed her example.

The broccoli and Stilton soup was delicious and quite unlike anything Opal had ever tasted before, and she cleared her dish in seconds.

'Lesson two,' Mrs King scolded. 'It is etiquette for a lady to always leave a little in her dish or on her plate.'

Opal flushed as she remembered the way her father had always loved to wipe his plate clean with a slice of bread after a meal, and she wondered what Mrs King would have thought of that? She could only assume that she had never gone hungry like they had, but she wisely didn't comment.

The second course was a rack of lamb served with seasonal vegetables and creamed potatoes, and it was so tasty that Opal found it hard to leave some on her plate. As far as she was concerned, it was an utter waste of good food, but even so she did as she was told. Finally, the dessert was carried in: a deep apple pie served with thick, creamy custard, and by the time she had finished, Opal was so full she feared she might burst. She had only ever been used to one course before, and then only when she was lucky enough to have anything!

'And now we shall retire to the drawing room, and you could perhaps read a little to me.' Mrs King rose from the table, leaning heavily on her ebony-topped stick.

Opal nodded obediently as she followed her. Her new life had begun and there could be no going back now – but then, what was there to go back for?

Chapter Twelve

After months spent incarcerated in a prison near the port, the day Charlie had dreaded finally arrived. Now, under a bright August sun, he shuffled across the dock to the huge ship that would transport the prisoners to Australia, with tears in his eyes as he thought of leaving the family he loved so far behind. He wished with all his heart that he could turn back the clock, and that he had never noticed the wallet lying on the ground – but it was too late for regrets now. What was done was done, and he would forever have to live with the consequences.

Each of the prisoners was shackled with chains on their hands and feet, which made walking difficult; but after being shut away for days in a prison with no daylight, it was a relief just to be outside again.

'Come on, let's be 'aving yer, yer motley lot!' one of the guards barked with a warning crack of his whip, and the men shuffled forward again, sick at heart. Very soon they would be packed into the ship like animals and who knew if they would ever see their homeland again?

Charlie was manhandled up a wooden gangplank and, just for a moment, he managed to glance across his shoulder for a last sight of dry land. A very long journey lay ahead, and from what he had heard from men in the prison, many of the prisoners wouldn't make it to the colony. Dysentery, typhoid and all manner of other serious illnesses were rampant aboard the ships, and it was common knowledge that many died before they even got there. For a fleeting moment, Charlie almost hoped he'd be one of them; but then he thought of Opal, and his resolve to survive returned. He hoped she was coping without him, and prayed that she would find a job to sustain her until they could be reunited.

He was rudely jolted out of his musings when a guard gave him a vicious push, and the sharp chains about his ankles chaffed at the blisters they had caused, making him wince with pain.

'Down 'ere, you lot!' A guard pushed them towards a ladder that led down into the dark bowels of the ship, and as he descended the stench made Charlie retch. It was a smell of illness, stale urine, vomit and something he didn't recognise and certainly didn't want to identify. Ahead of him a man panicked and turned with a scream to try to find his way back up to daylight, but a well-aimed whip across his back had him tumbling like a rag doll to the bottom of the ladder, taking the two men below him with him.

A guard instantly approached him and began to kick him until he managed to get to his feet and stagger on. Charlie watched helplessly. He felt as if he was descending into the bowels of hell as they came to yet another ladder, which somehow, though hampered by the heavy chains that shackled them, they managed to slip and slither down. At last they were led into an enormous room, with hammocks strung from the beams in the wooden ceilings. Buckets lined one wall – *no doubt for their toileting*, Charlie thought – and on the opposite side, a wooden bench ran down the length of the hull.

So, this is to be our home for the foreseeable future, Charlie thought with a sinking heart. There was no comfort of any kind and, once the guard had slammed the door behind them, they were left in darkness. He managed to get across to the bench and took a seat; and lowering his head, he began to pray. It was the only comfort that was left to him now.

When the ship finally sailed on the tide that night, a number of the men immediately became seasick. Most of them tried to reach the buckets, but others felt so ill they merely vomited on the floor in front of them, which made the stench overwhelming. Worse still, because it was dark, they had no way of knowing day from night. Eventually those who were strong enough claimed the hammocks and tried to lose themselves in sleep – no easy task when men were moaning and groaning all around.

But Charlie felt too stunned and too heartsick to move, so he stayed where he was on the bench.

At some point, the door was opened and the darkness lightened enough to reveal some guards bringing them food. It was very unappetising, mainly dry bread and salted beef or pork, and together with the disgusting stench of vomit and the sound of retching from some of the other men, the thought of food turned Charlie's stomach. But he knew he needed to keep his strength up, so he forced himself to eat what he could, washing it down with water from the jugs that had been provided. Finally, he curled up in a ball on the floor under the bench and tried to sleep. But he'd barely closed his eyes when the guards reappeared and poked and prodded the men up the ladder for their exercise, which consisted of a very short walk around the decks.

Charlie gulped at the salty air gratefully and shuffled over to the rails, only to be told, 'Get back in line, you, else you'll feel the length o' this!'

Glancing at the stern-faced guard who was holding a cat-o'-nine-tails, Charlie hastily did as he was bid. The way he saw it, he couldn't change what had happened, so he may as well keep his head down, do as he was told and serve his time as best he could. And then . . . he would go home to England and find Opal and Susie. It was only this thought that kept him going.

From then on, the days and nights blended into one, and life felt like a never-ending nightmare. After being confined in the dark, the men's tempers grew short and Charlie was sure that had they not all been kept in chains fights would have broken out. As it was, all the men could do was give out verbal tongue-lashings. And each day, when they were allowed a short break on deck for a shuffle about, the men were blinded by the bright light and had to squint to see where they were going. It was only thanks to these trips on deck that Charlie was able to keep a sense of how long they'd been at sea.

Charlie had thought conditions on the ship couldn't get any worse – but almost two weeks into the voyage they sailed into a storm and the men below were tossed about their prison quarters like corks. Charlie managed to wedge himself against the hull, where he lay steeped in misery; he tried to conjure up the faces of his beloved family to keep him going, but it proved impossible, and his despair deepened. Now it felt like even his memories were being stripped from him, and hopeless tears leaked from his eyes.

Some of the men were thrown so violently about the room that they suffered broken bones and were taken away to the ship's doctors' infirmary, and Charlie knew he wasn't alone when he found he was envious of them. To Charlie and those left below, it felt as if they were in a living hell and only the thought of returning home one day kept him going. For Opal's sake, he was determined to survive!

'At least they get to see daylight,' one of the prisoners grumbled, and a murmur of agreement rippled amongst them. They were surviving on almost starvation rations, though, and soon even talking took too much energy, and the men lay groaning, each lost in their own miserable world, as they gradually grew weaker and more of them fell ill.

Then one morning, there was a cry of disgust from one of the men. ''Ere, I reckon this chappie next to me is dead. A bloody rat was gnawin' on 'is feet and 'e didn't move an inch.'

Someone went to hammer on the door, but it was a few minutes before a guard shouted, 'What do yer want? What's goin' on in there?'

'We've got a body 'ere,' the man answered. 'An' it's going to begin to stink like 'igh 'eaven!'

'Leave it where it is. We'll move it when yer come up fer yer exercise,' the guard answered nonchalantly. 'We'll lob 'im over the side o' the ship then.'

The man at the door gritted his teeth with frustration, but there was nothing he could do, so he shuffled back to his place and sank down again.

Charlie stared dully at the dead man's motionless body and wondered whether this would be his fate too. To his surprise, the prospect didn't worry him, because right now the thought of being released from this torment and floating freely in the ocean seemed like heaven.

Chapter Thirteen

Two days after arriving at Mrs King's, Opal was summoned to the day room, where she found the old lady waiting for her with her dressmaker.

'Mrs Compton is here to take your measurements, Opal,' Mrs King advised her. 'Kindly take her to your room where it may be done in privacy.'

'Yes, ma'am.' Opal turned to lead the woman away, but then, remembering what she had been told, she hastily turned to dip her knee. The lessons on good manners and etiquette that Mrs King was determined to teach her had begun, and there was so much to remember that Opal's mind was reeling.

Her duties began at seven o'clock each morning when she rose, washed and dressed; then it was her job to go down to the kitchen and prepare a breakfast tray for her employer. It had to be set just so with a pretty, crisp, white tray cloth and a single bloom in a bud vase. She would then add the cup and saucer, sugar, milk and teapot and make the toast, which had to be just very slightly browned on the fire. The first morning she had been scolded and sent back to the kitchen to try again because the old lady insisted the bread was burned. She had clearly never known what it was like to be hungry, Opal had thought, for there had been times over the last months since the death of their parents that she and Charlie would have been glad of it. Thoughts of her brother had started the tears falling again.

Following breakfast, her next job was to sort out the clothes Mrs King wished to wear that day, lay them out for her and then help her to wash and get dressed. Opal had found this quite embarrassing as Mrs King had no qualms about her seeing her undressed, but then Opal supposed she was used to people helping her and so she had just got on with it.

Finally, Opal had to dress her hair, and she was somewhat struggling with that.

'I think I shall wear it in a French roll today,' the woman had told her on the first morning as she sat at her dressing table and Opal had stared at her blankly. What was a French roll?

Seeing her hesitation, Mrs King had tutted irritably.

'You twist the hair like so and pin it into place,' she had told her, trying to demonstrate and eventually Opal had managed it, but it brought home to her just how much there was to learn.

'There is much I need to teach you if you are to take your place in genteel society,' Mrs King had warned her, and so the lessons continued.

Once Mrs King had had her breakfast and was dressed and settled in the day room, Opal was free to enjoy her own meal in the kitchen with the servants, where she felt much more at home.

Mrs Tranter the cook was a kindly soul and Belle, the young maid who had first showed her to her room, went out of her way to be friendly to her. There was also Tilly, the general maid, whose job it was to clean and light the fires each morning before anyone rose, and Nancy, the kitchen maid; and then there was Ned, who tended the horses and did the outside work. Finally, there was Mrs Deep, the housekeeper, but she dined in her own rooms.

'We used to 'ave a butler an' all, but when 'e retired last year the mistress didn't replace 'im,' Belle had informed her with a giggle, her mouth full of scrambled egg. 'It's just as well cos he were very strict.'

After breakfast, Opal would then attend Mrs King to see if she had any visitors planned for that day for morning coffee. Visitors would leave little cards telling what day and time they would be calling and it was Opal's job to prepare a small tea trolley that Belle would wheel in when the visitors were seated.

'You will sit quietly to one side of the room,' Mrs King informed her. 'And you will not participate in the conversation unless you are spoken to, but sit with your hands folded neatly in your lap like so.' She had demonstrated and Opal had nodded. 'When I give you a slight nod, pour the tea or coffee for myself and the visitors. Remember, first you pour the tea or coffee, then add a little milk and offer the visitor the sugar bowl so that they may help themselves. White sugar for tea, brown sugar for coffee, and *never* splash any into the saucers! And then you will offer whatever biscuits or pastries Cook has sent in and ensure that their cups are refilled should they wish them to be.'

'Yes, Mrs King,' Opal had answered, feeling daunted. The cups and saucers were so delicate that she hardly dared handle them and she was afraid that her hands would shake so much she would slosh the drinks everywhere.

Now, Opal led the dressmaker up to her room and stood patiently while the woman seemingly measured every inch of her.

'Right, I think I have everything I need now,' the stout little woman informed her eventually. 'Let's go back down and see what Mrs King has in mind for you.'

In the day room, they found Mrs King inspecting the fabric samples Mrs Compton had brought with her.

'You will need two nice day gowns,' Mrs King commented. 'I quite like this navy material; it would look very smart trimmed with white. What do you think of it, Opal?'

'I-it's lovely,' Opal gulped. It looked very expensive, but that didn't seem to trouble Mrs King at all.

'And this silvery grey is nice also,' the woman went on as she fingered the material. 'Perhaps that one could be trimmed with black. She will also need a selection of petticoats and underwear and perhaps two lawn nightdresses. Oh, and of course a warm cloak. Perhaps in a dark grey with a fur trimming to the hood.'

'No trouble at all,' Mrs Compton crooned. They discussed styles, although Opal left that to them. She had no idea what was fashionable and what was not and truthfully would have been more than happy with the cast-off gowns she was wearing at present.

'And what about an evening gown?' Mrs Compton asked. 'Should you entertain guests at night, the day gowns would not really be suitable.'

'Hm, I dare say you're right.' Mrs King narrowed her eyes and stared at Opal for a few moments before asking, 'What colour would you suggest for her?'

'I think with her black hair and those lovely brown eyes she would look quite delightful in a sky blue,' the woman answered. 'Perhaps in a nice heavy satin, slightly off the shoulder and not too low cut as would befit her age? I could trim it with silk roses, perhaps in a nice pale pink colour, but keep it fairly simple, tight to the waist with a wonderful full skirt.'

'That sounds quite satisfactory,' Mrs King told her with a smile.

'In that case I shall get started on the order immediately.' Mrs Compton began to gather up her samples and once she had departed Opal hurried off to the kitchen to prepare the tea trolley in readiness for the visitors Mrs King was expecting for morning coffee.

This would be her first experience of waiting on visitors and she was feeling nervous.

'Don't worry,' Belle said kindly as she noticed Opal's hand shaking. 'Just relax and you'll be fine. Oh, hold on, there's the door. I bet that's them now.' She rushed away to answer the door.

After a final glance at the trolley to make sure she hadn't forgotten anything, Opal hurried back to the day room where Mrs King was waiting.

'Now, just remember, follow my lead and only speak when you are spoken to,' Mrs King warned her, as Opal took her place at the side of her chair.

Opal nodded just as Belle opened the door to announce, 'Miss Partridge and Mrs Partridge to see you, Mrs King.'

'Ah, Esther and dear Dorothy, do come in,' Mrs King said as a pair of enormously fat ladies waddled into the room. Opal assumed they were mother and daughter as one was an older version of the other, and she was proven to be right when they took a seat on the small sofa opposite Mrs King and removed their gloves.

'How are you both?' Mrs King asked when the greetings had been dispensed with.

'Oh, I am quite well, dear,' the older woman said with a curious glance at Opal. 'But my poor Esther has had a dreadful cold, the poor child. But then she has always been a delicate girl, as you know.'

Opal had to press her lips together firmly to stop herself from giggling. The younger woman was far from being a child. Opal judged her to be in her late twenties to early thirties and she was so solidly built that she looked the total opposite to delicate.

'But now tell me do, dear Winifred, who is this young lady?'

'Ah, this is my new companion, Miss Opal Sharp.' Mrs King introduced Opal.

She instantly stood and dipped her knee as she had been told to and said politely, 'How do you do, Mrs Partridge, Miss Partridge?'

'Really?' The older woman looked astounded while the younger eyed Opal coldly, although Opal had no idea what she might have done to offend her. 'Whatever made you choose one so young?'

'I happen to like having young people around me,' Mrs King informed her, and glancing towards Opal she told her, 'Perhaps you would like to ring the bell for the maid now? I'm sure our visitors will be ready for some refreshments.'

Opal quickly did as she was asked, before taking her place discreetly beside Mrs King's chair.

Belle appeared wheeling the trolley. 'Will that be all, ma'am?'

'Yes, Belle, for now. I shall ask Opal to pour the drinks.'

As Belle turned, she gave a sneaky grin and a wink towards Opal who stepped forward to ask the visitors, 'Would you like tea or coffee?'

Somehow, she managed to pour all the drinks and offer round the tiny pastries Cook had made without mishap and then, as she had been directed, she took a seat herself, listening with half an ear to the women's idle chatter as she looked longingly towards the window.

Somewhere out there in the big wide world were her brother and sister, but would she ever see either of them again or was this to be her life from now on? Admittedly she was aware that she was lucky to have a warm roof over her head, nice clothes to wear and food aplenty to eat, but she would gladly have returned to being poor and living in the derelict cottage if she could only have had her family back.

'Opal . . . did you hear me, child? Mrs Partridge is waiting for another drink!' Mrs King's voice brought her thoughts sharply back to the present and she started guiltily.

'I'm so sorry, what may I get for you?'

The younger woman glared at her, and the reason why became apparent when she asked, 'And how is *dear* Henry, Mrs King?'

Once more, Opal had to stifle the urge to laugh. So *that* was it: Esther was sweet on Mrs King's son and saw her as a threat.

Well she has no need to worry on that score, Opal thought as she again passed the pastries to the woman. *I have no designs on Henry King whatsoever; why he's almost old enough to be my father and if she wants him she's welcome to him. As if he would ever look at a girl from the slums like me anyway!*

As Opal patiently waited for the woman to load her plate yet again, she smiled sweetly. *It was no wonder she was the size of a house*, she found herself thinking, before resuming her seat. Once more her eyes strayed to the window as she again thought of Susie and Charlie, and unbidden tears pricked at the back of her eyes. She blinked them away, knowing crying now would not please her new employer.

The day before, Mrs King had told Opal that Belle would be giving her lessons on how to set a table correctly and then Mrs King would be instructing her on deportment.

'A young woman should never appear to walk into a room,' she had told her. 'She should appear to glide . . .'

Opal secretly wondered how learning all these useless things could ever be of any use to her, but she was there to please the old lady so she raised no objections, even though she found the majority of what she was being taught extremely boring. At least the lessons helped to pass the time – and time couldn't pass quickly enough for her, because in seven years Charlie would hopefully come home again and they could be a family once more.

Chapter Fourteen

The body had still not been removed when Charlie became aware that the boy sitting next to him was crying. Charlie had made an effort to keep his head down and had barely spoken to anyone since he'd been on board, but even so he had noticed the boy before, because he always put himself forward when the guards chose two prisoners to empty the buckets. Due to his small size, though, he was never chosen. He looked to be no more than eleven or twelve years old and Charlie's heart went out to him. He asked compassionately, 'Are you all right, matie?'

'I wants me ma,' the boy whimpered.

Charlie was at a loss for words. 'How come you ended up here?' he asked eventually.

The boy sniffed, wincing as he lifted his arm to wipe his nose along the sleeve of his tatty shirt. The skin on his wrists and ankles was red raw where the chains had rubbed them. 'I stole a loaf o' bread. Me ma and the kids were starvin', see? Me dad cleared off long ago an' I couldn't get no work an' I couldn't see 'em go 'ungry, could I?'

'Course not.' Charlie couldn't believe that a young boy should be punished so severely for such a trivial crime.

Stealing was stealing, admittedly, but a loaf of bread? It wasn't as if the poor little mite had robbed a bank!

'Look, stay by me, and I'll try to keep an eye out for you,' he said encouragingly. 'What's your name anyway?'

'Jimmy . . . Jimmy Bennett, mister.'

Unable to place an arm around his shoulders thanks to the chains, Charlie nudged him gently. 'I'm Charlie and I want you to try and cheer up. They'll be bringing our food soon, I reckon, such as it is, and you need to eat so's you can keep your strength up.'

The words had barely left his mouth when the door was unlocked and two guards appeared with a large basket of food, which they threw on to the floor before disappearing again. There was a mad scramble as Charlie and the other men made a rush for it and, as always, the weaker amongst them stood no chance. Most of it was gone by the time they even managed to get near the basket. It was survival of the fittest down there.

Charlie returned to his seat with a chunk of bread and a lump of salted beef and saw instantly that Jimmy hadn't managed to get anything.

'Here.' He broke his meagre rations in half and handed half to Jimmy. 'You'll feel better when you've got something inside you. How long is it since you last ate?'

He felt Jimmy shrug his slight shoulders. 'A couple o' days I reckon . . . fanks.'

Charlie sighed. 'I bet they feed the beasts they brought on board better than they feed us,' he remarked in disgust, as he forced himself to chew on the tasteless lump of meat, which he discovered very quickly was mainly gristle and fat. Jimmy nodded and they ate the rest of the meal in silence.

They were starting to get used to the stench, but after being on deck they always realised how truly dreadful it was. Thankfully, because of their meagre diet, the men's need to use the buckets had lessened, for they had so little in their stomachs; but it was still hard to force themselves to eat anything with the rancid stink all around them. And so it seemed to be proving for Jimmy, because not long after they'd finished their food, Jimmy leaned forward and vomited it back up again.

Later that day when they were allowed up on deck for a few minutes' exercise, little Jimmy stuck close to Charlie's side and Charlie was horrified when he was able to get a good look at the little chap in daylight. He wasn't as far through as a line prop and he looked grievously ill.

Nodding towards one of the guards, Charlie told him, 'I reckon this lad should see the ship's doctor. He isn't well.'

The guard sneered as he fingered the whip in his hand. 'Gerra move on there. 'E looks all right to me, 'e's standing, inn't he?'

Charlie gritted his teeth. He knew that to argue would earn him a whipping so he fell quiet, but when they were ushered back downstairs again he stayed as close to Jimmy as he could, fearing that he might fall down one of the ladders.

Over the next few days, Jimmy seemed to grow weaker by the hour, but apart from trying to get him a little food, there was little Charlie could do for him, much to his frustration. Finally one morning when the guards came to take them for their exercise the boy told him, 'You go up wivout me today, Charlie. I ain't feelin' so good.'

Charlie lifted his hands to feel for the boy's forehead in the dark and was shocked to find that the child was burning hot with a fever. He could feel the sweat running down his face and he instantly called the guard again.

'This lad has a fever,' he informed him, but the guard merely shrugged.

'An' just whar am I supposed to do about it?'

'Get the ship's doctor?' Charlie suggested bitterly, but the guard snorted as he elbowed another of the prisoners out of the door.

'Do you think we ain't got nothin' better to do than run about after you scum? Now get in line an' get up that ladder else I'll give you a taste o' me bloody whip!'

Charlie shuffled towards the door. There was nothing he could do, but he had never been so angry in his life. He was almost glad when the brief respite from the darkness was over so he could get back downstairs to Jimmy. Beside the door was a barrel of stale water and Charlie kept shuffling towards it and bringing a scoop back for Jimmy, but most of it just trickled out of his mouth as he struggled to swallow. It was clear the boy had begun to get delirious.

Sometime later, when most of the other men were sleeping, Jimmy's voice came out of the darkness, 'Are yer still there, Charlie?'

They were lying on the floor, for all of the hammocks were taken, and, pulling himself up on to his elbow, Charlie answered, 'Yes, I'm here, Jimmy.'

'Sometimes me mam used to tell us stories,' Jimmy confided in a croaky voice. 'She used to tell us 'ow one day we'd all go to live in a lovely cottage in the countryside wi' trees an' flowers and fields all around us. We'd 'ave a cow fer milk an' she'd 'ave a proper oven to bake in an' we'd never be 'ungry again.'

'And I've no doubt you all will when you get home again,' Charlie told him with a catch in his voice. 'After all, we're not going to be away forever.'

'I 'ope so,' Jimmy whispered. 'An' fanks fer bein' a mate, Charlie. I ain't been so scared since I met you.'

The boy's words touched Charlie so much he was too choked to answer him, and he stayed awake for as long as he could after Jimmy finally slipped into an uneasy sleep, listening to his laboured breathing, before finally he too slept.

The sound of some of the men moaning and shuffling about woke Charlie sometime later and, yawning, he turned to face Jimmy, asking, 'How are you feeling now?'

There was no answer, so tentatively he reached out into the darkness and recoiled as his hand met a warm furry creature sitting on Jimmy's chest and Charlie knew this could only mean one thing. Swallowing back the bile that rose to his throat, he moved his hand to Jimmy's arm – and sure enough it was as cold as ice, and he was lying very still.

Struggling to his feet, he shambled towards the door and began to hammer on it in a panic, 'Guards, for God's sake come quickly. I think the lad is dead!'

He could hear the guards beyond the door, laughing and drinking rum.

'Well, if he's dead there ain't no panic to move him, is there,' one of them shouted back and suddenly Charlie's temper erupted.

'*You heartless bastards!*' he screeched as tears slid down his cheeks. 'He's just a kid!'

He heard the sound of the locks and one of the big burly guards pushed the door open almost knocking him over.

'Who are *you* callin' a bastard!' he raged. 'You low life bleedin' scum.' His hand snaked out and caught Charlie's arm in a vice-like grip and before Charlie knew what was happening he was being hauled towards the ladder. 'Let's see if yer still as mouthy when you've 'ad a taste o' the cat-o'-nine-tails, eh? We can't have the likes o' you tryin' to cause a riot amongst the prisoners.'

Charlie was dragged unceremoniously up the ladder and on to the deck, and even as he was still blinking at the sudden bright sun, they had raised the chains that bound his hands above his head and placed them over a large hook nailed to the mast. He felt as if his arms were being ripped out of their sockets, but there was not a thing he could do.

'Now then, yer can cool off there, an' when the prisoners come up fer their exercise we'll show 'em what happens to those that wanna cause trouble.'

They walked away, leaving Charlie trembling in agony; he had never been so scared in his life.

By the time the first of the prisoners appeared on deck, every muscle in his body was screaming because of the unnatural position the guards had left him in.

'Form a circle,' he heard one of the guards shout, and out of the corner of his eye he saw the men begin to gather around him.

'Right you lot,' the guard shouted when they were all assembled. 'Now yer goin' to see what 'appens to prisoners who try to cause trouble aboard ship.'

Stepping behind Charlie, he grabbed his shirt at the back of his neck and tore it to the waist, leaving his back exposed. Then he waved a lethal-looking cat-o'-nine-tails at him.

'Let's see if you still feel so mouthy after fifty strokes o' this,' he said gleefully and went to take his place behind him.

There was a loud whistling noise and Charlie gasped as the whip cracked across his bare back. Blinking back tears of pain and humiliation, Charlie bit down so hard on his lip that he could taste blood.

'Now you lot, count fer me,' the guard ordered as he wielded the whip again, and too afraid to disobey the men reluctantly began.

'One . . . two . . . three . . . four . . . five . . . six . . . seven . . . eight . . . nine . . . ten . . . eleven . . .'

By this time Charlie was dangling almost unconscious, his back a bloody mess of ugly, ripped flesh. It felt as if he was on fire and he knew he wouldn't be able to take much more.

Just as he'd resigned himself to die, he dimly heard a voice bark, 'What the *hell* is going on here?'

The guard turned to face him, his face red with exertion. 'The prisoner were tryin' to cause a riot, cap'n, so I thought he should be made an example of in case any o' the others decided to join in.'

Clearly displeased with the situation, the captain raised an eyebrow and, turning to the nearest prisoner, he asked, 'What exactly did the lad do?'

'He were tryin' to get help fer the little chap at the side o' him; he thought he might even be dead,' the prisoner mumbled fearfully.

The captain seemed to swell to double his size. 'So if that's the case *why* didn't you get help?' he stormed at the guard, who was not looking so sure of himself now.

'Well . . . there weren't much we could 'ave done if the kid were already dead, was there, sir?' he muttered.

The captain's face turned puce with anger and, snatching the cat-o'-nine-tails from the guard's hand, he flung it on to the deck and ordered the other guard, 'Cut that young man down *immediately*. And *you*' – he stabbed a finger at the first guard, his eyes flashing fire – 'these might be criminals but they are *still* human beings and deserve to be treated as such. Report to my office *now*! You are relieved of your duties as of this minute and I shall be making a formal complaint about your behaviour to the governor of your jail on our return to England. From now on my men will see to the welfare of the prisoners and you and your colleague will be confined to quarters. Now get to my office immediately – I've nowhere near finished with you yet!'

His face surly, the guard slunk away as the captain beckoned two of his crew to him. 'Make sure these men have access to clean drinking water at all times,' he told them. 'And from now on, they will be allowed to exercise twice a day. I also wish to be informed of what they have been allocated to eat. Most of them look half starved. Now give them another ten minutes on deck.' He looked towards Charlie, who was now lying motionless on the deck, and beckoning another two sailors he told them, 'Get him into the infirmary and go gently on him.'

'Aye, aye, cap'n.' Bending over Charlie, they lifted him gently and carried him inside.

Charlie woke up some hours later flat on his stomach, and for a moment he wondered where he was and what he was doing there. But then, as it all came back to him, he tried to rise before gasping with pain as the weals on his back opened and began to bleed again.

'Lie still now, lad,' a man's voice told him, and turning his head fractionally he saw a man wearing a white coat. He was standing right beside the bed and was dressing Charlie's wounds.

'Sorry, son,' he muttered as he wiped one particularly deep wound and Charlie winced. 'I just need to get plenty of ointment on these to try and prevent infection.'

'I-it's all right . . . carry on,' Charlie told him bravely as he gritted his teeth. The pain was so severe that sweat was dripping into his eyes, but not once did he cry out.

'There.' At last it was done. 'Now that should start to ease the pain shortly,' the man informed him gently. 'Meantime, would you like a drink?'

Charlie managed to shake his head.

'Very well. I shall leave you to rest now, but I'll be back shortly; I'm Doctor Hardy by the way,' the doctor informed him.

Charlie stared at him through a haze of pain and saw a short, plump man with thinning grey hair and faded blue eyes. He looked weary, but his smile was kind and as Charlie closed his eyes, the doctor hurried away to find the captain.

'What those guards have done to that young man is barbaric,' the doctor raged as he paced up and down the captain's cabin. 'Even ten strokes of a cat-o'-nine-tails is too many let alone *fifty*. Thank God you happened along when you did or I'm sure he would have killed him!'

'I quite agree,' the captain said solemnly. 'And have no fear, it will not happen again. I have confined both the guards below decks and from now on my men will be responsible for the care of the prisoners for the duration of the voyage. But the young boy who has been whipped . . . will he recover?'

Doctor Hardy shrugged. 'It all depends. His back is cut to ribbons. I've done all I can but if he should develop a fever or the wounds should become infected . . .' He spread his hands. 'It's all in God's hands now!'

Chapter Fifteen

'Ah, here's my little darling,' Alicia crooned as Agatha ushered Susie into the room ahead of her. Alicia's parents were staying with them at present and they weren't at all sure about the adopted granddaughter their only child had presented them with. She was a pretty little thing, admittedly, with her lovely shiny black hair and beautiful deep-brown eyes, but she was very surly and barely said a word. In fact, in the three days they had been there, they hadn't even seen her smile as yet, although their meetings had been brief up until now.

Susie glared at Alicia resentfully. She hated being brought down and paraded in front of visitors as if she was some sort of prize, but she had no choice. She had learned to her cost that if she disobeyed Nanny, she would be smacked. She even had bruises to prove it but they were all where they couldn't be seen. Nanny always made quite sure of that, and seeing as it was always her that bathed her, Susie doubted anyone would ever see them.

'Come and say hello to your Grandmama and Grandpapa, darling,' Alicia coaxed, and resentfully Susie moved forward and dutifully bobbed her knee.

'You may leave her with us for a while, Nanny,' Alicia informed the woman. 'I'm sure Suzanne would like to take afternoon tea with us. Cook has made some lovely fancies and tarts that I'm certain she would like to sample.'

Agatha's face set. 'Begging your pardon, ma'am,' she said quietly. 'But it would be better if Miss Suzanne kept to her routine. She has her tea up in the nursery with me and too much sugar will be bad for her teeth.'

'It won't hurt the child just this once,' Muriel O'Gilvie, Alicia's mother, answered tartly, when she saw that her daughter was about to do as the nanny told her. She had taken an instant dislike to the woman and didn't care if it showed. 'Now go about your duties. We will ring for you when you are needed.'

With her cheeks flaming, Agatha bobbed her knee, turned and left the room, but inside she was seething. She could twist the mistress around her little finger, but her mother appeared to be a different kettle of fish altogether. Still, she supposed they wouldn't be staying for long and once they'd gone, she'd soon pull Suzanne back into line again and show her who was the boss!

Susie, meanwhile, was gazing at her newfound grandmother in awe. She was the first person she had ever heard stand up to Nanny and she liked her for it.

'So, child, how are you settling in?' the woman asked and Susie gave her a shy smile.

'All right, thank you.'

'Good. Now come and help me eat some of these delicious fancies or I shall eat them all to myself and get very fat.'

Susie really smiled then and Alicia was shocked. It was the first time she had seen her so relaxed and it made her wonder what she was doing wrong. She went to see the child before she went to bed every night and she spent half an hour with her and Nanny each afternoon, but she had never seen her like this before.

Alicia's mother, too, had noticed a change in the child the second the nanny had left the room and she began to wonder: was the child afraid of her? She would talk to her daughter about it later, she promised herself, and then set about making Suzanne smile again.

Half an hour later there was a tap on the door and Nanny entered with her hands folded neatly at her waist.

'I'm sorry to intrude, Mrs Darby-Jones, but it's time for Miss Suzanne's nap.'

Alicia's mother looked appalled. 'Her nap . . . but she's almost seven years old. Is it really necessary?'

'Oh, let her go, Mummy,' Alicia said hurriedly, afraid of upsetting the woman. 'I'm sure Nanny knows best. She has had far more experience of raising children than I have.' In actual fact, Alicia was almost as afraid of Agatha as Susie was, although she would never have admitted it.

The radiant smile instantly slid from the child's face and she hastily wiped the crumbs from her mouth as Agatha held her hand out to her and she quietly allowed herself to be led from the room.

Once Agatha had closed the door firmly behind them, Alicia's mother asked, 'How long has the nanny been with you, dear?'

'Oh, she came within days of us having Suzanne. Why do you ask?'

Her mother shrugged. 'I'm not sure, there's just something about her that doesn't feel quite right. Did she come with good references?'

'Well, with one reference, and yes it was excellent. She was nanny for a lord and lady before she came to us and only left when their child went to attend a boarding school.'

'Hm.' Muriel O'Gilvie still wasn't convinced. 'Then perhaps you should be spending a little more time with the child yourself,' she suggested.

'I have tried to, but Nanny gets annoyed and says that it interferes with Suzanne's routine.'

'And you allow her to dictate to you? Surely as her employer it should be the other way around? Don't you think, dear?' she said, turning to her husband, who had decided it was better not to get involved.

'Absolutely, my love. Servants should always know their place.'

'I suppose so.' When Alicia looked guilty, her mother sighed. Alicia was their only child and had been spoiled shamelessly.

'Look, we'll start this evening by going up and getting the child ready for bed ourselves,' she told her. 'Just show the nanny that you intend to be more involved with Suzanne and she'll have no alternative but to obey you if she wishes to keep her job.'

Muriel was greatly concerned. She prided herself on being a good judge of character and if she wasn't very much mistaken the little girl was afraid of her nanny. She had a sneaky idea that her daughter was too, but she hoped to remedy that before she and her husband set off for home. It was time someone let the woman know who was in charge and Muriel considered she was just the person to do it.

'In fact, why don't you let the child come down and dine with us this evening? It won't interfere with her bedtime,' she suggested tactfully and Alicia looked faintly surprised.

'I suggested that Matthew and I would like that when the nanny first arrived, but she said the food we ate would be too rich for her,' Alicia answered.

Muriel snorted. 'What utter rubbish. Suzanne isn't a baby and she just managed to stomach a number of rich pastries, didn't she? Leave it with me. I shall go up to the nursery presently and tell the nanny that Suzanne will be joining us for dinner myself. And furthermore, I think you should be thinking of hiring a tutor for her now. She's quite old enough to begin her lessons.'

'Oh, Mama, you're so wise,' Suzanne told her warmly. 'Thank you, I do so want to get raising Suzanne right.'

'You will eventually.' Her mother patted her hand and gave her a reassuring smile. She adored her daughter, but was aware that she had absolutely no idea how to run a household or raise a child. But still, she consoled herself, *before I leave I intend to put that obnoxious nanny firmly in her place.* It had broken her heart over the years to see her daughter longing for a child, and now that she finally had one she was going to ensure that she enjoyed her, if it was the last thing she did!

An hour later, while her husband dozed in the chair, Muriel made her way up to the nursery floor. She was amazed to find how quiet it was, and when she pushed the door to the nursery open, she saw why. Susie was lying in her narrow little bed facing the wall while Agatha sat drinking tea and reading the newspaper.

The woman started, clearly annoyed at such an un-announced visit and rose to her feet, saying primly, 'Can I help you, ma'am?' Her voice was icy cold but not as cold as Muriel's when she answered her.

'Yes, you can tell me why that child is lying there wide awake when she could be outside in the fresh air.'

Muriel sniffed indignantly. 'Miss Suzanne had her daily walk around the garden this morning, ma'am, and now she is having her afternoon nap.'

'Afternoon nap!' Susie had turned to peep out of the blankets at her and Muriel glared at Agatha. 'She doesn't look like she is napping to me. The child is wide awake and no doubt bored to tears. Get her up immediately and take her for a walk in the park at the bottom of the road. Let her use some of her energy up. And then when you get back, you can prepare her to dine downstairs with her parents and my husband and myself.'

'But I've already told her mother that I think the food would be too ri—'

'Oh, for goodness sake, woman! Don't talk such clap-trap!' Muriel barked. She had never been one to hold her tongue. 'Do as I say immediately.' And with that, she smiled at Suzanne and sailed from the room like a ship in full sail.

'*Why* . . .' Agatha was furious as she approached Susie's bed and yanked her none too gently out of it. 'Get yourself dressed,' she spat. 'It seems that your dear grandmama thinks she knows what's better for you than I do! And make it snappy or you'll be sorry!'

Susie did as she was told without a word, fumbling with the buttons on her dress and at last she stood before Agatha fully clothed. The woman looked her up and down; then, gripping Susie's hand, she hauled her towards the door, grumbling all the time.

Outside, Agatha stamped along the street, dragging Susie along beside her. 'Interfering old bitch!' she muttered, but Susie was too busy watching what was going on around her to hear her. She felt as if she had been released from a prison and was enjoying stretching her legs, even if it meant having to be in Nanny's company.

Once at the park, they took a turn around the lake and Susie was fascinated and envious as she saw some other children there with their nannies. Some were racing about, others were sailing little boats on the water, and others were kicking a brightly coloured ball across the grass, but Agatha kept a firm grip on her hand and yanked her straight by them, giving her no chance to say hello. There was a family of swans on the lake too and Susie would have liked to pause to watch them, but Agatha never slowed her pace and soon the little girl was breathless; her legs were nowhere near as long as Agatha's and she was having to run to keep up with her.

'Ca-can we stop for a minute? I have a stitch in my side,' she gasped, but Agatha merely grinned.

'Hm, I was right, you see. Didn't I tell the woman that you needed your rest?'

'I-it's not that,' Susie said breathlessly. 'It's just that you're walking too fast for me.'

'Don't you *dare* answer me back, you little guttersnipe!' Agatha warned her with a malevolent glare. 'Else you'll be sorry when I get you back to the nursery, my girl!'

'Sorry,' Susie whispered in a small voice, as she thought of the hard wooden hairbrush Nanny had hit her with the night before. And all because she had dared to tell her during teatime that she needed to go to the toilet.

'How *dare* you bring up such things while we are eating?' Agatha had ranted at her. 'That's disgusting. In future, you will go when I tell you and sit on the toilet until I tell you to get off.'

Susie had been too afraid to argue and now, as they marched along, she wondered what a guttersnipe was? Perhaps she could ask her new grandmama? She seemed to be kind and Susie bet she would know.

By the time they got back to the nursery, Susie's cheeks were glowing and her legs were feeling tired – but there was no time to rest, as Agatha took pleasure in telling her.

'It's time to get you ready for dinner downstairs and it will serve all of them right if you fall asleep halfway through,' she said maliciously. 'Perhaps then they'll listen to someone who knows what they're doing with children!'

Susie stood quite still while the woman yanked the dress she was wearing over her head then tried not to cry out as she viciously swiped the brush through her tangle of long dark curls.

'All this hair is so unnecessary,' Agatha grumbled, as she finally secured it with a blue ribbon to match her dress. 'I'm a firm believer that too much hair saps children's strength and I might have a word with your mama and ask her if I can cut it off. It would be so much more manageable if it were chin-length.'

Susie didn't like that idea at all, but again she said nothing – and when the maid arrived to take her downstairs, she followed her out of the room quickly, glad to get away from Nanny for a while.

Susie still found it hard to address Alicia and Matthew as Mama and Papa, but she had to admit that they were kind and she enjoyed the meal tremendously. There was a lovely thick soup to start with, followed by some sort of fish that had been cooked in butter, and finally there was a pudding that consisted of a chocolate sponge drizzled in fresh cream. It was certainly a far cry from the bread and butter that Nanny made her eat in the nursery, although unfortunately she had managed to spill some down the front of her dress.

'Don't get worrying about that, darling,' Alicia told her as she saw the child dabbing ineffectively at it with her handkerchief. 'Nanny can send it down to be washed. You have plenty more that you can wear.'

Her grandmother gave her a crafty wink.

Susie responded with a smile, before suddenly remembering something and asking innocently, 'What's a guttersnipe?'

Chapter Sixteen

It was as if time had ceased to exist for Charlie. For days after the barbaric whipping, he lay in the infirmary, which in actual fact consisted of no more than two beds in a cabin, drifting in and out of consciousness. But then, over a week after the event, he woke one morning and felt slightly better – until he tried to turn over that was, and then he groaned with pain.

'Ah, you're awake at last, old chap; how are you feeling?' the doctor asked. He had been tending Charlie night and day, and there had been times when he wasn't sure if he was going to make it – but now at last it appeared that he had turned a corner.

'A . . . little better.' Charlie licked his dry lips, and the doctor rose to fetch him a cup of water.

'Just a little sip at a time now, lad,' he cautioned, as he gently turned Charlie's head to the side and dripped a little water into his mouth. The open wounds on Charlie's back were beginning to scab now, so much so that he almost appeared to have grown a shell – but thanks to the doctor's care, none of the wounds had become infected.

'L-little Jimmy?' he asked.

The doctor patted his arm. 'Don't worry. I saw to it that he had a proper burial at sea. I even got the captain to say a few words as they committed his body to the deep. He's at peace now, son, so try not to think of it anymore.'

'Thank you.' Charlie turned his head to the wall, but couldn't prevent a tear from rolling down his cheek. A young life for a loaf of bread; what a price to pay!

They had been at sea for eight weeks when Charlie finally ventured out of bed; unfortunately the movement caused the remaining scabs on his back to split and bleed again, but it couldn't be helped. He felt if he lay there for much longer, he would go mad. Doctor Hardy tied a bandage soaked in lotion about him to stop the wounds from sticking to his shirt, and at least then he could sit in a chair and watch the activity on the deck. Meals were delivered to him three times a day, and although he had little appetite Charlie forced himself to eat them.

Thankfully conditions had improved vastly for the prisoners since the day he had been whipped. They were now allowed up on deck twice a day for exercise, and the captain had insisted that while they were confined below, their chains should be removed. They were also allowed to have water to wash with daily, which went a long way to improving the stench in their quarters, as did the fact that the toilet buckets were now also emptied on a more regular basis.

One day when the doctor was in the infirmary treating one of the prisoners who had developed a nasty ulcer on his leg, Charlie dared to ask him, 'I don't suppose you would have anything to read, would you?'

The doctor looked at him in surprise. 'You can read?' Most of the convicts he had known could only sign their names with a cross.

'Of course I can.' Charlie stared back at him. 'And I'm good with figures too.'

'I see. Then in that case you may be able to help me. I'm afraid I have nothing you might care to read on board, apart from medical journals. But I don't mind admitting I hate record-keeping. Would you be interested in having a go at that for me, if I told you what to write?'

Charlie nodded eagerly. He was prepared to do anything that might relieve the boredom of sitting there all day.

Doctor Hardy left his patient for a moment to fetch a large journal, which he placed on the table in front of Charlie. 'You need to write the date and time there; then here we put the prisoner's name.' He pointed to a box. 'We then enter what the problem was, in this case an abscess, and what treatment I used to remedy it. In this instance I have lanced it and dressed it with ointment. I will need to see the patient again tomorrow and should further treatment be necessary, you can enter that for me too.'

While he finished dressing the man's wound, Charlie did as he was told as neatly as he could, which was no mean feat as the boat was rolling quite alarmingly. After one of the sailors had escorted the prisoner back to the hold, the doctor took the journal from Charlie and examined what he had done.

'Your handwriting is actually a damn sight neater than mine,' he observed, grinning. 'Consider yourself hired. As it happens, there are a few entries I haven't got around to doing yet, so I'll tell you what they are and you can write them in for me.'

Charlie's chest puffed with pride and an hour later the journal was up to date. The doctor smiled at Charlie. 'Well done, son. I'm going to pop along and see the captain later. He might have something for you to read to keep you occupied. I can't see you being able to go below again before we reach Australia, not with some of those wounds still being open – it'd be risking infection. Come on, back to the bed. It's time we dressed them again.'

Charlie painfully did as he was told and as Doctor Hardy looked down at the wounds, he shook his head. This boy would be scarred for life and all because he had tried to get help for another young lad.

It was almost five weeks later when Charlie was writing in the journal one day that a shout went up. '*Land ahoy!*'

Instantly, those on deck flocked to the rails, chattering excitedly as in the distance they saw a coastline emerging from the ocean.

'I think we'll dock sometime this evening,' the kindly doctor told Charlie when he entered the infirmary shortly after.

Charlie was now able to potter about, although it still pained him to lift his arms. Many of the scabs had fallen away from the wounds now, leaving long, red weals in their place. The doctor had assured him that they would fade to a silver colour in time, but Charlie wasn't too concerned about that. At least he had survived, thanks to the intervention of the captain.

From that moment on, the ship was buzzing with excitement. It was now late in November, and back home they would be shivering in the cold of winter, so it was strange to think that here in this foreign country it was summer. Although it didn't feel like the summers he was used to: the sun was blazing in a cloudless blue sky and as they approached land, brightly coloured birds that Charlie had never seen before began to circle high above the ship. The doctor allowed him to go out on to the deck, and as the ship drew closer to land, Charlie saw a huddle of wooden huts and buildings. *Surely this couldn't be New South Wales?* he thought. He had imagined it would be a huge place, something resembling London, with grand buildings and ordered streets, but this was more like the shanty towns he had seen in books.

The ship dropped anchor some way off shore, and waited for a boat to come and guide it in to the dock. There were many people waiting for it, for as well as bringing a new influx of convicts, it also carried much needed supplies and animals: cows, sheep and chickens. Some of them had not survived the journey, but those that had would be fought over and highly prized.

Darkness was falling by the time the ship was led into the harbour, and as soon as it was secured, the sailors began to haul the gangplanks into place. First the supplies of wheat, flour and other food were unloaded and then the animals walked shakily down the gangplanks, looking confused after their long journey.

The doctor joined Charlie at the rail and, pointing to a number of men, he said, 'They are the convict overseers and the military guards. Once the convicts are delivered to them they will be segregated into groups. The most hardened criminals will be sent to prisons on the outskirts of the town. During the day they will do hard labour – digging roads and breaking rocks. Those with trades will be given work accordingly wherever possible. Every trade is welcome here from tailors to shopkeepers. The women convicts will probably end up doing domestic duties – cooking, cleaning washing and ironing. Troublesome female prisoners will be sent to the Female Factory, where they will make rope and spin and make carded wool. Most of them will marry quickly, though, and hopefully make a life here when they have served their time. There's only about one or two women to ten men here, so it's better if they do marry – it causes less hassle.'

'Convicts get married here?' Charlie asked in surprise.

'Oh yes.' He chuckled. 'If a man takes a fancy to a woman, all he has to do is approach her and drop a handkerchief or scarf at her feet and if the woman is willing and the governor approves it, the marriage can take place almost immediately. Those that work hard are rewarded; they can apply to the governor to bring their families here if they want to make a new life, and in some cases they can be assigned to free settler families, so I'd advise you to keep your head down and work hard. Have you had any experience of farm work?'

'Yes, sir,' Charlie replied. 'My father worked for a farmer and so did I once I left school.'

'In that case, I shall personally have a word on your behalf with the governor, Charlie. And thank you for the help you've given me during the voyage.' He had actually grown very fond of the lad.

'It should be me thanking you, sir,' Charlie told him. 'I doubt I'd have survived had it not been for you.'

The doctor shrugged to hide his embarrassment.

'But what happens when a prisoner's served his sentence?' Charlie asked then. The time couldn't pass quickly enough for him – he just wanted to get home and try to put what was left of his family back together again.

'The governor will issue you with an Absolute Pardon, which means that you are free to return to England should you so wish. But step aside, lad. It looks like they're bringing the first of the convicts up from below.'

Sure enough, the first of the men appeared from the holds and, once more chained and shackled, they shuffled towards the gangplank. When they reached the bottom and stepped on to dry land, just as the doctor had explained, Charlie heard the overseers shouting out names and the men being divided into groups before being marched away.

'So what do I do now?' Charlie asked as the captain joined them at the rail.

'I am giving you permission to stay on board for now,' the captain advised him above the rattle of chains and rumble of barrels being rolled down the second gangplank. 'The doctor and I are dining with the governor and his wife this evening and I am going to speak to him about you. That's his residence up on the hill there.'

He pointed up and for the first time, Charlie noticed a rather palatial residence perched amongst the trees on the hillside. He had expected Australia to be lush and green so was quite disappointed to discover that it actually looked very parched and dry. All the roads through the town were dry earth, and he could see clouds of dust rising into the air as people passed along them.

'Thank you, sir,' Charlie answered. 'I'll wait in the infirmary until you come back.'

But he didn't want to go back in there just yet. There was too much to see, so he stayed at the rails drinking in the sight of dry land after all the long, harsh weeks at sea.

Charlie watched one group of men being led away still in chains. As for the others, he noticed that some of the men had their chains removed and were led away by people who had been waiting on the quayside. Charlie guessed these might be settlers who were looking for workers on their farms.

Those men would be the lucky ones, so long as they behaved themselves, and he almost wished he was going with them. It would have been nice to work on the land again, although because of the climate, he imagined it would be a lot harder to grow crops, which accounted for all the supplies of flour and other foodstuffs that were being delivered.

When all the male convicts had been sorted, the women prisoners were brought up from their hold. It was the first time Charlie had seen them properly, apart from the odd glimpses of them from the window of the infirmary, for they had not been allowed on deck with the male convicts. They ranged from very young to middle-aged. Charlie saw that there were a number of men still standing below, no doubt waiting for a glimpse of them to see if there were any who would make suitable wives.

The captain and the doctor had been standing to one side of him, deep in conversation – but now the doctor approached him to say, 'Right, lad. I have people I need to see. Stay put and I'll see you later this evening.' Then he too went down the gangplank and disappeared amongst the people thronging the quay.

Charlie had no idea how long he stood there, but eventually the people wandered away and he returned to the infirmary to wait for the doctor's return. Just for a moment, he was tempted to make a run for it – after all who would notice him in the melee of people swarming on the dock? But he dismissed the idea. The doctor had trusted him and Charlie would not betray the trust.

Much later that evening, Charlie stood on deck staring up at the sky. It was a beautiful, balmy night, and the black velvet sky was dotted with stars – far more, he was sure, than he had ever glimpsed back at home.

'All right, lad?' Doctor Hardy's cheery voice made him look round, and Charlie was amused to see that he looked quite merry and his hat was askew. 'I've got some good news for you. I had a word to the governor – he's a good friend of mine, as it happens – and he's agreed to give you a trial working for him.'

Charlie's heart raced with excitement. 'Doing what?'

'Hm!' The doctor scratched his head, dislodging his hat even further. 'I dare say you'll be what might be described as "a jack of all trades"! You'll run errands, tend the grounds – do whatever he asks of you, really. So how does that sound? I'll tell you now, if you keep your nose clean you'll have it cushy.'

'It sounds excellent, sir. Thank you.' Charlie beamed at the doctor.

'The governor, Phineas Morgan, is a good man; firm but fair,' the doctor told him. 'And his wife is a lovely lady, so are his two daughters. I'll take you there first thing in the morning and you can get settled in.'

Charlie felt a lump form in his throat. 'I'll never be able to thank you enough,' he said quietly. 'If it wasn't for the captain's intervention and the care you gave me after I was whipped, I might not even be here now.'

'Oh, get away with you.' The doctor grinned. 'But now, if you'll excuse me, I'm going to turn in. I've had a bit too much wine tonight, I'm afraid, and it's been a busy day. Goodnight, lad.'

'Goodnight, sir.' Charlie watched with amusement as the man went unsteadily to his cabin. Then he leaned on the railings again, letting the peace and quiet wash over him. They had finally arrived at their destination and, for better or worse, this place would be his home for the next seven years, so he may as well make the best of it.

Chapter Seventeen

'That's right, arms to your side, head steady . . . turn . . . and walk!'

Opal felt ridiculous as she slowly turned, a book wobbling on the top of her head, to walk back to Mrs King. But it was no good, as seconds later the novel crashed to the floor yet again.

The old lady shook her head. 'Pick it up and try again. You know what they say – "practice makes perfect" – and deportment is so important for a young lady.'

Opal sighed as she did as she was told. It seemed that there was so much to learn if one was to become a lady, but she wondered how all these lessons could possibly benefit her. After all, she was only a companion to an old lady, so where would she go to practise such skills? But she was keen to please, so she continued until at last Belle appeared at the door with the afternoon tea trolley. She grinned fleetingly when she saw Opal wobbling along, before asking the old woman, 'Is there anything else, Mrs King? And would you like me to pour for you?'

'No, why should one have a dog and bark oneself?' she snapped, nodding towards Opal who had removed the heavy book and was rubbing the top of her head.

Belle dipped her knee and discreetly left the room, as Opal hurried over to pour the tea for her mistress.

'Oh . . . I forgot to mention,' the old lady said. 'My son will be dining with us this evening, so make yourself look respectable. Esther and Dorothy Partridge will also be joining us, so it should be a good evening. And it will give me a chance to see how your lessons in table manners are paying off.'

Opal's heart sank. She well remembered the Partridges and, if she were to be honest, she wasn't particularly fond of either of them, especially the daughter. *But still*, she told herself, *I'm here to obey and obey I will – for now at least.*

She poured the tea and then she helped Mrs King to her room, where she would rest until it was time to change for dinner. When it was just the two of them, she sometimes didn't bother, but she was a stickler for dressing up if they were expecting visitors.

'Is there anything I can get for you?' Opal asked, when she had helped the old lady on to the bed and placed a woollen blanket across her.

'No, just make sure you have all my clothes laid out ready for dinner. I shall wear the dark-purple satin gown this evening.'

Opal nodded, before quietly leaving the room to go and have a little time with Belle – if the other girl wasn't too busy. She enjoyed their chats, and because they were very close in age they had grown fond of one another. Belle had told her all about her home life. Her family lived in Attleborough, in a small cottage that was bursting at the seams – for she had six siblings all younger than herself.

Her father was a gravedigger at Chilvers Coton church, and when there were no graves to be dug, which was rarely, he tended the churchyard. Her mother took in washing and ironing, so their combined wages plus what Belle gave them out of her own money enabled them to live frugally. From the way she spoke of them, Opal had the impression that they were a happy family, and she felt envious of her.

For the first time in her life, Opal never had to worry about going hungry, she had a beautiful room all to herself, and was wearing clothes the like of which she had never thought she would own – but she would have given it all up in a sigh if things could only have gone back to what they had once been. Of course, she realised that this could never be, but hearing Belle speak of her family only made Opal all the more determined to be reunited with Charlie and Susie, for they were all she had left. It was this determination that made her get up each day and suffer her mistress's demands – although, in fairness, just as Henry King had told her, she had soon discovered that beneath her frosty exterior Mrs King wasn't so bad.

When she got downstairs, she found that Belle and the rest of the staff were almost run off their feet preparing for their visitors, so she asked Cook, 'Is there anything I can do to help?'

'Yes, you can lay the table in the dining room wi' the best cloth an' the silver cutlery,' the red-faced woman answered.

'I'd better do that,' Belle butted in good-naturedly. 'Opal laid out fish forks instead of dinner forks the other day when she was having a lesson off Mrs King on how to lay a formal table for three courses, and I don't think the mistress would be too pleased if everythin' weren't just so this evenin' with the Partridges comin'.'

Opal blushed. 'Perhaps I could peel those Brussel sprouts then, I've got a bit of spare time before I have to help Mrs King get dressed.'

When Cook handed her a knife, Opal sat down and got started, only too happy to let Belle set the table.

At last everything appeared to be under control, and Cook dropped thankfully into the chair at the side of the fire, lifting her feet on to a small stool.

'Make a cup o' tea, ducks,' she ordered the little kitchen maid. 'Me throat's as dry as the bottom of a birdcage. Why the mistress should insist on such fancy menus when we have company I'll never know. That duck 'as been cookin' slow all afternoon an' it still ain't quite done. Still, everythin's about ready now so I'm goin' to take the weight off me feet fer a few minutes. Me poor ankles are swellin' somethin' terrible.'

'I'd better go and help Mrs King get dressed or I won't have time to get changed myself,' Opal said, glancing at the clock.

'Are yer wearin' that lovely blue gown?' Belle asked eagerly. She and Belle had drooled over her new dresses when they had first been delivered, but the blue satin one was their favourite and Opal couldn't wait to wear it.

Opal shook her head. 'No, Mrs King thought it might be too grand to wear for dining at home,' she answered. 'And I think she's right. To be honest, I can't see me ever getting to wear it.'

'You will,' Belle told her, before hurrying away to place the large vase of flowers the florist had just delivered in the centre of the table.

Once Opal had helped her mistress to change, she walked her down the stairs and left her in the drawing room with a small glass of sherry as she awaited her guests' arrival, while Opal hurried back upstairs to get herself dressed. The navy dress fitted perfectly and Opal twizzled in front of the mirror as she admired it. But time was moving on, so she brushed her hair until it shone, twisted it into a long gleaming plait and hurried back down the stairs just as Belle was admitting Henry.

'Good evening, Miss Sharp.' His eyes raked her up and down approvingly, as he handed Belle his hat and coat. 'May I say you are looking most charming this evening?'

'Thank you, sir.' Opal bobbed her knee as she felt colour rise in her cheeks. 'Your mother is in the drawing room waiting for you.'

He nodded and made for the door as Belle winked at Opal. 'I reckon he's got his eye on you,' she whispered and Opal frowned.

'Don't be so silly,' she retaliated. 'What would a man like him want with the likes of me? If you must know I think Miss Partridge has her eye set on him.'

Belle smothered a giggle with her hand. 'That dowdy old spinster! You must be joking. Henry King wouldn't touch her with a bargepole, you just mark my words. He likes 'em young.'

And with that she waltzed off, with a cheeky grin on her face.

Soon after, Miss and Mrs Partridge arrived, and after showing them into the drawing room, Opal discreetly stood behind her mistress's chair, as she had been advised to do. She was actually glad to remove herself from standing next to Esther Partridge as she reeked of so much perfume that it was making Opal's eyes water. Her gown did nothing to flatter her either. In a bright-green satin, it clung to her, emphasising every ample curve, and it was so low cut that at times when she leaned towards Henry, Opal feared that her enormous breasts were going to spill out of it. Her cheeks were heavily rouged, making her look like a china doll that Opal had once seen in the toy shop window in the town, and from the moment she arrived she studiously ignored Opal and turned her whole attention on Henry.

'Is that a new waistcoat you are wearing, Henry, dear?' she purred, as she reached out to stroke it.

Henry frowned. 'Actually, I have had this one for some time,' he answered, looking mildly embarrassed.

'Well, it suits you very well. I must remember and buy you something that exact colour for Christmas,' Esther simpered.

Henry was saved from further embarrassment when Belle appeared at the door to tell them that dinner was ready to be served.

Henry took his mother's arm to escort her into the dining room, much to Esther's obvious chagrin, but she wasn't about to let him escape that easily. Once he was seated, she almost leaped into the seat next to him.

Belle served them each with the tiny triangles of toast and the duck liver pate that Cook had been slaving over, and once that was done she discreetly took her leave. Esther attacked her food with vigour and cleared her plate in seconds and Opal had to suppress a smile. So much for Mrs King telling her that a lady should always eat daintily and leave a little on her plate.

Cook's main course of duck à l' orange was a great success and the meat was so tender that Opal's knife sliced through it like butter. Unfortunately, though, the overpowering scent of the hot house flowers on the table and Esther's heavy French perfume was so cloying that Opal began to feel slightly queasy and she could hardly eat a thing.

'Is the meal not to your liking, my dear?' Henry asked with concern.

She smiled at him, which earned her a glare from Esther, and dabbed at her lips with the snow-white napkin. 'Oh no, it isn't that. It's quite delicious, but I'm not very hungry, thank you.'

'I hope you are not feeling unwell?'

Opal avoided glancing at Esther who was scowling at her and looking as if she was capable of murder.

'No, I'm feeling quite well, thank you.'

Mrs Partridge broke the uncomfortable silence when she hurriedly chipped in, 'Esther has joined the church choir. Of course, they are thrilled to have her, she has the voice of an angel.'

'Oh Mama, stop it, you'll make me blush,' Esther simpered, as she glanced at Henry coquettishly, fluttering her eyelashes.

He, however, pointedly ignored the remark as he told Opal, 'I wonder you don't consider doing something like that, Miss Sharp. I'm sure my mother would be more than happy to give you time off if you wished to take up a hobby.'

Esther looked so angry that Opal feared she was about to erupt as she answered hastily, 'That's very kind of you, but I'm quite happy to stay here with Mrs King.'

'A very wise decision,' Esther said spitefully. 'The vicar is very careful about what type of people join his choir and of course they have to have excellent voices. Have you ever had any training in that direction, Miss Sharp?'

Opal felt colour flood into her cheeks. 'No, I'm afraid not,' she answered with her chin in the air. Things were becoming uncomfortable, and she longed to leave the table. She would have much preferred to eat in the kitchen with the staff.

'I thought not!' Esther sat back, with a smug grin on her face.

Mrs King looked towards Opal. 'You may be excused if you're not hungry,' she said quietly and Opal was so relieved she could have kissed her.

'Thank you, I will.' She rose gracefully. 'Excuse me,' she said politely. And she was off like a hare in the direction of the kitchen, completely unaware of the way Henry's eyes followed her.

'Is sommat not right wi' the meal?' Cook asked with alarm when Opal appeared.

'The meal is wonderful,' Opal assured her. 'But Miss Partridge obviously didn't want a servant sitting at the table with her, so Mrs King kindly excused me.'

'Stuck-up little trollop,' Cook snorted. 'It's no wonder she's been left on the shelf. She's got a face on her that's enough to turn any man's stomach. But never mind, yer can eat in here wi' us if you've a mind to.'

With a grateful smile, Opal joined the staff at the table feeling decidedly more comfortable than she had in the dining room.

Chapter Eighteen

'Are you our new gardener?'

Charlie glanced up from the flowerbed he was weeding and found himself looking into the bluest pair of eyes he had ever seen. For no reason that he could explain his heart missed a beat, and he was suddenly all of a fluster.

'No . . . yes . . . Well, actually the governor has kindly given me a job as a sort of jack of all trades.'

'I see.' The girl smiled at him. Then, without a qualm, she held her hand out. 'I'm Francesca. The governor is my father. And that's my sister Juliet over there.'

Charlie self-consciously wiped his grubby hand down the leg of his trousers before tentatively taking her hand and giving it a brief shake. Then, looking to the side, he saw a slightly younger girl plucking some roses from a bush. They were both quite beautiful, with dark skin and hair that gave them a slightly exotic look.

As if she could read what he was thinking, Francesca suddenly told him, 'Our mother is Spanish, did you know?'

'Er . . . no, no I didn't.' He was finding it hard to take his eyes off her, as she carelessly twirled the parasol she was holding across one slender shoulder. She was dressed in a beautiful gown with a full skirt that was embroidered with tiny flowers and she grinned as she confided, 'Mummy insists that I should take this thing every time I go outside.' She was referring to the parasol. 'She says that too much sun isn't good for a young lady's skin. But how can you avoid being in the sun living here?'

Charlie had no idea how to reply and gulped, feeling suddenly very dirty and clumsy.

'What's your name anyway?' she asked with a smile that left him breathless.

'It's Charlie . . . Charlie Sharp.'

'I'm very pleased to meet you, Charlie Sharp. How old are you?'

'I just turned sixteen.'

'Really? What a coincidence. So have I, just last week.'

'In that case, happy birthday for last week,' he answered with a shy smile. She might be the governor's daughter, but she had no airs and graces about her and he felt himself begin to relax a little.

Just then, a stunningly beautiful woman entered the garden and, seeing Francesca, she wandered over to her. She too held a pretty lace-trimmed parasol that matched the soft green of her dress. She was tall and slim, with eyes that were the same startling blue as her daughter's and gleaming jet-black hair that hung down her back like a silken cloak. It reminded him of Opal's hair.

'Ah, so you must be the young man my husband told me about. Charlie, isn't it?'

'Yes, ma'am,' Charlie answered.

'The doctor and the captain were full of praise for you when they dined with us,' the woman said, and suddenly realising that she hadn't properly introduced herself, she smiled. 'I am Isabella Morgan, the governor's wife and Francesca and Juliet's mother. It is very nice to meet you, Charlie.' Her voice had a slight foreign ring to it and Charlie warmed to her immediately. 'So how are you liking Australia?'

He shrugged. 'I haven't really been here long enough to judge, ma'am, although I do already know it's very different to England – certainly out here in the garden. I don't even know what some of these flowers are. The only ones I recognise are the roses.'

'Ah yes, the roses. Phineas, my husband, had them brought out for me from England.' She sighed. 'Sadly, many of them died, but those over there in the shady corner have managed to survive. 'These here' – she pointed to some flowers – 'are waratahs, and these are part of the myrtle family, they are called callistemon or bottlebrushes because of their shape. And these are my particular favourites.' She paused in front of some cone-shaped, startlingly red flowers that he saw on closer inspection actually consisted of thousands of tiny flowers. 'These come in many different shades and are called banksia. They are quite beautiful, aren't they?' When he nodded in agreement, she smiled again. 'They are all native to Australia, unlike the roses.'

'I shall do my best to tend them well for you, ma'am,' he answered politely. 'Although I'm not sure there's much I can do to help the lawn.' He gazed at it with a frown. There was barely any grass to be seen and what there was was parched and brown.

'It will green up again when we have some rain,' the woman assured him. 'How are you settling in?'

'Very well, thank you.' He glanced towards the small shack tucked away in the corner of the garden that was his new home. It wasn't much, but it had a bed and a table and chair, and he considered that he was lucky. He might well have been sent to one of the prisons or forced to work long hours on a farm for one of the settlers; here he was allowed to eat with the rest of the staff in the kitchen, and the food was plentiful.

'I am glad,' she told him. 'My husband felt you deserved a chance after hearing the glowing report about you from the Captain. Should you need anything or have any concerns, do come and see me, Charlie.'

'Thank you again, ma'am; I will.' Charlie turned back to the job he was doing, and when he glanced up a few minutes later, the woman and her lovely daughters were gone. As yet he hadn't met the governor, but if he turned out to be half as nice as his family, Charlie knew that they would get on.

Since starting there, the staff had found him many small jobs to do in and around the house and grounds, and thankfully he had been able to turn his hand to all of them. He actually enjoyed living in his little shack, sitting outside of an evening staring up at the star-studded sky, although it did get lonely sometimes when he thought of home and his sisters. Every single day he wondered how they were and what they were doing, but not knowing where either of them were, he couldn't even write to them; all he could do was pray that they were safe.

He had been told that the governor would meet him when he had the chance, and that came early the following morning when one of the maids came into the garden to find him.

'The governor will see you now, Charlie,' she told him. 'If you come with me, I'll show you to his office.'

Charlie quickly flattened his hair as best he could and wiped his hands down his trousers, before following her through the large kitchen and into a beautiful hallway. There were highly polished black and white tiles on the floor, and Charlie almost felt afraid to walk on them. As they passed one doorway, the sound of a piano reached them and the maid smiled at him. 'That's Miss Juliet having her music lesson,' she whispered. 'She's very gifted musically and can play a number of instruments. But here we are.' She stopped in front of some oak double doors set to one side of the entrance. 'This is the governor's office. Just tap and go in; he's expecting you.'

Suddenly nervous, Charlie gulped. Then he straightened his back and rapped on the door.

'Come in!'

Charlie stepped into an enormous office. One wall was completely covered in shelves from floor to ceiling, and he found himself gazing at the hundreds of books crammed on to them. In the centre of the room, almost hidden behind a pile of papers, a man sat at a huge desk.

He stood up and smiled a greeting. 'Ah, Charlie Sharp, I believe. Take a seat. I'm sorry I haven't had time to meet you before, but as you can see, the paperwork is endless. I never seem to get on top of it.'

He was a very tall man – well over six foot, Charlie thought – and he was powerfully built and handsome, with thick fair wavy hair and grey eyes.

'It's all right, sir.' Charlie took the seat in front of the desk, and when the governor sat back down, he eyed him for a moment before informing him, 'You have the doctor and the captain to thank for being here. I do not usually employ convicts, so perhaps you could tell me why you were sent here. I would appreciate your honesty.'

Charlie licked his lips, praying that he wasn't about to lose his position. 'I was sentenced for theft, sir.'

'I see.' The governor steepled his fingers and stared at him as if he could see into his very soul. 'And were you guilty of the crime?'

'Not of the one I was sentenced for but . . .' He paused for a moment. 'I was guilty of stealing some time before this incident happened. You see, our parents died and myself and my brother and sisters took shelter in a derelict cottage . . .' The terrible story of what had happened to his family poured out of him, and he found it was a relief to finally get it off his chest. 'So you see, even though I did intend to hand the wallet to the magistrate when he dropped it, I was guilty of another theft and I deserve to be here . . .' His voice tailed away, as he stared miserably down at his clenched hands.

There was silence for a moment, but then the governor said, 'I appreciate you being honest with me, Charlie. Not many people would be. But even so, you must accept that you are only here on a trial. To be honest, there isn't really enough work in and about the house and garden to keep you busy full-time, but the captain told me that you had kept his log for him while you were at sea and that you can read and write, so I was wondering . . . well, the thing is, my deputy of some years had to leave to return temporarily to England recently because of a family bereavement and as you can see the paperwork is piling up and getting rather out of control.' He spread his hands towards the teetering piles of paper and sighed. 'As the governor of the island, it is part of my job to keep a record of each of the prisoners that are brought here. Do you think you would be capable of writing the reports the overseers bring in if I showed you how to do it?'

Charlie nodded eagerly. 'I could certainly try, sir.'

'Hm!' The governor sat back and surveyed him closely for a moment, before making a decision. 'In that case I am prepared to give it a go, but I must point out that if it doesn't go well, I shall have you placed with one of the settlers and you will work out the rest of your sentence with them.'

Charlie nodded. 'I understand fully, sir, but I won't let you down, I promise. I can turn my hand to most things and I'm willing to tackle any job, big or small.'

'Then we shall need to get you some clothes more suitable for working in the house.'

Charlie looked down at the only clothes he possessed and flushed. He had tried to wash them as best he could each evening so that they dried overnight, but they were very old and shabby.

The governor unlocked a drawer in his desk and pulled out some money, which he handed to Charlie. Could Charlie have known it, this would be his first test.

'I want you to go down into the town and visit Mr Schwartz. He has a tailor's shop in the main street; you can't miss it.' He hastily scribbled a note and handed it to Charlie. 'Give him this, and then when you're done there, go to Mr Jones, the bootmaker. He is three shops down, and give him this one.' He scribbled another note and handed that to Charlie too. 'And that's all for now,' he said quietly, still intently studying the young man in front of him. 'When you've finished, come back and report to me.'

'Yes, sir . . . and thank you, sir.' Charlie rose hastily from his chair.

Once he had left the room, the governor crossed to the window and watched the boy's progress down the drive.

'You took my advice then and decided to give him a chance . . . yes?'

A gentle touch on his arm made the governor start and, turning, he found his wife standing close behind him. He put his arms around her as he rested his chin on the top of her shining black hair. She was dressed in a bright-yellow satin gown today and reminded him of one of the exotic butterflies that often landed in their garden. He and Isabella had been married for almost twenty years, and he didn't regret a single day of it. If anything, he adored her more now than he had on the day they had wed, and he set great store by her opinion.

'Yes, I took your advice,' he answered quietly. 'And I hope I don't live to regret it. I just sent him off with a sum of money, so it will be interesting to see whether he comes back or tries to escape with it.'

'He will come back,' she said with conviction. Then, standing on tiptoe, she kissed him on the lips, and for a while the governor forgot everything but the beautiful woman in his arms.

Chapter Nineteen

'Your father and I have decided to extend our stay for another week,' Muriel informed her daughter over breakfast one morning. 'And during that time, I'm going to give you a few lessons in parenting.'

Alicia flushed but she did not argue.

'And while I'm at it, I'll give you a few on how to keep your staff in order as well. Or that nanny at least.'

Alicia sighed as she dabbed at her lips with her napkin. 'I know I should be more assertive, Mama, but I'm afraid Nanny is a very forceful woman.'

'All the more reason to put her in her place and let her know who is mistress here, then,' her mother replied. 'And there is no time like the present. We shall go up together and get Suzanne dressed in clothes of your choice and then take her for a stroll in the park. It looks set to be a beautiful day and the child will benefit from the fresh air.

'I think your mother is right, darling,' Matthew piped up, as he saw the look of fear flit across his wife's face. As he had discovered since their marriage, Alicia was beautiful and she had a good heart, but she was completely out of her depth when it came to running the house or making decisions. 'I can't say that I'm too keen on Agatha either,' he admitted.

'And if you are afraid of her, imagine how Suzanne must feel. She's more like a sergeant major than a nanny.'

'As usual, Alicia, your mother is quite right,' Alicia's father said drily.

Muriel smiled at her husband as she and Alicia rose from their seats and left the room, leaving the men to enjoy their coffee in peace.

'Just leave this to me,' Muriel told her daughter as they mounted the stairs, and Alicia nodded docilely.

Muriel swung the nursery door open just in time to see Nanny tugging an underskirt none too gently over Suzanne's head while the child stood like a statue.

'Ah, Nanny.' Muriel smiled at Suzanne. 'I'm glad to see we are not too late. My daughter decided she wanted to choose what her little girl would wear today.'

'B-but I've already laid her clothes out ready,' Agatha stuttered indignantly.

Completely ignoring her, Muriel marched across to the small armoire and swung the doors open. 'So, what do you think?' she asked her daughter. 'This blue dress is very pretty. Or perhaps this pink one?'

With her cheeks flaming, Alicia joined her, studiously avoiding looking at Agatha, who was staring at them with eyes that were as cold as ice.

'I, er, well, er . . . what about this one?' Alicia lifted down a pretty cotton dress covered in little sprigs of forget-me-nots. 'Do you think this one would be suitable, Mama?' she asked timidly.

'It doesn't matter what *I* think, or anyone else for that matter,' her mother replied, with a pointed look at Agatha.

'Suzanne is *your* child and so she should do and wear what *you* wish her to. Isn't that right, Nanny?'

Agatha's mouth opened and closed but no words came out, and as Suzanne peeped at her out of the corner of her eye, she was reminded of one of the goldfish she had seen when her parents had taken her and the rest of her siblings to a fair once.

'Very well . . . she will wear this one today.' Alicia handed the dress uncertainly to the nanny who slipped it over Suzanne's head without a word. She would be glad when her mistress's mother cleared off back home. The young mistress was as soft as butter and very easy to manipulate, but her mother was another matter entirely, the interfering old busybody.

'Oh, darling, you look *so* sweet,' Alicia cooed when Susie was dressed and the nanny had brushed her hair, far more gently than she usually did. 'Grandmama thought you might perhaps like to come for a little walk with us now? We could go to the park. And perhaps we could scrounge some stale bread from Cook and feed the ducks while we are there, and then we could get an ice cream. Would you like that?'

Suzanne nodded eagerly. Anything was better than being left to the tender mercies of the spiteful nanny.

'Yes, please.'

Muriel nodded her approval. 'Good. Then we shall leave you to get your shoes on while we get ready ourselves,' Muriel told her. Then, turning to Agatha, she ordered, 'See to it that she is waiting in the hallway in ten minutes.'

'But she usually learns her letters in the morning,' Agatha objected, finally finding her voice again.

'There is absolutely no need for her to be doing that just yet – at least, not with you,' Muriel told her. 'I have already suggested to my daughter that it is time to bring in a tutor to teach Suzanne. You are merely the nanny, responsible for seeing to her creature comforts. Kindly remember that in future.' She sailed from the room with her daughter, leaving Agatha looking so red in the face that it appeared she might burst a blood vessel.

'The jumped-up sanctimonious old *cow*!' The words were out before Agatha could stop them and, rounding on Suzanne, she snapped, 'You didn't hear that; do you hear me?' She gave the child a vicious pinch on the arm.

Susie nodded as she blinked back tears. 'Y-yes, Nanny.'

'Good, now get yourself off down them stairs an' it'll be woe betide you if you say so much as one word out of place while you're gone, just remember that!'

She pushed the child none too gently ahead of her, and soon they were down in the hallway, where Agatha inclined her head before making her way back upstairs. Once there, she reached under the cushion of the rocking chair and removed a bottle of gin from which she took a large gulp. There were bottles of the stuff hidden all about the room, but she was careful never to drink it while Susie was about.

She sat for a time seething with rage. But eventually, as the gin worked its magic, she began to calm down. This was turning out to be the best position she had ever had, and it would be a shame if anything were to spoil it. The old bag couldn't stay forever; she had her own home to go to, and then hopefully everything would return to normal. Feeling slightly happier, Agatha took another long swig from the bottle, before settling down in the chair for her morning doze.

As they headed for the park, Muriel watched Susie carefully. The child walked sedately beside them to start with, but the further away they got from the house, the more she seemed to relax. It troubled Muriel. The child was clearly afraid of her nanny, but as yet the woman had given Alicia no reason to dismiss her.

'Can we feed the swans, please?' Susie asked eagerly, as they turned into the park gates. She was clutching the bag of stale bread that Cook had given her, and Alicia smiled fondly as she nodded and released her hand.

'Of course, darling. You may run ahead, but don't go too close to the edge of the water, mind.'

She smiled as the little girl raced off, her skirts flying around her. 'She's a lovely child, isn't she?' she asked her mother.

'Yes, she is . . . but rather withdrawn for a child of her age while we are in the house, don't you think?'

Alicia glanced at her mother and frowned. 'Whatever do you mean?'

Muriel shrugged, choosing her words carefully. 'I just wonder if she isn't a little afraid of her nanny. She came with a good reference you, say?'

'Oh yes, it was glowing. She worked for a Lord Albans somewhere in Sussex.'

'Hm.' Muriel said no more as they hurried to join Susie, but she promised herself that just as soon as she arrived back home, she would begin to make a few discreet enquiries.

They spent a delightful hour wandering around the park and at one stage Alicia bought Susie an iced bun that made the little girl's eyes light up. There were numerous nannies in the park, some wheeling perambulators with gurgling babies in them, while others played hide-and-seek amongst the trees with their young charges. Somehow, Muriel couldn't picture Agatha doing anything like that with Susie – the woman appeared to be happiest upstairs incarcerated in the nursery.

'So, have you thought any more about employing a tutor for Suzanne?' Muriel enquired. They were returning home and Muriel had noticed that Susie had gone quiet again.

'Oh yes. Matthew and I were talking about it only last night,' Alicia told her. 'Matthew is going to place an advert in the paper and we'll see who applies.'

'Good.' Muriel would feel a good deal happier when she knew that Susie wasn't being left to the nanny's tender mercies all day long.

'Had a good time, did you?' Agatha asked nastily when Susie tentatively walked back into the nursery. Her lips were curled back from her teeth, but her expression changed when Alicia and Muriel walked in right behind her. She hadn't been expecting that.

'She had a *very* good time,' Muriel informed her acidly. 'And in future, if the weather is fair, I want you to ensure that she visits the park each day. Exercise and fresh air are so good for children, don't you find? And now she is going

178

to wash her hands and face, and join us downstairs for an hour before lunch. See that she is tidy.'

She walked regally away with Alicia close behind her as Agatha's temper rose again. But she was wise enough not to take it out on Susie. Not yet! She would wait until the old bitch had gone home and then make sure the child knew exactly who was in charge again.

Over the next few days, Susie seemed to blossom. She dined downstairs with her new parents and grandparents each day and slowly she became more talkative, much to Alicia's delight.

Matthew had placed an advert for a tutor in the newspaper as promised, and two days before Muriel left for home, the first one arrived to be interviewed. He was an elderly man who to Muriel appeared to be almost as strict as Agatha was.

'It's up to you who you employ, of course, my dears,' she told Alicia and Matthew after sitting in on the interview. 'But if you were to ask my advice, I would go for a female and preferably someone a little younger. Learning should be fun and I fear the gentleman who just left might be rather stuck in the old ways. A "spare the rod and spoil the child" type. I'm afraid she has quite enough of that from Agatha.'

'You really don't like Suzanne's nanny do you, Mama?' Alicia said.

Muriel shook her head. 'No, I'm afraid I don't, and I have an idea were you to ask Suzanne, she would say she didn't like her either. But there – I am interfering. Who you choose to employ is up to you, but I just ask that you keep a close eye on things.'

'We will,' her son-in-law promised. He set a lot of store by his mother-in-law's opinion, and often wished that his wife could have been a little more like her. He loved Alicia but was forced to admit that her head was full of nothing more than the latest fashions most of the time. Although he couldn't deny that she did seem to love the child in her own way, sometimes he wondered whether she had only wanted a child so that she could dress her up and parade her in front of her friends like a little doll, for she didn't seem to have a clue how to care for her – or even wish to learn how to, if it came to that. But Susie was here now, and despite his own initial misgivings, Matthew had grown fond of the child and wanted to do right by her.

There were tears on the day that Alicia's parents departed, and Alicia stood on the front step dabbing ineffectively at her eyes with a little scrap of lace handkerchief.

'You be a good girl for your mama now,' Muriel told Susie, as she patted her cheek affectionately. 'And rest assured Grandpapa and I will be back to see you very soon.'

Susie bobbed her knee as she had been taught to do and Muriel sighed. The only time the child seemed to act like a six-year-old was when she was away from the house, but there was nothing she could do about it for now.

Alicia stood on the steps with Susie and waved until the carriage was out of sight before leading the little girl inside.

'Pop back up to the nursery to Nanny now, there's a good girl,' Alicia told her. 'I have some friends coming to take tea with me shortly and I really must get changed.'

Lifting her skirts, she hurried away up the stairs and Susie sighed as she followed her with a heavy tread. It was as if her new mother had forgotten all about her already – but then, she was getting used to it by now. Just for a second a picture of Opal's kind face flashed in front of her eyes and, gulping down tears, she went on her way.

Chapter Twenty

Charlie looked around him as he strode down the rough road that led to the town. He passed ramshackle shacks that looked as if a single gust of wind might blow them away, and every step he took caused a cloud of dust to rise up. He stared in wonder at the brightly coloured birds in the trees; he had seen one just like them back in a pet shop in England once, and could scarcely believe that here they thrived and flew free. In the distance, he could see the quay where the ship he had come on had docked, but there were only small fishing boats bobbing on the azure-blue water now. As he continued down the hill, the main road in the settlement became busier, with horse-drawn traffic and people milling everywhere. There were far more shops dotted along the main street than he had expected. There was a dressmaker's shop displaying a colourful gown in the window, and next to that was a bakers' with a variety of loaves and cakes resting on a counter inside. Next to that was a milliner's and slightly further on a hardware shop with many items displayed outside, from buckets and bowls to gardening tools.

He paused outside a shop with a sign above the window that said 'Ezra Schwartz, Tailor'. This was the one he was looking for, so he opened the door, setting a small bell tinkling. It was quite gloomy and dusty inside, despite the glorious sunshine outside, and for a moment he stood as his eyes adjusted to the dim light. A tailor's dummy dressed in a multicoloured waistcoat stood just in front of him, and beyond that was a long, roughly hewn wooden counter that ran the width of the shop. It was covered in offcuts of material, tape measures, needles, pins and scissors, and as Charlie stared at it, a door behind the counter opened and a tiny, smartly dressed man stepped through it. He was almost completely bald with a small skullcap – which Charlie later discovered was called a kippah – perched on his head and he was almost as far round as he was high.

The man smiled a greeting. '*Boker tov*, young man. Ezra Schwartz, at your service. What can I do for you?'

'Er . . . good day, sir. The governor asked me to give you this.' Charlie handed him the message the governor had written, and after quickly reading it, the elderly man nodded.

'You are to be fitted for new clothes, it seems,' he said approvingly. 'So first we shall take your measurements and then we shall look at material. Please . . . stand so.'

Charlie held his arms out as requested, and the man began to measure every inch of him, writing down the measurements with a stub of pencil in a little book he produced from his pocket.

'And now, if you could just take your shirt off. I must be precise.'

Charlie froze as his hands flew to the buttons of his ragged shirt. He hated the thought of anyone seeing his back, but realising he had no choice, he sighed and slowly undid them, slipping it off.

When the old tailor saw the zig-zag of angry scars across his back he winced, but he said not a word as carried on taking his measurements, and when it was done, he told Charlie, 'You may put your shirt back on now, son.' He looked at him curiously. 'Forgive me asking, but why would the governor wish you to have new clothes?'

'It's because I shall be working with him in his residence.' Charlie was fumbling with the buttons on his shirt. 'He told me that his assistant has recently returned to England and I am to help him with his paperwork.'

The tailor looked impressed. 'Ah, so you can read and write then. This is most unusual; never in the time I have lived here have I known the governor to employ a convict in his home. Make the most of the opportunity, and I wish you good luck. You never know, should he be pleased with your work, you may earn an early pardon.'

'Thank you, I shall try hard,' Charlie assured him. 'But now if you could let me know how much the clothes will cost, I am to pay you.'

Again, the tailor was surprised. Normally the governor would be presented with a bill after the clothes were made, and yet today he had sent this young man with money to pay for them. Could it be that he was setting Charlie a test? His hand flew deftly across a piece of paper as he reckoned up what everything was going to cost and handed it to Charlie, who paid him and tucked the change safely away in his pocket. 'I shall do my best to have everything ready within the week,' the tailor promised.

Charlie left and made his way to the bootmaker. They decided on a soft brown leather that would go nicely with the light tweed Mr Schwartz had chosen for his suit. Once again, when the measurements were taken, Charlie paid the man, took his receipt and tucked the change into his pocket.

When he walked out of the shop, he was shocked to find how the temperature had risen and he soon began to sweat. The heat was taking some getting used to, but he didn't have long to think about it as he suddenly noticed a straggly line of men in chains being marched through the settlement. Walking alongside them were a number of overseers wielding evil-looking whips, and by the way they were barking at the men they would not be afraid to use them. As he watched, one of the men stumbled and the overseer closest to him was on him in a second. 'Get up, yer bleedin' mangy cur!' he growled. 'Else you'll feel the length o' this leather across yer back.'

The man struggled to his feet, a look of despair and defeat on his face. These were obviously the more hardened criminals, who were forced to break rocks or work for long hours in the harsh sun, and Charlie couldn't help but feel pity for them; it brought home to him how lucky he was to have been given a chance to work in a civilised manner. The men moved on in a cloud of dust as flies and mosquitoes buzzed all around them and Charlie turned to make his way back to the governor's house. He would have liked to stay a while and explore the settlement a little more, but he dared not risk upsetting the governor.

Two hours after he had sent Charlie into the town, the governor looked up from the pile of paperwork on his desk when someone tapped at the door.

'Come in,' he answered irritably. He didn't seem to be making any progress whatsoever, and wondered if he would ever catch up.

When Charlie appeared he looked momentarily surprised but he nodded towards the seat in front of his desk. Part of him had wondered if Charlie would take the money and make off to other parts, but it appeared that Isabella had been right to place her trust in him. It was a good start.

'Your change, sir.' Charlie took the money and two receipts from his pocket and laid them on the desk. The governor did a quick check and found that the money was correct, right down to the last penny.

'I'm told that the new clothes and the new boots will be ready within a week.'

'Good!' The governor narrowed his eyes and, making a decision said, 'Come here and let me show you what you will be expected to do.' He took a large register from the drawer and opening it he pointed to rows of names and numbers. 'These are the names of the convicts,' he explained, 'and each has a number against them. Every day the overseers visit, usually during early evening, and if there is anything to report they will write it down. For instance, here is one.' He pointed to a piece of paper on which was written in a crude hand, 'Williams, Convict Number 146, 50 lashes for causing a fight amongst the convicts.'

'It will be your job to enter this into the journal, along with the date. It might not sound like much of a job, but believe me when you are dealing with many convicts, the paperwork can soon pile up, as you can see. We also receive reports regularly from the settlers who have taken convicts to work on their farms. If they give good reports then that is written into the ledger too, and it can sometimes earn a convict an early pardon if they work hard and keep their nose clean. Do you think you are up to it?'

'I shall certainly give it my best shot, sir,' Charlie answered enthusiastically. After all, how hard could it be?

'In that case, there is no time like the present.' The governor smiled at him. 'I have to go out, so why don't you make a start now? This is the pile I would like you to deal with first and I shall have some food sent in to you at lunchtime. Then, when I return, we'll see how you've got on.'

'Yes, sir.' Charlie took a seat, and the governor was heartened to see that before he had even properly left the room, the boy had dipped the pen in the inkwell and was concentrating on the pile he had placed before him.

'So . . . he came back then, my love,' a teasing voice behind him mocked, as he quietly closed the door behind him.

He grinned. 'Yes, he did; you were right as always,' he conceded.

'My papa told me when I was a little girl always to go with my instinct,' she said, laughing up at him. 'Which is why I agreed to marry you, my love. Instinct told me that you were the perfect man for me.'

'Then I shall never question your judgement again, my love. Clearly you have the finest instincts in Australia – if not the world.' He grinned and kissed her swiftly on the lips, before striding away.

Smiling happily, Isabella watched him go, admiring his broad back and the way the sunlight streaming in through the windows turned his hair golden.

At lunchtime, a maid appeared with a tray for Charlie. On it was a jug of lemonade, a selection of dainty sandwiches and a variety of small cakes and pastries. He thanked her and ate hungrily, but then got straight back to work, and by the time the governor returned in the late afternoon, he was impressed to see that Charlie had made an excellent start on the backlog of work.

He examined the pages carefully, before nodding his approval. 'Your handwriting is almost better than mine,' he told him with a wry smile.

'Thank you, sir. I'm really enjoying it,' Charlie answered.

'Very well, carry on, but knock off at six o'clock and make your way to the kitchen for your evening meal. Oh, and present yourself back here at seven o'clock tomorrow morning.' He turned to leave, but then, remembering something, he paused and added, 'And please ensure that this and the kitchen are the only rooms in the house you enter. This is my home and I have daughters and a wife. I would not wish you to invade their privacy.'

'Of course, sir.'

Satisfied, the governor left, and Charlie once again became absorbed in the paperwork.

Late that evening, as Charlie was sitting outside his tiny shack admiring the balmy night, Francesca and Juliet appeared and, seeing him, they hurried across.

'So you are working inside for Father now.' Francesca gave a tinkling little laugh that set Charlie's heart thudding. He was sure she was easily the most beautiful girl he had ever seen. 'I am so pleased. Father hates all the paperwork that his position involves, and he is always so grumpy when he gets behind with it.' She sank down on to the patchy grass next to him, oblivious to the beautiful gown she was wearing.

While Juliet wandered off to examine the flowers, Francesca asked, 'So tell me about yourself, Charlie, and what led to you being here. You do not seem like a convict to me.'

Haltingly, Charlie began with his mother's death and then told her everything that had happened to him and his family since, and by the time he was done, there were tears in her eyes.

'So I suppose when you have served your sentence, you will wish to return to England and find your family again?'

He nodded.

'I can understand that.' She sighed. 'But at least until then we shall have the pleasure of your company. That is one of the drawbacks to living here. Juliet and I do not have many young people our age to associate with.'

'Well ...' Charlie looked slightly uncomfortable. 'No offence intended, miss, but I don't think your father would be very happy about you associating with me. I am a convict, after all, and you are a lady.'

Francesca scowled and tossed her head. 'Huh! You are still a human being, Charlie Sharp, and circumstances led you to do what you did! Perhaps I would have done the same had my family been in such dire straits. My mother always taught us that we should not judge others, and so if I wish to speak to you I will!'

Charlie said not a word but his smile spoke volumes as they sat quietly side by side enjoying the peace and quiet.

Chapter Twenty-One

December 1852

'The mistress asked me to tell you that Mr King will be dining with her this evening, Cook,' the housekeeper announced.

Cook sighed. 'What again? That'll be four times this week in all.'

'Well, I dare say the mistress may have her son to dinner whenever she wishes,' Mrs Deep answered and, turning in a rustle of stiff bombazine, she left the room.

'I reckon he's got designs on Opal,' Belle whispered to the cook. ''E can hardly keep his eyes off her an' when Miss Partridge came to dinner last week an' kept fawnin' over 'im, he were all but downright rude to 'er!'

'You can hardly blame 'im for that,' Cook snorted, as she continued to roll out pastry for a rabbit pie. 'You'd think she'd 'ave given up by now, after all this time. She must 'ave skin as thick as a rhino's if she ain't took the hint that he ain't interested by now!'

'If who hasn't taken the hint?' Opal asked innocently, as she strolled into the kitchen just in time to catch the end of the conversation. She had changed vastly in the time she had worked there and had blossomed from a young girl into a very beautiful young woman. She was still slim, but her figure had filled out in all the right places, and thanks to Mrs King's tutoring, she carried herself proud and erect. Although, to give her credit, her nature hadn't changed at all, and she still felt more at home with the staff than she did with her mistress's guests. Today, she wore her long dark hair in an elegant chignon.

'We was just sayin' as how Miss Partridge tends to throw 'erself at Mr King every time she sees him but how he won't have a bar of it!' Cook answered.

Opal grinned. 'You're not wrong there. She's so blatant in her attentions to him that it can get quite embarrassing at times.'

'Hm, but has it not occurred to yer that his attentions might be directed elsewhere?' Cook asked, and when Opal frowned and looked confused, she laughed.

'We're on about *you*, yer daft thing,' she teased. 'Surely it's dawned on you by now, that he's right taken wi' you?'

Opal looked shocked. '*Me!*' Her hand flew to her throat. 'But Henry King must be old enough to be my father.'

'Happen he is, an' happen that's why he sees you as the next Mrs King. You're young enough to give him sons – sommat his poor late wife couldn't do, God bless her soul. Why else do yer think he brought you here to have the old lady teach yer social skills? He could 'ardly marry a workin'-class maid, now, could he? But a lady's companion is a different kettle o' fish entirely.'

Opal sat down heavily on the nearest chair and gulped. Surely Cook was joking? But no, one glance at her face told Opal that she was deadly serious.

'Think on it,' the cook rambled on as she expertly transferred the pastry to a prepared pie dish. 'He's been comin'
more an' more regular these last few months, an' I doubt it's
been to see his mother.'

'B-but I don't *want* to be the next Mrs King . . . I don't want
to marry anyone, if it comes to that. I'm only just eighteen.'

'Huh! I was married wi' two little 'uns by the time I were
your age,' Cook informed her. 'But don't get worryin' about
it. He can't make yer marry him if you've no wish to. Though
what I'll say is this – he might not be a young, dashin' blade,
but yer could do a lot worse. Married to him yer'd have servants to wait on yer an' yer'd never want fer nothin'. It beats
bein' married to a drunkard an' bein' knocked from pillar
to post, never knowin' where the next penny were comin'
from. Think on it, me girl.'

But Opal didn't want to think on it and, rising, she quietly
left the room. Thankfully Mrs King was having her afternoon nap, so once in the privacy of her room she crossed
to the window and stared down on to the lawns below. The
sky was heavy and grey, and she wouldn't be a bit surprised
if they had snow before the day was out. It had been threatening for days. With tears in her eyes, her thoughts turned,
as they so often did, to her parents. They had never had
much but they had been content with each other and she
had always hoped that one day she would meet someone she
could love as much as they had loved each other.

Her eyes strayed to the small desk beside the window,
where a half-written letter to Charlie lay unfinished. She had
written a number of letters to him, as Henry had told her

that he'd made enquiries and believed that her brother had been shipped to the convict colony in Tasmania. But not one of her letters had been answered, and now she was wondering if they had ever even reached him, for perhaps the convicts were not allowed to have any correspondence from loved ones while they were serving their sentence.

Henry was trying to track down Susie for her too, and she was forced to admit that he had been more than kind to her. Without him, she had no idea what might have happened to her. She supposed that in a way she had grown fond of him, but she had never in her wildest dreams considered him to be a suitor! Cook must be wrong, she told herself, and she would go on as before. Nothing had changed, not really. Feeling better, she tapped on her mistress's door to see if she was awake yet. Mrs King liked a cup of hot chocolate when she woke from her nap each afternoon.

'Ah, there you are,' Mrs King said, when Opal stepped into the room. 'I forgot to mention that Henry will be joining us for dinner again this evening. His cook is in bed with a bad case of influenza, so I dare say we'll see a lot of him until she's up and about again. But now go and get my drink and then I'll decide what I'm going to wear to dinner. I thought perhaps you could put that nice new dress on that you got a couple of weeks ago. I haven't seen you wear it yet and that bronze colour suits you.'

'Yes, ma'am.' Opal slipped away to fetch the chocolate, and for the rest of the afternoon she was too busy seeing to her mistress's needs to think of much else.

That evening, Mrs King chose to wear one of her favourite gowns in a deep-purple colour, and with it she wore her amethysts, which sparkled in the light of the oil lamp as Opal fastened the necklace about her neck. To go with the necklace she had a matching ring, bracelet and earrings, and when she was ready she looked quite regal.

'I'm afraid jewellery is my weakness.' She chuckled as she stroked the gleaming gems about her neck and Opal didn't doubt it. Her mistress had jewels in all the colours of the rainbow: emeralds, sapphires, amethysts, diamonds and rubies, to name but a few. When she had first gone to work for her Opal had been almost afraid to touch anything so valuable, for she guessed that one single stone alone would probably be worth more than a whole of her year's wages. But now she was used to handling them and was even entrusted with cleaning them when the old lady thought they needed it.

'Right, m'dear, you'd better go and get yourself ready. Henry will be here any minute, but first you can help me downstairs and get me a glass of sherry.'

Opal did as she was told, before hurrying back upstairs to put on the newest dress Mrs King had bought her. She now had four very nice day gowns, but as yet there had still been no occasion to wear the lovely blue silk one, and secretly Opal doubted there ever would be. Even so, she gazed at it longingly as she lifted her newest dress from the armoire.

She was halfway down the stairs when she heard the front-door bell sound, and almost instantly Belle rushed forward to admit Henry King.

'Why, Opal, my dear, you look quite charming,' he remarked admiringly, and after handing his hat and coat to Belle, he offered his arm, which she took self-consciously, allowing him to lead her to the drawing room.

'Ah, here you are, Henry. Come and sit by the fire to get warm. Would you like a brandy?'

'No, thank you, Mother, not before dinner.' He bent to peck her on the cheek and hurried on, 'I have something rather nice to tell you. My dear friend Peter Dawson-Myres has invited me to a ball. You too, of course, and you, Opal.'

Opal gawped wordlessly. *A ball!* Surely there must be some mistake; since when were servants invited to attend a ball?

But his mother took it all in her stride. 'Do shut your mouth, my dear,' she advised. 'You look like you are catching flies and it is most unladylike! And yes, of course you must come too. You are my companion and as such it is fitting that you should be invited.' Then, turning back to her son, she asked, 'And when is this grand occasion to be?'

'On Christmas Eve and it looks set to be a very fine affair.'

'Hm, I shall have to get Opal to check my wardrobe,' the old woman said thoughtfully. 'It's been a while since I last attended such an event. I just hope the moths haven't got into my gowns.'

'Order a new one if necessary,' Henry told her. 'And allow me to pay for it for your Christmas present.'

His mother scowled at him as she sat forward, leaning heavily on her walking stick. 'I'm not quite a charity case yet,' she scolded.

Thankfully Belle appeared in the doorway then to inform them that dinner was ready, and with the ladies on each arm Henry led them to the dining room.

'Is the ball to be at his place?' his mother asked as Belle served the first course.

'Yes, I believe he has hired caterers from London.' And then realising that Opal had no idea where 'his place' was, he told her, 'Peter has a wonderful home in Caldecote. It's very grand, so it looks set to be a wonderful evening. I'm sure you will enjoy it. All the local dignitaries will be there, as well as many he knows from London.'

Opal inclined her head and, as the meal progressed, Henry could speak of nothing but the ball ahead. 'I've been to see my tailor today. He's making me an evening suit,' he informed his mother.

'Very nice, dear,' she answered, only half listening. Then, turning to Opal, she told her, 'This will be a nice opportunity for you to wear your blue satin gown, dear, and also to show off all the lessons I have taught you on how to conduct yourself as a young lady when in company.'

'Yes, Mrs King,' Opal answered, with mixed emotions. As the old lady had said, it would be a wonderful opportunity to wear her beautiful dress – but there was just one problem.

'The only thing is . . .' she said hesitantly. 'I don't know how to dance. At least, not the sort of dances they will be doing at a ball.'

'Oh, don't get worrying about that.' Henry grinned at her as he laid his napkin across his lap. 'I shall give you a few lessons here before we go. It's very easy really, you just follow me and you'll get the hang of it in no time. In fact, we'll start this very evening when we've finished our meal.'

Opal flushed at the thought of him holding her, but she could hardly object so she simply smiled.

Once the meal was over, Henry led the ladies back to the drawing room.

'We'll start with a waltz,' he told Opal, and somewhat reluctantly she allowed him to place his arm about her waist, as her mistress looked on. 'Hold my hand up here like so . . . that's it, now put your other hand here and just follow me while I hum a tune.'

Opal suddenly got a fit of the giggles, but instead of being annoyed as she had feared, Henry began to laugh with her as he guided her around the room, and she found that she was quite enjoying herself.

'One two three, one two three,' he chanted.

Soon Opal felt that she was getting the hang of it. It wasn't nearly as difficult as she had feared, and Henry was turning out to be a surprisingly patient tutor. Eventually, as she grew more confident, he quickened his steps and before long they were whirling about the room.

'There, first lesson over. That wasn't so bad, was it?' he asked when he finally released her.

Laughing, she shook her head. 'No, it was quite fun, actually,' she admitted breathlessly.

'Good, and by the time the ball rolls around you'll be good at it. I shall make a point of coming to teach you every chance I get.'

As the old lady looked on, her lips curled into a smile. *So, I was right*, she thought. *Henry* has *set his sights on her*.

She didn't mind in the least, for in the time Opal had worked for her she had grown very fond of the girl. She could only hope that if Opal did see the merits of becoming Henry's wife, he would treat her better than he had the last one.

Chapter Twenty-Two

It was Christmas Eve and Mrs King's house looked resplendent. A tall Christmas tree decorated with candles and glass baubles stood in the entrance hall, and another smaller one stood beside the fireplace in the drawing room. Opal had been out and picked bunches of holly sporting bright-red berries, and had placed them in crystal vases in almost every room.

The kitchen was bustling as Cook prepared an enormous goose for the next day, when Henry and Miss and Mrs Partridge would be coming for lunch. Opal was so excited at the prospect of the evening ahead that she could hardly stop smiling. It had been arranged that she would help Mrs King to dress early, so that she would have time to get herself ready, and Belle had offered to help her with her hair. Henry would be calling for them at seven o'clock promptly, and Mrs King had lent Opal a beautiful velvet cloak with a fur-trimmed hood to go over her gown. She had also bought her a pair of blue satin slippers that matched her dress perfectly as her Christmas gift, and Opal could hardly wait to put them on.

Opal had risen early that morning to bathe and wash her hair, which she had then dried by the fire, and now it fell about her shoulders in shining waves.

When it came to lunchtime, Opal was so nervous that she could barely eat a thing, but Mrs King had told her not to worry as there would be plenty to eat at the ball.

'Peter and his wife Emma always lay on a grand spread for any guests they have, so you can eat then if you wish to,' she told Opal kindly. It was nice to see the girl looking so happy.

After lunch, Opal read to her mistress for a time, but her mind was clearly not on it and eventually Mrs King told her to stop. 'I'm going up for my lie-down,' she informed her. 'And if you've any sense you should do the same. It's going to be a very late night, so rest while you can so that you enjoy it.'

Opal did try to do as she was told, but as she lay on her bed watching the snow gently falling outside the window, her eyes kept straying to the beautiful gown and the dainty slippers she would be wearing that evening.

When it was time to start getting Mrs King ready, Opal was glad of the distraction; the snow was still falling and she had begun to worry. What if Henry's carriage couldn't get through it? What if the roads became impassable? She voiced her concerns to Mrs King, who snorted. 'Huh! Henry will be here, never you fear. I think he is looking forward to it almost as much as we are.'

Opal helped her to dress, this time in a burgundy satin gown that she had never seen her in before. 'I think I shall wear my rubies tonight,' Mrs King said thoughtfully as Opal dressed her hair.

Eventually, she was ready.

'Will I do?' Mrs King asked, as she stared at herself in the looking glass on her dressing table.

Opal smiled broadly. 'If you don't mind me saying, ma'am, you look quite . . . quite' – she searched her mind for the word she was looking for – '*majestic!*'

'That'll do nicely.' Mrs King chuckled. 'I don't scrub up bad for an old lady, even if I do say so myself. But now help me downstairs, girl, and settle me by the fire with a glass of sherry. Then go and get ready. I don't want you showing us up.'

Belle was already waiting in Opal's room when she there, stroking the blue dress enviously.

'Eeh, I don't think I've ever seen a lovelier gown,' she sighed. 'You're going to look grand in this.'

'I hope so,' Opal told her, as she wiggled out of her dress and petticoats. Belle helped her into the petticoats that went with the dress and finally it was time to slip the gown on.

Belle lifted it over her head, then began the task of doing up the many tiny, satin-covered buttons at the back of it. 'Ooh, I'm all fingers an' thumbs,' she groaned, but at last it was done and she guided Opal to her dressing table. 'I thought we might pile all your hair on the top o' yer head like so,' she demonstrated. 'Then I'm goin' to tease it into little ringlets that fall all down the back. I've bought some o' me own clips cos I don't think you have any. What do yer think?'

'It sounds lovely, if you think you could manage it,' Opal said uncertainly as she stared at her reflection in the mirror.

'Oh, I'm good at dressin' hair; I used to practise on me mam,' Belle assured her as she began.

Finally, Belle finished to her satisfaction. 'Yer can look now. Come on over to the cheval mirror.'

When Opal went and stood in front of the looking glass, she gasped. Her hair looked lovely and the dress, which was off the shoulder and a little lower cut than anything she had ever dared to wear before, made her feel like a princess. It was tight into the waist, making it look tiny, and then it flared into shimmering folds that rustled with every movement.

'You look *really* beautiful,' Belle told her with a catch in her voice. 'An' I don't mind bettin' me next quarter's wages every bloke at the ball will want to dance wi' you.'

'Oh!' Opal was momentarily speechless. Never in her wildest dreams had she ever imagined owning a gown so fine or looking like this and in her excitement she did a little twirl.

'Right, missie. It's time you were getting' yourself down-stairs.' Belle giggled. 'An' you just be sure to enjoy yourself. I only wish I were comin' with you.'

'I wish you were too,' Opal told her earnestly, as she turned to face her. 'And thank you so much for doing my hair.'

'It were my pleasure.' Belle ushered her out of the room and lifting her skirts, Opal raised her chin and floated down the stairs. She had just reached the bottom when Henry appeared out of the drawing room and at the sight of Opal, his mouth dropped open.

'Why, my dear girl, you look . . .' He shook his head as if he was seeing her for the first time. 'Absolutely splendid.'

'Thank you, sir.' Opal dipped her knee and blushed as he gently took her arm and led her into the drawing room where Mrs King was waiting for her.

She too told her how lovely she looked, before beckoning her over. She was holding a black velvet box and holding it towards Opal, she told her, 'I thought you might like to wear these tonight. My dear husband bought them for me on our first wedding anniversary many years ago and I thought how well they would complement your gown.'

Opal gasped as Mrs King snapped open the box to reveal a string of perfectly matched pearls. 'O-Oh, that's very kind of you,' she stuttered. 'But I'm afraid they must be worth a great deal of money and I would be too afraid to wear them.'

'Oh, fiddlesticks! Henry, come and fasten them about her neck for her.'

Henry did as he was told, enjoying the feeling of her creamy skin as he fiddled with the clasp.

'You were right, Mother,' he said approvingly. 'They match her gown beautifully. But now it's time we were leaving, ladies, if we wish to arrive on time.'

Lifting the velvet cloak, he slipped it across Opal's slender shoulders and then, after helping his mother into a long mink coat, they made for the door. Belle was waiting in the hallway to open the front door for them, and she gave Opal a little wink as she passed.

In the carriage, Opal sank back against the leather squabs, her face glowing with excitement. The snow was still falling and beyond the carriage windows the world looked as if it had been coated in fairy dust, which only added to her happy mood.

The carriage rattled through Weddington and once they were in Caldecote it turned through some enormous iron gates that led on to a winding, tree-lined, gravel drive that was lit by lanterns strung from the branches. When they arrived at the large forecourt, people were descending from their carriages and the horses were being led away to the stables by smartly dressed grooms. Lights spilled from every window, and a footman in livery stood beside the open front doors welcoming the guests.

Opal began to feel as if she were caught up in a fairy tale as the carriage door was opened and she was helped down. After climbing the steps, they walked into the most enormous hallway that Opal had ever seen; it was as if she had stepped into another world.

'Your cloak, miss.' A fresh-faced maid in a navy dress and a mop cap and apron trimmed with *broderie anglaise* took Opal's cloak and pointed down the hallway. 'The ladies' powder room is down there, miss, if you wish to tidy yourself.'

'Go on,' Mrs King urged her. 'I want a word with Emma, Peter's wife; it's some time since we have seen each other. I shall wait here for you.'

Opal started off, passing many beautifully dressed women coming and going on the way. Another young maid held the door to the powder room open for her and she went inside.

She stood for a moment, admiring it. All along one wall were tiny gilt-legged chairs with a long mirror in front of each, where women of various ages sat powdering their noses and putting the finishing touches to their hair. Along the other wall was a row of closets. A voice she recognised came to her from the far end of the room and, looking towards it, she saw Esther Partridge deep in conversation with a woman sitting beside her.

'It's more than obvious that the little chit has set her cap at Henry,' she heard Esther sneer. 'And her nothing more than a so-called lady's maid as well . . . Huh! As if he would ever look at someone like *her*! Why, Henry and I have had an unspoken agreement ever since his wife died. It will be only a matter of time before he makes me the next Mrs King. He would *never* lower himself to marry that little trollop. I can't even understand why dear Mrs King even bothers to employ her.'

It suddenly struck Opal like a blow between the eyes that Esther was talking about her and as hot colour rose in her cheeks, she turned and fled back out into the corridor in a most unladylike manner. Further along, she could see Henry and his mother talking to their host and, trying to remember all she had been taught, she managed to compose herself. This was a special evening – a wonderful evening – and she was damned if she was going to let that woman spoil it for her. And so she lifted her chin, took a deep, steadying breath and went to join them.

'Ah, here you are, my dear.' Henry smiled at her. 'Peter, may I introduce you to Miss Opal Sharp.'

'Charmed, I'm sure,' the tall, dark-haired gentleman said as she dipped her knee and inclined her head. 'My wife is about somewhere; I shall introduce you as soon as I can find her.'

'Thank you for inviting me, sir,' Opal said politely.

'You are most welcome, Miss Sharp.' The man smiled at her.

Mrs King took her arm then and led her away, as Peter told his friend, 'What a delightful young lady, Henry.'

'She is indeed,' Henry agreed and, keen to be at her side again, he excused himself and hurried after them.

Once all the guests had arrived, they were led into a large dining room, where a feast fit for a king was laid out on crisp, white tablecloths. Opal had been introduced to Peter's wife, Emma, by then, and the two took to each other instantly. Maids were mingling amongst the guests with trays of tasty hors d'oeuvres and glasses of champagne and Opal accepted a glass, hoping that it would calm her nerves. The bubbles tickled her nose, but she found that it was rather pleasant so drank it too quickly – but strangely it did seem to calm her a little, and she tried to put the unpleasant episode in the ladies' powder room out of her mind.

Staying close to Henry and Mrs King, she mingled with the guests and Henry noticed proudly that she was attracting more than a few admiring glances. Then, suddenly, Esther was in front of them.

'Henry, my dear,' she crooned, completely ignoring Opal. 'How very smart you look in your evening suit. Quite dashing, in fact.'

'How very kind of you to say so,' he answered politely.

She clutched at his arm and in a girlish voice she purred, 'I do hope you have reserved the first dance for me?'

Henry looked mildly embarrassed. 'It would have been my pleasure, but unfortunately I have promised it to Miss Sharp.'

'I see.' She flicked open her fan and glared at Opal, then smiling at him sweetly, she said, 'Perhaps later then?'

He gave a little bow. 'Of course. It would be my pleasure.'

She turned and waddled away in a swathe of pink satin that did nothing to complement her ample figure.

'Shall we make our way to the ballroom, ladies?' Henry suggested. 'I think I can hear the orchestra tuning up.'

The ballroom proved to be equally as grand as the other rooms Opal had seen, if not even more so, and she gazed about in awe as Henry led her and his mother to one of the many little velvet sofas positioned around the edges of the room. Enormous crystal chandeliers lit by a multitude of tiny candles were positioned here and there across the vast ceiling and the parquet floor was so highly polished that Opal was sure she could almost see her face in it. Once the women were seated, Henry took more champagne from a passing maid and handed the ladies a glass each, and slowly Opal began to relax.

On a raised platform at the end of the room, the orchestra were tuning up and soon they took their places as someone announced, 'Take your partners for the first waltz please.'

'Shall we?' Henry stood and gallantly offered his arm as Opal peeped at Mrs King. Her two hands leaning heavily on her ebony-topped walking stick, the old woman gave the briefest of nods, so Opal took his arm and allowed him to lead her on to the dance floor as the orchestra began to play.

She felt so self-conscious as she became aware of eyes watching her that she stumbled a few times. Thankfully, Henry had his arm tightly about her waist and, forcing herself to relax, she began to enjoy it – and soon they were whirling about the floor, her satin skirts and petticoats billowing about her as he smiled indulgently down at her.

She smiled back up at him, lost in the joy of the moment, and it suddenly struck her that although he was somewhat older than her he actually looked quite handsome. He had lost a little weight and in his smart evening suit with his hair neatly trimmed, he looked quite distinguished.

She was breathless and flushed by the time the music stopped and she laughed as he led her back to her seat. But she had no sooner sat down, than a young man approached her and, offering his arm, he asked, 'Would you care to dance, miss?'

She glanced at Henry and when he nodded somewhat sullenly, she went back on to the floor to dance a polka this time.

Minutes later, she noticed that Esther had claimed Henry and she had to stifle a giggle as they danced past. Esther was clinging to him as a drowning man might cling to a raft and, seeing how uncomfortable Henry looked as he tried to hold her at arm's length, she almost felt sorry for him.

The rest of the evening passed in a pleasant blur. Opal was in great demand and rarely sat down, and she couldn't remember when she had ever enjoyed herself so much. And then, halfway through the evening, a tall fair-haired man approached her and, once they were on the dance floor, he said, 'I'm sorry, I didn't catch your name?'

Opal blushed, 'It's Opal . . . Opal Sharp, sir.'

'It's very nice to meet you, Opal.'

Her stomach did a little flip as she looked up at him; he was the most handsome man she had ever met. He was nice too.

'Are you from Nuneaton, sir?' she asked tentatively, trying to remember Mrs King's lesson on polite conversation.

He shook his head. 'No, I live in Mayfair in London, actually. Oh, and by the way, I'm Matthew Darby-Jones. I almost forgot to introduce myself then.' His eyes were twinkling as he smiled down at her, and once again her stomach did a little flip.

'I'm down here with my wife to spend the holidays with our friends, Peter and Emma. That's my wife over there dancing with Peter now, and our daughter is up in the nursery with Peter's children and their nanny.'

Opal glanced in the direction he was nodding and saw that his wife was a very beautiful woman. Her hair shone silver blonde and she was tall and slender, and for no reason that she could explain, she felt a pang of envy. She felt as if every nerve in her body was tingling and was painfully aware of the warmth of his hand on hers, to the point that she was almost glad when the dance ended and he chivalrously delivered her back to her seat. No man had ever affected her that way before, and she felt guilty for being attracted to another woman's husband.

The instant she sat back down, Henry again claimed her for the next dance, and her heart settled back into rhythm – but for the rest of the night she found her eyes straying back to Matthew Darby-Jones.

It truly had turned out to be the most magical evening, one that she knew she would never forget. Particularly the moments she had spent in the arms of Matthew Darby-Jones, who had asked her to dance twice more – much to Henry's ill-concealed annoyance. Just for a time she had managed to forget about Susie and Charlie, but all good things must come to an end, and just before midnight the last dance was announced and Henry took her arm possessively before someone else stepped in.

'May I?'

'Of course.'

It was another waltz and as they glided about the floor, he asked her, 'Have you enjoyed yourself, my dear?'

'Oh yes!' She answered without hesitation. 'It's been truly wonderful. I feel a little like Cinderella.'

He threw back his head and laughed. She was so innocent and unspoiled; that was what he most liked about her, and he also knew that with her on his arm he was the envy of every man there.

'Then let us hope this will be the first of many such evenings for you.'

Suddenly shy again, she lowered her head as she thought back to what she had heard Esther saying in the powder room. Could it be true? Could Henry possibly be considering her as the next Mrs King? She hoped not, because as much as she had enjoyed the evening, all she really wanted was to see her family back together again. The thought put a slight blight on the occasion, and in the carriage on the way home Henry and his mother noticed that she was unnaturally quiet. Could they have known it, she was thinking of her family – and Matthew – although she was wise enough to say nothing. It would be some long time before she saw Charlie, and as for the handsome stranger . . . it was doubtful their paths would ever cross again.

Chapter Twenty-Three

It was hard to get up the next morning after the late night, but Opal rose at her usual time to serve her mistress with breakfast in bed.

'And we have another busy day ahead of us,' Mrs King commented, as Opal plumped her pillows and placed them behind her back, before laying the tray across her lap. 'Oh, and Merry Christmas, Opal. I almost forgot it was Christmas Day.'

'The same to you, ma'am.' Opal crossed to the window and swished the curtains aside, to reveal a white world. The snow was still falling and on the lawn below a little robin was busily pecking away searching for worms, his bright-red breast a brilliant splash of colour against the snow.

'What time will the visitors be arriving, ma'am?'

Mrs King took a sip of her mint tea. 'Not before twelve o'clock hopefully. I have instructed Cook to have the lunch ready for one. But first we are going to attend church with Henry. He should be here within the hour, so we need to get ready.'

The Sunday morning church service was a ritual now and Opal enjoyed it, but today's service would be extra special, and as she helped the old lady get dressed, Opal couldn't help but think of Christmases gone by when the family had all been together. Just two Christmases ago she and Charlie had spent the festive season in the derelict little cottage in Rapper's Hole, and the one before that had been spent with their parents and siblings! *Such happy times*, she thought with a pang of sadness – but they could never come again and she wondered what Susie and Charlie were doing now. Wherever they were, she prayed they were well and happy and had enough to eat.

The service was beautiful and the church looked magical nestled in the snow with the light shining through the stained-glass windows. The church pews were decorated with holly and ivy and the choirboys looked angelic in their starched white surplices as they sang much-loved carols. The many candles added to the atmosphere and the congregation was light-hearted as they left to shake hands with the vicar at the door and wish him a Merry Christmas.

When they arrived back at Mrs King's house, they found that their visitors had already arrived. Belle had served them morning coffee in the drawing room and when Henry walked in Esther rushed over to greet him effusively, clutching a sprig of mistletoe.

'Merry Christmas, my dear Henry,' she gushed, as she planted a sloppy wet kiss on his cheek. Opal was amused to see that she had aimed it at his lips but he had just managed to turn his head away in time.

Looking slightly annoyed at her failed attempt, Esther greeted Mrs King while ignoring Opal, which bothered Opal not a jot.

'I suggest we open our presents now before we go into lunch,' Mrs King said, reaching for one of the gaily wrapped presents beneath the tree.

'This is for you,' she told Mrs Partridge. 'Just a token gift, you understand?'

The woman opened the package and smiled. 'Why, they're lovely, thank you,' she said admiring the lavender bath salts and scented soap.

Esther then opened hers, which proved to be exactly the same only rose-scented. Henry was next and he looked genuinely pleased as he examined a gaily coloured waistcoat, and finally Mrs King handed Opal hers.

Opal flushed with pleasure as she unwrapped the present and found a fine, deeply fringed silk shawl in a lovely pastel green colour.

'Thank you very much, ma'am,' she muttered, aware of Esther's disapproving glare. 'But the slippers were quite enough!'

Then it was Henry's turn to hand out the gifts he had bought. There were dainty white handkerchiefs embroidered with their initials for the Partridges, and a pair of fine leather gloves for his mother. Finally, he turned to Opal and handed her hers.

She opened it carefully, sorry to have to rip the pretty paper, to reveal a long, black leather box and when she opened it she gasped as she saw a gold fine-chain bracelet with a heart charm dangling from it.

'Oh . . . Mr King . . . thank you, it's lovely,' she said breathlessly.

Pleased to see her looking so happy, Henry said, 'Here, let me fasten it on for you.' All the time, Opal was aware of Esther's eyes boring disapprovingly into her back.

The Partridges had also brought gifts for Henry and his mother, and these too were duly handed out and exclaimed over, by which time Belle had appeared to announce that lunch was ready to be served.

The food was excellent, although Opal didn't really enjoy it, for Esther went out of her way to exclude her from the conversation and she was just grateful that the Partridges hadn't been invited to stay for tea as well. They would dine on cold cuts that evening because Mrs King had given the staff the rest of the day off to have their own little Christmas party in the kitchen.

Opal was shocked at the amount of food Esther managed to eat, and at one point Henry gave her an amused wink, showing that he had noticed too. At last the meal was over and Esther suggested, 'Why don't we retire to the drawing room for a game of cards, Henry? I'm sure my mother and Mrs King can keep themselves entertained and I imagine Miss Sharp will have duties that need attending to.'

'As it happens, Miss Sharp is my mother's companion, not a household maid,' he responded somewhat coldly. 'But I dare say we could have a game of cards if Opal wishes to join us.'

'I-I'm not really very good at cards,' Opal told them, and he nodded.

'In that case we shall all take our coffee in the drawing room.'

Opal saw the dark stain spread up Esther's neck at what she had clearly taken as Henry's rebuff, but by the time they had risen from their seats she was fluttering her eyelashes at him again as she rushed to take his arm. He looked slightly annoyed but led her from the room, leaving Opal to bring her employer and Mrs Partridge through to them, and for the rest of the afternoon, Opal made sure that she sat well apart to avoid any unpleasantness.

At five o'clock, Mrs Partridge glanced towards the window and said, 'Well, it's been quite delightful, Winifred, and compliments to your cook for the lovely meal, but I'm afraid we really should be going now. Do you think you could have our carriage brought round to the front for us, please?'

'Of course,' Mrs King answered graciously. 'Henry, could you go through to the kitchen and ask Ned to see to it, dear?' Ned was her jack of all trades about the house and garden and lived in the rooms above the now empty stables. Until a couple of years before, Mrs King had kept her own horses and carriage but now she no longer ventured out so frequently, she had given them to Henry and relied on him to take her wherever she wished to go.

Henry looked slightly relieved as he rose to do as she asked, and he soon returned to say, 'Ned will have it around at the front for you in ten minutes, but he said can you please be ready to leave as he doesn't want the horses standing out in the cold. I'm afraid the snow is coming down thick and fast still.'

There followed a busy few minutes as the Partridges got into their outdoor clothes and collected their things together, and after taking their leave of Mrs King and studiously ignoring Opal yet again, Henry showed them to the door.

'I was thinking,' Esther said as she stroked her finger suggestively down the lapel of Henry's jacket. 'That you might like to come and dine with me and mother tomorrow? It must be so incredibly boring for you having to be entertained by your mother all the time.'

'In actual fact, I enjoy my mother's company, and Miss Sharp's if it comes to that,' he said coolly, as he firmly removed her hand. 'But thank you for the invitation all the same.'

Just for a moment her face set in an angry mask, but then it was all sweetness and light again as she turned and trilled, 'Goodbye for now then, dearest Henry.'

And he watched her as she was swallowed up by the snow, before closing the door firmly behind her.

'Well,' Mrs King said, 'I'm afraid I am going to have to leave you to entertain yourselves for a while. I'm in need of a rest and a lie-down.'

'I'll help you up the stairs,' Opal offered instantly as, leaning heavily on her stick, Mrs King struggled to her feet – but the old lady shook her head.

'You'll do no such thing. I'm quite capable of climbing the stairs myself, thank you very much. You just stay here and keep Henry company, and I'll see you both in a couple of hours. Belle informs me they have laid food out for us in the dining room, so when we're hungry we can help ourselves.'

Opal sank back into her seat, feeling slightly uncomfortable. She had never been left truly alone with Henry before and after hearing what Cook thought Henry's intentions were, she was suddenly nervous.

'I'll just throw a bit more coal on the fire, shall I?' Henry said cheerfully when his mother had left. 'I don't want you getting cold.'

She watched him as he stoked the fire and then her heart missed a beat when he said, 'Actually, I'm glad of this chance to have you to myself for a time, because there's been something I've been meaning to ask you.'

Opal squirmed in her seat, but remained silent as he came and sat uncomfortably close to her on the sofa. 'First of all, I just want to say how proud I was of you last night,' he began. 'I have no doubt I was the envy of every man at the ball when I walked in with you on my arm, and you conducted yourself like a true lady, my dear.'

Opal licked her suddenly dry lips. She didn't like the way the conversation was going at all, but she didn't know how to stop it.

He leaned forward and rested his elbows on his knees as he stared into the flames, wondering how she was going to react to what he was going to say next.

'I know you are only eighteen and I am double your age, but I have to tell you that since the day I met you I have been very taken with you, my dear.'

Opal gulped and blinked rapidly, wishing she was a million miles away.

'I-I am very fond of you too, Mr King, you have been very kind to me,' she muttered, which made him frown and wave his hand.

'I have asked you before . . . please, call me Henry!'

'Sorry,' she mumbled, as she gripped her hands together and pressed them tightly into her waist.

He coughed and went on haltingly, 'The thing is, Opal . . . I am *more* than a little fond of you. So much so that I would like to ask you to be my wife.' Suddenly he dropped down to one knee in front of her and her eyes stretched wide with panic. 'Please don't be afraid,' he pleaded. 'I truly have only the best of intentions towards you. Think of it . . . as my wife, you would want for nothing. I shall take you all over the world, wherever you wish to go, and you will dress in the latest fashions. You will never have to work again, and you will have servants to wait on you.'

Her head was wagging from side to side now as she tried to think how she might turn him down without hurting his feelings. What she had said was true; she had grown fond of him, but the problem was she didn't love him. Suddenly, a saying of her mother's popped into her head, 'Tell the truth and shame the devil!' And so, taking a deep breath, she said, 'I am truly flattered that you should ask me, Mr . . . er, Henry. You are a lovely man and you have shown me nothing but kindness, for which I am truly grateful . . . but the thing is, it wouldn't be fair of me to marry you. You see . . . I am fond of you, but I don't love you, not in the way a wife should love her husband, and I think you deserve a woman who will. Perhaps someone like Miss Partridge, who clearly has feelings for you?'

'*Pah!*' He grunted. 'I'm sure you are mistaken, and even if you weren't I wouldn't look at that shrivelled-up old spinster if she were the last woman left on earth. Without wishing to sound cruel, I believe Esther would marry anyone who was

219

brave enough to ask her. And as for your feelings – love will come in time. Fondness is a good place to start to my way of thinking . . . I do realise that this proposal may have come as somewhat of a shock to you and I also realise that you may need some time to think about it. So . . . would you at least consider it and not dismiss me out of hand?'

'But the thing is . . .' She hesitated before rushing on. 'I still have a family somewhere, Henry. One day, when he has finished his sentence, Charlie will come home and I still have to find Susie.'

'I can understand that, and I assure you I am still doing my best to trace them for you. But even if Charlie does come home and we find your little sister, it need make no difference to us. They would come and join us in my home and be part of our family. So, I ask you again . . . will you please just consider my proposal?'

'Yes . . . yes I will consider it,' she told him gently, but deep inside she very much doubted that she would change her mind.

Chapter Twenty-Four

At the governor's residence everything was hustle and bustle as the staff worked to get ready for the annual New Year's Eve ball that night.

Things had improved vastly for Charlie since he had started working there. He no longer lived in the small shack tucked away in a corner of the garden, but now had his own room up in the servants' quarters of the house.

It had been another strange Christmas for him. They were now at the peak of summer and the heat was almost unbearable, as were the flies and mosquitoes that came with it. And yet, being British-born, the governor still strived to celebrate a traditional English Christmas. A huge tree had been erected and decorated with tiny candles and baubles in the entrance foyer, but because of the heat it had instantly begun to shed its needles – much to the annoyance of the maids, who were forever sweeping up – and within a week it was drooping.

Charlie and the other staff had been allowed down to the beach on Christmas Day after dinner to swim in the azure-blue sea, although Charlie had been warned not to swim out too far – the place was a favourite with sharks and many people had lost their lives there. After the snowy

Christmases of days gone by, Charlie had struggled to adapt and even sometimes missed the cold. At least when you were cold you could huddle in a blanket, but here there was no escaping from the heat and humidity, and it was draining.

He pitied the men who worked on the roads, for they had no respite whatsoever from it, and were expected to work from morning till evening beneath the burning sun with nothing but dry bread and water to sustain them. Still, at least the governor had declared that Christmas Day and New Year 's Day were to be holidays for all, although Charlie doubted they would have found much comfort in the huts they were forced to live in. Every day he thanked God that he hadn't been sent to the prisons and he showed the governor his gratitude by working hard. He had completely updated the filing system so he could put his hand on each convict's file in seconds should it be necessary, and there were no longer teetering piles of paperwork all over the office. Charlie was proud to know that he was now the governor's right-hand man.

The governor had been so pleased with his efforts that the year before he had allowed Charlie to sit in with Juliet and Francesca's tutor for three hours each day to improve his mathematics. It had paid dividends and now, as well as keeping the files for the governor, Charlie was also able to keep a check on the household budget. On top of that, when there wasn't a lot of paperwork to do, Charlie was still more than happy to get his hands dirty on manual jobs about the house, unless it needed a specific tradesman, and so all in all he was happy; or as happy as he could be while he waited for his freedom. But he still worried constantly about Opal and Susie, and prayed that they were faring well.

Today, he was on his way to help the male staff set out the large tables for the buffet that would be available to the guests that evening, and when he entered the dining room he found it in a state of organised chaos.

'I think we should put the tables over there,' a harassed-looking footman said, pointing to the wall by the door.

Charlie had other ideas. 'Actually, if you put them down there on the far wall, you would leave the entrance to the room clear and there would still be space for the guests to mingle when they've helped themselves to the food,' he suggested.

The footman, a middle-aged man with a rather pious attitude, stared about thoughtfully, before grudgingly having to admit that Charlie was right.

The staff in the kitchen had been working for days preparing the food, and delicious smells were floating around the house, making Charlie feel hungry as he pitched in to help get all the tables into position. They had no sooner finished than Isabella appeared with Francesca and Juliet close behind her.

'Ah, very good,' she said approvingly as she fanned herself with a pretty little fan that she had brought with her from Spain many years ago. Then, looking towards the maids, she told them, 'Hurry and get the best linen tablecloths. We shall need to start bringing the food in soon if we are to be ready to receive our guests. And you, gentlemen' – she smiled at the men – 'perhaps you would be so good as to go and prepare the stage in the ballroom for the orchestra?

There is still much to do, I'm afraid.' She wandered away in that direction to supervise as Francesca caught up with Charlie.

'You're sweating,' she said, laughing.

Charlie mopped his brow with the back of his hand and grinned. 'So would you be; it's hot work lugging heavy furniture about.'

The last year or so had wrought a great change in both of them. Charlie had thought Francesca was a pretty girl when he had first met her, but she had developed into a beautiful young woman. Her figure was curvy, her hair gleamed and she had a beautiful tanned complexion. He, too, had grown some inches and towered almost a head above her, and his once skinny frame was muscular and bronzed from the sunshine.

But for Francesca, growing up had brought with it its problems. Sometimes she missed having company of her own age, and she was aware that had her family still lived in London she would have been being introduced into society, whereas in the colony she had only the occasional ball to look forward to – and they were far too few and far between.

The governor was fiercely protective of both his daughters, although strangely he didn't seem to mind Francesca associating with Charlie, but then Charlie realised this was probably because their meetings only ever took place in the house where they were always under scrutiny. Charlie accepted this. After all, he was still a convict, and it wouldn't do at all for the governor's daughter to be seen outside with the likes of him.

'So, have you got a new gown for this evening?' he asked.

She giggled prettily. 'Yes, I have. Luckily the last convict ship delivered some wonderful bolts of material and some magazines with pictures of the latest London and Paris fashions in them.' Her face became serious, and she sighed. 'It seems that we may be returning to London soon. Apparently, there will not be any more convicts being shipped to New South Wales now, and once the ones that are here are freed, what will my father have to do? They will all be free men to make a life here or return home. Were you aware that they are to stop transporting convicts?'

'Your father did mention it,' he said, trying to keep his feelings from showing on his face. He hated the thought of not being able to see Francesca every day. And what would become of him if the governor left?

'And what do you think of it?'

'Well, obviously for convicts it will mean that if they are sentenced they will have to serve their time in English jails and, seeing as they're already grossly overcrowded, I can see problems arising.'

They had reached the ballroom by that time and Francesca's maid hurried over to her. 'If we're to bath you and wash your hair, you'd best come now, miss, else we'll never have you ready in time.'

'Very well, Gertie, thank you.' She turned to Charlie. 'I wish you were coming to the ball too, Charlie,' she said with a smile, before following after her maid.

By the time the first guests were due to arrive, everything was ready and Charlie positioned himself on the landing, where he squatted down behind the balustrade to watch. In the ballroom the orchestra could be heard tuning their instruments and there was an air of excitement as maids dashed to and fro, looking smart in frilled white aprons with matching mop caps. He was so engrossed in watching what was going on that he jumped when he heard a slight cough behind him. He rose to his feet so quickly that he almost overbalanced and, whirling about, he found Francesca grinning at him.

The sight of her almost took his breath away. She always looked beautiful but this evening she was positively stunning and he was momentarily lost for words. Her hair was piled on top of her head in loose curls, which made her appear older, and the heavily embroidered cream satin gown she was wearing had an off-the-shoulder design that showed off her flawless skin to perfection.

'How do I look?' she asked teasingly as she gave him a little twirl, setting her satin skirt dancing.

Charlie nodded, unable to take his eyes off her. 'You . . . you look . . . magnificent,' he gasped, and a blush rose in her cheeks as he stared at her intently.

'Why, thank you, kind sir.' Her eyes twinkled as she smiled at him, but peeping over the balustrade she saw her mother and father standing in the foyer below greeting their first guests and she told him reluctantly, 'I'm sorry, but I shall have to go and join them, Charlie.' She paused as if there was something else she would have liked to say but then, thinking better of it, she flitted past him and glided down the stairs.

In no time at all, the governor's residence seemed to be bulging at the seams and Charlie barely knew where to look first. Maids carrying silver trays loaded with sparkling glasses of champagne circled amongst the guests and the air was full of laughter and chatter.

Opal and Susie would have loved this, Charlie thought regretfully, as he followed Francesca's progress. She seemed to have every young man there trailing behind her and he didn't blame them in the least. She was easily the most beautiful girl in the place, although he noted that she didn't seem to be paying particular attention to any one of them.

Eventually, the guests drifted towards the dining room, where the buffet had been laid out and Charlie slipped away to his attic room where he flung the window wide to stare down at the town with the sea sparkling beyond it. Suddenly, he had the urge to feel the cool water on his skin – so, snatching up a towel, he headed for the servants' stairs and let himself out of the house. Shortly after he was walking through the throng of ramshackle buildings that made up the main street of the town and when he came to the beach he kicked off his shoes and strung them about his neck, relishing the feel of the soft, warm sand beneath his feet.

It was that special time between day and night, and he saw that there were some other young men slightly further along the beach, who clearly intended to swim as well. Glancing about to make sure there were no ladies to be seen, Charlie

227

stripped down to his long johns and, after neatly folding his clothes, he headed for the surf.

He recognised one of the young men as the son of the deputy governor and wondered why he wasn't at the ball. It seemed that everyone who was anyone was there, but the youth's absence was explained when Charlie heard him tell his friends, 'Why would anyone want to go to a stuffy old ball when he could be here enjoying himself?' His comment was followed by guffaws of laughter as the young men hurtled into the sea.

Charlie had been gently swimming along the shoreline for some minutes when a commotion behind him made him glance over his shoulder.

'Julian . . . look out . . . behind you!' A shout went up and looking about Charlie saw that the young man was some way out in deep water. His friends were frantically swimming back towards the shore, choking and swallowing salt water in their haste to get back on the beach. And then Charlie realised why they were in a panic. Further out and heading straight towards the boy was a large black fin slicing through the water.

'Julian, *swim* for, God's sake! There's a shark!'

The youth looked behind him and panicked when he saw the fin heading towards him. The fear took hold of him for a moment and he disappeared beneath the waves, only to come up seconds later splashing and screaming.

Without thinking, Charlie struck out in the youth's direction, as the young men who were now all safely back on the beach shouted encouragement. In no time Charlie had reached him and, grasping Julian round the neck, he struck out for the shore, swimming for all he was worth as every hair on his body stood to attention. Every second he expected to feel the shark's teeth sink into him, but he kept going as the young men screamed encouragement.

And then, after what seemed like a lifetime, Charlie felt the sand beneath his feet and he dared to glance back over his shoulder, just in time to see the shark turn and, with a sharp flick of his tail, disappear beneath the waves.

Hauling the young man up the beach, Charlie dropped him unceremoniously on to the sand as he sank to his knees, trying to get his breath back.

'Lord, that was a close call,' one of the chaps exclaimed, as Julian coughed up salt water. Then, turning to Charlie he told him admiringly, 'If it wasn't for you, he'd have been a goner for sure then. Well done, mate.'

Charlie shrugged. As far as he was concerned, he had only done what anyone who was able to would have done. He was just thankful that things had turned out as they had and that he had learned to swim in the blue lagoon, a reservoir back in Nuneaton.

'Perhaps it would be a good idea if you told your pal not to go so far out next time he decides to go for a swim,' he suggested caustically. Shock was setting in now and Charlie was shivering uncontrollably as he rose and made his way to where he had left his clothes.

'Th-thanks,' Julian gasped. Then, as he looked at him properly for the first time, recognition flared in his eyes. 'Aren't you the chap that works for the governor?'

Charlie nodded as he pulled his shirt on. The last thing he wanted was for them to see the scars on his back.

'Well . . . all I can say is thanks again.' The young men watched Charlie walk back up the beach.

He was suddenly exhausted as what might have happened struck him and now all he wanted was his bed.

Chapter Twenty-Five

'Are you going to keep this sulking up for much longer?' Matthew asked, as he gazed into Alicia's dressing table mirror and straightened his tie.

Lifting her perfume, Alicia lavishly applied it to her neck and wrists and pouted.

'Why shouldn't I sulk?' She patted the ringlets that cascaded over her slim shoulders as her eyes met his in the mirror. 'I can't forget how you held that girl at the ball at Peter's house last week. And did you *really* have to dance with her *three* times?'

Matthew grinned and raised an eyebrow. 'Hold on, darling. I don't recall you sitting any of the dances out. In fact, you were in such great demand that I barely got a chance to claim you for a dance myself.'

She shrugged. 'I can't help it if I'm pretty,' she said coyly.

Matthew sighed as she handed him a strand of pearls to fasten about her neck. He had to admit she looked ravishing. Tonight she had chosen to wear yet another of her new gowns in a deep sky-blue colour, heavily adorned with sequins and pearls that set off her fair beauty to perfection – but as he had discovered, in some ways, Alicia's beauty was only skin deep. She was incredibly vain, thanks to her parents, who had spoiled her shamelessly, and she tended not to think of much at all apart from her jewels and what she would wear.

It had been she who had wanted to adopt a child and, although Matthew had had grave misgivings about the idea, he had finally given way to her wishes, just as he always did. Unfortunately, the novelty of having a daughter had worn off very quickly for her and strangely it was he who had become fond of the child, to the point that it hurt him to know that poor Suzanne was left in the care of the dreadful nanny in the nursery upstairs for most of the time now. Had it been up to him, he would have given the woman her marching orders in seconds, but Alicia had insisted that she knew what she was doing, so he had reluctantly kept his own counsel – for now at least.

Once the necklace was fastened, he stood back, and as he watched her, admiring the pearls – a gift from him for Christmas – he suddenly found himself thinking of the girl he had danced with who Alicia had taken such a dislike to. In fact, it was clear that she had more than disliked her and was insanely jealous of the girl. He could picture her shining jet-black hair and gentle face, but it was her eyes that he most remembered. They had been quite striking: an unusual nut-brown colour with long dark lashes. In fact, now he thought about it, they were remarkably similar to Suzanne's, and they even had the same haunted look about them. Opal, she had said her name was, he recalled, and he wondered why Alicia was so jealous of her. She normally didn't mind who he danced with when they were at such events, so long as she herself was surrounded by admirers.

'You're thinking of her now, aren't you?' she suddenly accused crossly.

Bringing his thoughts back to the present, Matthew flushed guiltily. 'Of course I'm not. Now, are you quite ready? If so, I shall just pop up and say goodnight to Suzanne before we leave.'

'Oh Matthew, must you?' Alicia pouted again as she picked up a tiny satin evening bag that matched her dress. 'You do know how disgruntled William and Fiona get if their guests are late. And I do so want to show off my new gown before we go in to dinner.' She had started to resent the fact that Suzanne seemed to prefer Matthew to her, even though she never called him 'Father'. Instead she called him by his first name, and Matthew didn't seem to mind at all. She found it most improper. When she was Suzanne's age, she would never have dreamed of addressing a grown-up man by his first name!

'Then you go down and I'll join you in a moment.' He bent to kiss the soft skin on her shoulder and hastily left the room, taking the stairs that led to the nursery two at a time.

He found Suzanne sitting in a chair with a book in her lap and the nanny with her feet up on a stool as she sat in the chair next to the fire.

Agatha rose hastily, but barely giving her a glance, Matthew strode past her towards Suzanne, who was sitting as still as a statue.

He hunkered down next to the child and asked with concern, 'Are you all right, Suzanne? You look as if you've been crying?'

Before Susie could say a word, Agatha said silkily, 'No, she hasn't, sir. She has a bit of a cold that's making her eyes run.'

Matthew didn't believe a word of it as he rose and stared at her stonily. 'In that case, I suggest you summon the doctor to look at her first thing in the morning.'

'Oh, there'll be no need for that, sir,' Agatha smarmed. 'She just needs to be kept in for a few days.'

'But surely fresh air is good for a child if they are well wrapped up?'

'Not when it's as cold as this, sir.' Agatha just wished he would clear off and stop interfering. He was becoming a nuisance lately, popping in and out of the nursery when he wasn't expected.

'I see.' Matthew hovered uncertainly. He couldn't abide the woman. There was something about her that he hadn't taken to, but then he knew very little about raising children, so he supposed in this instance he would just have to trust her judgement. When he turned his attention back to the child, she gave him a faltering smile. 'Be a good girl for Nanny then, my dear, and I'll pop in and see how you are when I get back.'

'I'd rather you didn't, sir.' Agatha stared at him boldly. 'Suzanne will be fast asleep by then and I wouldn't wish her to be disturbed.'

He supposed she was right on that count, so he nodded. 'Very well, but I shall come up here first thing in the morning and if she isn't any better I shall have to insist that she sees the doctor.'

Agatha's lips set in a grim line, but she nodded, knowing she had no alternative. Thankfully the interfering busybody turned and left, leaving Susie to the nanny's mercy again.

Still, Susie thought miserably, at least she had some respite from her now that she had a tutor come in for a few hours each day.

Thankfully Matthew had had the final say on who they should employ, which was just as well, for Alicia didn't seem to have a clue when it came to interviewing the applicants. He had finally decided on a younger woman called Elizabeth Collins who had come with an excellent reference from her former employers who no longer needed her because their two boys were now attending a boarding school. Elizabeth was in her early thirties, slim to the point of being thin and not at all pretty in the traditional sense; her hair was light brown and unfashionably straight and her nose slightly too big for her face, but she had a wonderful sense of humour and twinkling brown eyes.

'I think learning should be fun,' she had told Matthew enthusiastically during the interview, much as his mother-in-law had said, and he had taken to her immediately. She soon proved that she wasn't afraid to stand up to the strict nanny either, which Matthew took as a point in her favour when Agatha tried to interfere.

'I see no need for you and Suzanne to closet yourselves away in the school room,' Agatha had told her bossily the first time she arrived to give lessons. 'She can work just as well in here with me to make sure she behaves herself.'

Miss Collins had drawn herself up to her full height and glared at her coldly. 'Thank you for your concern, Nanny, but I'm quite sure we shall do very well on our own.'

And from that moment on they had barely spoken, apart from when they had to, which suited Miss Collins right down to the ground.

Susie loved the time she spent with her new tutor. Miss Collins would take her out to the park on nice days, much to Nanny's disgust.

'I thought you were supposed to be teaching her not gallivanting about,' Agatha had said stroppily.

Miss Collins had merely stared her out. 'There is a lot more to learn than English and mathematics,' she had informed her coolly. 'It is important that a young lady learns about birds and flowers and wildlife, so I suggest you leave her teaching to me.'

From that moment on the two women were at war, and could the gentle Miss Collins have known it, it was no good for Susie whatsoever, for when she returned to the nursery Agatha would vent her wrath on her with vicious pinches or slaps where the bruises would not be seen.

Sometimes Susie wondered if she should tell the woman who professed to be her new mother about it, but her fear of the bullying nanny kept her silent, and anyway she doubted that Alicia would believe her. Her visits to the nursery floor had waned somewhat over the time Susie had lived there, although she was still taken downstairs from time to time and paraded in front of Alicia's friends.

Susie hated such times. The tiny teacups and saucers she was handed were so fine that she was terrified of breaking them or spilling tea everywhere, and she was too afraid to take any of the tiny cakes or pastries she was offered for fear of spraying crumbs, although the sight of them made her mouth water. That was another thing she hated. Nanny was very strict about Susie's diet and insisted that anything sugary was no good for a growing girl, although she never seemed to mind stuffing her own face with cakes and sweets.

Every night when she went to bed she thought of Opal, Charlie and Jack, and wondered where they were and what they were doing. For some long time, she had lived in hope that they would come and find her, but as time passed the hope died, and now it felt as if there was nothing to look forward to other than living under Agatha's strict reign.

Downstairs Matthew was helping Alicia on with the new mink cloak he had bought her, another present for Christmas, and soon after they left in their fine carriage, unaware that Susie was watching them enviously from the nursery window.

'Come away from there and get yourself into bed,' Agatha barked, making Susie almost jump out of her skin. 'You can have an early night tonight because I want to go down and have a game of cards with Cook.'

'But isn't it a little early to be going to bed?' Susie plucked up the courage to ask – and instantly wished she hadn't when she saw angry colour flood into Agatha's cheeks.

'You are questioning me?' Agatha's words came out more as a threat than a question and before Susie could answer she was across the room and gripping her arm so tightly that Susie winced with pain. She had no doubt that tomorrow there would be another bruise to add to the others that had not yet faded. There were so many of them now that Agatha had taken to locking the door when Susie bathed or got undressed in case anyone should come in and see them. Agatha shook her viciously, making her teeth rattle as she dragged her towards the bed where she flung her onto the bedspread.

'Now, you just stay there an' make sure I don't hear a peep out of you, else you'll regret it,' she warned, waggling a plump finger in the terrified girl's face.

Susie dragged the blankets back and crawled beneath them as the nanny headed for the door, then she lay there listening to the sound of the woman's footsteps receding as hot tears spilled down her pale cheeks.

And it was then that she made her decision. She was going to run away and find her family.

Without waiting to think about it, she crept out of bed again and, after throwing her nightgown over the back of a chair, she hastily dressed in the clothes that Agatha had laid out ready for her to wear the next day. Her heart was hammering as her ears strained for the sound of Agatha returning, but all was quiet, so she grabbed a bag from the bottom of her small wardrobe and began to ram some clothes into it. Next, she slid her arms into the sleeves of the fancy little red coat Alicia had bought her for Christmas and pushed her feet into tiny black leather lace-up boots.

It was only then that the enormity of what she was about to do hit her and she chewed nervously on her lip. She didn't think that her new mother would much care if she was gone, but she thought that perhaps Matthew would – so, snatching up a book that she had been using to practise her alphabet she licked the end of a pencil and hesitantly began.

Dear Matew,

I'm sorry but im runnin away cos nanny is crewl to me an I don't want to live ere any moor. Yu ave bin very kind to me but I want to find my reel family so I'm goin to luk for them, luv Susie

After reading the note through, she propped it up against the inkwell on the table – but then, thinking better of it, she decided she would leave it somewhere else, for she was sure that if Agatha found it, it would end up on the fire.

She pulled the bonnet that matched her coat on to her springy curls. Then, grabbing the note, her bag and the beautiful china-faced doll that had been a gift from Matthew for Christmas, she left the room and crept along the landing. Because Alicia and Matthew were out for the evening, the house was quiet as the staff made the most of their absence. Most of them were in the kitchen drinking tea and gossiping, and the hall was deserted.

Susie quickly propped her note up against a crystal vase full of flowers standing on the gilt console table in the hall – then, with her heart in her mouth, she crept towards the door, praying she would be able to open it.

After what seemed like a lifetime, she finally managed to turn the key in the lock and as the door opened an icy blast of air hit her full in the face, making her gasp. But she didn't hesitate and, stepping out on to the step, she closed the door as quietly as she could behind her.

She glanced up and down the rows of fine terraced town houses, realising that she had no idea where she was going. But there was no time to lose; if anyone was to discover her note and find her out there on the step, she had no doubt that Agatha would relish punishing her severely. The thought added wings to her feet as she fled down the street, a tiny figure flitting beneath the pools of yellow light spread by the gas lamps.

Chapter Twenty-Six

Early in January Mrs King came down with a bad cold that confined her to bed and when she told Opal that Henry would be dining there that evening Opal flew into a panic.

'But does that mean that he and I will have to dine alone?' she asked in alarm.

Mrs King chuckled as she pulled the blankets up around her neck. She found that she was either freezing cold or roasting hot and couldn't seem to get comfortable. 'Don't worry, my dear,' she croaked. 'There will be plenty of food as always, so I'm sure he won't eat you.'

Opal bit her lip as she filled the old lady's water glass from the jug at the side of the bed. Henry had not as yet broached the subject of his proposal nor asked her for an answer, but Opal had no doubt that he would that very evening if they were to dine alone.

'B-but what shall I talk to him about?'

The old woman sighed. 'Haven't I taught you how to hold polite conversation? This will be your chance to put it to the test.'

Seeing that she had made up her mind about Henry coming to dinner, Opal said no more – but as the afternoon wore on, she became more nervous by the hour. The old lady was living on a diet of soup at present, insisting that she could stomach nothing more, and when Opal carried her tray up to her Mrs King said, 'Thank you. Now I suggest you go and make yourself presentable for Henry. Perhaps you could wear that nice yellow gown I bought you at the end of last year? Oh, and do something with your hair. It looks very stern tied back in a bun like that. When you're ready, you can come in and let me have a look at you.'

With a sigh of resignation, Opal placed the tray on the old woman's lap, and when she had ensured she had done all she could to make her comfortable, she went to her room to change for dinner.

The dress Mrs King had suggested she should wear was in a pretty shade of lemon yellow. It was fashioned in a very fine, silky wool and Mrs King had bought her hooped under-skirts to wear beneath it. It was high-necked, with tiny little navy buttons running all up the bodice and the hems of the sleeve and the neckline were trimmed with navy braid that made it look quite elegant. Opal had been looking forward to wearing it, but tonight, after thoroughly washing every inch of herself, she felt no pleasure at all as she slipped it over her head.

Once she was dressed, she released her hair from its pins and, after brushing it until it gleamed, she fastened it into a loose chignon on the back of her head, leaving a few strands to curl about her face.

When she was ready, she stared at herself in the mirror. She was barely recognisable now compared to what she had looked like when she arrived, yet she would have given up her new easy life and the fashionable clothes she now wore in a sigh if only she could have had her family back. As they often did, her thoughts turned to Charlie. She had been reading everything she could get her hands on about Australia and as she gazed at the hoar frost on the lawn beyond her bedroom window it was hard to imagine that where he was, they would now be at the height of their summer.

The sound of Mrs King ringing her bell yanked her thoughts sharply back to the present and after a final glance in the mirror she hurried away to see what the old lady wanted.

'Ah, very elegant!' Mrs King studied her approvingly. 'I thought that colour would suit you. Now, pass me my book, my dear, and get yourself downstairs. Henry should be arriving any minute.'

Even as she spoke they both heard the sound of his carriage wheels and the horses clip-clopping down the drive; so, reluctantly Opal turned to make her way downstairs.

Henry was in the hall handing his hat and coat to Belle as she reached the bottom of the stairs and he smiled at her, his eyes openly approving. 'May I say how very charming you look this evening, my dear?' To her huge embarrassment, he took her hand and kissed it, much to the amusement of Belle, who was struggling not to grin. He held his arm out and, feeling that she had no choice, she slipped hers through it and allowed him to lead her to the drawing room, where he instantly headed for the cut-glass decanters that the old lady insisted were filled daily.

'A little sherry perhaps?'

Opal shook her head and sat down on one of the fire-side chairs, spreading her skirts neatly about her. Suddenly she felt tongue-tied, but she needn't have worried as Henry asked, 'So, how is my mother today? Did the doctor call in again?'

'She is no worse, and yes he did. He has left her a tonic; but other than ensure that she drinks plenty of fluids, there is little else I can do for her.'

He nodded. 'Quite right. She's lucky to have you looking after her.' He flashed her a smile. 'How are you, my dear? This is the first time I have had a chance to speak to you alone for some time.'

Thankfully, Opal was saved from having to reply when Belle tapped at the door and entered to tell them, 'Dinner will be served in the dining room in ten minutes.'

'Excellent, and what is on the menu this evening, Belle?'

'I believe it's broccoli and Stilton soup followed by roast lamb, sir.'

He nodded his approval and turned his attention back to Opal, his expression serious. 'I'm afraid I have some bad news for you,' he told her solemnly. 'And as it has been weighing on my mind and there is no easy way to say it, I may as well tell you now and get it out of the way. It's about your brother, Charlie.'

Opal's heart began to beat a mad tattoo, and she felt the colour drain from her face as she fixed her eyes on him.

'The thing is . . . I have written a number of letters to the penal colonies, as you know, to try and trace his where-abouts and today I heard back from one of the governors. I'm so sorry, but he believes that Charlie might have been one of

244

the men who died of typhoid on the journey out there. They can find no trace of him in the prisons there.'

Opal gasped as her hand flew to her mouth and her eyes filled with tears. 'B-but he can't be dead!'

Henry crossed over to her and put his arm about her shoulders, and she was so shocked that she made no move to prevent it.

'I'm afraid there is a grave possibility that he is,' he told her grimly, the lies tripping easily from his lips. 'And I'm heartily sorry to have to be the one to tell you. The only consolation is that you can start to think of getting on with your own life now.' In truth, Henry had no idea if Charlie had survived the sea trip; he only knew that he had been transported and the chance of any of the prisoners who were sent to the colony returning was so slim that he had no need to worry about lying to her if it achieved his aims.

'No, until it's confirmed I shan't believe it! And I still have to find Susie . . .' she said desperately .

He gave her a gentle squeeze. 'Have no fear, if she is out there, I shall find her for you eventually. You may be assured of that. But perhaps you should prepare yourself for confirmation of Charlie's death. But now, shall we go in to dinner?'

Opal was in a daze as she allowed him to take her arm and lead her into the dining room. Belle brought course after course, but each one of Opal's was returned to the kitchen untouched as she sat there so steeped in misery that she forgot all about Henry's presence. He in turn seemed to realise that she was in shock and he remained silent as he did justice to the food. At last the meal was over, and they retired to the drawing room again to wait for Belle to serve them coffee.

It had just been brought in when the sound of the door-bell echoed in the hall and a moment later Esther Partridge appeared in the doorway. It was all Henry could do to hide his annoyance, but remembering his manners, he greeted her, 'Why, Miss Partridge, what a pleasant surprise. We were not expecting you.'

'I came to see how your mother is,' she told him as she pulled her gloves off, ignoring Opal. 'Mother and I have been so concerned about her. Is she any better?'

'Thanks to Opal's care she is no worse. But do come in and sit down. Would you like some coffee?'

'Yes, please.' She sat down heavily on the nearest chair and it was all Henry could do to stop himself from groaning aloud. It seemed like Esther intended to stay and he had been looking forward to having Opal to himself all day, drat the woman!

'Would you mind pouring for us all, my dear?' Henry asked Opal and as she rose from her seat she was aware of Esther glaring at her. This evening she was dressed all in black and she reminded Opal of a great fat crow.

'While she is doing that, I think I shall go and tidy myself after my journey, if you would excuse me.'

Opal was all fingers and thumbs as she poured the coffee into the cups, and an awkward silence settled on them as they waited for Esther to return.

Outside in the hall, Belle was just about to enter the kitchen when she saw the back of Esther's dark dress disappearing up the stairs. Why would she be going up there? Perhaps she was going to see the mistress. With a shrug, Belle went on her way, but for no reason that she could explain something didn't feel quite right.

Shortly after Esther returned and told Opal, 'I believe I just heard dear Mrs King calling for you as I came down the hallway.'

'Then will you excuse me?' Opal hurried from the room, but when she got upstairs to peep in on her mistress, she found her fast asleep, so reluctantly she returned to the drawing room.

The next half an hour passed in somewhat stilted conversation until at last Esther rose from her seat. 'Well, dear Henry, I suppose I should be going,' she simpered, starting to pull on her gloves. Suddenly she paused and gasped. 'Oh dear, I seem to have misplaced my emerald ring.'

Henry frowned and asked impatiently, 'Are you quite sure you were wearing it?'

'Oh yes.' She continued to stare at her hand for a moment and then suddenly smiled. 'Ah, I believe I took it off to wash my hands earlier. It belonged to my grandmother and is very valuable. Would you mind going and looking?'

She gazed pointedly at Opal, who instantly rose from her seat. 'Of course.' She hurried to the bathroom but there was no sign of the ring, so after a thorough search, she went back to the drawing room.

She had barely got through the door when someone tapped on it and Belle appeared.

'Excuse me.' She bobbed her knee as she looked at Esther. 'But I found this in the bathroom a few minutes ago. Is it yours, miss?'

Esther looked dumbfounded for an instant, but quickly forced a smile as Belle held out the missing ring. 'Oh, er . . . yes, yes it is . . . Thank you.' She took the ring and rammed it on to her finger and, after saying a quick goodbye, she left.

'I rather think it's time I was retiring too, if you don't mind, Henry,' Opal told him, and hiding his disappointment he nodded.

'Of course. I didn't realise how late it had become. And I'm so sorry I had to be the bearer of bad news. Goodnight, my dear.' He crossed to Opal and lifting her hand he gently kissed it, making the colour rush to her cheeks.

Opal made a hasty exit while Belle hurried away to fetch Henry's hat and coat.

A little while later, as Opal was taking the pins from her hair, there was a gentle tap on the door and Belle stuck her head around it and whispered, 'May I come in fer a minute?'

'Of course.'

'Look, I just came to warn yer that Esther tried to set yer up tonight,' Belle told her, in a hushed voice. 'Earlier on I saw her disappearin' up the stairs, then as I passed the drawin' room door I heard her askin' you to go an' look for her ring. It got me to thinkin', so I checked the bathroom, then sneaked upstairs to check your room, an' there was the ring sittin' on your dressin' table bold as brass. The stuck-up madam was tryin' to make it look like you'd stolen it, so just be on yer guard.'

Opal was shocked. 'But *why* would she do that?'

Belle snorted. 'It's as clear as the nose on yer face. She knows that Henry is taken wi' you an' she's green wi' envy. She wanted to try an' make you out to be a thief to put him off you.'

'She must *really* hate me,' Opal whispered. 'And she'd hate me even more if she knew that Henry had proposed to me.'

Belle chuckled. 'Per'aps yer should tell 'er that an' that you've accepted him,' she suggested with a wicked grin. 'I'd love to see the look on 'er face then!'

Opal shook her head, stunned. All in all, it had been a terrible evening. 'Thank you, Belle,' she breathed when she'd managed to compose herself a little. 'Had she succeeded, it could have cost me my job and I would have been homeless again.' Esther had never tried to pretend that she liked her, but even so Opal was shocked at the depths she would sink to to discredit her.

'Well, now yer know just watch yer back,' Belle advised as she left.

Reeling, Opal dropped on to her stool. What Esther had tried to do on top of the news about Charlie possibly being dead was just too much, and lowering her face into her hands she sobbed broken-heartedly. After a time she sniffed and raised her chin. Charlie couldn't be dead! She would feel it in her heart if he was, surely? She refused to believe it; there must be hundreds of prisoners in the penal colonies and eventually they would trace him and this would all be a terrible mistake. Gazing from the window, she determined that she would not believe otherwise.

Chapter Twenty-Seven

'So, it seems you are the hero of the hour.' The governor grinned when Charlie reported for work the day after New Year's Day. 'Everyone in town is saying that had it not been for you a certain young man would probably be in a shark's belly by now.'

Charlie flushed a dull, brick red. 'I only did what anyone else would have done,' he mumbled just as Francesca burst into the room, her cheeks glowing.

'Is it true what I'm hearing? That you rescued Julian from a shark?'

Charlie shrugged as Francesca clapped her hands. 'I just spoke to his mother and father and they are *so* grateful to you,' she gushed as Charlie squirmed uncomfortably.

'Well, it's done now so let's just forget about it, and hope he isn't daft enough to try swimming out so far again.'

The governor, Phineas, chuckled. 'Such modesty, but I think you'll find Julian's parents feel you should be rewarded.'

'There's really no need.' Charlie crossed to the desk and began to shuffle through the paperwork that had mounted in the few days they had had off. He'd never been one for blowing his own trumpet and just wanted to forget the incident had ever happened. It was all too embarrassing.

Sensing the boy's discomfort, the governor ushered Francesca from the room, leaving Charlie to get back to work, but in the early afternoon the governor came back after a visit to the prison with some very exciting news.

'It appears that gold has been discovered about thirty miles south of here,' he told Charlie. 'And suddenly everyone is flocking there staking claims on parcels of land hoping to find some.'

'Then good luck to them,' Charlie said good-naturedly, turning back to his work and forgetting all about it.

A little later, through the open door of the office, Charlie saw the governor and Julian's father in the hallway walking towards the office, deep in conversation. A moment later the door was pushed open and Julian's father, with a broad smile on his face, strode over to the desk.

'So, I believe I have you to thank for saving my son's life,' the deputy governor said, reaching out to shake Charlie's hand. Before Charlie could reply he went on, 'Governor Morgan had already brought you to my attention before this happened, saying what a great help you had been to him, so we've had our heads together and have decided that you should be rewarded.'

'There's really no nee—'

The man held up his hand. 'From where I'm standing there *is* a need, and the governor here agrees with me. And so we've discussed it and have something to tell you, but I'll let Mr Morgan do that.'

The governor grinned. 'The thing is, Charlie, neither of us believe that you should have been sent here in the first place,' he said. 'And you've certainly proved that you're honest and hard-working. So, in light of that, I've decided that I'm going to grant you a free pardon. You will be free to leave whenever you wish. I'll even arrange a passage on a ship home for you, if that's where you want to go. I shall miss you, but I feel you deserve it a dozen times over. My family and I will be leaving here shortly to return to England and you would be very welcome to travel with us, should you so wish. There will be no more prisoners transported here, and Edward will take my place as governor until those that remain have served out their sentences. So, what do you think?'

'I . . . I . . .' Charlie was so shocked the words stuck in his throat as Julian's father clapped him on the back.

'You're a fine young man,' he told him. 'And if I'm not much mistaken, you'll go far in life. But take a few days to decide what you'd like to do. Some prisoners opt to stay here and farm the land; it will be your choice.'

'Th-thank you, sir,' Charlie stuttered and when the men had left the room, he rose and crossed to stare sightlessly from the window on to the parched lawn. He was *free*! It was taking some getting used to, and it hadn't quite sunk in yet.

He blinked as tears burned at the back of his eyes. If only there were some way he could let Opal know – but he had no idea where she was or even what she was doing. Still, God willing, it wouldn't be long until they were reunited.

The door suddenly burst open, and Francesca exploded into the room in a froth of lemon satin and lace. 'Oh, Charlie, I am *so* thrilled for you,' she gushed. 'Father just told me the wonderful news.' And before he knew what was happening she flung her arms about him and rested her head on his chest setting his heart thudding erratically. 'But . . . I must admit . . . I shall miss you.' There was a tremble in her voice and as she raised her face to look up at him he saw tears glistening on her long dark lashes. Without thinking his arms tightened about her and his lips settled on hers in a hungry kiss that she returned eagerly.

Charlie came to his senses first and, with an effort, he pushed her away from him and held her at arm's length. 'I . . . I'm so sorry. I shouldn't have done that.' His hand rose to swipe a lock of hair from his brow and, confused, he turned to gaze from the window again.

'But *why* are you sorry?' Her voice was gentle. 'I have been waiting for you to do that for a long time.'

Suddenly angry he wheeled about. '*Why*, you ask? Surely you know the answer to that question? What would your father have said if he had walked in and caught us kissing? I don't think he would have been too pleased, do you?'

Her brow creased. 'But you are a free man now,' she pointed out as a tear slid down her cheek.

'That's as maybe but I'm still an ex-criminal.' Francesca's lips trembled and his voice softened. 'Look, Francesca, you are the most beautiful and interesting girl I have ever met and had things been different there might have been a future for us. But as it is . . .' He spread his hands in a helpless gesture. 'We come from different worlds. Your parents will want you to marry someone with position and wealth; someone who can keep you in the manner to which you are accustomed. They would never consider a chap like me, not in a million years.'

She sniffed and raised her chin. 'If that is how you feel, then there is no more to be said,' she whispered, and with what dignity she could muster she sailed from the room, closing the door quietly behind her.

Charlie was in a quandary. Since the moment he had met her, he had dreamed of kissing her and holding her in his arms and yet now that he had he had sent her away. *But what choice did I have?* Charlie asked himself, and the answer came back: *none at all.* With a heavy sigh, he turned back to the window. He needed to channel his thoughts into what he wanted to do now, but right at that moment he had no idea whatsoever.

Later that evening when the worst of the heat had died down, Charlie wandered into town and strolled along the main road, such as it was. Eventually as he neared the harbour he came to the Mermaid Inn, and after checking that he had some coins in his pocket he decided to go in and have a celebratory pint of ale. It wasn't every day a man was granted a pardon, after all, and he thought he should celebrate.

The air inside was heavy with tobacco smoke, and the sawdust on the floor was grubby. Even so, every table was full and after ordering a tankard of ale, Charlie soon discovered that almost every man in there was talking about the latest gold found in Ophir – a town close to the Macquarie River north-east of Orange.

'They reckon there was almost a riot in the prison when the convicts heard of the gold,' one old chap at a table close to him told his companions with a chuckle. 'They were planning on escaping so they could go an' try their hands at gold prospecting, but the guards soon put paid to that plan, by all accounts. Some of 'em were whipped then thrown into the hell hole for twenty-four hours, poor sods!'

Charlie shuddered as he listened to the conversation. The hell hole, as it was nicknamed, was a small wooden box, barely big enough for a grown man to stand or turn around in, and prisoners were locked in there as a punishment. He could only imagine how unbearably hot and uncomfortable it must have been for them, and from what he had heard there were many who didn't survive it.

'Hm, it seems like everyone's caught gold fever,' an old man, who Charlie recognised as Mr Schwartz, the tailor, said glumly. 'My apprentice took off yesterday without a by your leave to go and buy a plot of land. And I'm left to manage on my own. I've no doubt he'll come back with his tail between his legs if he has no luck, but I shall send him packing with a flea in his ear if he does, the ungrateful young bastard!'

There was a mutter of assent around the table, but suddenly Charlie's mind was working overtime. Would it be worth trying his hand at gold prospecting? As things stood, if he returned to England now he would go with very little, but if he should strike gold he could return home a rich man and change the lives of his sisters – when he found them again! The more he thought of it, the more appealing the idea became. He had hardly spent a penny of his meagre wages since arriving there and it didn't amount to a lot, but even so there would be enough for the tools he would need and to feed him for some weeks if he was careful. He hastily drained his tankard and stepped outside again with his mind working overtime. Perhaps he should ask the governor's opinion? He passed the barber shop, the butcher and the ladies' dress shop without so much as glancing in their windows, suddenly keen to get back to the governor's house.

Unfortunately, when he arrived back, the governor and his wife were entertaining visitors. There would be no chance of speaking to him that evening, so Charlie made his way to his room where he tossed and turned for most of the night.

The next morning, as he entered the kitchen to eat his breakfast with the rest of the staff, the air was buzzing with the news of his pardon.

'Is it true, lad? That the governor's giving you your freedom?'

Charlie blushed self-consciously. 'Er ... yes, yes, it is, actually.'

'Then good on you!' The rosy-cheeked cook slapped him heartily on the back. She'd always had a soft spot for Charlie. 'So when are you planning on goin' an' what are you goin' to do?'

Charlie shrugged as he took a seat at the table and lifted an apple from the dish. 'I thought I might try my hand at gold prospecting.'

The cook laughed. 'Oh, not you an' all! Half the town has gone harin' off to Ophir from what I've heard of it. I doubt there'll be enough gold there for everyone. But then I suppose you never know unless you try, so if that's what you decide then I say good luck to you, lad.'

As he was making his way to the governor's office after breakfast, Charlie passed Francesca in the hallway. Today she was wearing a pale-pink linen gown sprigged with tiny rosebuds and she looked so pretty that Charlie's heart skipped a beat at the sight of her, although she merely acknowledged him with a slight incline of her head. He had clearly hurt her feelings, and his heart was heavy as he entered the office.

The governor glanced up from his desk and smiled. 'Ah, Charlie, I didn't expect to see you today.'

'I still have a few things to finish before I leave, so that you're all up to date.' Charlie nodded towards a pile of paperwork on the end of the desk and the governor gave him a grateful smile.

'I appreciate that. But have you given any thought as to what you're going to do?'

'I have, as it happens.' Charlie went on to tell him about his idea and Phineas listened carefully.

'Well, all I can say is you have the same chance as anyone else of making a strike,' he said musingly. 'So if that's what you want, then you should do it. Now it's in your mind you may well live to regret it if you don't try, and life is too short for regrets.' He held his hand out and Charlie shook it, and in that moment his mind was made up.

He was going to go gold prospecting to seek his fortune!

Chapter Twenty-Eight

Susie had no idea how long she had been running, nor even where she was running to, but eventually a stitch in her side made her pause to catch her breath and lean against a fence. A thick smog had descended, coating the streets in an eerie yellow glow, and there was a damp chill in the air that seemed to creep into her very bones. The fog restricted visibility to a few yards in front of her, and as she tried to catch her breath, she peered nervously into the gloom. Running away had seemed such a good idea at the time, but now she wasn't so sure. Even so, she knew it was too late for regrets now. She wouldn't be able to find her way home, even if she wanted to. Nanny had never taken her further than the park and back so she didn't know the area at all well, so now she was just going to have to make the best of things.

Eventually she walked on a little further down the street where she came to some shops, but she could see shapes huddled down in boxes inside the shop doorways so nervously she hurried past them and kept on walking. Sometime later, she passed some wrought-iron railings that were clearly surrounding a park, and when she came to the gates she slipped inside them. It was even more eerie in there, though, as there were no streetlamps to guide her way and for the first time tears pricked at her eyes.

After what seemed like an eternity, what appeared to be a large bandstand loomed ahead of her and she climbed the steps and huddled down in a corner of it. Her teeth were chattering with cold and her hands and feet were numb, but she was so exhausted that very soon she fell into an uneasy doze and knew no more.

Back at the house in the room next to the nursery, Agatha stretched and yawned in her comfortable feather bed. Downstairs she could hear the maid going from room to room as she lit the fires and she knew the kitchen would be busy as the cook prepared breakfast. Deciding to go down for a cup of tea before she roused Susie she rose, shivering as her feet connected with the cold floorboards, and after washing and dressing hastily, she pinned up her hair and crept to the door that led into the nursery. There was no sound, so she gently inched the door open and stared across at the mound in the bed. Confident that Susie was still fast asleep, she made her way down to the kitchen.

'Morning, Agatha,' the cook greeted her, as she fetched a string of sausages from the cold shelf in the pantry; the master was partial to a bit of sausage with his breakfast. 'Was it a cup of tea you were after?' When Agatha nodded, she pointed towards the large brown teapot on the table. 'Help yersen then. It's just made so it'll be nice and hot. Good job an' all. It's enough to freeze the hairs off a brass monkey out there.'

In actual fact, the cook didn't care much for Agatha, and neither did the rest of the staff, but they had learned to be civil to her. In any house, the nanny came high in the hierarchy and it paid to keep on the right side of her.

Agatha poured a cup of tea and sat down.

'So what have you got planned for today?' the cook asked.

Agatha sniffed. 'Much the same as always. Being a Sunday, I shall take Susanne to church this morning, then it's my afternoon off so I shall probably go out for a walk if the weather warms up a little.'

'I wouldn't count on that.' The cook lifted the large frying pan and as the conversation seemed to be at an end, Agatha drank her tea and went back upstairs to wake Susie.

In the nursery she threw some coal on to the dying embers of the fire and drew aside the curtains, revealing the murky grey clouds beyond the window.

'Come on, let's be having you, girl. Your breakfast will be here in a minute and we have to get you ready for church,' she barked.

When her order was met with no response, she scowled and moved to the side of the bed, where she impatiently threw back the blankets – only to gasp with dismay. What she had thought was Susie lying beneath the covers was actually a pillow the girl had placed there in case Agatha should glance into the room during the night.

But of the girl, there was no sign.

Agatha's heart began to pound as she stared around the room, as if expecting Susie to somehow miraculously appear.

'Oh bugger!' she swore, as she wondered how she was going to tell the master and mistress. What would they say?

But first she would discreetly check all around the house to make sure the child wasn't hiding somewhere.

To start with, she checked the rooms on the landing, before quietly hurrying down the stairs to make sure that Susie wasn't in any of the downstairs rooms. Her search proved fruitless, so she hurried back to the nursery. Her heart sank as she opened the wardrobe door to find that the girl's hat, coat and boots were gone. There was nothing for it now but to go and tell her employers. So, steeling herself, she set off down the stairs again.

The maid raised an eyebrow when she saw Agatha marching along the hallway but she had no time to comment before Agatha snapped, 'Where are the master and mistress?'

'I've just served them breakfast in the dining room.'

Without a word of thanks, Agatha stomped off and tapped on the dining room door, before entering without waiting to be invited in. The mistress was seated at the table while the master was helping himself to some devilled kidneys and sausages laid out on silver serving dishes on the sideboard. They both blinked with surprise when she barged in, but before they could utter a word Agatha burst out, 'It's Miss Suzanne. She's missing . . .'

'What the hell do you mean she's *missing*?' Matthew's forehead creased in a frown. 'If this is some sort of joke, woman, I have to tell you I am not finding it in the least funny!'

'It's no joke, I assure you, sir.' Agatha's knees were knocking with fear. 'I just went in to wake her to find her bed empty and her coat and boots are gone. She must have left the house sometime during the night while we were all asleep.'

Alicia's hand flew to her mouth as she stared out of the window. It looked terribly cold outside. Why would Suzanne venture out there without telling anyone?

'Have you made *quite* sure that she isn't hiding somewhere in the house?' Matthew's voice was a growl and Agatha's fear increased.

'I . . . I checked all the rooms as best I could, sir.'

'But why would she run away? Was she all right when she went to bed?'

'Oh yes, sir. Quite all right,' Agatha told him hastily as he dropped his plate on to the sideboard. 'And you didn't hear her get up?'

When Agatha shook her head, he stormed towards the door. 'Right, I want everyone in the house to search it from the attics to the cellars,' he said. 'And then if we don't find her we must go to the police. She's just a child. Anything could happen to her out there all on her own.'

Within minutes everyone was calling Susie's name and methodically searching every room they came to, but all in vain. Finally, Matthew summoned the parlour maid and told her, 'Run to the police station as fast as you know how and tell them I need to see someone. We must report a missing child. And keep your eyes peeled for a sight of her on the way.'

'Yes, sir.' The young maid bobbed her knee, and after snatching her coat from the hook on the back of the kitchen door, she was off, running like a hare. In the meantime, all they could do was wait and pray that the child would soon be found safe and well.

When Susie first woke, she stretched out on the cold floor painfully. Every bone in her body ached and her stomach was growling with hunger as she knuckled the sleep from her eyes and stared about fearfully. She had no idea where she was, so, rising slowly, she clattered down the steps of the bandstand and set off. She could hear the noise of traffic in the city and it drew her like a magnet. At least there would be people there who might be able to help her find her way back to Nuneaton and Opal.

Gradually the streets she walked down became busier, but she might have been invisible for no one gave her so much as a second glance. The roads were busy here too and her heart began to thud as the many carriages rattled past her. It seemed that she had been walking forever. At one point she passed smart shops, their bright windows displaying all manner of goods, but eventually she found herself in the poorer streets again and in time she came to a bridge that spanned the River Thames. To one side of it was a small footpath leading down to the water's edge and she slipped and slithered her way down it. There she found some poor, tumbledown huts, and she eyed them warily, just as the door to one of them opened and a plump woman in a large wrap-around apron appeared. The woman eyed her cautiously for a moment, noting Susie's fine clothes and the expensive doll she was carrying, before asking, 'So what brings you down here, dearie? Lost, are you?'

Susie was reminded of the old cottage she had stayed in so briefly with Charlie, Jack and Opal before being taken to the workhouse, and she gulped before replying in a small voice, 'I, er . . . Yes, I am lost . . . Well, in a way. I've run away, you see.'

'Have you now?' The woman narrowed her eyes and stroked her double chin. 'Run away from whom?'

Before Susie could stop herself, the whole sorry story came pouring out as tears ran down her cheeks unchecked.

'So you see . . .' she sobbed. 'I have to find my way home to Opal . . . she'll be worried about me.'

'Of course she will. But look, it's cold out here. Come inside and we'll see what we can do for you.'

Susie cautiously followed the woman inside and was shocked to see three cradles in a row along one wall. Inside each lay a tiny baby, all unnaturally pale and quiet. Against another wall was a wooden table and two mismatched chairs and an iron bed stood behind the door. Another door led into what appeared to be a small kitchen, and a fire burned in a small grate, over which a large kettle was suspended.

'I dare say you're hungry an' thirsty?' the woman said and Susie nodded, her eyes huge in her pale face. 'Right, so sit yerself down an' I'll rustle something up for you.' The woman crossed to the table and sawed a large chunk of bread from a loaf then pushed it towards Susie with a pot that contained some dripping. She then poured her a lukewarm cup of tea, and although it was unsweetened and there was no milk in it, nothing had ever tasted better to Susie as she drained the mug thirstily. The bread and dripping followed in a remarkably short time and, with something inside her, Susie began to feel slightly better.

'So, will you help me to get home to our Opal then?' the little girl asked innocently when she had finished.

Before she could answer, one of the babies started to cry feebly and, rising, the woman poured a small amount of milk into a glass feeding bottle before adding some drops from a tiny chemist's bottle. She then placed a teat on it and held it to the baby's mouth. It drained it thirstily and within seconds the infant was silent again.

The woman turned her attention back to Susie and eyed her thoughtfully. The clothes the girl was wearing and the doll would fetch a fine price at the pawnbroker's if she wasn't very much mistaken and with a girl around to help her, she could take it easy.

'Yes, I'll help you,' she said eventually. 'But I should warn you it could take time to track your sister down. Meantime, you can stay 'ere wi' me, if you like? I'd expect you to help with the babies in return, o' course.'

'Oh, I would,' Susie promised as she crossed to stare down into one of the cribs. 'But are they all your babies?'

'Good lord, no.' The woman chuckled, as she packed tobacco into the bowl of a pipe and lit it, and when Susie looked confused, she explained, 'I 'elps out young women who've got theirselves in a bit o' bother, like. You know . . . they find they're havin' a baby afore they're wed? Anyway, they brings the babes to me an' I finds 'em a new family.'

'That's kind of you,' Susie said innocently.

The woman smirked. 'Yes, it is, ain't it? Oh, an' I'm Mrs Dyer by the way. You'll 'ave to sleep on the mat in the kitchen, mind, an' I'll teach you how to make the bottles up for the babies. You puts a quarter milk an' four drops from this little bottle 'ere.'

Susie eyed the bottle curiously. 'What does that do?'

'Oh, er . . . it just 'elps 'em to sleep. I've got another girl bringin' another one tomorrow.'

'But there aren't any more cots,' Susie pointed out.

Mrs Dyer grinned. 'Don't you go worryin' about that, me dear. Two of these will be gone by tomorrer . . . To nice new homes o' course,' she added hastily. 'But now I'm goin' to trust you to watch 'em while I run up to Paddy's market. If you're goin' to be stayin' 'ere fer awhile, you'll need some different clothes. You'll stick out like a sore thumb in them yer wearin' now.'

'But what about finding Opal?' Susie's lip wobbled. 'I can't stay for too long.'

'Don't get worryin' about that. I'll write to her for you.'

It never occurred to her that the woman didn't even know where Susie was from and she smiled at her trustingly; it felt like a long time since anyone had been this kind to her.

Once the woman had gone, Susie looked at the babies more closely and her eyes wrinkled as she leaned over the cots. They all smelled appallingly of urine and she guessed that their bindings must need changing, but as she had no idea how to do it, she decided to leave well alone and crossed to the grimy window. The Thames was lapping gently against the shore only yards away from the door to the hut, and as she stood there a boat sailed by. Even so, it was far from a pretty sight. The water was a sludgy brown colour and the water reeds that edged it were clogged with debris washed in by the river. It smelled nasty too, and Susie found herself hoping she wouldn't have to stay there for too long.

Eventually, Mrs Dyer came back with what appeared to be a bundle of rags under her arm, which she handed to Susie. 'I had to guess yer size,' she told her. 'But they should fit near as damn it. Go an' slip 'em on in the kitchen. I'll keep them yer wearin' an' that doll nice fer you till you go home to your sister.'

Her eyes shone greedily as she watched Susie unfasten the dainty little button boots and the warm coat, and soon after Susie appeared, looking very different. The dress she was wearing reached to mid-calf and the material was so faded that it was hard to distinguish what colour it might once have been. The neat little boots had been replaced by wooden clogs that chaffed her toes, and the smart coat by a shabby shawl. But she didn't complain; if Mrs Dyer really was going to help her find her way back home, she would have done anything for her.

That night, she settled down on the bare earth floor in front of the fire with a thin blanket to cover her and, as she drifted off to sleep, she heard the hut door open. Seconds later she heard two large splashes, but it had been a long day and soon she was snoring softly.

The next morning two of the cribs were empty and Susie smiled. 'Their new families came for the babies then?'

Mrs Dyer gave a grin. 'Yes, last night just after you'd gone to sleep. But look lively now, I've another one due any minute.'

The words had barely left her lips when there was a tap on the door, and when she opened it Susie saw a young woman with a tiny baby in her arms. She was plainly but decently dressed, and Susie wondered if she was perhaps a nanny or a governess?

'Come in, miss.' Mrs Dyer ushered the young woman to a chair, but the instant she sat down she began to cry as she stared down at the baby.

'A-are you quite sure she will go to a good home?' the young woman asked tremulously and Mrs Dyer reached across to tap her arm sympathetically.

'The very best; it's already arranged,' she assured her. 'But shall we get the financial bit out of the way now?'

'Oh yes . . . yes of course.' The girl fumbled in her bag, and placed what appeared to Susie to be quite a large sum of money on the table.

Mrs Dyer's plump hand shot out to take it and she shoved it down the front of her dress.

'There, that's that bit out of the way,' she said cheerfully. 'How's about you give her to me? There's no sense in drawin' out the goodbyes.'

The poor young woman was openly sobbing as she planted a tender kiss on the baby's downy blonde curls. 'Her name is Charlotte. Do you think the new family will let her keep it? And there's a bag of clothes I bought for her here,' she said with a catch in her voice. 'I couldn't bear to think of her going to her new family with nothing.'

'Course not, dearie. I'll see as they gets 'em.' She took the baby from the young woman's arms, and watched as she rose from her seat and staggered unsteadily towards the door. She was clearly greatly distressed at having to part with her baby, and Susie's young heart went out to her – but the second the door had closed behind her Mrs Dyer threw the baby none too gently into one of the empty cribs and she began to cry lustily at such treatment. Fetching the small bottle from the table the woman tipped a few drops straight into the infant's mouth making her choke and gurgle, but soon afterwards her eyelashes fluttered on to her cheeks and she was still.

'There, that should keep her quiet for a while,' the woman said. 'Now, we'll have us somethin' to eat, shall we?'

With that, she began to carve some slices from the loaf on the table, as Susie looked silently on.

Over the next few weeks, there were many such unfortunate babies brought to Mrs Dyer's door, but never once did Susie meet any of their new families. She would just wake one morning to find the cribs empty before a new baby arrived, and all she could do was hope they had gone to happy homes. Sometimes she would question Mrs Dyer and ask if she had heard anything from Opal yet, but the answer was always the same.

'No. It could take a while to track her down, so just be patient.'

With that, Susie had to be content as she cooked and cleaned and cared for the babies as best she could. Thankfully she never grew too close to them, for none of them were there for more than two or three nights at the most. And all the time, her hope kept her going.

Chapter Twenty-Nine

At last spring arrived and cast her magic over the land. Daffodils and primroses pushed their way through the earth, tender green buds appeared on the trees and dog roses clambered across the bushes.

'About time too,' Mrs King grumbled one morning in late March as Opal dressed her hair. 'My old bones can't cope with all that cold weather. But now, get a move on, girl. Henry will be here soon to take us to church.'

Opal stifled a sigh of relief. For the last few weeks, the old lady hadn't felt well enough to go, which had meant she had been forced to go alone with Henry, who was keen for an answer to his proposal. She knew that she wouldn't be able to stall him for much longer, and wondered what the consequences would be when she turned him down. She doubted Mrs King would want to keep her on once she had spurned her son, and already she had been making tentative enquiries about other jobs – not that any of them had amounted to anything. With another sigh, Opal hurried away to fetch Mrs King's bonnet and coat. Then, once she was ready, she rushed off to her room to get her own.

Henry was waiting in the hall for them when they descended the stairs, and Opal fancied she saw a look of annoyance flash in his eyes when he saw that his mother would be accompanying them. Even so, he was the perfect gentleman as he helped them into the carriage and soon they were on their way.

'I suppose you'll be staying for lunch when we get back?' his mother questioned as they rattled along and he nodded.

'If it wouldn't be an imposition,' he replied. Then, his face grave, he said, 'I have something I need to speak to Opal about, as it happens.'

Opal's stomach sank. Ah well, she had known it was coming sooner or later, so in a way she supposed it would be a relief to give him his answer and get it out of the way.

To Opal, the church service seemed to take twice as long as usual that morning, and by the time they returned to Mrs King's, she was a bag of nerves and barely able to take a bite of the delicious roast Cook had made for them. At last the pots were cleared away, and Mrs King asked Opal to help her upstairs for her ritual afternoon nap.

'I shall be back shortly,' Opal informed Henry politely, as she led the old woman from the room, and he inclined his head.

When she returned, she sat down in the wing chair next to the fireplace, folded her hands primly in her lap and looked at him.

Henry rose from his seat and began to pace up and down the room with his hands clasped behind his back, until presently he came to a stop in front of her. 'The thing is, my dear – and it pains me to have to tell you this – but I'm afraid I have some very bad news for you.'

Opal was surprised. She had been so sure he was about to speak of his proposal, but there was clearly something else on his mind and she had no idea what it might be . . . unless it was more news about Charlie!

Her heart began to thump painfully as he took a deep breath. 'As you know, I have continued trying to trace your brother for you for some time now, and at last I have managed to find his whereabouts. He was actually in New South Wales, not in Tasmania as I had originally thought, and that's why they could not find him. But the governor there informs me that, sadly, Charlie passed away with a fever that swept through the colony some time ago and this time there is no doubt about it. I'm so *very* sorry, my dear.'

Opal gasped as tears burned at the back of her eyes, and she tried to digest the news. Charlie, her wonderful brother, was dead! She would never see him again. Never be able to tell him how very much he had meant to her. As the tears spilled down her cheeks, Henry dropped to his knees beside her and, fumbling in his pocket, he pulled out a clean, crisp white handkerchief.

'That's it,' he breathed, his eyes full of false sympathy. She had clearly believed every word he had said. 'You let it all out now. There's no sense in keeping grief locked inside.'

It seemed natural when his arms came around her to lay her head on his chest as she gave way to her grief, and Henry made the most of every second as he crooned comforting words in her ear. Eventually, with an enormous effort, Opal managed to pull herself together and gently disentangled herself.

'I'm sorry,' she muttered miserably. 'It . . . it was just a shock.'

'Of course, I quite understand.' He patted her hand but made no effort to rise. 'But please, don't think this will stop me continuing my search for your little sister. Oh Opal,' he groaned, grasping her hand. 'This is so hard for me. If only you would agree to be my wife, I could look after you properly.'

She sniffed as she looked at him long and hard. All hope of her ever forming a life with her brother was gone now, and with each month that passed her hopes of finding Susie faded just a little bit more. *So what lies ahead for me now?* she asked herself.

At least with Henry she would have a home and stability, and perhaps even a family of her own one day.

Finally, she took a deep breath and said quietly, 'I believe you would look after me, Henry . . . so, I accept your offer.'

'*What?* You mean you'll marry me?' He looked both shocked and elated.

Opal wished with all her heart that she could have raised a glimmer of a smile, but she felt dead inside. 'Yes, Henry, I will. And I promise I will do my very best to be a good wife.'

'But this is excellent!' He rose and began to pace again. 'We must tell Mother the moment she gets up. Oh, and we'll have to have an engagement party. And then we'll need to set a date for the wedding.'

Seeing the look of distress on her face he looked instantly repentant. 'I'm so sorry, my dear. I'm rather rushing you into things, aren't I? Of course you won't feel like thinking of such things so soon after hearing about your brother's death. Do forgive me. It's just that I'm so thrilled you have accepted my proposal.'

She rose slowly, and offered him a weak smile. 'I hope you will excuse me,' she said quietly. 'But I think I'd like a little time alone in my room now. Perhaps we could continue this conversation tomorrow?'

'We certainly will,' he agreed, taking her arm and leading her to the door; and then he suddenly drew her into his arms and before she could stop him, he kissed her firmly on the lips. 'Just to seal our betrothal.' He grinned and Opal found herself blushing. No one had ever kissed her like that before, and she wasn't sure she liked it, although it hadn't been unpleasant.

As she made her way up the stairs on legs that felt like lead, she could feel his eyes boring into her back and she felt vaguely uncomfortable. Once they were married, he would be entitled to see every inch of her, and just the thought of it made her hot with embarrassment. Opal had always thought that when she married it would be to someone who had swept her off her feet, but that was hardly the case with Henry.

Unbidden, she remembered the man she had danced with at the Christmas ball. She could remember the way his arms had felt about her and the way her heart had started to thud as she had gazed up into his eyes. She had felt as if they were the only two people in the room – in the whole world, if it came to that – but she was forced to admit she had never felt that way about Henry. But still, he was kind and thoughtful and generous to a fault, so she could only pray that in time love would grow. Meantime, she craved the time alone to grieve for her brother.

Opal refrained from telling her employer that she was about to become her daughter-in-law. Somehow she felt that it was Henry's place to break the news to her and she didn't have long to wait long for she and Mrs King had barely finished their breakfast the next morning when they saw Henry's carriage rattling down the drive.

'Henry's early today,' she commented as Opal squirmed and refilled her teacup. 'I wonder what's so important that it couldn't have waited until this evening?'

Opal took a deep breath to prepare herself, as Mrs King raised an eyebrow. Opal had told her about her brother's death, and the woman could see that she was grieving, so the last thing she would expect to hear was that her son was now engaged to be married again.

Seconds later, he burst into the room with a smile on his face that stretched from ear to ear.

'Good morning, ladies,' he boomed. 'And what a fine morning it is!' He kissed Opal's cheek, making the old woman's eyes bulge.

'So . . . has she told you the wonderful news?' he asked his mother as he gripped Opal's hand in his own.

'No . . . but I have a funny feeling I might have guessed what it is,' she responded shortly.

'Opal has done me the very great honour of agreeing to become my wife.' He smiled at Opal and suddenly she had the urge to run from the room.

'Hm, well I can't say it comes as a surprise.' Mrs King narrowed her eyes as she stared at Opal. 'But are you quite sure about this? I know you are grieving for your brother. Perhaps Henry should have waited until you had had time to come to terms with your loss.'

'I suppose I should have,' Henry admitted, shamefaced. 'But we can't bring him back and life must go on. Surely you will be the first to congratulate us, Mother?' Then before the woman could answer, he produced a small velvet box from his pocket and sprang the lid, holding it out for Opal's inspection.

Opal stared down at a ring. It was a large sapphire surrounded by diamonds and looked like it must have cost an awful lot of money. Probably more than she could have earned in years.

'Oh, I . . .' She was quite at a loss as to what to say but Henry took it from the box and before she could protest, he had slid it on to her finger.

'There,' he said with a satisfied smile. 'This was my late wife's ring. I want you to have it.'

'In that case, it doesn't really matter what I think, does it?' his mother said testily. She could see all too clearly that Opal wasn't at all happy with accepting a dead woman's ring, and wondered why he hadn't thought to buy her a new one. But it was done now, so they would just have to make the best of it. Her thoughts then turned to more practical issues. 'But we shall now have to rethink our staffing arrangements, because we will have to announce the betrothal in the newspaper and it would hardly do for you to have to introduce your future wife as my lady's maid, would it?'

'No, I don't suppose it would.' Henry frowned, but it seemed that his mother had everything worked out.

'Opal must stay here from now on as my house guest until the wedding, and Belle will take over as my lady's maid until I engage another. And when is the wedding to be? Or haven't you had time to think of a date yet?'

'N-no I hadn—' Opal stuttered.

'I think June is a good month for a wedding,' Henry interrupted and Opal closed her mouth abruptly, wondering what she had let herself in for.

'But that hardly gives us any time at all to make the arrangements,' Mrs King objected. Then turning to Opal, she asked, 'How do you feel about that date?'

'Er, well, it does seem a little soon and I only want a small wedding,' Opal said shakily. 'It wouldn't feel right having a big affair while I am still grieving for my brother. Perhaps we could wait until later in the year?' she suggested hopefully.

Henry was clearly not happy with that suggestion. 'I see no reason why we should have to,' he said shortly. 'You and your brother have been apart for a long time so we hardly need to observe an official mourning period. He was a convict!' Then seeing the colour drain from Opal's cheeks, he realised he had been thoughtless and added hastily, 'Although I realise that you were very fond of him, my dear. I merely wish to give you something happy to focus on. And how about a party to mark our engagement?'

'No . . . I really don't think so.' Opal stared at him solemnly, and his face dropped with disappointment.

Since meeting him, Henry had shown her nothing but kindness, but for the first time she had glimpsed a side of him that she hadn't liked and she wondered if this was a sign of things to come. Already, she knew that she had accepted his proposal for all the wrong reasons. There was no hope of being reunited with Charlie now, and very little hope of ever finding Susie without his help. He could offer her a life of comfort and stability, but would that make her happy? She thought of her parents. They had never been rich, but they had been happy and clearly very much in love with each other. Her eyes fell to the glittering ring on her finger. It felt strangely out of place – but then, she told herself, she wasn't used to wearing jewellery. No doubt she would grow accustomed to it, and it was too late to back out now.

'Perhaps just a very small party?' she suggested tentatively.

Henry smiled. 'Excellent. I shall speak to the staff at my house about it immediately, and of course you must come with me to be introduced as my future wife. I'm sure Mrs Wood will arrange everything; she is very efficient. But now, Mother, should we not raise a glass to celebrate the occasion?'

Mrs King snorted. 'What? At this time of the morning? I think not. Go about your business and leave us in peace.'

Henry maintained his smile with an effort and, after kissing Opal's hand, and inclining his head towards his mother, he left without another word, leaving the two women to stare at each other.

'Well!' It was Mrs King who eventually broke the silence. 'I must confess that I thought my son had his eye on you from the minute he brought you to me, but I had come to the conclusion that you had no romantic attachment to him. Would I be right in thinking that?'

Shamefaced, Opal bowed her head and nodded. She knew better than to lie to the woman who she sometimes thought could see into her very soul.

'I . . . I have to confess that I'm not in love with Henry,' she said quietly. 'But I have told him that and he is still happy to marry me. He says that love will come in time and while I don't love him, I do trust him so I hope he will be right. Whatever happens, I promise that I shall try to be the best wife I can be for him.'

Mrs King nodded. She couldn't fail to notice that Opal looked nothing like a newly engaged girl should look. In fact, she looked more as if she were preparing for a prison sentence than a marriage. Henry was her only son and she loved him, but she was also aware of his many failings and now that she had grown fond of Opal, she too wondered if the girl was doing the right thing in marrying him. She was painfully aware that his first marriage had not been a happy one for his late wife, once the initial novelty of having a younger woman at his beck and call had worn off, and now she could only pray that the same thing wouldn't happen to Opal. But the girl had chosen her path, so there was not much she could do about it.

'I have no doubt whatsoever that you will try, my dear,' she said quietly. Then, leaning heavily on her stick, she rose and walked out of the room, leaving Opal to stare down at the sparkling ring on her finger, wondering what the previous owner had been like.

Chapter Thirty

The governor's house was buzzing with activity as servants rushed in and out, bearing boxes full of the family's possessions that were being loaded on to a large cart before being taken to the ship that stood in dock. Isabella was flying about frantically, trying to make sure that the girls had not forgotten to pack anything, and Charlie was in the office showing the deputy governor how the filing system he had devised worked. After shaking Charlie's hand and thanking him again for saving his son's life, the man left and Charlie set to putting the last-minute paperwork into the right place.

He had almost finished when the door opened and Francesca stepped into the room. Since the night they had kissed, Charlie had studiously avoided her whenever he could, although it had hurt him to do so. She haunted his dreams every single night and he wished things might have been different – but he knew that as much as the governor respected him, there could never be a future for them; they were from two different worlds.

'I . . . I came to say goodbye, Charlie, and to wish you luck.'

He was shocked to see that there were tears on her lashes, and he felt heat rise in his cheeks. She looked so beautiful that it was all he could do to stop himself from rushing across and taking her in his arms, but he knew that he mustn't. It would only make things worse.

'I wish you luck too.'

She detected the tremor in his voice and smiled. 'It was good of you to stay on after my father granted your pardon to help him prepare for the new governor.'

Charlie shrugged. 'It was the least I could do. He gave me a chance when others in his position may not have, and I'm grateful to him for that.'

'So, when will you be leaving?'

'Later this afternoon, just after your ship has sailed. I shall be travelling with a chap called Digger Barnes – we got talking one day because it turns out he comes from Nuneaton like me, although he's been here for thirty years now. He's off to try his luck at gold prospecting too, so we decided we may as well go together. He's a bit of a character, so it should be fun if nothing else.'

'But what will happen if you are not lucky?' Her voice held concern now.

'Don't worry. Your father has kindly given me a more than generous bonus, and I shall be leaving enough for a passage home here just in case I'm going on a wild goose chase. I intend to prospect for a few months and then if nothing comes of it, I'll come back and book a passage on the next ship home.'

She stared at him for a moment, then hesitantly held out a piece of paper on which she had written her London address. 'I thought perhaps you could write to me . . . or perhaps one day if you do return, you might pay us a visit. I know everyone would love to see you again.'

'I might just do that.' He reached out to take the paper from her, but as their fingers brushed he groaned and within seconds she was in his arms and he was raining kisses down on her face.

'Oh Charlie, I shall miss you *so* much,' she gasped, as she stroked his thick hair. She was crying now, and it was almost more than he could bear.

'I love you, Francesca,' he told her in a choked voice. 'I think I have since the first time I saw you. And if things could only have been different . . .'

'Shush!' She raised her small finger to his lips. 'I do understand. You must go away and make your fortune and then who knows what the future holds?'

The sound of her mother's voice calling for her wafted into the room and Charlie quickly released her. 'This is it then . . . this is goodbye.'

She shook her head. 'Not goodbye, *never* goodbye. It is only *en attendant de retrouver, mon amour*. We shall see each other again. I *know* it. But until then, take care, and know that I will be thinking of you.'

Then she lifted her skirts and was gone, leaving only a waft of her perfume behind, as Charlie lowered his head and brushed the tears from his eyes.

It was much later that afternoon before Charlie left the governor's house for the final time, and at the end of the drive he paused to take one last look at it. He had been happy there, but now it was time to try to make something of himself so that he could make Opal, Susie and Francesca proud of him.

He found old Digger in the inn waiting for him.

'All ready for this, are yer, lad?' Digger enquired, as he drained the ale from his tankard. Digger was a well-known character in the district and had been earning a living on the neighbouring farms doing any odd jobs that needed doing. Charlie thought he might be somewhere in his mid-fifties, although his long straggly hair and grey beard made him appear older.

'Ready as I'll ever be,' Charlie said, and went outside where the cart that was to be their transport stood waiting on the dusty road, a donkey harnessed to it and patiently munching on a nosebag. The back of the cart was already piled with everything they might need: tarpaulins to sleep under, pans for sieving the contents of the riverbed, shovels, bedding, plus bags of groceries and supplies consisting mainly of dried beans and rice. 'We'll hunt for us meat,' Digger had told Charlie and it had made him think back to the times when he had caught rabbits for his mother or Opal to make a stew from back home. Happy times that could never come again.

Charlie tossed his bag into the back, then clambered on to the plank seat beside Digger. As they set off, the older man handed Charlie a map. 'I've been to the land office an' staked us a claim on a piece o' land down by the creek just west o' Ophir,' he explained as Charlie studied the map. 'There ain't no better place for findin' gold than close to runnin' water, you believe me. Trouble is there ain't many places yer can find water in the outback.'

On the way out of town, they passed the penal prison and Charlie shuddered. Had it not been for the kindness of the ship's doctor and the governor, he might still be incarcerated in there. Instead, he was free to seek his fortune as he wished. His eyes strayed to the sea and on the horizon, no more than a tiny dot in the distance, he saw the ship that was bearing Francesca away from him. Purposefully he turned his eyes to the front again. There was no point in yearning for what he could never have, but if things worked out as he hoped, he might at least have a chance to earn enough to return home and look after his sisters again.

Many days later, they finally arrived at the patch of land where Digger had staked his claim, and at first sight Charlie was concerned. They were miles from anywhere and he felt vulnerable, but Digger was optimistic as they stood on the banks of the creek.

'We'll make a camp a way back from the water,' he told Charlie. 'Durin' the summer months, the creek is little more than a dribble, but with the rains due it'll turn into a ragin' river in no time an' we don't want to get washed away. You go and set up the tarpaulins and I'll start to unpack the cart. Then we'll each take a rifle an' go huntin' for our dinner. The woods should be full o' livestock an' I've a yen for a bit o' meat after livin' on beans and rice for days. A nice juicy wallaby or wombat wouldn't go down amiss an' there should be plenty o' them about here. But watch out for spiders an' snakes.'

Charlie shuddered. He'd never been keen on spiders – or snakes, for that matter – particularly some of the venomous ones that were native to Australia.

By teatime, as the sun began to sink in the sky, they had erected a fairly comfortable camp and a wallaby was roasting on the fire they had built, along with a pan of rice to go with it. Digger had proved to be a very good hunter so Charlie was at least reassured that they wouldn't starve while they were there, although he was already wondering if he had been right in his decision to try his hand at prospecting.

'We'll make a start on this part o' the creek first thing in the mornin',' Digger decided as he carved the meat on to two tin plates. 'You can dig an' I'll do the sievin'.'

Charlie was only too happy to do as he was told. Never having tried his hand at prospecting before, he had very little idea what he was doing, whereas Digger seemed to be an old hand at it. Now that they only had each other for company, Charlie realised that he actually knew very little about Digger, aside from the fact that he had come from the Midlands. The man never spoke of his personal life so as they were eating, he asked, 'Do you have a family, Digger?'

The man shook his head as he wiped the juice from his beard with the back of his hand. 'Nah . . . not anymore, nor never will again.'

'So, you did have a family then?'

With his stomach full, Digger crammed tobacco into his pipe and, after lighting it, he stared into the flames thoughtfully for a moment, before answering, 'Aye, I had a family once, a long time ago . . . A wife and a child.'

'What happened to them?' Charlie was curious now; he had never seen Digger as a family man.

'They both died o' the fever.'

'Oh . . . I'm sorry.' Charlie wished he hadn't asked.

Digger shrugged, although his eyes looked haunted. 'It's just one o' them things, lad. An' when it happens, you either pick yerself up an' get on wi' life, else you go under. I decided to think meself lucky I had 'em, even if it were only for a very short time. The trouble is, when you've had the best there's no point in searchin' for somethin' better. My wife were the best lass in the world, an' when I lost her I decided that from then on I'd be tied to no one. We had a little farm, but once I lost her an' the nipper I left it lock, stock an' barrel, an' I ain't never been near the place since. I just goes from one place to another makin' a livin' as best I can. But that's enough o' this maudlin' talk. We've got a busy day ahead of us tomorrer, so let's get some kip.'

Realising that Digger didn't wish to say any more on the subject, Charlie threw some more wood on the fire to keep the wild animals at bay and crawled beneath the tarpaulin with his bed bale, and within minutes he was fast asleep.

By the end of the first day prospecting, every muscle in Charlie's body ached, but they hadn't found so much as a single nugget. For all that Digger was somewhat older than him, Charlie had been surprised to see that he could work tirelessly. They took it in turns with the spades, filling the pans and rinsing the contents in the creek for signs of yellow gold – but all they had unearthed up to now was rocks and mud.

Digger laughed at Charlie's glum expression as they sat at the side of the campfire.

'Don't look so disheartened, lad. No one ever said it was goin' to be easy. Happen we'll shift a bit further down the creek come mornin'. We might have more luck there.' He glanced at the darkening sky and sniffed the air. 'I reckon the rains will be on us any day now. Can you hear the dingos howlin' in the woods? That's a sure sign.'

Charlie hotched a little closer to the fire as he stared nervously towards the trees. 'You don't reckon they'll come close, do you?'

Digger laughed again and took a gulp of the gin he had brought with him. 'Not so long as we keep the fire burnin'. What you have to remember is they're as scared of us as we are o' them. Most times they'll only attack if they're starvin' or they've been cornered.'

Charlie nodded miserably. His hair was caked with dust and he smelled of sweat and mud, so he decided to go down to the water's edge for a swim.

The creek was quite shallow, but Digger had warned him that it could be very deep halfway across.

'Don't get goin' in too far,' he warned. 'Evenin' time is a favourite for water snakes an' it ain't unknown for crocodiles to be found in there neither. Now they are nasty critters an' they'd have your leg off in the blink of an eye.'

Disconcerted, Charlie decided that he'd settle for a wash instead and after paddling into the shallows he threw off his shirt and sat down in the water as he washed the dust from his body. He still didn't feel completely clean, but at least he felt better than he had now the sun had gone down. But the midges and mosquitoes that had plagued him mercilessly ever since they had arrived were still intent on biting, and so he hastily pulled his shirt back on and set off back to the camp.

They had been panning for over two weeks, in which time the rain had come down in torrents, turning the slow, trickling creek into a raging river. The scrubby barren land was transformed as fresh grass sprouted from the earth, and suddenly all manner of wildlife was to be found drinking there. With every day that passed now, Charlie was becoming a little more disheartened, to the point that he was seriously considering going back to the port and catching the first boat home. Already, he hardly resembled the smart young man who had left the governor's house. A beard was sprouting on his chin, his hair was growing long and he'd forgotten what it felt like to be properly clean.

But then, as they toiled side by side, he heard Digger take a deep breath and, glancing up from his own pan, he saw him holding up a small yellow nugget.

'There, y'are, Charlie lad,' he chortled gleefully, jumping up and punching the air triumphantly, sending a flock of cockatoos that had been perching in the trees fluttering into the sky. 'Our first piece an' where there's one,

288

there's more. Come on now, put yer back into it, we're gonna be rich.'

Suddenly forgetting how cold, wet and miserable he had been feeling, Charlie set to with a vengeance. At last all their hard work was beginning to pay off.

Chapter Thirty-One

It was now mid-April and the stench from the River Thames was overpowering. The little hut Susie shared with the babies and Mrs Dyer had been bitterly cold when she first arrived but now it was at least a trifle warmer as the weather heated up. But the warmer weather brought the flies. They buzzed everywhere and Susie had given up trying to keep them from going inside.

Mrs Dyer now spent most of each day lazing in her old rocking chair drinking gin, which reminded Susie of her nanny, leaving Susie to care for the babies and do the housework and the shopping. The only time the woman ever made an effort to look smart was if she had a young woman delivering a baby to her. In actual fact, the babies were very easy to care for. The medicine Mrs Dyer insisted they have saw to that. They slept for most of the time, and as soon as the poor little things so much as whimpered, Mrs Dyer would make Susie dose them up again.

Sometimes Susie thought longingly of the comfortable little bed and the pretty clothes she had had back at the house in London. She missed Matthew too, but even that couldn't tempt her back to the nanny – not that she'd know how to get back even if she wanted to. Even thinking about the spiteful Agatha could bring her out in a cold sweat, so all she could do now was wait for Mrs Dyer to hear back from Opal. Almost every day Susie asked if she had heard from her, but the reply was always the same: 'Not yet,' and Susie was becoming increasingly upset. Surely Opal should have replied to Mrs Dyer's letter by now? Or perhaps she didn't want her anymore? Sometimes she thought of running away again, but then what if she did and Opal replied? And so she stayed and one long day ran into another.

On this particular morning, after changing the babies' bindings and giving them a pitifully small amount of milk, Mrs Dyer pressed some coins into her hand.

'Get yourself off to the market an' get us some meat an' vegetables for dinner,' she instructed. 'An' make sure you only spend what you have to an' bring the change back, else I'll skelp yer backside.'

The threat held no fear for Susie. Mrs Dyer had many faults, but she had never once lifted her hand to her, unlike her nanny back at Matthew's house. It was funny, she thought, how she always thought of it as his house and not Alicia's. Perhaps it was because after the initial novelty of having her there had worn off, Alicia had paid her little heed whereas Matthew had always taken the time to give her a kind word.

Susie took the money and ran her fingers through her matted hair. She had no hairbrush, so she tied it back with a length of string and set off in her ragged clothes for the market, attracting more than a few sympathetic glances on the way. She knew that she must look a sight, but it was hard to keep clean when there was only the dirty river water to wash in and she only possessed the one set of clothes Mrs Dyer had bought her. On odd occasions, she had tried to wash them in the river, but the nights by the water's edge could still be nippy so most times they were still wet when she put them on again the next morning.

Today, however, the sun was shining brightly, so she set off with a wicker basket over her arm and a smile on her face. Once at the market, she bought some green beans, potatoes and peas still in the pod, then she visited the butcher and bought some mutton. Satisfied that she hadn't overspent, she retraced her steps back to the bridge that spanned the river. It was noisy up there with the horses and carriages rattling by, but Susie stopped for a moment to watch the boats as she always did. Suddenly she heard a shout, and a passing carriage pulled up with a jolt just yards ahead of her and a man jumped out the back.

'Suzanne!'

Her jaw dropped as she saw Matthew racing towards her, and without stopping to think she turned to run. But it was too late. His legs were much longer than hers and he had her arm in a grip within seconds.

'Suzanne . . . it *is* you, isn't it?' He looked a little uncertain as he stared into the grimy face of the child who was struggling to get away from him.

'*Get off me!*' Susie's basket went flying, sending vegetables rolling along the pavement.

The second he heard her voice, he knew he hadn't been mistaken and now his face was kindly as he told her, 'Oh, my dear girl, you can have no idea how worried we've been.

We've had every policeman in the city out looking for you. Why ever did you run away?'

Knowing that she had nothing to lose anymore, Susie glared at him. 'I ran away because . . . because of my nanny. But I left you a note – didn't you get it?'

Matthew looked grim as he shook his head. He had always had his concerns about Agatha, but each time he had raised them with Alicia, she had insisted that she was exactly what Susie needed. His mother-in-law had once promised to check Agatha's references, but shortly after returning home, her husband had suffered a mild stroke so her mind had been occupied with other things. And now Susie was confirming that the woman wasn't what she had made herself out to be, just as he had feared, and his blood boiled. Why hadn't he checked the references himself? he wondered, as guilt sliced through him.

'Was she nasty to you?' he asked, and the concern in his voice made tears burn into her eyes.

Susie nodded miserably and lowered her head. 'Y-yes, she smacked and pinched me, but I couldn't tell you because she said that if I did, she would punish me even more.'

'I *knew* it!' Matthew was furious, but he forced his anger back and loosening his grip on her arm, he bent to her level. 'I am so sorry, Suzanne. Or should I call you Susie? You prefer that, don't you? But listen, if you'll just come back home with me, I promise I shall have Nanny out of the house this very day. And furthermore, we'll enrol you in a nice local school so that you can mix with children your own age. How does that sound?'

He wished now that he had sent the woman packing after Susie had disappeared. She had had it cushy since then, sitting on her fat backside doing nothing, but Alicia had insisted she should stay until they found Susie. What a fool he had been!

Susie stared at him uncertainly. Could she trust him? 'I can't come back,' she said eventually. 'I have to help Mrs Dyer with the babies.'

Mathew frowned. 'What babies? And where are the nice clothes you were wearing when you left us?' He realised it was a silly thing to ask the second the words left his lips. Susie had grown taller since she had left home and the clothes probably wouldn't fit her now.

'Mrs Dyer told me she would keep them nice for me until my sister came to take me home. She's written to her you see . . . to tell her where I am.'

'Really? And were you able to give her your sister's address?' The more Matthew heard of this Mrs Dyer, the less he liked the sound of the woman.

Susie chewed on her lip for a moment. 'Well . . . I told her that Opal lived in Nuneaton, so the letter she wrote is bound to reach her, isn't it?'

Not wishing to upset the child, Matthew smiled. 'I tell you what, let's get you home and settled in then I'll come back and ask Mrs Dyer to send any reply she might have to our address. How does that sound?'

Susie was more than a little tempted, especially if the nanny was not going to be there. 'Erm . . .' She thought for a moment. Matthew had never lied to her before, so she had no reason to doubt him now. 'But will . . . Mama be *very* angry with me for running away?' Alicia had always insisted on Susie addressing her as Mama, whereas Matthew had been happy for her to call him by his Christian name, which was another thing that had endeared him to her. And oh, the thought of clean hair and a lovely hot bath was so tempting! 'And you *would* tell Mrs Dyer where I had gone?'

'Of course. Where does she live?'

Susie pointed over the bridge. 'In a hut down there. It isn't very nice, though.'

Matthew managed to hide his outrage. What sort of woman was this Mrs Dyer to keep a child from her family and not even try to trace them? But his voice was calm as he answered, 'Very well. But now will you *please* come home? I have missed you so much.'

It was the first time for a very long while that anyone had spoken kindly to the child and, overcome with emotion, she wrapped her arms about Matthew's neck and he held her close, heartbroken to feel her thin body through her clothes. This Mrs Dyer certainly hadn't been overfeeding the child, he observed, and she'd feel the length of his tongue when he came back to see her. In fact, for two pins he would report her to the police. But for now, his priority was getting Susie back to the house, so after gently lifting her into his arms he placed her in the carriage and told his driver, 'Back to the house, please, James, as fast as you know how.'

'Right y'are, sir.' The driver touched his cap and the horses set off at a trot as Susie leaned back against the comfortable leather squabs.

When the carriage pulled up again, Susie chewed on her lip fearfully. What if Matthew had been lying and he didn't send

Nanny away? She would be very angry with her, and who knew what she might do when Matthew was out of the way.

But she needn't have worried, for after taking her hand and leading her into the hall he barked at the housekeeper, 'Send Agatha Deverell to me immediately, and go and find my wife.'

'Yes, sir.' The woman was beaming from ear to ear at the sight of the little girl. All the staff, apart from Agatha, had missed her, and she was happy to see her home.

'And then when my wife has seen Susie, you can ask Molly if she would kindly see to it that Miss Susie has a bath, a change of clothes and a good meal. Tell Miss Deverell that I shall be waiting in the drawing room.'

The housekeeper scooted away, still smiling broadly.

When Alicia appeared in the doorway of the drawing room, she clapped her hand to her mouth at the sight of Susie. 'Oh Suzanne, is it *really* you?'

'From now on she will be called Susie; it is the name she prefers,' her husband informed her sternly, reluctantly relinquishing his hold on the little girl's hand so that his wife could greet her.

The greeting however was very short-lived, for as Alicia gracefully bent next to the child, she got a whiff of her and hurriedly drew back. Thankfully Molly appeared at that moment and after giving Susie a hug she led her away upstairs.

Alicia asked her husband, 'Wherever did you find her?'

'I'll tell you all about it later,' he answered shortly. Usually he had all the time in the world for his wife, but today he had other things on his mind, especially as Agatha had just appeared from the kitchen.

'Would you come with me, Miss Deverell?'

'Of course, sir. I can't tell you how thrilled I am to hear that darling Suzanne has been found safe and well and—' She stopped talking abruptly as she saw the angry look on Matthew's face, and meek as a lamb she followed him into his study, closing the door softly behind her.

Matthew went to stand behind his desk and facing her he told her, 'You are to go and pack your things *immediately*. I want you out of my house within the hour.'

'But *why*, sir?' she simpered innocently, and it was all Matthew could do to stop himself from leaning across the desk and slapping her.

'*Why?*' he roared. 'You have the bare-faced audacity to ask me *why*? Then I'll tell you, I know *everything* now. Susie and I had a little chat in the carriage on the way home and I know all about your cruelty to the child. My mother-in-law expressed her concerns about your treatment of her some long while ago, and I only wish to God that I had listened to her.'

'Why . . . I have never been so insulted in my life!' Agatha snorted indignantly. 'I have never so much as laid a finger on the girl; she's a little liar. But I won't stay where I am not wanted! If you would kindly sort out my wages and give me a letter of reference, I shall leave as soon as possible!'

Matthew narrowed his eyes as he leaned heavily over the desk towards her. 'Make no mistake, you will not be getting so much as another penny piece out of me *or* a reference. I think I have kept you in comfort sitting on your lazy back-side eating me out of house and home for quite long enough. You would have been long gone had it been left to me. In fact, you should think yourself lucky that I'm letting you go without involving the police.'

The colour drained from Agatha's cheeks like water down a drain. She knew when she was beaten. 'In that case I shall leave immediately,' she stated, and with what dignity she could muster, she walked from the room on legs that suddenly felt as if they had turned to jelly.

Upstairs in her room she fetched her carpet bag from the bottom of the wardrobe and began to throw her clothes into it, along with a few rather nice pieces of china and silver she had stolen from the cabinets downstairs. This had been one of the cushiest jobs she had ever had and goodness knew where she would go now. Why hadn't the little brat stayed lost? In the time since she had been gone, she had managed to wrap the mistress around her little finger, but the master was a different kettle of fish altogether. But one day, she promised herself – one day she would make that little brat wish she had never been born, just see if she didn't!

Chapter Thirty-Two

'What is *this*?' Esther Partridge threw the newspaper that contained the announcement of the engagement down on the desk in front of Henry, as her eyes flashed. *'Please* tell me that it is some sort of awful joke!'

Henry frowned as he looked up at her. He didn't at all appreciate her barging into his home unannounced, but now that she had, he supposed he would have to deal with her.

'Good morning, Esther.'

'Oh, don't trifle with me,' she fumed. 'Answer my question and tell me this isn't true. Surely you would never consider marrying a nobody from Rapper's Hole? Think of your position, Henry.'

He steepled his fingers and stared at her across the top of them. 'Very well,' he answered calmly. 'Yes, it is quite true, my dear. And yes, I have considered my position and I believe that Opal will make a wonderful little wife, regardless of where she came from. She is honest and she has principles, which is all a man could ask for in a wife.'

Esther began to march up and down the room, her stiff skirts rustling. 'B-but I always thought we had an unspoken agreement,' she said eventually. 'I thought that I was to become the next Mrs King in time.'

'Really?' Henry looked surprised. 'Well, I really don't know what gave you that idea. In truth, until I met Opal, I had no intention of there ever being a next Mrs King. I'm sorry if I ever gave you that impression. I value your friendship, but have never considered us to be anything more than friends.'

'I see.' Painful colour burned into Esther's cheeks as she realised what a fool she had been. She had dreamed of becoming Henry's wife, of being driven about in his fine carriage and of the children they would have, of living in his house, the mistress of all she surveyed – but that dream was gone now and humiliation and cold fury coursed through her.

'You'll live to regret this,' she told him through gritted teeth, her plain face mottled with rage, making it look even more unattractive. 'You're going to be a laughing stock when word of this spreads, you just mark my words.'

He surveyed her calmly, and even though his stomach was churning, his voice was dangerously quiet when he said sarcastically, 'So I take it you won't want an invitation to the wedding?'

'*Huh!*' She tossed her head, making the feathers on her bonnet sway alarmingly. 'You think *right*! How could I bear watching you throw yourself away on such a little *trollop*!' With that she turned and flounced from the room.

Henry took a deep breath and sank back in his chair. Esther had made it more than plain for some long time that she harboured feelings for him, but he had never, so far as he knew, given her any encouragement, so it was her fault if she had taken the news of his engagement to Opal badly.

Picking up the newspaper she had thrown on to the desk, he read the announcement and a smile crossed his face as he imagined making Opal his wife. She was young and innocent, just as he liked his women to be. Even if he had never met Opal, Henry knew that he would never have wed Esther; she was a little long in the tooth for his liking! He had felt just as he did now when he had married his first wife, but as soon as the first bloom of youth had faded from her his interest in her had waned, and he wondered if the same would be true of Opal.

With a sigh, he laid the newspaper aside and concentrated on the pile of paperwork teetering on his desk.

The next person who seemed very unimpressed with his choice of wife was his housekeeper, who rapped smartly on the door some two hours later and strode into his study without waiting to be invited.

'Is what I am hearing true, Henry?' She always addressed him by his first name when they were alone, although used his title in company, as was expected of her.

'And what have you been hearing?' Once again, he laid his pen down and prepared himself to face a woman's wrath.

'That . . . that there is to be a new mistress in the house shortly.'

'That is correct, Blanche. Have you come to congratulate me?'

She was at a loss for words as she thought of all the evenings she had entertained him. In truth, she had never really expected him to make an honest woman of her – she was merely a housekeeper – and yet here he was about to wed a girl who had come from the slums in the worst part of town.

'I . . .' Her voice trailed away. She could think of nothing to say.

Seeing her dither, Henry informed her, 'I was going to tell you and the rest of the staff later today, but no doubt you won't mind sharing the news with them instead, now that you already know? And have no fear, things will go on just as before . . . Well, most things.'

She gulped. She wanted to tell him that she wouldn't stand for it; that she had always served him loyally – in every way – but then common sense took over. She had a cushy position here and didn't wish to lose it and so, swallowing her pride, she inclined her head. 'Of course . . . *sir*!' And with that she turned and strode from the room, her back as straight as a broom handle.

'God save me from silly jealous women,' Henry muttered to the empty room, and with a grin he again set to work.

Up at Mrs King's house, Opal was preparing for a visit to the dressmaker in town, where she was to choose the material and pattern for her wedding gown. 'Money is no object,' Henry had told her generously. 'You must have the dress of your dreams. I believe a wedding gown is something all young ladies dream of?'

'I think I already have just the style that would suit her in mind,' Mrs King had answered enthusiastically. 'Never you fear, son. I shall see to it that she looks the part.'

So now Opal stood in the hallway, waiting for the carriage to arrive, feeling more than a little nervous. She felt as if she had started something she was in no position to stop, and she was already wondering if she had done the right thing. It was all right Henry telling her that she would grow to love him in time, but what if she didn't? She would have to spend the rest of her life living with a man she had no feelings for, and the thought was terrifying.

Too late she realised that she had agreed to the marriage when she was at her lowest ebb, trying to take in the news of her brother's death. Even now, she was struggling to come to terms with it, but there could be no going back. Already her status in Mrs King's house had changed dramatically. She was no longer a lady's maid but a guest who was waited on, and it was taking some getting used to. In fact, she was becomingly increasingly bored with nothing to do all day but embroider and read. The staff there had been kind about it and had wished her well, but Opal doubted that she would get the same reception at Henry's house. She had seen the way his housekeeper looked at him and had an idea that she, at least, would resent her.

Her gloomy thoughts were interrupted when she saw Belle helping Mrs King down the stairs.

'Ah, here you are, punctual as ever,' the old woman said approvingly, as the sound of the horses' hooves on the drive outside reached them. 'Come along then. You must be very excited. It isn't every day you get to choose your wedding gown.'

When they entered the dressmaker's shop Mrs King started to search enthusiastically through bolts of material.

'This blue is quite nice,' Opal suggested hesitantly but the old woman waved it aside.

'No, no, I think ivory or cream would be better. Much more suitable for a bride. Ah, what about this one?' Her gnarled hand rested on a heavy ivory satin and the dressmaker pulled it out so they could have a better look at it.

'A very good choice,' the woman said. 'It's of the very finest quality and would make up beautifully.'

'That's the one then.' Mrs King's mind was made up and Opal smiled wryly. 'Do you have a pattern in mind for her?'

'Hm.' The plump little woman rubbed her double chin as she eyed Opal's slim figure speculatively. 'Well . . . I think we should go for a style nipped in tight to the waist to show off what a lovely figure she has. And perhaps a sweetheart neckline and short sleeves, seeing as it's going to be a summer wedding? A very full skirt with hooped petticoats and a train, and I could embellish the bodice with sequins and pearls so that it sparkles?'

Opal was feeling as if she needn't have even been there. The two women seemed to have in mind exactly what she should wear, and it was becoming increasingly clear that she wasn't going to have a say in it. However, seeing as she didn't much care, she was happy to leave them to it and remained silent.

'Perfect.' Mrs King smiled her approval. 'And perhaps we could have a bonnet made to match in the same material, with a little veil in front, I think, don't you?'

The dressmaker nodded in agreement, and then all that remained was the measuring. Opal stood patiently as the woman measured every inch of her and at last it was done.

'I shall have it ready for the first fitting in three weeks,' the little dressmaker twittered happily. It would be the most expensive commission she had undertaken for some time.

As they left the shop, Mrs King decided, 'Seeing as we're in town we may as well go and place our order for your bouquet with the florist. I think cream roses and freesias, don't you? They have such a heavenly scent.'

'As you wish.' Opal was trying to sound interested, but in truth she didn't much care what her bouquet would consist of. And so, the florist was the next stop, and after that they called in at the shoemaker, where Mrs King ordered a pair of satin slippers to be made for her. 'We shall have to have a few more nice day gowns made up for you as well,' she mused in the carriage on the way home. 'As Henry's wife, you will be expected to entertain and it wouldn't do for you to wear the same gown too often.'

By the time they got back to Mrs King's house, Opal felt exhausted, although she had hardly done anything.

'Run along and make yourself look pretty.' Mrs King patted her arm. 'Henry will be calling to see you shortly, and you'll want to look your best for him, won't you, dear? Now that you are engaged, I think it would be quite suitable to allow you both a little privacy in the day room after lunch.'

Opal was dismayed at the thought. Since she had accepted his ring, which still felt strangely out of place on her finger, he had become a little more amorous and only the night before he had kissed her fully on the lips. In fairness it hadn't been awful, but there had been no tingling or wanting more, and Opal had been glad when it was over. Although she was a virgin, having lived on a farm she had a good idea what went on in bed between a husband and wife, and now she was beginning to dread it.

Once upstairs in the privacy of her room, she slid out of her dress and petticoats and went to stand in front of the cheval mirror. A young woman with a sad face stared back at her as she studied her body appraisingly. Her breasts were pert and high, although nowhere near large enough to be considered voluptuous, and her hips were rounded but still slim, as was her flat stomach. She had never really bothered to study her own figure before, but now suddenly she was very aware that Henry would be seeing her undressed soon and she wondered if she would be a disappointment to him? Just the thought of standing naked before a man made her break out in a hot sweat, and she hastily pulled a clean gown on as she turned abruptly from the mirror.

Henry arrived soon after and Opal reluctantly went downstairs to greet him.

'So, did you manage to choose your gown?' he asked, smiling.

She nodded as he linked her arm through his, and led her into the drawing room where his mother was reading the newspaper. Mrs King loved her newspapers; she said they helped her to keep abreast of what was happening in the world and she read each one from cover to cover every day.

'I was thinking that we should really be putting together a list of who you wish to invite to the wedding,' she told them after greeting her son. 'Then we shall have to choose the invitations.'

'Oh . . . but I did say I didn't want a fuss,' Opal said in a panic. 'And I don't really know many people to invite, except perhaps my old neighbours.'

Mrs King laughed and patted her hand. She had no intentions of allowing such lowly working-class people to attend, although she didn't tell Opal that. 'You just leave that side of it to us,' she advised. 'Oh, and I forgot to tell you that I've spoken to the vicar at Chilvers Coton church and arranged for you both to go and see him tomorrow to set the date. He thinks he has the second Saturday in June free.'

Opal gulped but said nothing. It was all becoming very real now.

Oh Charlie, I miss you so much! she cried silently. But as Henry squeezed close to her on the sofa, she managed to raise a weak smile.

Chapter Thirty-Three

'Will Henry not be dining with us this evening?' Opal enquired, as she and Mrs King took their seats at the dining table on the eve of the wedding.

'He most certainly will *not*!' Mrs King opened her napkin and laid it across her lap. 'He isn't happy about it, but I told him in no uncertain terms that he would not be welcome. It's bad luck for the groom to see the bride on the eve of the wedding.'

'Oh.' Opal wondered why, although she felt vaguely relieved.

'And anyway . . .' For the first time since Opal had known her, Mrs King seemed to be slightly uncomfortable. 'I thought it would give us a chance to have a little chat . . . you know, about the birds and the bees.'

Deeply embarrassed, Opal nodded.

'You see, it suddenly occurred to me that, seeing as your mother isn't here to talk to you, you might not know what to expect on your wedding night?'

'I, er . . . think I have a good idea.'

'Good.' Mrs King became silent as Belle entered carrying the soup tureen. Once she had served them both and left, the old woman went on, 'I'm afraid sex' – she said it as if it was a dirty word – 'is something we women have to put up with as part of married life. The men always seem to enjoy it far more than we do, but I would advise you to just lie back and endure it. They say that if a wife keeps her husband happy in the bedroom, it will stop him straying, although I have to say I know of many instances where this hasn't been the case. My own husband had a wandering eye.' She chuckled. 'He thought I didn't know about it, but I actually welcomed his little flings. While someone else was keeping him satisfied, I didn't have to.'

Opal blushed and almost choked on the mouthful of soup she had just lifted to her mouth.

'Is there anything you would like to ask me, my dear?'

'I don't think so.' Opal's voice came out as a croak, and thankfully the subject was dropped.

Soon after dinner, she excused herself to go to her room, although sleep eluded her and the dawn was breaking before she fell into an uneasy doze.

The day of the wedding dawned bright and clear. As beautiful a day as any bride could wish for, and Belle woke Opal early with her breakfast and a pot of tea on a tray.

'I thought the bride should have breakfast in bed,' she chirped brightly as she laid the tray down and crossed to swish the curtains aside, allowing the morning sun to flood into the room. She frowned as Opal stared groggily back at her. 'What's up? Had a bad night, have you? That'll be pre-weddin' nerves. But come along now; get something inside you and then we'd better start to get you ready. You have to look your best today of all days!'

'Eh, miss.' There was a catch in Belle's voice sometime later, as she stared at Opal's reflection in the cheval mirror. 'You look just *beautiful*.' She raised her hand to pull the tiny veil on Opal's bonnet down over her face. Then, crossing to the dressing table, she picked up the fragrant bouquet that had been delivered earlier.

'Mrs King said to tell you she'll see you at the church, miss. She's already gone on ahead.'

Opal nodded and stared into the mirror; she hardly recognised herself. The dress Mrs King had chosen for her was beautiful – everything was beautiful. *So why am I not feeling happy?* she wondered.

They both started at the sound of a carriage coming down the drive and after running to the window, Belle clapped her hands. 'Ooh, your carriage is here, miss.' She leaned forward and, lifting Opal's veil, she kissed her gently on the cheek. Opal was touched to see that there were tears in her eyes. 'Good luck an' don't forget us. I'll . . . I'll miss you.'

'I shall miss you too,' Opal admitted, but Belle flapped her hand at her.

'All right, but don't start cryin'. The mistress will have me guts for garters if she thinks I've upset you.' She gently ushered Opal towards the door.

At the bottom of the stairs, Opal found the rest of the staff assembled to see her off. Cries of ooh and aah were heard as they caught a glimpse of her, and then they were all wishing her well as she went out to the carriage. Her clothes and personal things had been taken to Henry's house during the previous week, so all that remained now was to become his wife. The next time she visited Hollow's House, it would be as Mrs King's daughter-in-law.

The staff poured out on to the steps to wave her off, and when they were lost to sight Opal settled herself back as the horses clip clopped down Griff Hollows.

Once at the church, she walked to the entrance, wishing with all her heart that her father was there to give her away. But then the organ began to play and everyone turned to catch a glimpse of the bride, so she gathered her courage and began her lonely journey down the aisle. Henry was waiting for her looking very smart in a grey tail suit and an intricately embroidered waistcoat with matching cravat, and he stared at her so hungrily that she almost felt as if he was already undressing her.

The service, conducted by the Reverend Lockett, went without a hitch and after what seemed like a lifetime the newly-weds emerged into the sunshine to a shower of rice and rose petals. Opal looked around at the sea of smiling faces, realising with a little jolt that she hardly knew any of them, except for Esther Partridge and her mother. Esther's face was as black as thunder and Opal hastily averted her eyes, surprised that Esther had bothered to come – but then, she supposed, this had turned into something of a society occasion, and Esther wouldn't want to miss that. Suddenly two more faces she recognised advanced on her and her new husband with broad smiles on their faces. They were Peter Dawson-Myers – whose ball she had attended on Christmas

Eve – and his wife, Emma, who looked resplendent in a light-green costume with a matching bonnet

'Congratulations.' Peter shook Henry's hand and pecked Opal on the cheek. And then, to her shock, a face that she had dreamed of on so many occasions stepped from behind him and Opal's heart lurched. It was Matthew, the man she had danced with at the ball – the man she had been unable to forget. He too congratulated Henry; then he turned to Opal, whose cheeks were suddenly burning.

He smiled. 'May I say you look beautiful?' His eyes were twinkling just as she remembered them. 'I'm so sorry my wife couldn't be here. She hasn't been well recently and felt that the journey might be too much for her, but I didn't want to miss the chance to come and congratulate you both. Henry and I have known each other for a long time.'

'Thank you . . . I hope your wife will be well again soon.' Opal was at a loss as to what to say to him. He had that effect on her, although she couldn't imagine why that should be. He was just a man she had met at the ball after all. 'W-will you be staying long?'

He shook his head. 'No, I have to get back to my wife and daughter. I shall be setting off back to London later this afternoon. Probably round about the time you and Henry are leaving for your honeymoon. I hope you enjoy it.'

Thankfully she was saved from answering as Henry turned back to her and placed his arm possessively around her waist. She watched, her heart aflutter, as Matthew stepped back and was lost amongst the crowd gathered around the church doors. Henry led her to the waiting carriage and they set off for the George Hotel in the marketplace, where Henry had organised a wedding breakfast fit for a king for them and their guests.

As they took their seats in the lavishly decorated dining room, Opal scanned the room for a sight of Matthew, and she felt inexplicably sad when she didn't see him. The wine began to flow like water, and she was faintly disturbed to see that Henry was drinking glass after glass. She was aware they had a very long journey ahead of them that day, as they would be taking the train to Dover later in the afternoon before boarding a ship to France, and she was alternately looking forward to it and dreading it. She had never ventured even as far as the coast before and it felt as if she would be going to the other side of the world.

Finally, though, Henry lurched to his feet to make a toast and she had no more time to think of it. He was clearly more than a little drunk as he raised his glass and stared down at her.

'I would like you all to raish a toasht to my little virgin wife,' he slurred, and she lowered her eyes as humiliation flooded through her. Thankfully his mother was close at hand and she instantly stepped in.

'Henry, I'm sure that is quite enough,' she said with a cold smile at the guests. 'And now perhaps we should continue with the meal.'

Henry sat back down like a naughty little boy who had been reprimanded, and the waiters and waitresses brought out course after course of delicious food. Under other circumstances, Opal was sure that she would have enjoyed it, but today everything tasted like sawdust and seemed to stick in her throat, so she ate very little.

At last it was over and the guests began to drift away. Henry had booked a bedroom where they could change into their travelling outfits and he grinned at her lewdly as he suggested, 'Shall we go to our room then, my dear?'

'Opal can; I've booked a maid to help her get changed and you can go up when she comes down,' his mother informed him bossily.

Just for a second Henry scowled, but then he nodded. 'Very well. I shall have another little drink down here while I wait.'

'You most certainly will not! I think you have had far too much already,' Mrs King scolded. 'I have ordered us a pot of coffee, so come and sit down here by me. And you, dear, go up and get changed.'

In that moment, Opal could have kissed her and, only too happy to do as she was told, she fled from the room. Just as Mrs King had promised a young maid was waiting on the landing of the hotel for her and after leading her to a bedroom Opal saw that her outfit was laid out ready for her. It was a pale-bronze colour and was definitely the most beautiful two-piece costume she had ever seen, with a fitted jacket and a full skirt; there was also a little hat trimmed with feathers, with a bag and shoes to match. Once again Opal barely recognised herself as she looked in the mirror.

'You look lovely, if yer don't mind me sayin' so, Mrs King,' the young maid said and Opal gasped. Mrs King she had called her! *Mrs King!* She was no longer Opal Sharp but Mrs Henry King. From now on she would be addressed as ma'am rather than miss. It was going to take some getting used to.

'Thank you.' She inclined her head and after picking up her bag, she descended the stairs where she waited with her mother-in-law while Henry got changed.

Henry was still somewhat inebriated when he rejoined them, and his mother tutted disapprovingly.

'Come along, the carriage is waiting outside to take you to the station,' she told him and once outside she pecked Opal on the cheek and whispered, 'Don't forget what I told you, just lie back and it will be over in no time.'

Despite feeling nervous, Opal enjoyed the train ride, even more so because within minutes of the train pulling out of the station, Henry's head lolled to one side and he started to snore loudly enough to wake the dead. She smiled wryly as she stared at the passing fields beyond the window. *If this is the effect drink has on him, I shall have to encourage him to drink more often*, she thought, and a wicked little grin played about her lips.

Hours later, they boarded the ship that would take them across the Channel. A steward showed them to their cabin and despite being nervous about the night ahead Opal was looking forward to visiting France.

'I shall go to the bar and give you time to get changed, my dear,' Henry told her, and she nodded as she began to unpack the small overnight case that Belle had packed for her. Once undressed she washed hastily, took the pins from her hair then leaped into bed with her heart thudding as she stared fearfully at the door. The minutes ticked away and Opal felt her eyes grow heavy, and then she knew no more until the steward knocked on the door. Starting awake, Opal was shocked to see Henry lying beside her fully clothed with his mouth hanging slackly open, making him look like a goldfish. Light was pouring through the porthole, and after hastily climbing out of the bed and putting her wrap on, she opened the door for the steward who was bearing a tray of tea.

'We should be in port within an hour, ma'am,' he informed her, and she smiled her thanks. Once he had gone, she poured herself a cup, but Henry snored on, so she dressed quickly and fixed her hair. Mrs King had instilled in her the importance of wearing it up at all times now – apparently, it was only unmarried women who wore their hair loose. When she was ready, she peeped out of the porthole. She could see the dock in the distance and was a little disappointed to note that it looked no different to the one they had sailed from. Then, knowing that she had no choice, she reluctantly shook Henry's arm.

As his bloodshot eyes flickered open, she smiled at him apologetically. 'I'm sorry to wake you but we shall be arriving in the port shortly. Would you like a cup of tea?'

He groaned as his hand rose to his head. Then realising where he was, he dragged himself up on to one elbow, looking very sorry for himself indeed.

'My dear Opal. I cannot apologise enough for my behaviour. I only meant to have one drink, but I was feeling so happy that somehow one turned to two and . . .' His voice trailed away as she handed him a cup of tea.

'It's quite all right,' she assured him, as she began to repack her small valise. 'But perhaps when you have drunk that we should be going up on deck?'

'Of course.' He gulped at the tea as she tried to suppress a smug little smile that came to her face. But it didn't last for long; she had avoided the inevitable the night before, but it still lay ahead of her and very soon she would have to become Henry's wife in all ways. The thought filled her with dread.

Chapter Thirty-Four

'The chateau is very pretty, isn't it?' Henry said, when they finally arrived late that evening. It had been another long day travelling and Opal felt as if she could have slept for a week.

'In truth it was too dark for me to see much of the outside,' Opal admitted. 'But the inside is charming.'

Henry had hired the chateau for a week for the first part of their honeymoon and they would be alone there apart from a cook and a maid. As she spoke, she was undoing one of their cases but Henry snapped the lid shut again.

'Leave that for now. I shall get the maid to unpack it. Let's go down for a meal, shall we? I'm so hungry I could eat a horse.' The journey had taken them much longer than Henry had thought it would, so he was grateful that there was a meal waiting.

Opal reluctantly followed him from the room and as she passed a window on the landing she saw the moon shining down on the sea beyond.

'I believe we have our own private beach here,' Henry told her cheerfully. 'Perhaps tomorrow we could go and have a look at it?'

'Yes, that would be nice.' They descended the stairs where a young French maid directed them to the dining room in broken English.

The dining room was very elaborate and lit by candles in crystal chandeliers hung over the entire length of the enormous mahogany table. Places had been set at one end of it, and they were barely seated before the maid bustled in carrying a large silver soup tureen.

'It is *soupe à l'oignon*.'

As Opal looked at Henry questioningly, he explained, 'It is a French soup made of onions and beef stock with croutons and melted cheese on top.'

Opal had thought she would be too nervous to eat, but when she tried a mouthful it was so delicious that she suddenly realised how hungry she was and cleared her bowl in minutes.

The main course was beef bourguignon followed by a very light chocolate soufflé, and by the time she had finished, Opal felt as if she might burst. Henry had had two helpings of everything, which he'd washed down with copious glasses of wine, and she wondered if there was to be a repeat of the night before. Hopefully he would be so drunk by the time they went upstairs that he would fall straight to sleep again.

While the maid cleared the pots from the table, they went to sit on a small veranda that led off the dining room while they waited for their coffee to be served and Opal instantly fell in love with the view. The chateau was perched on the side of a hill overlooking the sea and she was sure she had never seen anything so pretty. The moon made the waves look as if they had been sprinkled with diamond dust.

Seeing her expression, Henry smiled. 'You approve of my choice?'

'Oh yes, it's just beautiful here.' She couldn't lie and felt quite guilty when he looked inordinately pleased. Perhaps she was being too hard on him. After all, he had never shown her anything but kindness and he wasn't a bad-looking man. Perhaps she should try a little harder to fall in love with him. Her thoughts were interrupted when the same little maid, who introduced herself as Sophia, appeared with their coffee on a tray.

'Is very lovely here, yes, madame?'

'Oh yes.' Opal smiled at her and after bobbing her knee, which made Opal blush, the girl disappeared back the way she had come, leaving the newly-weds alone again.

Opal fiddled with the cups and poured the coffee, and as she handed Henry his he caught her hand tenderly and told her, 'You've made me a very happy man, my lovely Opal. I think we shall be very happy together indeed.'

'I hope so,' she responded, meaning it, but her heart was hammering again and she fell silent as she stared at the silver waves crashing on to the sand below. She had had two glasses of wine, hoping it would help her relax, and although she was far from drunk, thankfully it had certainly helped.

'Perhaps you would like to go to our room and get changed before I join you?' Henry suggested when they had drained the coffee pot.

Blushing prettily, Opal nodded and made her way upstairs.

Once in the privacy of their room she washed hurriedly in the warm water that Sophia had left for her and, pulling the pins from her hair, she brushed it and slid into the soft lawn, lace-trimmed nightdress that had been a wedding present from her mother-in-law, before jumping into bed and pulling the thin blankets up to her chin.

The sound of the waves breaking on the beach below her was soothing, but when she heard Henry's footfalls on the landing outside her heart began to race. The smell of whisky hit her as Henry entered the room and Opal realised that he had been drinking heavily again while she was upstairs.

He stared at her for a moment, then began to undress, dropping his clothes in an untidy heap on the floor. Deeply embarrassed, she turned her head to stare at the window so she wouldn't have to look at his flabby stomach.

'Opal, come here.' Reluctantly she sat up and blushed, as she saw him there with his manhood standing to attention. She had never seen a completely naked man before and she began to tremble. 'Come here!' he snapped, growing impatient.

On legs that had turned to jelly, she slowly swung her legs out of the bed and crossed the floor to stand in front of him and, before she knew what was happening, his hand snaked out and tore her nightdress from the neck to her waist, exposing her breasts. She gasped in fear, but didn't have time to react before he instructed, 'Get it off!' His voice came out as a growl and too afraid to do anything else, Opal slipped her arms free and allowed the ruined gown to slide to the floor.

Humiliation coursed through her as she saw him run his tongue across his lips. His hand shot out and he grabbed one of her breasts brutally, making her cry out. 'Turn around . . . I want to get a good look at you.'

Opal slowly turned as his hands nipped and stroked at her body. She felt as if she were caught in the grip of a nightmare, but in fact, the nightmare was barely beginning. 'Now get back on the bed.' His hand was rubbing at his penis and tears burned at the back of her eyes as she slowly did as she was told.

She tried to pull the sheet over her but he tore it savagely away and suddenly she didn't recognise him anymore. 'You're my *wife*,' he spat. 'And if I want to look at you, I shall.' And then he was on top of her, sucking and biting at her tender breasts like a frenzied animal. She could feel his penis, hot and erect against her stomach.

'P-please . . .' she whimpered, but it was as if he couldn't hear her as he reached down and roughly threw her legs apart – and then he was thrusting himself inside her, and pain ripped through her as he began to buck and rear up and down. She was openly crying now. This was nothing like she had imagined it would be, and the pain was such that she was sure he was going to kill her.

When she was sure that she couldn't bear it anymore, he suddenly froze and made a feral sound deep in his throat, then collapsed on top of her. She lay quite still, terrified he would do it again. But he seemed to be spent, so she managed to push him off her and was horrified to see that he was asleep, his flaccid penis lying limp now.

With a sob, she rolled off the bed and crossed to the washstand. She felt battered and bruised as she took a flannel and began to wash between her legs and every other inch of her that he had touched. Yet even as she did it, she knew that she would never feel clean again, even if she was to soak in hot water for a month. Already bruises were beginning to show on her breasts and she was so sore down below that even the cooling water stung. Again and again she washed herself. Then, crossing to the drawers, she took out another nightdress and slid it on, keeping a wary eye on Henry the whole time. She was too afraid to climb back into bed, so after hiding the torn nightgown in her valise, she crossed to the chair by the window and there she spent a restless night, alternately catnapping and keeping a watchful eye on her new husband.

She woke when Sophia tapped on the door the next morning. She had brought the newly-weds breakfast in bed, so Opal hastily donned her dressing robe and made sure that Henry was decently covered before letting her in.

'Good morning, madame.' Sophia wheeled in a trolley, just as Henry made a loud snorting noise and opened his eyes.

'Ah, excellent, food.' He smiled as if nothing untoward had happened the night before.

Sophia wheeled the trolley closer to the window and after bobbing her knee she left, leaving Opal to pour the tea.

'Sleep well, did you, my dear?' Henry clambered out of bed stark naked and came to sit beside her, making Opal blush and avert her eyes. 'What would you like to do today? I thought we might do a little sightseeing?' His hand snaked out to squeeze her breast through the thin material of her nightgown making her flinch away from him and he frowned. 'What's wrong? Are you not feeling well?'

he asked, beginning to load his plate with slices of a long baguette, still hot from the oven. There were dishes of butter, jam, honey and syrup to spread on it. There was also a jug of grapefruit juice and another of freshly squeezed orange juice, and Opal was surprised that the French breakfast was so different to the English ones.

'I . . . I am quite well,' she forced herself to say. 'But last night . . . you were very brutal with me.'

'Poppycock,' he answered unfeelingly. 'Sex is a normal part of married life.'

'I agree, but does it have to be so . . . so rough?'

He scowled as he rammed another piece of bread into his mouth, and she shuddered as jam ran down into his neatly trimmed beard. This was a side of him she had never seen before; had she have done, she knew she would never have married him, and already she was deeply regretting it.

Suddenly his smile was back in place and, reaching out, he patted her hand. 'I apologise if I was a little too rough with you, my love. I can only blame the fact that I was so intent on making you mine, I gave no thought to your feelings. It will be different in the future, I promise.'

Opal stared bleakly out of the window, praying that he was telling the truth, for she knew that if he wasn't there was no way she could stay with him, even if her leaving caused a scandal.

After breakfast they dressed and left the house to stroll around and acquaint themselves with their surroundings. At the bottom of the lawned garden, there were deep, stone steps that led down to the beach and as Opal stared in awe at the rolling waves, she was happy again for a time. She had never seen the sea before and was as excited as a child. 'I just never realised it was so . . . so . . . immense . . . and so . . . so *blue*!'

He laughed as he tucked her arm into his, and they strolled along the beach with Opal bending now and again to examine the shells that the sea had washed up.

'I have a carriage at our disposal for the whole of the time we are here, so we could perhaps go for a ride out into the countryside this afternoon, if you wish . . . Unless you would rather spend the time in our room?' he added suggestively.

'Oh no . . . no, a ride would be lovely,' Opal told him, her words almost tripping over each other.

He chuckled, and for the next half an hour they walked in silence, before climbing back up the steps to the chateau where they found hot chocolate and croissants waiting for them, and once again Henry ate like a pig.

'Cook wishes to know if you will be requiring lunch?' Sophia said when she popped her head round the door, but Henry shook his head.

'Thank you but no. We shall eat out, but you could have the carriage brought round for us.'

'I shall take you to visit a vineyard while we are here,' Henry told her as they clip-clopped along in the carriage. 'And there you will see how wine is made.'

Opal nodded, smiling again and almost forgetting the indignities of the night before for a time.

They visited a tiny town where market stalls were set out along the main street, and Opal wandered amongst them, stopping to exclaim over a little jewellery box that was made entirely of shells from the beach. 'Oh, look, Henry, it even has a little hinged lid,' she said, laughing as she examined it. The next second Henry was haggling in French with the stallholder and once they'd finally agreed on a price, he handed it to her.

She was thrilled. 'Thank you, I shall treasure it.' She tucked it safely away in her bag, listening to the stallholders shouting their wares and revelling in the atmosphere of the place.

At lunchtime, they visited a small restaurant where they enjoyed a light lunch.

'Won't you try the snails? They are a French delicacy,' Henry encouraged, but Opal grimaced and shook her head.

After last night, she was tired, as well as being sore, but she somehow kept her smile in place. She knew she had to try to make her marriage work. After all, she was lucky compared to many of the girls from where she had come from. Most of them were married at sixteen and had a baby every year, making them old before their time. They frequently had no money for rent or food, and yet here was she, married to a very wealthy man, honeymooning in France. She now wore fine clothes and would never have to worry about where the next meal was coming from again.

Yet for all that, as she thought back to the tiny cottage in Rapper's Hole where she had briefly lived with Charlie, Jack and Susie, she knew in her heart that she would have given up everything to be able to go back and have that time with them over again.

Still, I am Mrs Henry King now, she told herself and a saying of her mother's came to mind, 'You've made your bed and now you must lie in it!'

And lie in it she would, for better or for worse.

The day passed pleasantly, but once they returned to the chateau for their evening meal, Opal began to dread the night ahead.

By the time she went to their room to get changed, her stomach was in a knot, but she had made a decision. She had married Henry and even though she didn't love him, she was determined to be the best wife that she could be. But that didn't mean she would allow him to continue to hurt and abuse her, and she realised that if there was to be any chance of the marriage working, she must let him know how she felt. And so that evening when he followed her upstairs, he found her sitting in a chair at the side of the bed with a determined expression on her face.

His eyes instantly glazed over with lust as he saw the outline of her breasts through the thin nightgown she was wearing, and he began to throw off his clothes.

As he approached her, she rose and faced him squarely. 'I'm sorry, Henry, but I feel I should tell you I have no intention of letting you treat me as you did last night!'

'What?' Shock registered on his face. 'But you are my wife and you should do my bidding!'

'And I shall,' she assured him. 'But I refuse to let you treat me like some street woman whose services you have paid for! As your wife I deserve a little respect.'

An ugly scowl appeared on his face. It appeared that his innocent little wife knew more about life than he had given her credit for.

'You will submit to my demands when and if I wish you to,' he ground out. 'Just remember I saved you from the gutter, girl. You're just a nothing from Rapper's Hole.'

'I may well be, but I still have my pride,' she shot back indignantly. Could he have known it, their marriage was doomed from that moment on, and she would never forgive him for what he had said. She climbed beneath the sheets and stared at him defiantly. 'Now you may have your way, but I warn you, if you attempt to treat me like you did last night again, I shall fight you with every ounce of strength I have.'

He was so flabbergasted that his mouth hung open for a moment – but then, snatching up his clothes, he began to dress. 'I think I may go down and have a drink. And don't worry, I shall not be troubling you tonight.'

'As you wish.'

He left the room, slamming the door so loudly behind him that it danced on its hinges – and only then did Opal give way to her emotions as she began to tremble. Tears slid down her cheeks and soaked into the pillow as she realised that she was clearly not the young woman Henry had thought her to be. He had obviously thought she would be so grateful to him for saving her from poverty that he could treat her any way he wished, but she had too much spirit to allow that to happen. She had hoped she would grow to love him in time, but now she knew this would never happen and she sobbed as she thought of the loveless life that lay ahead of her.

She thought again of the family: her parents, Charlie and Jack were gone forever; all she had left were her memories of them now. But there was still a slim chance that one day she might find Susie again and this would keep her strong.

Chapter Thirty-Five

At last the honeymoon was over and, as the carriage pulled up in front of Henry's house, Opal stifled a sigh of relief; at least she was back on home ground now. Thankfully, there had been no repeat of what had happened in the bedroom on their first night together, and although Henry had claimed his rights, he had been much gentler and she had been able to lie there submissively and bear it.

Now he climbed from the coach and, after instructing the driver to unload their luggage, he helped Opal down the steps and to the front door.

The staff were waiting to greet them in the hallway and Opal immediately noticed the set look on Mrs Wood's face.

'Welcome home, sir . . . *madam.*'

'Mrs Wood.' Opal inclined her head. It was obvious that she was not welcome there, at least not by the housekeeper, if her face was anything to go by; but as Henry had soon discovered, she wasn't as subservient as he had thought, and Mrs Wood would have to discover that too. She was the new mistress of the house and the woman would just have to accept it.

'Could you see that our cases are taken up to our room and unpacked, Mrs Wood?' Opal said, as she took off her gloves and hat and handed them to the maid. 'And then my husband and I shall have tea in the drawing room.'

Mrs Wood looked so angry that Opal feared she might explode, but she made no comment as she bobbed her knee and instructed the maid to do as her new mistress had asked.

'Oh, and perhaps we could have some sandwiches too? We missed lunch travelling, so we'll have our dinner early this evening. The sandwiches will keep us going until then.'

The housekeeper gulped and hurried away to organise it, and Opal went into the drawing room, closely followed by Henry, who was grinning.

'You might want to go a little easy on Mrs Wood,' he suggested. 'She has run this house for many years and may find it a little difficult to hand the reins over to a new mistress.'

Opal shrugged. 'Mrs Wood must know her place,' she said shortly. 'If I am to be mistress here, she must get used to taking her orders from me. If she cannot do that, then she will have to look for another position.'

In the kitchen, the startled cook glanced up from the evening meal she was preparing as Mrs Wood stormed in.

'Tea and sandwiches, if you please, Cook. By order of . . . *Her Ladyship*!' Mrs Wood's face was red with temper. 'The jumped-up little trollop! Who does she think she is coming here into my house throwing her orders about!'

The cook gave a wry grin as she lifted the kettle on to the range. 'I take it they're back then?'

'Oh, they're back all right.' Mrs Wood thumped the table. 'Though I wouldn't like to hazard a guess as to how the honeymoon has gone. She's as white as a sheet and there are bags big enough to do your shopping in under her eyes – though it hasn't stopped her being bossy and throwing her weight around!'

'Hm, well happen the lass is just finding her feet,' Cook commented innocently. 'The thought of running a big house like this must be a bit daunting for her.'

'Huh! *I* run this house,' Mrs Wood ground out through clenched teeth. 'I have everything running like clockwork, so why should she want to interfere? The last Mrs King was quite happy to leave everything to me.'

'Yes, but the last Mrs King were a timid little thing who wouldn't say boo to a goose,' Cook pointed out. 'If truth be told, I used to feel a bit sorry for her. The master had her well and truly under his thumb. But from what you've said, happen the new bride has a bit more spirit and won't be so easily ruled.'

'Just so long as she doesn't try to interfere with how I run things.' Mrs Wood sniffed, and sailed away to her private sitting room to make herself a cup of tea and lick her wounds. The new mistress had already rubbed her up the wrong way, and she had a feeling that things were about to change – and not for the better!

After a light snack, Opal went up to see her new bedroom. The walls were covered in a deep-burgundy flock paper and with the heavy velvet curtains that hung at the windows, she found it very dark and dismal.

'So, what do you think of our room?' Henry asked.

Opal tried to be tactful. 'It's, um . . . a little dark for my taste, to be honest.' And then as a thought occurred to her, she asked tentatively, 'Was this the room you shared with your late wife, Henry?'

He nodded. 'Yes, it was. She died giving birth in that very bed, as it happens.'

When Opal shuddered, he looked concerned. Such things didn't trouble him, but they clearly did her and things were strained enough between them as it was. 'Do you have a problem with that?'

Opal took a deep breath. 'I do, I'm afraid. Is there not another room we could have, or perhaps we could have a room each, if you wish to continue sleeping in here?'

Her hopes of that happening were dashed when he shook his head. 'Our own rooms? Fresh off honeymoon? Why, the staff would have a field day with that. Can you imagine what they would say? However, there is another room of equal size at the back of the house, if you'd prefer that?'

'I think I would,' Opal answered, and so he led her along the long landing to a room that overlooked the garden. Opal looked around the room, it was a good size but the wall paper was somewhat faded.

'Perhaps we could have it decorated?' she suggested.

Just for a moment, his lips set in a grim line. Henry was a wealthy man, but all that knew him knew that he would never part with a penny if a ha'penny would do. Even so, he still had hopes of moulding Opal into the woman he had expected, so he nodded.

'I dare say that would be acceptable. I shall instruct a decorator to bring some wallpaper samples for you to look at.'

She smiled – *really* smiled for the first time in days. 'Wonderful, and perhaps we could have some new furniture too? This is very heavy and outdated.'

He sighed. 'Very well, but we shall have to stay in the other room while all this is being done.'

Opal nodded her agreement and they went back to the other room to wash and change for dinner.

Thankfully, there was no sign of Mrs Wood for the rest of that evening and as they made their way to bed Henry told Opal, 'I'm afraid I shall have to return to work tomorrow, my dear.'

'Of course, you must. I quite understand.' Opal tried hard to hide her elation.

'However, should you wish to shop or visit my mother the small carriage is at your disposal and Jenkins has orders to take you wherever you wish to go.' Jenkins was the groom who lived above the stables at the back of the house.

'Perhaps you could send out some visiting cards for ladies to attend morning tea or afternoon coffee here with you?' Henry suggested.

Opal refrained from answering. From what she had seen of many of Mrs King's visitors, the majority of the women were terrible snobs.

'Actually, I think I might quite enjoy having a few days here acquainting myself with the house and the staff.'

'As you wish, my dear.'

It felt strange getting ready for bed in the bedroom where Henry's first wife and baby had died, but the thought left her mind once they had climbed between the sheets and Henry again demanded his rights. She lay passively, staring up at the flickering shadows on the ceiling, and thankfully it was soon over.

His mother was right, Opal thought, when Henry lay snoring beside her. This is a part of marriage that women must endure. But surely there should be more to it than this? Having come from a family that lived in a very small cottage she had sometimes heard her parents making love, and her mother had always sounded as if she was enjoying it as much as her father – so why did she herself feel nothing? she wondered. Perhaps it was because she didn't love him? Again, she wished she could turn the clock back and decline his proposal. Things had to improve or she didn't know how she would bear it.

Opal spent the next day relaxing. Henry was home in time for dinner but once the meal was over, he told her, 'I'm so sorry, my dear, but I have to go out this evening. I have clients to see.'

'That's quite all right,' she assured him. If truth be told, she would have liked him to go out every night.

Once he had left, Opal retired to bed early with a book, but she found it hard to rest and decided that she would speak to Henry about having their new room decorated as soon as possible. She just couldn't relax lying in a dead woman's bed. Eleven o'clock came around and still there was no sign of Henry and soon Opal slipped into an uneasy doze. She was woken when he barged into the room smelling strongly of whisky and she peeped fearfully over the covers at him. Glancing at the clock on the mantelpiece she was surprised to see that it was after midnight, but she had no time to say anything because Henry was clearly in a very happy mood.

'Here she is waiting for me, my little bride,' he chuckled, almost falling over as he tried to take his trousers off. Seconds later they sailed over his shoulder as he righted himself. 'Have you mished me?'

Opal sighed. He was drunk again and she knew only too well what that would mean, and she lay back and closed her eyes as he pawed at her. This time, he was very rough with her, and she knew she would be bruised in the morning. *But what can I do?* She had married him for better or for worse. The trouble was, she was still waiting for the better.

'I'm sorry, but I think when you are going out you should retire to your own room when you get home so as not to disturb me,' she told him primly over breakfast the next morning.

Henry glared at her. 'We are husband and wife,' he reminded her coldly. 'And that means we shall share a bed until I say otherwise.'

The rest of the meal was passed in silence and when he left for work shortly after Opal breathed a sigh of relief.

However, her relief was short-lived. Very soon, she began to feel bored as she wandered about inspecting each room. There was actually quite a lot she would have liked to change in each one, but already she understood her husband enough to know that she would have to take things easy. *What do ladies of leisure do with themselves all day?* she wondered. She had thought her life was easy as a lady's maid to Henry's mother, but she still had plenty to occupy her, but now she was feeling at a loose end.

And then a thought occurred to her. Perhaps it was time to stake her claim as the mistress here? And she would start by telling Mrs Wood that she would plan the menus for the forthcoming week. She would also do what her husband had suggested and send out some visiting cards inviting ladies to morning tea.

Taking a deep breath, she went downstairs ready to do battle, for she had a feeling that Mrs Wood was not going to welcome any interference whatsoever.

'Ah, Mrs Wood.' The lady in question was just crossing the hallway when Opal got to the bottom of the stairs. 'I thought perhaps I would plan the menus for the forthcoming week?'

Mrs Wood's lips set in a grim line as she joined her hands primly at her waist. 'There will be no need for that, Mrs King,' she answered, trying to keep her voice civil. 'I know exactly what the master prefers and have planned the menus for some long time now.'

'I'm sure you have,' Opal told her with a courage she was far from feeling. 'But now I feel as I am mistress here, I should be taking some of the household chores from your shoulders. So . . . shall we go into the day room while I decide what we should have?'

Mrs Wood took a deep breath and for a moment Opal feared she was going to explode but then with a curt nod of her head she followed Opal into the day room where they sat together while Opal planned the meals.

'I think on Monday we shall have braised beef for the main course.'

'We *usually* have chicken on Monday,' Mrs Wood pointed out, barely able to contain her displeasure.

Ignoring her comment, Opal smiled and continued, 'And I think we shall have lamb for the main course on Tuesday.'

Once it was done, Mrs Wood took the sheet of paper from Opal and sailed out of the room, her full skirts billowing about her like the sails of a ship, and Opal heaved a huge sigh of relief. She had taken the first steps towards showing the woman that she intended to be the mistress here. All she had to do now was keep it up, but she sensed that this was not going to be easy.

Chapter Thirty-Six

It was early in September and at last the new bedroom was ready to move in to. The dark, heavy wallpaper had been replaced by a pale-blue silk, complemented by navy curtains, a light-blue carpet and furniture in a pretty rosewood that made the room feel light and airy.

'Do you like it?' Opal asked Henry, when he returned home from work that evening. The maid had transferred all their clothes into the two new armoires that afternoon, and there was a fire burning brightly in the marble fireplace.

'To be truthful I find the blue somewhat cold.' Henry was appalled at what the room had cost.

'Really? I find it bright and airy. And I know I shall be happier sleeping in here.'

'In that case, I dare say I shall get used to it,' Henry said begrudgingly.

'Of course, on the nights when you visit your club and you are home late you could always sleep in your own room?' Opal suggested hopefully and was rewarded when Henry nodded his agreement.

'I dare say I could.' Already he had discovered that Opal was not the compliant little wife he had expected her to be, but he still had high hopes of her giving him a son and so he was prepared to keep her happy; for now at least. 'Oh, and by the way,' he said, as he remembered something. 'I shall be giving a dinner party next week. There will be twelve people including ourselves on Friday evening. Could you arrange the menu with Mrs Wood?'

'Of course. May I ask who is invited?'

'I don't believe you will have met many of them except very briefly at the wedding. They are mainly work colleagues – magistrates and such – although you may remember Peter Dawson-Myers and his wife, Emma. Oh, and Matthew and Alicia Darby-Jones from London will be coming too. They are here on a visit to Peter for a week with their daughter.'

Opal's heart did a little jerk as she remembered gliding around the dance floor in Matthew's arms, but she said nothing.

This would be the first dinner party they had hosted since their marriage. They had attended a few at other people's homes, and although the hostesses had always been icily polite, Opal was sure that they felt Henry had married far beneath himself. She also had a good idea why. Esther Partridge had dripped poison whenever they met at a social event, and Opal was convinced she was the reason why everyone she had so far invited for morning tea or afternoon coffee had politely declined. If truth be known, Opal was not that concerned and had only sent the invites out because Henry had wished her to. She could think of far better ways to spend her time than to have to pander to these spoiled ladies. Luckily, apart from Mrs Wood, who also never lost an opportunity to belittle her, Opal got on well with the rest of the staff, particularly Eve, the young maid who was only a year younger than herself.

And so, all in all life was bearable – but only just. Now, however, she would have something to focus on and she intended to make this dinner party something people would talk about long after it was over.

'Will you be going to your club this evening?' she enquired, and Henry nodded. He seemed to go out more and more in the evening of late – not that Opal was complaining, for as she had suggested, he now slept in his old room if he came home late and that suited her down to the ground.

'Er . . . yes.' He flashed an apologetic smile before saying, 'And may I ask, is there any sign of an addition to the family as yet?'

Opal blushed. She had just started her monthly course. 'No . . . I'm afraid not.'

He sighed and continued with his meal, while Opal counted the minutes until he was gone and she could relax and have the evening to herself. Admittedly there were times when she felt terribly lonely, but even that was preferable to having Henry at home pawing at her like a dog to a bitch in heat.

After the dining room had been cleared and Henry had gone, she decided to go for a short walk.

'It's hardly seemly for a lady in your position to be seen walking the streets alone of an evening,' Mrs Wood said disapprovingly, as Opal put on her bonnet and coat. It seemed that there were many things that were unseemly for a married woman, but Opal didn't care.

'Please don't concern yourself, Mrs Wood.' Opal drew herself up to her full height. 'I merely need a breath of fresh air and I shan't be gone for long.'

The woman turned with a toss of her head, and with a wink at her, Eve opened the door to let Opal out into the chilly night air.

She had not gone far when she became aware of someone following her and, stopping beneath one of the gas lamps, she turned hurriedly to look behind her – only to find a rather mangy-looking dog who was limping badly and looking up at her hopefully.

'Oh, you poor thing.' Opal was instantly sympathetic. He was clearly a stray and was so thin that she could see his ribs through his patchy fur coat. He stopped beside her and unable to stop herself she bent to stroke him. 'I'm afraid I have no food to give you,' she apologised and he gave a little wag of his tail as he stared up at her trustingly from limpid, velvet-brown eyes. It was then that she made a decision. 'Come along.' She fondled his floppy ears. 'I shall take you home with me and feed you. How would you like that?'

His tail wagged again as if he understood what she was saying, and when she turned about to retrace her steps, he limped along beside her. It was only then that she began to worry. Mrs Wood would have a fit when she took this poor dirty little creature back to the house. *But then,* I *am the mistress there*, she told herself, *so Mrs Wood can like it or lump it*!

When she arrived at the house, she took the back entrance leading to the stable yard and the back door. The cook and Eve, who was washing pots at the sink, looked up in surprise when she came into the kitchen.

'Crikey, ma'am, that were a quick walk. Did you . . . ?' Eve's voice trailed away as she stared at the mutt who crept into the kitchen behind her mistress.

'This poor little thing is starving,' Opal told the women. 'You haven't thrown the scraps from dinner away yet, have you?'

'No, ma'am. They're all scraped on to that plate on the table there. I was just about to put them in the pig bin for the pig man to collect.'

To the women's amazement, Opal took the plate and set it in front of the dog, who wolfed it down within seconds.

'Eeh! The poor little mite.' Eve's eyes filled with tears as she saw the state of the creature. 'He's been through the wars an' no mistake. It looks like someone's hit him with a belt, look.' She pointed the welts on his back. 'He's been beaten and starved an' all by the look of it.'

Opal noticed the scars on his back for the first time and chewed on her lip. How could she turn him back out into the cold? He clearly had nowhere to go.

Making a hasty decision she told them, 'I'm going to keep him!'

'What?' The cook looked horrified. 'Eeh, are yer sure, ma'am? I reckon the master will have somethin' to say about that. Not to mention Mrs Wood!'

As if speaking her name had conjured her up by magic, Mrs Wood suddenly appeared from the hallway and stared at the animal in horror.

'And what is this?' Her voice was clipped, but Opal knew now more than ever that she had to stand her ground if she were ever to stake her claim as the mistress of the house.

'I would have thought that was quite obvious, Mrs Wood.' Her voice was as icy as the housekeeper's as she stared calmly back at her. 'It's a dog – a poor stray dog who has been severely mistreated – with nowhere to go . . . And so, I intend to give him a home.'

Mrs Wood's face turned an alarming shade of red. 'I'm afraid that won't be possible, ma'am. The master would never allow it. And anyway, it is too unhygienic. Ugh, I have no doubt it's covered in fleas and carrying all manner of diseases.'

'That can be remedied. I intend to give him a good bath and in the morning I shall get the veterinary surgeon to come out and inspect him and I'll make him better. But make no bones about it: this is *my* house and I say he stays!'

Mrs Wood looked as if she was in danger of bursting a blood vessel as her face turned from red to purple. 'Then . . . I insist if the cur *must* stay that he lives in the stable block.'

'He will stay in the kitchen.'

The two women eyed each other like opponents in a boxing ring.

Mrs Wood seemed lost for words for a moment – but then, containing her rage, she nodded. 'Very well, ma'am. It shall be as you wish.' And with that she stormed from the room so fast that she almost tripped over her skirts.

'Eeh, I reckon you've upset her good an' proper,' Cook said worriedly.

Opal shrugged. 'It couldn't be avoided. Eve, would you fetch the tin bath in? I think he'll look and feel a lot better when we get all these layers of dirt off him.'

'I certainly will, an' I'll help yer bath him an' all, ma'am,' Eve answered enthusiastically, as she headed for the back door to drag the tin bath in from outside.

An hour later, the dog was almost unrecognisable. Beneath the layers of dirt, his coat was a light tan colour and he had the sweetest nature. His ears were long and he had a curly tail, although it was impossible to tell what breed he might have been. Cook had found him a blanket to lie on by the fire and after another meal he curled up contentedly and was fast asleep in seconds.

'So, if he's to stay, have yer thought of a name for him?' Eve asked, as she carried the bathful of dirty water towards the back door.

'Yes . . . I shall call him Charlie.' A lump formed in Opal's throat as she thought of the dog's namesake, but then she rose and shook the damp patches on her gown.

'Well, yer can leave him here wi' us now, ma'am,' the cook said good-naturedly. 'We'll see as he's all right, won't we, Eve?'

Opal smiled. It seemed that Charlie had two more allies as well as herself. Now she just had to wait to see what Henry's reaction to the new addition to the family would be, and she had an idea it wasn't going to be a very good one. No doubt Mrs Wood would break her neck to tell him about Charlie the second he walked through the door, but she would cross that bridge when she came to it.

Sure enough, some hours later Henry entered their bedroom with a face like thunder.

She smiled a welcome as she laid the book she had been reading aside, but he asked instantly, 'What's this I'm hearing from Mrs Wood? That you've brought some mangy mongrel into the house?'

'That's right.' Outwardly she was calm, but inside she was quaking. 'He is a stray who has been badly neglected and I thought he might be company for me.'

Henry frowned. 'But *surely* you have enough to fill your days without having to waste time on some stray dog?'

'As it happens I don't,' she told him boldly. 'And I have an idea that this might be something to do with your friend, Esther Partridge. She has made no secret of the fact that she thinks I am not good enough to be your wife, and I suspect she has poisoned the minds of the ladies who I have sent invites to, who have all politely declined.'

Henry looked vaguely uncomfortable. He had no doubt that she was right, although he hoped that with time people would accept Opal.

'I can assure you that you won't even know the dog is here,' she went on. 'He will not be allowed into the main part of the house while you are in and at least I can take him for walks when you are out, which will keep me entertained and give me a purpose.'

'But if you had wanted a dog, I would have bought you one that had been well bred. There is no need for you to take in a mongrel.'

'But I like him and I don't care what breed he is.' Opal had sat up in bed now, and through her nightgown he glimpsed the shape of her pert nipples and instantly felt himself hardening.

'In that case, I suppose he may stay . . . just as long as you keep him out of my way.'

He was clumsily throwing his clothes off now and Opal lay back against the pillows knowing what was to come. Yet strangely this evening, she didn't mind. She felt as if she had scored a minor victory over Mrs Wood now that Henry had agreed to allow the dog to stay, and if this was the price she had to pay, then so be it.

The vet called the next day and, after examining Charlie, he left a pot of ointment for his wounds and another to treat his mange. He had told Opal that he thought the dog could be anywhere between two and four years old and that, apart from his wounds and being grossly underweight, he appeared to be healthy.

Charlie already had the cook and the maids eating out of his paw, and the outside staff seemed to have taken a shine to him too. Opal bought him a collar and lead, and soon she was a regular sight in the area walking him. Suddenly she felt as if she had someone she could confide in again, and the second Henry left the house he was allowed to have free run of the rooms, although she wasn't quite brave enough to let him into the bedroom. She felt Henry would have put his foot down at that. Charlie made Opal's life a little more bearable, and in no time at all she loved the little mutt unreservedly.

As well as looking after Charlie, she turned her efforts to the forthcoming dinner party, determined to make it as good as it could be. She sat for hours planning the menu with the cook, much to Mrs Wood's disgust, who felt that this should have been her job – but like Henry, she was discovering that the young mistress wasn't quite as pliable as they had expected her to be.

On the day of the party, fresh flowers were delivered and Opal spent the morning making table decorations that would be dotted amongst the silver candelabra. Delicious smells were issuing from the kitchen, and soon it was time to go and change into the new gown that Henry had insisted she should have especially for the occasion.

It was much more elaborate than anything she had ever owned before in a pale-green silk that clung to her waist before billowing out into a full embroidered skirt. It had a low-cut neckline and once she was dressed and Eve had helped her pile her hair into curls on top of her head, the little maid declared, 'Eeh, you look like a princess, ma'am.'

'I feel like one, actually.' Opal chuckled as she fingered the strand of fine pearls about her neck. They had been a wedding present from Henry, and she had rarely worn them before.

There was a little bubble of excitement growing in her stomach, and although she tried to deny it to herself, she knew it was due to the fact that very shortly she would be in Matthew Darby-Jones's company again. Even though she knew nothing could ever come of her feelings, no other man had ever made her feel the way she had when she had danced in his arms, and she doubted that anyone ever would again. She could not wait to see him.

Chapter Thirty-Seven

'I think this is the end o' the road fer me, me old mate,' Digger told Charlie one evening, as they sat round their campfire eating roast wombat. The weather was improving, but the winter had taken its toll on him, leaving him with a hacking cough, and now he was ready to cash in their stash of gold and move on to pastures new. Digger never stayed at any one thing for long, especially when he had money in his pocket.

They had gained another helper a couple of months before in the shape of an Aboriginal chap called Nullah. He had come across them and offered to stay to help, and they had welcomed him with open arms. Since he had arrived they had never gone short of meat. Armed with his slingshot, Nullah had ventured into the woods each evening and had proved to be a dab hand at hunting. He had also directed them to some good seams of gold, and although they hadn't found enough to make a fortune, they knew that once they had weighed it in there would be enough for both of them to live comfortably for some months to come.

'This outdoor life is fine fer a while,' Digger went on, fingering his long, greying beard. 'But then I gets a yearnin' fer a drink or two an' a soft feather bed, so I'm throwin' the towel in come mornin' an' headin' fer civilisation.'

Nullah looked between the two men, frowning. 'We can go to weighing shop in Orange County,' he told them. 'They pay fair money, an' then per'aps you an' me, boss, could head for Lightning Ridge? Good opals to be found there, worth even more than gold. Black opals, much wanted!' He stared at Charlie hopefully.

Charlie shrugged noncommittally, trying to hide the jolt of pain that had lanced through him when Nullah had said 'opal'. How he longed to be reunited with his sister. He hated to think what could have happened to her during the years they had been apart. What if she had succumbed to fever, as his parents and Jack had? Could all his attempts to make enough money to go back and support his sisters be for nothing?

He cleared his throat as he choked back his emotion. 'I'm not so sure, Nullah. To be honest, I wouldn't know an opal if one hit me in the eye.'

'Ah, but I would.' Nullah thumped his chest.

'Hm, I'll sleep on it,' Charlie promised. If they were to pack up camp the next morning, they had a long trek ahead of them through gruelling forest and countryside before they reached Orange County, so there would be plenty of time to make up his mind. But for now, he was dog-tired; so, throwing some wood on to the fire to keep the critters away, he crawled beneath his tarpaulin and almost instantly fell asleep.

As they trudged wearily into the town some days later, Charlie suddenly felt claustrophobic. He had spent so long isolated in the forest that to be surrounded by people and noise again made him panic, although outwardly he was calm. He no longer resembled the young man he had been when he first set out on his adventure nearly six months before. Through hours and hours of tirelessly digging and sifting, his arms were now heavily muscled and his shoulders were broad. He had grown too and now towered over six foot tall. His skin was deeply tanned from long hours spent out in the sun and his long hair was tied with string in a ponytail at the nape of his neck. His beard was so long that it touched his chest and Digger saw him glimpse longingly at the barber's shop as they headed for the stables.

'We'll see to the old girl here an' get her settled, an' then we'll go an' weigh our gold in.'

Charlie nodded in agreement, aware that they must look a very strange sight. Charlie thought longingly of a nice hot bath with real soap to wash with. Their only means of bathing for the last months had been a dip in the river, and their clothes were stiff with dirt.

Noticing that Nullah was hanging back, Charlie paused to ask, 'Is everything all right, Nullah?'

The man shook his head. 'I not comfortable in towns, boss. I prefer to sleep in the wild.'

'But when we've given you your share, you can come and stay in a hotel with us,' Charlie told him.

The man took a step backward. 'No . . . I go now. If you decide you want to go to Lightning Ridge, you be here each night at six o'clock. If you not come for a month, I go on my way.'

'But what about your share of the money?'

Nullah grinned, revealing a row of strong white teeth in his black face. 'I have all I need out there. Goodbye for now, boss.' And with that he was gone, leaving Charlie to stare after him.

'So are yer goin' to stand there gawpin' all day?' Digger's voice brought his attention back to what they were doing and once again they set off for the livery stable where their old donkey would get a well-earned rest.

Two hours later, after settling the animal in the stable and coming out of the weighing office with a pocketful of money each, Charlie and Digger stood facing each other in the main street of the town.

'So, shall we go and find a hotel where we can have a good meal and get a good night's sleep?' Charlie suggested.

Digger shook his head. 'No, lad. I'm back off to the colony afore I do that. I allus end up back there, probably because it's close to where me missus an' me little 'un are laid to rest. I'll spend some o' me dosh then. No doubt I'll hit the trail again on me next money-makin' adventure but this is the partin' o' the roads fer us.' He held out his hand and shook Charlie's warmly. 'But I have to say, it's been a pleasure spendin' time wi' you, lad, an' I wish you all the best. Just take a word of advice though . . . don't leave it too long afore you decide to go back to yer roots. From what you've told me you still have kin in England, an' as I know to me cost there ain't nothin' as precious as family – not any amount of gold or gems.'

Charlie felt a lump rise in his throat. For all his rough and ready ways, he had grown close to Digger during the time they had spent together.

'But what shall I do about the cart and the donkey and all the tools? They're half yours by rights.'

Digger waved his hand airily, already looking towards the open road beyond the town. 'Keep 'em. I'll have no use of 'em for some time, an' if need be I'll replace 'em. Goodbye, lad.'

With that he swung his heavy bag on to his shoulder and set off whistling merrily, leaving Charlie to chew thoughtfully on his lip. Digger was right. He did still have sisters somewhere back in England and never a day went by when he didn't think of them . . . but was he ready to go home yet? It would need some thinking about, he decided, as he turned and strode towards the hotel.

After booking into the hotel, he soaked for an hour in a steaming hot bath then made his way to the barber where he had a shave and a haircut. The next stop was the tailor, where he was measured and told that the tailor could alter one of the suits he had already made ready for Charlie the next day.

Charlie was too embarrassed to go down to the dining room that evening in the clothes he had, so he dined alone in his room and slept like a baby from the second his head hit the pillow. He had forgotten what it was like to sleep in a comfortable bed, and not have to keep one eye open for critters that might stray too close.

Bright and early the next morning, he set off for the tailor and when he emerged almost an hour later with his old work clothes in a bag, he was unrecognisable.

Over the next week, as he rested, Charlie tried to make up his mind about what he should do. On the one hand the thought of following Digger back to the colony, so that he might get a passage on the next ship home, was tempting. But on the other hand, if he were to go with Nullah to find opals and become rich, then when he went home he would be in a position to give Opal and Susie an easy life. He might even pluck up the courage to go and see Francesca. And so, his mind kept swinging first one way and then the next.

Already he was growing bored of having nothing to do, so that evening he set off to the saloon bar up the street. The raucous sound of laughter and music hit him the second he set foot through the door and the smell of cigarette smoke and cheap perfume was so overpowering that it made his eyes water. Within seconds of getting a tankard of ale, he found himself surrounded by a crowd of gaudily dressed, heavily made-up women wearing dresses that were so low cut they were almost indecent. They flirted with him shamelessly, each vying for his attention, but all Charlie could see was Francesca's face before his eyes. So, draining his tankard as quickly as he could, he left hurriedly, without giving them so much as a backward glance.

Late the following afternoon as he sat staring moodily from the window of his hotel, he made a decision. Tonight he would go and meet Nullah and tell him that he was going with him. With his mind made up, he set off and sure enough just as the clock on the little wooden church chimed six, the Aborigine appeared.

'You make your mind up what you do, boss?'

'Yes, I'm coming with you,' Charlie told him, clapping him on the shoulder.

'Then we need to go to hardware store and buy pickaxes and shovels. Mining for opals very different to mining for gold.'

Charlie nodded. 'We'll do that first thing in the morning, then we can settle the bill at the livery store and set off, if you want to.'

Nullah grinned happily as he turned and walked away, leaving Charlie to enjoy his last night of comfort for goodness knew how long.

After a leisurely dinner in the dining room that evening, Charlie went to sit outside and smoke a cigar as he watched the world go by. His one regret was that he couldn't write to Opal or Susie, for he had no idea where they might be by now. But even so, he had no doubt that when he did return home he would have no trouble finding Opal, at least. Nuneaton was only a small market town, so surely somebody somewhere would know where she was, and then he would buy them a little house to live in where they wouldn't have to worry about paying the rent. Perhaps Opal would already have found Susie and they could all live together. His thoughts flew back to the old dilapidated cottage they had stayed in at Rapper's Hole, and he sighed. Somehow thoughts of the cottage strengthened his resolve to do well and make enough money to make up to his sisters for all the hardships they had suffered.

The next morning, he ate a hearty breakfast and after packing his new clothes carefully away he got back into his work clothes and went downstairs to settle his bill. Next he headed for the livery stable, only to find Nullah already there and waiting for him. The donkey, too, was well rested, so after harnessing her to the old cart they stopped at the grocer to buy food supplies and finally the hardware shop, where they purchased everything they would need. In no time at all they were heading out of town towards Lightning Ridge, and Nullah grinned. 'I have feeling in my bones that we be lucky, boss,' he told him.

Charlie grinned back as he urged the donkey forward. 'Let's just hope you're right, Nullah; my future depends on it.'

Chapter Thirty-Eight

Peter and Emma, with Matthew and Alicia close behind them, were the last to arrive. Once the maid had taken their hats and coats, Henry ushered them into the dining room, where the other guests were already seated at the table enjoying a glass of wine.

The conversation was lively; everyone clearly knew each other well, and Opal felt slightly out of things. To make matters worse, the Partridges had been invited and Esther had been glaring spitefully at her all evening. Thankfully, Mrs King was also there, to make sure she was included in the conversation, for it was soon clear that some of the ladies – friends of Esther's – were studiously ignoring her.

'I must say, my dear, the table looks lovely,' Mrs King praised loudly enough for everyone to hear her. 'I have no doubt you will be a real asset to my son.'

A murmur of grudging agreement rippled round the table.

'Dear Opal has already made a start on redecorating the house, haven't you, dear?' Mrs King went on. 'And a rather grand job she's making of it too. If any of you need any tips on interior design, you should call on her. She seems to have a flair for it.'

Thankfully the conversation moved on then, but not before she noticed Matthew give a cheeky grin across the table. Opal was painfully aware that he was sitting just yards away from her. She had also noticed that his wife didn't look at all well, and this was explained when Alicia told the ladies, 'I wasn't sure that I would be able to make this trip, but Matthew thought it might do me good to get out of the house for a while. I've been quite unwell for a time, although the doctors cannot say why. I think I must just be a little run down.'

The ladies began to recommend remedies while the gentlemen's talk turned to business, and once again Opal sat quietly feeling almost as if she needn't have been there.

Esther was in full flow, as usual, hogging Henry's time and fluttering her eyelashes at him every opportunity she got, but Opal didn't care. One course followed another, each even more delicious than the last, until eventually the meal was over and coffee was served.

Occasionally, Opal would catch Matthew's eye and he would smile at her, as if he could sense that she was feeling uncomfortable; and each time she smiled tentatively back at him as her heart gave a little skip.

'Right, gentlemen, I suggest we retire to my study for some port and a cigar while the ladies entertain themselves in the drawing room,' Henry said, and a murmur of agreement went through the men as they rose to follow him. Opal meanwhile led the ladies to the drawing room, where Eve was waiting to serve them with sherry or coffee should they wish it. This was the part that Opal had been dreading, but Mrs King took control of the situation immediately.

'I must congratulate you on an excellent meal,' she told Opal approvingly. 'And I'm sure the ladies will agree with me.'

Some of them had the good grace to look embarrassed as they nodded in agreement and settled themselves on to the chairs and sofas that were dotted about the room. And then the gossiping began in earnest.

'Did you hear that Daphne Davenport is expecting again?' Esther said cattily. 'Her youngest is only five months old. Really, I'm sure she thinks she is a rabbit the way she is churning babies out! Still – I suppose that's normal where she comes from. Her father is a greengrocer and she has no breeding whatsoever. I really can't imagine why dear Rupert ever married her. He could have done so much better for himself.'

'Perhaps it was because he loved her! He certainly seems happy enough.' Mrs King knew that Esther was having a sly dig at her daughter-in-law and was more than a little put out.

Esther smiled sweetly and looked pointedly at Opal. 'And have you any happy news to share with us yet? We all know how much dear Henry longs for a son. It would be so awful if you were unable to present him with one, after the tragedy of his first wife.'

Opal wished the ground would open up and swallow her, but she was getting fed up with Esther trying to belittle her and knew that it was time to stand her corner. She had done it with Mrs Wood, so, she told herself, she could certainly put Esther in her place.

'Not as yet,' she answered with a dimpled smile. 'But it isn't for the lack of trying. Henry is such a devoted husband, so we are hoping to have happy news for you all very soon. In fact, I think I might turn my attention to a nursery next, so that it's all ready for when the time is right.'

Dull colour blazed into Esther's cheeks, and Mrs King had to raise her hand to hide the smile that played about her lips as she looked at Opal approvingly. That was one up to her.

Esther quickly changed the subject then, and soon after Opal excused herself to visit the ladies' room.

She had taken no more than a few steps along the hallway when she glanced up to see Matthew coming towards her, and she was instantly tongue-tied.

'Ah, Mrs King.' As he took her hand in his, her heart began to beat faster. 'Married life is obviously suiting you; you look quite radiant. And I must thank you for the delicious meal.'

'You're very welcome.' She wished she could stand there all night with her hand in his. But of course, she knew she couldn't. So, bobbing her knee, she gently withdrew her hand and hurried on her way. It was only when she reached the privacy of the ladies' room that she let out a long breath and leaned heavily against the sink.

What was it about Matthew that made her go weak at the knees every time she saw him? she wondered. He was good-looking, admittedly, but then so were many other men she had met and none of them had affected her the way he did. With a sigh, she splashed her face with cold water and, after tidying her hair and patting her skirts into place, she went back to join the women, counting the minutes until the night would end.

'Well done, my dear,' Henry praised her, when he had closed the door on their last guest later that evening. 'The meal was perfect and so were you.' His eyes fell to her bosom and with a sinking feeling, she knew what he had in mind. But then this was part of married life, so when he took her arm to lead her upstairs she went without protest.

Two months later, Opal woke feeling unwell. She felt sick and her breasts felt tender. Struggling to the chamber pot, she vomited everything she had eaten the night before back up then sat on the floor feeling weak. She was still there when Eve brought her a tray of tea shortly after, and the young maid raised an eyebrow.

'What's this then, ma'am? Are yer not feelin' well?'

Opal shook her head. 'I'm afraid not, Eve. I wonder if I've eaten something that disagrees with me?' Although she couldn't think of anything out of the ordinary she had had that Henry hadn't also eaten, and he had been fine when he set off for work.

'Hm!' Eve gave a knowing grin. 'Or per'aps we're about to hear the patter o' tiny feet? When did you have your last course?'

Opal looked stunned. She hadn't given it a thought but now that she came to think of it, she had missed at least one, possibly two. 'I . . . I'm not sure,' she stammered. 'You don't think I could be having a baby, do you?'

'I think it could be a possibility.' Eve chuckled as she helped her up from the floor and led her back to the bed.

'Per'aps we should get Doctor Lewis in to have a look at you?'

'Oh no . . . not yet.' Opal dropped back against the pillows. 'It's a bit early to be calling him out just yet. Let's wait a little longer and see if it happens again. It could be just something I've picked up. I'll probably be as right as rain tomorrow.'

'If you say so, ma'am.' Eve grinned as she poured the tea and handed the delicate china cup and saucer to her young mistress. 'Now, is there anythin' else I can do for you?'

'No, thank you.' Opal managed to raise a smile, but when the girl had left the room, she placed the cup down and gnawed worriedly on her lip as her hand dropped to her belly.

Could it really be possible that she was carrying Henry's child? And if she was – would she want it? And then the answer came . . . Yes . . . Oh yes, she would! Once again, she would have someone to call her very own. She tried to imagine what the baby would be like. Would it be a boy or a girl? Would it look like her or take after its father? She realised that she really didn't care what sex it might be or even what it looked like. It would be *her* very own baby to love and to cherish, and there would be no more lonely days and nights with just Charlie for company, for she would have a child to fill her time.

Now stop it, she scolded herself then, you're not even sure that you are with child yet. As she lay there, she started to feel much better and the nausea passed. So much so that as she climbed back out of bed, she wondered if she had imagined it. Only time would tell, so she would say nothing to Henry until she was sure.

Later that morning, she put Charlie on his lead and they set off on their favourite walk. Henry had informed her before leaving for his office that morning that he would not be home for lunch, so the day was hers to do with as she pleased. They set off up Tuttle Hill with Charlie's tail wagging furiously, and when the five-sailed windmill came into sight they took the footpath down to the towpath that ran alongside the canal. On the way, they passed a row of pit cottages and one of the women who lived there who was out scrubbing her front doorstep shouted a greeting.

'Mornin', Mrs King, luvvie. Nippy day, ain't it?'

'It certainly is, Mrs Jennings. It's almost cold enough for snow.' Opal had come to know most of the occupants of the cottages, and she smiled a greeting as she moved on, Charlie off his lead and prancing ahead of her now.

To the other side of the path was a deep quarry and Opal kept well away from the edge of it until they reached the towpath. The leaves underfoot were still rimed in frost and she didn't want to slip, especially now. Opal loved to wander along the towpath watching the brightly painted barges that delivered the coal and goods being dragged along by the huge horses, but today there wasn't a barge in sight; so, after walking for a while, she sank down on to a fallen tree trunk and after removing her bonnet she hugged her knees as Charlie licked her face.

'So how would you feel about having a little playmate, boy?' She grinned as she stroked his floppy ears and their breath fanned like lace on the air in front of them.

He was almost unrecognisable from the mangy stray she had taken in off the streets. His coat was thick and shining and he had gained weight. It was no wonder, because everyone fed him scraps and the staff seemed to love him almost as much as she did. Sadly, Henry didn't share their enthusiasm for a pet, so while he was at home Charlie was confined to the kitchen – but for the rest of the time he was constantly by Opal's side.

As her hand dropped to stroke her flat stomach, she felt a little bubble of excitement. How wonderful it would be if she really was pregnant. If she was correct, to her reckonings the baby would be due sometime in June the following year. Her thoughts raced ahead and she smiled again. Boy or girl, this baby would be loved, she vowed, and could hardly wait to have it confirmed.

On arriving home, she was surprised to find Henry there, so she hastily banished Charlie to the kitchen, much to his disgust.

'Here you are. Where have you been?' he asked shortly, as she undid the ribbons of her bonnet.

'I took Charlie for a walk. I didn't expect you home so early.' She removed her gloves and blew on her cold fingers as he looked on disapprovingly.

He scowled. 'I really don't think it's seemly for my wife to be seen walking a mongrel,' he muttered, clearly in a bad mood. 'Esther Partridge broke her neck to tell me that she'd seen you at the top of Tuttle Hill on more than a few occasions.'

Opal nodded. 'That's correct. I like to take Charlie down on to the canal towpath where he can run without his lead. Seeing as you're home early, would you like me to have a cup of tea or coffee sent in to you?'

Henry shook his head. 'No, although I'm early I won't be staying. In fact, I'm afraid I have to be away from home this evening . . . Business, you know?'

'Oh, that's all right. Would you like me to pack you an overnight bag?'

He shook his head. 'Mrs Wood has already done it.'

'Very well. May I expect you home tomorrow then?'

Henry shrugged churlishly. He didn't appreciate being questioned. 'It all depends on how long the business takes.' Thankfully, Opal had no idea of the shady dealings he was involved in, and he intended to keep it that way. To everyone in their circle, Henry was a pillar of the community and a well-respected magistrate; but unknown to them, he also had his hands in a very great number of illegal dealings. He rose then and after giving her a perfunctory peck on the cheek he left.

Opal frowned; Henry had seemed preoccupied, and she wondered if all was well, but as she thought of the baby again the smile returned to her face and she forgot all about it. It would be nice to have the bed all to herself; in fact she might even allow Charlie to sleep with her. What Henry didn't know, he couldn't complain about. Unless Mrs Wood told him, of course. She sighed. It seemed that both the housekeeper and Esther Partridge were out to cause her as much grief as they possibly could, although as far as she was aware she had never knowingly done anything to upset either of them. She shrugged. Let them do their worst; she was Henry's wife now and there wasn't a thing either of them could do about it.

Henry meanwhile was heading for the train station to catch a train to Birmingham where, unknown to anyone, he owned a number of slum properties that he let out at exorbitant rents. He had bought them shortly after meeting Opal, when he had seen the state of the cottage she was living in. He had never realised that people would live in such appalling conditions and had instantly seen the purchases as a way to take advantage of those who were desperate for somewhere to live. The houses were streaming with damp and rat-infested, but his tenants soon learned that it wasn't wise to complain. Unfortunately, though, the man he paid to collect the rents had cleared off with a great deal of his money, so he needed to be tracked down and punished. Luckily, Henry knew just the man to do it. Tricky Norman was a hardened villain and Henry had no doubt he would have slit his own granny's throat for sixpence.

Henry also ran a very profitable, if somewhat questionable, money-lending business. The interest he charged was so high that many of his clients could never get out of his clutches and should they try to Tricky was on hand to show them who was boss and keep the payments coming in. He had no compunction whatsoever in breaking someone's kneecaps if asked to, and over the years he had become Henry's right-hand man. He was also a dab hand at directing Henry to young ones who had fallen on hard times – girls or boys, it really didn't matter to Henry, so long as they allowed him to have his way with them. Already the novelty of having a young wife was wearing off. Opal's figure had filled out slightly since the wedding, and she no longer held the same appeal for him – so hopefully during this trip he would be able to satisfy his sexual needs as well. Feeling in a slightly more optimistic frame of mind, he boarded the train and set off on his journey.

Chapter Thirty-Nine

'Right, this has gone on for quite long enough,' Henry's mother stated one morning early in December. She had called to have coffee with Opal and once again found her looking pale and ill. 'Eve, go and tell Mrs Wood that I wish her to send someone to the doctor to ask him to attend your mistress immediately!'

'No . . . really,' Opal protested weakly, but it was too late. Eve had already shot off to do as she was told.

'So, young lady' – Mrs King raised her eyebrow – 'do you have any idea why you might be feeling this way?'

Opal avoided her eyes as she nodded numbly.

'I thought as much. I'm no fool, you know? But why haven't you sent for the doctor before?'

'I suppose I just wanted to make sure it wasn't a false alarm before I asked him to confirm it.'

Mrs King smiled. 'Hm, I rather doubt it, looking at you, and I'll tell you something – this is going to make Henry a very happy man indeed if it is confirmed. But off upstairs with you. The doctor can hardly examine you down here, can he?'

The older woman shooed her away, and Opal climbed the stairs wearily, each step an effort. Even so, she was secretly relieved that she was going to find out one way or another, although she knew she would be heartbroken if she wasn't having a baby. It had been all she could think about, for once it was born she would have someone to love again.

Sadly, she still hadn't managed to fall in love with her husband as she had hoped she would, and with each day that passed her hopes of ever finding Susie again were fading. She had come to terms with the fact that Charlie and Jack were gone forever, but once she had this baby in her arms, she would have someone to focus on again and she knew that it would change her life. It might even improve her relationship with Henry, for if they had a child together, they would be a proper family. She lived in hope of that happening.

When the doctor arrived some short time later, he found Opal pacing the floor of her room and smiled. 'So, young lady.' He placed his black bag down and peered at her over the pair of tiny steel spectacles perched on the end of his nose. 'And what appears to be the problem? Tell me your symptoms and how long you've been experiencing them.'

When Opal had haltingly told him he nodded.

'Very well, hop on to the bed and let's have a look at you, eh?'

He gently felt her stomach, then he straightened and gave her a broad smile. 'Well, my dear, it would appear that congratulations are in order. You're with child. About three months I should say, so the baby should be due early in June.'

Opal felt as if all her Christmases and birthdays had come at once and she beamed. 'Oh, thank you. Thank you so much. I hoped I was but was afraid I might be wrong.'

'Well, you weren't.' He picked up his bag. 'I shall keep a check on you from now on, and nearer to the time we'll engage a midwife for you. Meanwhile go on as normal. Gentle exercise and eat well. And don't worry about the morning sickness. It should pass any time now. The first three months are usually the worst, so it's nothing at all to worry about. Good day, m'dear, and congratulations again.'

She followed him down the stairs, feeling as if she were floating on air, and the second she had seen him out she dashed into the drawing room to her mother-in-law.

'You were right,' she told her joyously. 'I am having a baby! It should arrive early in June.'

Mrs King smiled. She was no fool and had realised that marriage to her son was not turning out to be as Opal had hoped, but she seemed very happy about the baby.

'Then I'm thrilled for you. And Henry, of course! Goodness, he's going to be like a dog with two tails when you tell him. He has wanted a son for so long.'

The smile momentarily left Opal's face. 'But what if it's a girl?'

'I'm afraid he'll have to take what comes.' Her mother-in-law raised herself painfully from her chair and leaned heavily on her stick. 'Now tell me, is Henry coming home for lunch today?'

When Opal nodded, she made for the door. 'In that case I shall be on my way. You should have some privacy to tell him the happy news. Take care, my dear.'

And with that, she left, leaving Opal to hug herself with delight. She could hardly wait to tell Henry the good news, and found herself glancing at the clock every few minutes.

Thankfully he arrived on time, and once they were seated at the table in the dining room she waited for Eve to serve their meal before saying, 'I, er . . . have something to tell you, Henry.'

'Oh yes?' She could tell that he was only listening with half an ear, but her next statement made his head snap up.

'The thing is . . . your mother encouraged me to see the doctor this morning. I've been feeling unwell for some time and he told me . . . that I – we – are going to have a baby!'

'What?' A look of incredulity crossed his face and for a moment he seemed lost for words before he blustered, 'But . . . are you *quite* sure?'

She nodded. 'Very sure. The doctor thinks it should be born early in June.'

It took a lot to make Henry lose his appetite. Usually he could eat like a horse, but suddenly he pushed his plate away and, hurrying round the table, he dragged her from her seat and waltzed her round the room.

'But . . . but that's *wonderful!*'

She was delighted to see how thrilled he was. He had paid her so little attention for the last few weeks, but now he was elated.

'There is a nursery already prepared for when my last . . .' His voice trailed away and he hurried on. 'But of course,

I give you free rein to redecorate it as you see fit. I want my son to have the best of everything – the best clothes, the best education . . . just *everything*!'

'But it could be a little girl,' she gently pointed out.

But nothing could spoil his good mood. 'Then if it is, we shall perhaps have a boy the next time,' he said stoically, and Opal felt happy – really happy – for the first time in some long time.

That afternoon when he had reluctantly gone back to work, she passed on the good news to the staff, and asked Mrs Wood for the key to the nursery. She had never ventured in there before, but now she wished to see it. Everyone apart from Mrs Wood seemed thrilled that there was to be a baby in the house, and the woman reluctantly handed over the key saying spitefully, 'Let's just hope the same thing doesn't happen to you as to the last Mrs King.'

But even her spite couldn't dampen Opal's spirits that day and, taking the key, she walked away from her.

The minute she entered the nursery, her mood became sad as she thought of the poor dead baby it had been prepared for. Clearly a lot of thought and money had gone into it but Opal wanted to put her own stamp on the room and she began to plan how she wanted it. *I shall have white walls*, she thought, *and then it won't matter if it's a boy or a girl. And I shall order a new crib too.* It seemed just too sad to think of putting her baby in the crib that had been bought for another. That very afternoon she walked into town and bought some wool. Cook had told her that she would teach her how to knit and she wanted to make some little matinee coats.

Charlie was disgruntled at being left behind, but today all Opal's thoughts were centred on the baby.

'I think we should throw a little dinner party to celebrate,' Henry told her that evening as they sat by the fire after dinner.

Delighted that he was so happy with the news, Opal smiled at him indulgently. 'Of course, if that's what you'd like. I'll speak to Mrs Wood about a menu. You just let me know how many people will be coming.'

He reached across to pat her hand. 'I have a feeling this is going to be the best Christmas ever!'

Opal could only hope that he was right.

The next week passed in a pleasant blur, and Opal found that Henry had once again become the man he had been before they were married: kind, considerate and generous.

'I'm going to start paying you a monthly allowance. You'll need new clothes when you, er . . . you know?'

Opal giggled. 'Get fat, you mean?'

She had already had two enormous Christmas trees delivered, which she had decorated with candles and shining glass baubles and now with vases of holly everywhere the house was looking very festive. Then one morning, she woke and lay there waiting for the usual nausea to set in, but it didn't. Usually the second she opened her eyes she would end up leaning over the bed heaving into the chamber pot, but this morning there was nothing. She lay still for a few minutes more, hardly daring to hope the morning sickness had passed then tentatively sat up and swung her legs out of bed, but there was still nothing. If anything, to her delight, she felt as fit as a fiddle and suddenly she was ravenously hungry.

The dinner party was set for the following week, the week before Christmas, and Opal started to look forward to it, although she doubted that their good news would come as a surprise to any of the guests. Henry was so thrilled at the prospect of becoming a father that he was telling anyone that would listen, and Opal suspected their guests would already know by then.

One of the first to arrive on the evening of the dinner party was Esther Partridge and her mother, and as Opal and Henry greeted them at the door it was clear they had heard the news.

'I hear there is to be an addition to the household,' Esther commented bitterly, pointedly ignoring Opal as Eve took her hat and coat.

'There certainly is.' Henry couldn't stop smiling, and didn't even seem to notice that Esther seemed to be rather scathing about it.

'Opal has already had decorators in to start work on the nursery and she's costing me an absolute fortune. Not that I mind, of course.'

Luckily the doorbell rang again then, and he and Opal turned their attention to greeting the next guests to arrive as Esther stamped into the drawing room. Soon everyone was there and after drinks they were all shown into the dining room. Opal had dressed the table herself and it looked very festive. The mood was light – apart from Esther's that was, who seemed to be drinking rather a lot of wine.

They were on the main course when Esther suddenly asked, 'So when is the child due?'

'The beginning of June,' Henry answered, and Esther's lip curled as a silence momentarily settled around the table.

'Hm, so you won't have quite so much time to spend up Tuttle Hill then? I just wonder what the attraction is there for you.'

'Pardon?' Opal felt herself blush. 'I go there because I like walking Charlie along the canal.'

Esther sneered, but thankfully someone else spoke at that moment and the subject was dropped.

By the time the meal was over, it was quite clear that Esther was more than a little drunk; even her own mother looked slightly embarrassed as she began to grow louder and slur her words.

'Well, I have to shay for a girl from Rapper's Hole you've done quite well for yourshelf, haven't you?'

A deadly silence settled on the room until Mrs Partridge suddenly said loudly, 'It's been a lovely evening but I think we should be going, Esther. The snow has held off up to now but I think we should get back in case it starts and I'm rather tired.'

Esther left without protest, but the night was ruined for Opal and she wondered why Esther seemed to hate her so much. She'd always known that the other woman had had her eye on Henry for some long time, but even so surely

375

there was no need for her behaviour towards her. It wasn't
as if she had forced Henry to marry her, after all.

As they were getting changed for bed, Opal mentioned it
to Henry. 'I really don't know why Esther is so rude to me.'
She could still clearly remember the time Esther had tried to
make it appear she had stolen her ring.

He grinned. 'Don't worry about it, my dear. Esther made
it more than clear to me after the death of my first wife
that she would like to become the next Mrs King, but I can
assure you she holds no attraction for me whatsoever. To be
quite blunt, I wouldn't marry her if she were the last woman
on earth. But there – forget about her and don't let her spoil
the evening. It went well, didn't it? Oh, and I have a little
gift for you.'

'But it isn't Christmas yet,' Opal pointed out.

Henry chuckled. 'This is my gift to you for making me
a very happy man.' He fetched a long, velvet box from his
dressing table drawer and when Opal opened it, she gasped.
It was an emerald and diamond bracelet.

'Oh, but it's beautiful.'

He laughed as he fastened it about her wrist. 'You deserve
it. You are going to make my dream of becoming a father
come true, and this will be the first of many.'

Opal smiled up at him. In truth she wasn't overly fond of
jewellery, but it was nice to see him so happy. 'You really
don't have to spend your money on things like this for me,'
she assured him. 'I already have everything I need.'

But he waved her words aside.

They got into bed but Henry made no move towards her. In fact, she realised, he hadn't since she had told him the good news. He was so afraid of anything going wrong that he didn't want to risk hurting her. Opal smiled into the darkness. Perhaps this would be a turning point in their relationship. She hoped so.

Chapter Forty

They spent Christmas quietly at home with Henry's mother and, despite the fact that Opal often thought of the family she had lost, she enjoyed it. It had started to snow two days before and everywhere looked clean and bright, but Henry was concerned about her going out on walks with Charlie.

'What if you slip and fall?' he fretted.

She laughed. 'I'm very careful, and the doctor assured me that gentle exercise is good for me and the baby.'

He sighed, but said no more. For Christmas, he had bought her the necklace to match her bracelet, and although Opal thanked him profusely, for she didn't wish to appear ungrateful, she wondered where she would ever go to wear it. It was beautiful and she guessed it must have cost a great deal of money, so she tucked it safely away in her drawer, certain that it would rarely see the light of day. He had bought her a number of costly pieces of jewellery now and she didn't have the heart to point out to him that she rarely wore them.

But as it turned out she got to wear them sooner than she expected when on New Year's Eve they again attended a ball at Peter's house in Caldecote, and for the first time, as she got ready, Opal noticed that her clothes were getting rather tight about the waist.

'Eeh, I'm strugglin' to do the buttons up on this,' Eve said as she helped her into her gown.

Opal giggled. 'I'm not surprised; I'm eating like a horse. I shall be the size of a house at this rate by the time the baby comes.'

'Ah, but you're eatin' for two now,' Eve answered with a happy smile. She was looking forward to having a baby in the house.

When Opal went downstairs, she found Henry waiting for her in the hall, and he smiled when he saw that she was wearing her emerald necklace and bracelet. They complemented the pale-green satin gown she was wearing and with her skin glowing she looked radiant.

'You'll be the most beautiful woman at the ball,' he told her as he helped her on with her new fur-lined cape – another Christmas present from him – and smiling they went out to the waiting carriage.

When they arrived at Peter's splendid home, Opal scanned the room and was vaguely disappointed when she saw no sign of Matthew – but then she gave herself a mental shake as she kept her smile firmly in place. She was a married woman and an expectant mother into the bargain, so she must put him from her mind.

It was Emma who explained his absence sometime later as they stood chatting. 'Poor Matthew couldn't attend this time,' she said regretfully. 'Alicia is far from well again and he's growing really concerned about her. Still, we won't speak of sad things this evening. Come along and I'll introduce you to some of the guests you may not have met.'

The evening passed pleasantly, although Opal was glad when it was over and they could go home. She still felt a little out of place at such events and was finding that she tired more easily nowadays – no doubt due to the little life growing inside her. At the thought of the baby, she smiled as the carriage rattled along, and her hand fell to stroke the tiny mound of her stomach. In just a few months' time, she would be a mother and she could hardly wait.

The winter was harsh and worse still for the people who lived in the pit cottages in Tuttle Hill, for at the end of December the miners went on strike and soup kitchens were opened in the town. At least two or three times a week, Opal got the cook to fill a basket with food that they could share amongst them, which she delivered when she took Charlie on his walk. It wasn't much, she knew, but she supposed that every little helped. She couldn't bear to think of the children going hungry. She was painfully aware that Henry wouldn't approve of what she was doing, but she reasoned that what he didn't know wouldn't hurt him, and Cook assured her that he would never find out from her.

On a wet and windy day early in March, Opal set off with a loaded basket and Charlie on his lead. She was thoughtful as she walked along, for the night before she had woken to find Henry was not in bed in the early hours of the morning, and when she'd gone downstairs to find him she had seen him coming out of Mrs Wood's room, which she had found rather strange.

He was clad in his dressing robe and when he had caught sight of her coming along the hallway he had almost jumped out of his skin.

When she had looked at him enquiringly, he had blustered, 'Sorry if I disturbed you, m'dear. I was sure I heard something downstairs and thought I'd better ask Mrs Wood if she had. She hadn't as it happens, so let's go back to bed, shall we?'

It was the second time in as many weeks that this had happened, but she put it from her mind as she concentrated on staying upright in the strong wind.

As soon as the cottages came in sight, she let Charlie off his lead and tapped at the door of the first one she came to.

'Hello, luvvie,' the woman said, her eyes dropping to the contents of the basket. 'I didn't expect to see you on such a cold and blustery day.'

'Charlie here needs his exercise whatever the weather,' Opal told her with a smile as she handed the basket over. 'There's a loaf and a few bits for each of the cottages in there, Mrs Green, if you wouldn't mind sharing them out.'

'Bless you,' the woman said gratefully. 'But just mind how you're going now.'

'I shall,' Opal promised as she set off again. During the last month, her stomach had swollen to twice its size, and Eve teased her that she now waddled instead of walked. She was smiling as she made her way down the steep lane leading to the canal, and careful to keep away from the edge of the quarry as the drizzly rain had made the path slippery. She had not gone far past the cottages when she happened to glance across her shoulder just in time to see what appeared to be someone in a dark-green cape hurry into the shelter of the trees. She frowned; but then, thinking it was probably just one of the children from the tiny homes she had just passed, she went on her way, laughing at Charlie who was gambolling along some way ahead of her.

And then suddenly she felt a pressure on her back. She had no time to turn to see who it was for someone was pushing her to the edge of the quarry.

'No . . .' she screamed but before she could say any more, she slipped on the wet mud. For a moment she felt as though she was flying as the deep quarry below rushed up to meet her. She was vaguely aware of Charlie growling and barking furiously as the bushes and broken trees growing from the quarry face tore at her clothes and then suddenly a tree stump was looming out of the steep sides of the drop. As she crashed into it, an excruciating pain ripped through her and the breath was knocked from her body, and then a welcoming darkness rushed towards her and claimed her.

Mrs Green had just knocked on her neighbour's door to deliver the food Opal had asked her to share when Charlie raced back up the lane towards her.

'Hello, Charlie, what are you doin' back here?' she asked as she peered past him for a sight of his mistress, but she was nowhere in sight. 'Where's your mistress then, boy?'

The dog was clearly agitated and running around her in a circle, before running a few paces back the way he had come and back again as if he was trying to tell her something.

Her neighbour opened the door at that moment and she too frowned as she saw the dog.

'So where's Mrs King then? It ain't like Charlie to leave her,' Mrs Green said, worried.

'I know,' her neighbour replied. 'I'm wonderin' if somethin' is amiss. It's as if he's tryin' to tell us somethin'. Do yer think we should go an' have a look where she is?'

'Aye, I do, an' I'll get our Will to come wi' us.'

Will was her son. He and his father were employed by the local pit and when his mother called him he threw his coat on and went willingly with the women down the lane as Charlie pranced ahead of them.

Eventually Charlie stopped abruptly and, standing dangerously close to the edge of the quarry, he began to bark even more furiously.

'So what's to do then, boy?' Will asked gently as he tentatively picked his way to stand by the dog. As he stared down into the deep quarry his face paled. '*Mam!*' he yelled, throwing off his coat. 'Run back home an' tell me dad an' any men yer can find to come straightaway. An' tell 'em to bring a length o' long rope. The young mistress 'as gone over the edge but she's caught on one o' the trees. We have to try an' get her up afore she falls.'

His mother was off like a shot from a gun and soon she was back with a number of the miners from the cottages.

'One of us is goin' to 'ave to go down an' try to bring her back up,' Mr Green said and Will instantly volunteered.

'I'll go, Dad. Tie that rope round me waist an' lower me down gently as yer can. I'll try an' bring her back up across me shoulder. But make sure you all hold on tight, else the two of us could end up at the bottom o' the quarry.'

He began to tie the rope securely about his waist and once the rest of the men had a firm grip on it he gingerly swung himself over the edge, finding footholds wherever he could. After what seemed like a lifetime, he finally reached the jutting tree but he realised that this had been the easy part; now he had to find a way to get a heavily pregnant woman back up the steep and slippery incline.

'Is the poor lass alive?' his mother shouted down to him.

'I think so,' he called back. 'But for God's sake, keep a tight grip on that rope while I try to get her over me shoulder.'

Soon he was panting with the effort of trying to lift Opal. She was a dead weight and unable to help herself and he was painfully aware that one false move could send both of them crashing to their deaths. At last, however, he had managed to manoeuvre her on to his shoulder where she hung as limp as a rag doll. And then the really hard work started as he began the long climb back up. He had climbed no more than a few feet when the heavens opened and the rain came down in torrents, which made it even more difficult, but thankfully the men were all strong from the many hours they spent toiling down the pit and inch by inch they dragged them up. At last, Will's head appeared and strong hands reached out to pull him and Opal to safety. While the women turned their attention to Opal, Will lay gasping and shaking from the effort.

'We'd best get her back to my cottage,' Mrs Green said worriedly. 'Then someone had best run to tell her husband what's happened and fetch a doctor, though by the look of her I doubt the poor lass will last till he gets here.'

'I'll go.' Will stood up shakily and after catching his breath he was off like the wind as the men bent to lift Opal between them as gently as they could.

Once back at Mrs Green's cottage, the men laid Opal carefully on the bed while Mrs Green began to tap her cheeks. There was no response and she groaned. 'Eeh, I wish we had a drop o' brandy to give her.'

'Huh!' This from Mrs Jennings. 'We can't even afford bread for us little 'uns, let alone brandy.'

'Well, we can at least get her out o' these wet clothes,' Mrs Green said as she began to unbutton Opal's coat. 'Fetch me that clean nightdress from over the fireguard, I'll put her in that an' try an' get her warm again.'

Charlie was sitting at the side of them with his tail down and one of the men stroked him. 'Well done, ol' chap,' he praised. 'If it weren't fer you, your mistressus would 'ave been a gonner for sure.' He frowned. 'But I wonder what made her walk so close to the edge that she slipped over?'

Will arrived back with the doctor shortly after, telling them that Opal's housekeeper had sent word to her husband.

The doctor ushered them all away and, his face grave, he leaned over to examine Opal before shaking his head. 'Her arm is broken,' he told them. 'I shall have to splint it as best I can, but worse still, I fear she is about to have the baby and she's in no state to help bring it into the world.'

'But she's only six months along,' Mrs Green fretted. 'It's too soon.'

The doctor shrugged. 'Too soon or not, it's coming.' He took off his coat and rolled his sleeves up, telling her, 'I shall need hot water and towels and it might be as well if the rest of you go next door.'

Only too happy to escape, Opal's rescuers hurried from the cottage leaving the doctor and Mrs Green to do what they could for her, although deep down the doctor didn't hold out much hope for Opal or the baby.

Chapter Forty-One

It was over an hour later when a fine carriage pulled up outside and everyone in the row of cottages peeped through the curtains at it.

Grim-faced, Henry got out and strode to Mrs Green's door and rapped on it impatiently.

'Come in, come in, your wife is through there wi' the doctor,' she told him tearfully.

'What's happened?'

She told him haltingly how Charlie had run back to the cottages as if to warn them that his mistress was in danger, ending with, 'If it hadn't been fer him, happen she would 'ave died!'

'*Bah!* If it hadn't been for her obsession with walking the damn mutt she would never have been here in the first place,' he stormed. 'I warned her time and time again that that path was dangerous, but would she listen?'

He made to move towards the bedroom but Mrs Green stayed him with a gentle hand on his arm. 'I wouldn't go in there if I were you. The doctor sent for the midwife to assist 'im an' I reckon the baby could come any minute now.'

'What? But it's too soon,' he ground out through clenched teeth. 'Can't they do something to stop it?'

'I'm afraid not.' Mrs Green ushered him towards a chair. 'But you just sit down now an' I'll make us a nice cup o' tea.'

Henry angrily shook her hand from his arm, and began to pace the room like a caged animal. 'So what will the baby's chances be if it comes now? Opal wasn't due to have it for another three months.'

Mrs Green studiously avoided his eyes as she filled the kettle from a bucket that stood on the wooden draining board. 'We'll just 'ave to wait an' see. It's all in God's 'ands now.'

She had noticed that not once had he asked after his wife. His only concern seemed to be the baby, and she felt sorry for the young woman lying in the other room. While she made the tea, he looked about scornfully at the hard-packed earth floor and the mismatched furniture but he had no time to say anything for at that moment the doctor appeared. He was covered in blood and he looked weary.

'Well . . . has she had the baby?' Henry instantly asked.

The doctor nodded. 'Yes, it's a boy . . . but I'm afraid he didn't draw breath.'

Henry sat down heavily in the nearest chair, his face the colour of putty as all his dreams turned to ashes. He had had a son, but thanks to Opal's stupidity he had lost him. He became aware that the doctor was still talking to him then and he looked up at him vacantly. It was as if he was only hearing odd words that he was saying.

' . . . gravely ill . . . bleeding heavily . . . hospital . . .'

'What?' Henry shook his head to clear it. 'What did you say?'

'I said your wife is very gravely ill and needs to be taken to the hospital immediately, otherwise I think her chances of survival are slim. Can we carry her out to your carriage? I'm really not happy about moving her but we have no alternative.'

'Yes . . . yes, I suppose so,' Henry answered dully. He was clearly in shock.

'I'll go an' get the men folk to lift her,' Mrs Green volunteered and hurried away as Henry sat staring into space.

The doctor travelled in the carriage to the hospital with Opal and Henry, and once there two men with a stretcher hurried out to carry her inside.

The doctor was shocked when, as soon as they had taken her from the carriage, Henry told his driver, 'Drive on. Take me home.'

'But aren't you going to come in and see how your wife fares?'

Henry glared at him and shook his head, and after slamming the door, the carriage rattled away as the doctor stood for a moment watching it open-mouthed. With a shake of his head, he hurried after his patient.

When Henry entered the house sometime later, he found the housekeeper waiting for him.

'What's happened?' she asked. 'I had some man turn up here all of a fluster saying that we had to get word to you that Opal had had an accident.'

He moved past her into the drawing room where he crossed to the cut-glass decanter and filled a crystal goblet with a generous measure of whisky, which he knocked back in one gulp.

'Well?'

He looked at her now before snarling, 'She went over the edge of the quarry. The baby has been born but didn't draw breath. It was a boy, but he was born too soon and it's all her fault!' And then the tears came, streaming down his face and blinding him, as she hurried over to wrap her arms about him.

'And your wife?'

He shrugged. 'She's in the hospital, but from what the doctor said it's uncertain whether she will survive.'

He failed to see the look of satisfaction that flitted across her face but her voice was sympathetic as she told him, 'How awful for you, Henry. Once more, you have been cheated of a son.'

He shook his head as he disentangled himself from her arms and poured himself another whisky. 'At the moment I don't much care if she dies. I'll never forgive her for this, Blanche. She killed my baby and all for the sake of taking that damn dog for a walk.'

'But how did it happen?'

'How should I know? She was clearly walking too close to the edge. Either that or the dog tripped her up. The bloody thing – it'll not come in this house again, I swear!'

'But shouldn't you be at the hospital?'

He drained his glass again before answering, 'The way I feel, I never want to see her again!'

'I can understand that. But think how it will look, Henry, if anything happens to her and you are not there. I know she doesn't deserve your consideration but you have your reputation to think of.'

'I suppose you're right,' he admitted as the anger drained out of him. 'I'll just pull myself together and then I'll get back down there.'

She hovered uncertainly for a moment before saying, 'Actually there's something I need to speak to you about. I know this is probably not the right time, but it must be said . . . you see, you might be having a son after all.'

He frowned and as her hands dropped to her stomach his eyes stretched wide. 'You mean . . . ?'

She nodded. 'Yes, I am carrying a child.'

He was so flabbergasted that he dropped on to the nearest chair as if someone had sucked all the air out of his lungs. 'But you . . . you assured me that you were unable to have children. And . . . is the baby mine?'

'Of course, it is yours.' Her mouth set before she ground out, 'And I *did* think I was unable to conceive, but it appears I was mistaken.'

'Good lord!' Henry dropped his head into his hands as he tried to take in what she had told him. It seemed that everything was happening today.

'So what are we going to do about it?' she asked.

He gulped deep in his throat. 'Well . . . I clearly can't acknowledge the child. Opal is my wife. How would it look if I was to admit to being its father? As you quite rightly pointed out just now, I have my reputation to consider.'

'Ah, but if Opal should not survive, there would be nothing to stop us getting married, would there? And truthfully, it's highly unlikely that she will after falling down the quarry face. It would seem a little disrespectful, admittedly, if you didn't observe a proper period of mourning, but needs must.'

'She didn't fall all the way down, as it happens,' he answered woodenly. 'A tree growing out of the side of the quarry broke her fall otherwise she would have stood no chance.' He stood and made dazedly for the door where he paused. 'As you say, I should get to the hospital. We will talk about this later.'

And with that he strode away, leaving her scowling after him.

'Mrs King is in that ward there, sir,' a young nurse told Henry when he arrived at the hospital, and without a word, he marched towards the double swing doors that led into it.

'Can I help you?' a sister in a crisp white apron and navy dress immediately approached him.

'My wife, Mrs King, she was brought in a short time ago.'

'Ah yes.' She pointed towards a bed with the curtains drawn about it. 'The doctors are still with her but if you would care to take a seat, I'm sure they will speak to you when they've finished examining her.'

He inclined his head and did as he was told, but it was some time before the curtains parted and two elderly doctors appeared. Henry saw the sister say something to them and nod towards him before they approached him.

'If you'd like to come this way?' The taller of the two led him towards a small office and once inside he closed the door and motioned to a seat. 'I'm afraid your wife is very gravely ill,' he told Henry without preamble. He had never been one to give false hope. 'The next twenty-four hours will be critical. Her body has suffered a severe shock and that added to the birth . . . She also has a badly broken arm and at least two cracked ribs but as yet we haven't been able to establish if there are any internal injuries.' He shrugged. 'We have set her arm but there is little more we can do for her now, except to give her laudanum for the pain.'

'I see.' Henry pursed his lips before asking, 'May I see her?'

'Of course, although she is deeply unconscious and will not know you are there. At this stage we have no way of knowing if she will wake up, I'm afraid.'

When Henry followed him back out into the ward, a young nurse led him to Opal's bedside. He was shocked when he looked down on her still form. Her face was so swollen that she was almost unrecognisable, and purple bruises were beginning to bloom all across her face. She also had a nasty gash that ran the length of one cheek that had been stitched. Another young nurse was there, gently bathing her face with cool water, and she smiled at him sympathetically.

'Don't worry,' she told him. 'You can be sure we shall give her the very best of care.'

He inclined his head, and without a word he turned and marched away, his lips set in a straight, grim line.

Darkness was falling that afternoon when a tap came on the kitchen door. Eve hurried to answer it to find a young man standing there with Charlie on a length of string.

The dog's tail started to wag ecstatically at the sight of her and, dropping to her knees, she wrapped her arms about his neck and was rewarded with his wet tongue licking her face.

'I, er ... thought I'd better bring 'im 'ome,' the young man told her, then introducing himself he said, 'I'm Will, by the way. It were me as managed to get Mrs King up the quarry face wi' a bit of help.'

'It seems you're the hero of the hour then, lad. Come on in out o' the cold. It's enough to cut yer in two out there.' The cook and Eve had been crying on and off all day after the news of what had happened to their dear mistress had reached them, but now they smiled to see Charlie again.

'Actually, it's this 'un 'ere who should take the credit.' Will patted Charlie's head. 'It were 'im as run back to the cottage to warn us that sommat were wrong, otherwise she could have died there if no one 'ad spotted her.'

'What a good clever boy you are,' Eve told Charlie – but before she could say any more, the door banged open and the master appeared, his face as dark as a thundercloud.

'Just what the *hell* is that murdering mongrel doing back here?' he stormed as Will's mouth dropped open. 'I shall have him destroyed *immediately*. It was that damn cur that killed my unborn child and I'll not have it under my roof for a second longer than necessary.'

Will stared back at him coldly before saying, 'Mrs King's fall was nothing to do with Charlie 'ere, I'm sure. She allus let him off his lead when she got to the lane that runs by our cottages an' he bounds on ahead of her. If anythin', yer should be thankin' him fer savin' her life.'

'How *dare* you come into my home and speak to me like that!' Henry thundered, but unperturbed Will stood his ground as the cook and Eve looked fearfully on. 'Give the mutt to me this *instant*. I'll take it outside and shoot it myself.'

'No, you'll not,' Will snapped, a muscle in his cheek twitching with anger. 'Charlie is a gentle creature, an' if you don't want 'im then I'll take 'im back 'ome wi' me. At least that way your poor missus will be able to come an' see 'im from time to time. If the poor soul survives, that is.'

And with that, he turned and banged back out into the cold night air, leaving Eve staring admiringly after him.

The master was fuming. 'Damn *peasant*!' he raged. It hadn't even crossed his mind to thank Will for his part in Opal's rescue. Then, to the women's relief, he turned on his heel and slammed away.

Eve sighed dreamily. 'Eeh, weren't Will just the most *'andsome* chap you ever saw? And brave an' all to stand up to the master the way he did.'

The cook gave a wry smile, sensing they might be seeing a sight more of young Will in the future if Eve's reaction to him was anything to go by, for if she wasn't very much mistaken her young helper was well and truly smitten!

Chapter Forty-Two

Opal was aware of someone groaning and whimpering, but it was some moments before she realised that it was herself as her eyes slowly blinked open. But it was too bright and the light was like burning needles stabbing and she quickly closed them again.

'Mrs King . . . Mrs King . . . can you hear me?'

A gentle voice made her try again, and as she narrowed her swollen eyes, a face swam blearily into focus. It was a man in a white coat, but where was she? She ached in every bone of her body, and when she tried to breathe it hurt so badly that she dared not move. And then it all came rushing back to her. The last thing she remembered was walking Charlie down to the canal when suddenly she had caught a glimpse of a dark-green cloak before someone had pushed her. But who would do such a thing to her?

'Mrs King, can you try to follow my finger with your eyes? Can you hear me?'

She tried hard to do as she was asked, but the pain in her head was so bad that she just wanted to sleep again.

'Wh-where am I?' Her voice came out as a croak and she felt her lips crack.

'Don't worry, you're quite safe. You're in hospital; you had a bad fall from the side of the quarry.'

'N-no . . . I didn't fall.' She tried to shake her head. 'I was pushed. Some . . . one pushed me.'

The doctor frowned as he glanced at the young nurse who was standing beside the bed.

'Let's just concentrate on getting you well again before we think about that,' he soothed, as the nurse stepped forward and gently held a glass of cool water to Opal's parched lips. She gulped at it greedily, which set her coughing and almost crying out with pain.

'I don't mind telling you, you had us worried for a while there,' the doctor went on as the nurse laid her head gently back on the pillows. 'We weren't sure if we were going to lose you, but now you're awake we can concentrate on getting you well again.'

Opal tried to move her hands and became aware that one of them was firmly strapped up. The other fell to her stomach and panic set in. It was soft and wobbly, so where was her baby?

'M-my baby? Please, where is it?' She gripped the doctor's hand with her one good one, tears rolling down her cheeks and smarting as they came into contact with the stitches.

Looking very sad the doctor shook his head. 'I'm afraid we couldn't save it. You had a little boy. He was born far too soon, but the shock of the fall would probably have killed him anyway. I'm so very sorry, Mrs King.'

'*No, no!*' Heedless of the pain it caused, Opal's head wagged from side to side. 'It can't be true. I want my baby. *Please . . .*'

She saw the doctor nod at the nurse, and suddenly she felt a sharp sting in her arm and within seconds the darkness was claiming her again and she welcomed it. Anything was better than having to face the heartbreak she was feeling.

Back at the house, Blanche Wood was humming to herself as she delivered the week's menus to the cook. Opal had been lying in hospital at death's door for four days, so Blanche felt it was highly unlikely she would wake, and that would suit her just fine. The timing couldn't have been better now that she was carrying Henry's child. With Opal gone, he was sure to make an honest woman of her, if only for the sake of the baby, and then at last she could assume what she had always considered should be her rightful place in the household. She had just left the kitchen when Henry appeared from his study and she asked innocently, 'Is there any change in the mistress?'

He shook his head, his expression dark. 'I haven't contacted the hospital as yet today, but there was no change last night when I called in and the doctor did say that the longer she remained unconscious, the less likely it would be that she would ever wake up. She'll probably just slip away in her sleep.'

Much as my son did, he thought bitterly, although he didn't voice it.

Blanche was tempted to ask him what his intentions towards her were now that she was with child, but he had been walking about like a bear with a sore head, so she decided it was probably wise to bide her time. Best to wait till the jumped-up bitch from Rapper's Hole was dead and gone before making her move.

'Is there anything I can get for you?' she simpered. She had waited on him hand and foot since the day of the accident – she wanted him to see how indispensable she was – but he merely waved her aside.

'No, nothing. I have to get to court now. Oh, and don't bother with a meal for me this evening. I shall be going straight out when I've finished.'

Disappointment clouded her face. With the upstart out of the way, she had been hoping to dine with him, but she kept her voice even as she forced a smile and answered, 'Very well.' She glanced about to make sure they were alone then, before whispering coyly, 'But just in case you should feel in need of a bit of company when you get in, I shall leave my bedroom door unlocked.'

He glared at her before snatching his hat and coat from the tall mahogany coat stand that stood next to the grand-father clock, and stormed out of the house, banging the door resoundingly behind him.

In the kitchen the mood was low. 'Do you reckon Mrs Wood might give me an hour off this afternoon so I can go to the hospital and see how the young mistress is?' Eve asked the cook. They had both been so worried about Opal that they had barely been able to concentrate on anything.

'You could ask; she'd have to be pretty heartless to refuse yer.' The cook paused in the act of kneading the dough and sighed. 'Though from what the master said, I don't hold out much hope fer the poor soul now. God bless 'er!'

'I'll go and ask her right now,' Eve decided and before she lost her nerve she hurried away.

She found Mrs Wood going through the household accounts, and as the woman glanced up Eve blurted, 'Please may I have an hour off this afternoon to go an' see the mistress, Mrs Wood?'

A refusal hovered on the woman's lips, but then she thought better of it. Henry hadn't really kept her properly informed of Opal's condition but Eve would when she got back, she was sure.

'Yes, of course you may.'

'Oh . . . thanks.' Eve looked vaguely surprised, before bobbing her knee and disappearing before the housekeeper could change her mind.

And so, just before four o'clock that afternoon, the official visiting time, Eve stood in a queue of visitors outside Opal's ward, clutching a rather bedraggled-looking bunch of flowers. She wasn't even sure if her young mistress would be awake to see them, but she hadn't liked to come empty-handed.

On the stroke of four, a fresh-faced young nurse appeared to admit them, and as Eve walked down the ward, her heart was in her throat, wondering what she would find. However, she was delighted to see that Opal was awake, at least, even though she looked as if she had been in a boxing ring with a heavyweight champion. An ugly scar ran down one side of her cheek and her lovely face was so badly cut and bruised that Eve almost didn't recognise her. But her delight at seeing her awake made her face glow.

Opal was propped up on pillows with one arm heavily strapped in a thick bandage, but at sight of Eve she managed a weak smile.

'Eeh, ma'am. Yer give us a right scare,' Eve told her, as she sat down on the chair at the side of the bed. 'We thought yer was a gonner fer sure fer a time back there . . . an me an' Cook, we're so sorry about the baby.'

Tears instantly started to roll down Opal's discoloured cheeks, and Eve could have bitten her tongue out as she reached to take the unbandaged hand lying limply on top of the bedspread. 'Oh, me an' me big mouth. Cook's allus tellin' me it'll get me hanged one o' these days! But how are you? Have they given you any idea how long yer might be in 'ere?'

Opal shook her head. 'Not yet, although they've said it could be a while.' She really didn't care. In truth, she didn't much care about anything at the minute. All she could think about was the beautiful baby boy she would never hold in her arms.

'It were a rum do, you slippin' like that,' Eve said sadly.

Opal shook her head. 'But I *didn't* slip.' Her eyes were two great pools of misery in her bruised and battered face. 'Someone pushed me, Eve, I know it!'

Eve looked shocked, but before she could comment, someone stopped at the end of the bed and, glancing up, Opal saw Emma Dawson-Myers standing there, looking very pretty in a matching bonnet and cloak. She recognised her from her visits to the house.

She smiled at Eve. Then, rounding the bed she placed a gentle kiss on Opal's swollen cheek. 'Oh, my poor dear, Peter and I were so upset when we heard what had happened.' Emma's eyes were kindly, which made Opal cry all the harder. 'Is there anything at all I can do for you?'

Opal shook her head. She wanted to say, *Yes you can give me my baby back*, but the words stayed trapped inside as Eve stood up to give Emma her seat.

'I, er . . . ought to be gettin' back now,' she mumbled. 'But we'll look forward to havin' you back home again, ma'am. Bye fer now.'

Opal smiled at her – a smile that didn't quite reach her eyes – and Eve's kindly heart went out to her. 'Thank you, Eve. Goodbye for now.'

Eve set off down the ward, her mind whirling. What could the mistress have meant? *Someone pushed her!* The poor soul was clearly in a bad way, so perhaps her mind was playing tricks on her? Eve could only assume so, after all, Opal was one of the kindest people she had ever met, so who would want to hurt her?

'How was she?' Cook asked the second Eve stepped through the door.

'Well, she's awake at least, but I think she's a bit confused.' As Eve removed her bonnet, she went on to tell her what Opal had said.

Cook frowned. 'The only one I can think of who don't like the mistress is Esther Partridge,' she said thoughtfully. 'An' come to think of it, she were the one who told the master she'd seen the missus by the quarry. You don't think she could 'ave had anythin' to do wi' it, do yer?'

Eve shrugged as she took her coat off. 'I doubt we'll ever know now. But one thing's for sure, the way the master is carryin' on he'll never forgive her fer losin' that baby.'

'Hm, I think yer could be right,' Cook agreed, turning to fill the kettle as Eve fetched cups and saucers.

It was not until the following day that Henry bothered to call in to the hospital again, and for the first time since the accident, he found his wife awake.

Her eyes filled with tears as he stared at her with contempt. With her ugly scar and disfigured face, she looked nothing at all like the lovely young woman he had married.

'So . . . you're awake then?' he commented rather unnecessarily, and his face told her all she needed to know. He wished that she wasn't.

'Y-yes I . . . Oh, Henry, I'm *so* sorry about the baby. I know how much you wanted a son. But believe me I am hurting too and—'

He held his hand up to silence her, his eyes flashing fire. 'Had you listened to me this need never have happened,' he spat through gritted teeth. 'Didn't I tell you to avoid walking that way? But would you listen? No, of course not. You knew best!'

'Henry . . . please . . . you don't understand,' she cried. 'I didn't fall, I was pushed. I saw—'

'Pah!' His raised voice made the patients in the nearby beds glance towards them in alarm. 'Just send word when they are going to discharge you and I will send a carriage for you!'

And with that he walked away leaving Opal to stare help-lessly after him. She knew then that their marriage was over. Henry was never going to forgive her for the loss of their son. At the same instant a face flashed into her mind and she gasped. The dark-green cloak! *Esther Partridge.* It must have been her who had pushed her – who else could it be? She had been a thorn in Opal's side since the day Henry had proposed to her. Not that she could do anything about it – she had no proof. Once again tears coursed down her face and she sobbed for the child she had lost as if her heart would break.

Chapter Forty-Three

Henry returned home late that evening to find Blanche waiting for him.

'So, she's awake?' she said tartly, her hands folded primly at her waist.

He nodded as he threw his hat in the direction of the coat stand. It was clear that Blanche was no more pleased with the news than he was. She had been hoping that Opal would never wake up, which would leave the way clear for herself and her unborn child, but now she would have to rethink what they were going to do.

After following him into the drawing room, she watched as he poured a large measure of whisky into a glass and swallowed it back in one gulp.

'What are we going to do about *this* child then?' Her hand rested on her stomach. 'This is yours just as much as the other one was, and I can assure you I shall take far better care of it than that hussy did of hers.'

Henry suddenly looked weary as he ran his hand across his eyes. 'Do we *have* to do this this evening?' he said. 'It's been quite a long day.'

But Blanche was not going to be put off so easily. Her hopes of becoming his wife had died when Opal woke up, but she was determined to make sure that he shouldered responsibility for their child.

'I'm afraid we *do* have to do it today,' she told him calmly and he looked at her in amazement. She had always been so pliable but now her eyes were cold.

'It's obvious that I shan't be able to remain here,' she went on. 'This is not a condition that I will be able to hide for much longer and so I have already started to look for a small cottage. I shall have the child there and you can visit us when you can.'

Henry's eyes stretched wide. '*What?* You are telling me that you want me to establish you somewhere as my mistress and keep you both?'

'That is *exactly* what I am saying.' Her nostrils flared as she leaned towards him. 'At least that way we can continue to be discreet. What is the alternative? After all, you wouldn't wish it to become common knowledge that you had put me in the family way and abandoned me and your unborn child, surely? Think of what that would do for your reputation!'

Henry was astounded. She had clearly given this a lot of thought, and the worst of it was he knew she was right. It was acceptable for a man of his social standing to have a mistress tucked away somewhere, but he would be classed as a cad if he were to turn her out with nowhere to go and not a penny to her name.

'In that case I suppose you had better continue to look for somewhere,' he answered.

She smiled. It wasn't the outcome she had hoped for, but at least this way she and her baby would be sure of a comfortable life with no money worries.

'I shall begin to make enquiries immediately.' She inclined her head and sailed out of the room, leaving Henry feeling as if bad luck was coming at him from all directions. Once again he was to become a father, but to a child he could never lay claim to, for it would be a bastard. Life seemed very unfair.

Over the next two weeks, Opal slowly improved. The bruises faded to pale yellows and lilacs and the stitches were taken out of her cheek, although they left an ugly scar. Her broken arm and ribs still pained her, but physically she grew a little stronger with each day that passed. Mentally, though, it was another story, and sometimes she wondered how she would ever get over the loss of her child. She had started to have nightmares in which she saw Esther creeping up behind her and shoving her over the edge of the quarry. She would wake in a lather of sweat and tangled damp sheets, and the nurses would rush to give her laudanum.

But at last the day came when the doctors decided that she was well enough to go home.

'Can you arrange for someone to come and pick you up tomorrow?' one of them asked her.

Opal nodded, not at all sure that she wanted to go home – if she could call it that. The only visitors she had had were the cook, Eve and Emma. Henry had not so much as shown his face once since the evening he had blamed her for the baby's death.

'Yes,' she answered dully.

When Eve visited later that afternoon, Opal asked her to relay the news to Henry. 'Of course, I'll let the master know,' the good-natured girl told her. 'But you'll never guess what – Mrs Wood has left.'

Opal raised her eyebrow. 'What do you mean, left?'

'Just that.' Eve spread her hands. 'She told us a couple of days ago that she was going to live in a little cottage in Church Lane in Weddington and this morning a cart came and she were off wi'out so much as a backward glance.'

'Really?' If truth be told Opal wasn't sorry; Mrs Wood had made her feel like an interloper in her own home and Opal wouldn't miss her. 'But she's a little young to be retiring, isn't she? Or has she taken up another position?'

'I ain't got no idea.' Eve grinned. 'But don't you get worryin' about it. We'll muddle along just fine.'

Opal nodded.

'Anyway, I'd best get home an' get everythin' ready for you.' Eve could see that her young mistress was getting tired. 'An' I want to call in an' see me family on the way home, so if you're sure there's nothin' you need, I'll be off.'

'Yes, of course, thank you.' As Opal watched the maid walk away, she was envious of her. Eve's parents and her younger brother lived in a small two-up, two-down house in Stratford Street, and although they weren't rich they were close, and Eve adored them. Opal blinked back tears as she thought back to the time when she too had had a family, but she had no one now and suddenly the loneliness threatened to choke her.

The next day Eve arrived at the hospital, with a valise containing Opal's clothes, to take her home. The clothes she had been wearing on the day she fell were ruined beyond repair, and anyway they would have been far too big for her now. Eve pulled the curtains about the bed to offer them some privacy, but with Opal's injured arm and ribs it took some time to help her struggle into her clothes and by the time they were done Opal was exhausted.

'Come on, ma'am. Let's get you home an' tucked up safe in yer own bed, eh?' Eve said kindly, as she tied the ribbons of Opal's bonnet beneath her chin. 'The carriage is just outside, so lean on me.'

On the way out, Opal thanked the sister and the nurses for their care, and soon after she sighed as she settled into the seat in the carriage. In a strange way, she almost didn't want to go home. She had felt safe in hospital, but now she was nervous about facing Henry again after his outburst. He clearly blamed her for the loss of the baby, and she knew she would be wasting her time if she tried to convince him that someone had pushed her. Even so, she knew that she had to go home sometime so she decided it was just as well to get it over and done with. Suddenly, she thought of Charlie and guilt stabbed at her.

'Charlie.' She gripped Eve's arm. 'He is safe at home, isn't he?'

Eve licked her lips and avoided her arms. 'Actually, he isn't at home . . . but he is safe,' she quickly assured her as she saw the fear in her young mistress's face. 'The master got it into his head that it was his fault you had the accident, and he wouldn't have him back in the house. So that nice young man, Will, took him back to live with him an' his family at the cottages. I saw him yesterday, as it happens, and he asked me to tell you that you can go and see Charlie an' take him for a walk whenever you want.'

Opal noticed the blush on her cheeks. If she wasn't very much mistaken, Eve was quite taken with the young man. She herself now had something else to thank him for. He had saved her life and given a home to her beloved pet. So, as soon as she was able, she would make sure he was reimbursed for his trouble; it was the least she could do. But oh, she would miss Charlie so very much! He had become her confidant and faithful companion and it was hard to imagine her life without him.

Cook was hovering by the front door when they got home, and she rushed out to meet them. 'Oh, ma'am, it's so good to 'ave you home,' she greeted Opal. 'We've missed yer somethin' terrible, but come on in out o' the cold. Eve got a lovely fire goin' for you in the drawin' room afore she left to fetch you home an' I've got a nice tray o' tea just waitin' to be poured, an' some o' yer favourite shortbread biscuits.'

Opal gave her a wobbly smile, shocked at how weak she still felt as Eve helped her up the steps and into the hallway.

'That's really kind of you, but I'm not very hungry at present,' Opal told the cook.

Cook frowned as she waved a plump finger at her. 'Well, you need to get your strength back now. Look at you – yer not as far through as a line prop so try just one at least for me.' Without waiting for a reply she left to arrange the tea tray.

'Yes, an' when you've had that, we'll get you tucked into bed. The doctor at the hospital said yer not to overdo it and yer need to rest.'

Twenty minutes later, after Cook had stood over her while she nibbled at a biscuit, Eve helped her upstairs. The second she set foot in the bedroom, she knew something was different. Henry's cologne and hairbrush were absent from the dressing table and as Eve saw her looking towards it, she told her in a small voice, 'The master's had us move all his stuff into the other bedroom. No doubt he wants you to rest.'

Not much caring, Opal nodded.

'Now I've brought you some books and magazines to read,' Eve told her kindly once Opal was settled against the pillows. 'And I'll bring you yer lunch up on a tray. Cook 'as made yer some chicken soup. She reckons it's good for convalescents, so hopefully we'll have you back to your old self in no time.'

Opal doubted that very much. How could she ever be her old self again when she had lost everybody in the world that she loved? They were all gone: her parents, her brothers, Susie, her baby. Even her beloved pet was gone now. As she stared up at the ceiling tears rolled down her cheeks until, eventually, she slept.

It was the following day before she saw Henry.

'So, you're back,' he said curtly as he entered her room and stared down at her. 'How are you?'

She shrugged. 'As well as can be expected, but hopefully I shall be up and about again soon.' And then thinking of something she said, 'Eve tells me that Mrs Wood has left? That was rather unexpected, wasn't it?'

Looking decidedly uncomfortable, he ran his finger around his collar as if it was suddenly too tight for him. 'It was her choice,' he muttered, and then his manner became stern again as he told her, 'I dare say you will have noticed I have had my things moved into the other room. I thought it would give you more of a chance to recover and rest if you were alone.'

Opal could have answered that she had felt alone ever since the day she had set foot in the door, but she merely nodded.

'Well, should you need anything, I'm sure Eve or Cook will attend to you. I shall be away for a few days. I'm going to stay with Matthew in London. I have some business to attend to there. Expect me when you see me.'

Seeing the loathing and disgust in his eyes as he stared down at her scarred face, she merely nodded, and without another word, he turned and left abruptly. He didn't seem to have any regard for her feelings at all. Suddenly the years stretched ahead of her, lonely and empty, and she wondered how she would bear it.

The next day, she had two visitors. Mrs King came to see her in the morning and Emma called in with a basket of fruit and a wonderful bouquet of flowers in the afternoon.

It was Emma who told her, 'I know what has happened to you is dreadful, Opal, but you must try to get over it and go on now. You're young, and there'll be time to have lots more babies. Not that I'm saying you shouldn't grieve over the one you have just lost, of course, but accidents happen.'

It was on the tip of Opal's tongue to tell her her suspicions about Esther Partridge pushing her, but at the last moment she decided against it. What would be the point? She had absolutely no proof and if she was accused, Esther would obviously deny it and it would simply be her word against Opal's. She had no doubt whatsoever who everyone would believe and so she kept it to herself, a terrible secret that would haunt her for years to come.

Chapter Forty-Four

November 1859

Clutching an enormous bunch of flowers, the handsome young man standing on the steps of the smart house in Mayfair nervously fiddled with his cravat – then, straightening his back and lifting his hand, he pulled at the rope hanging to the side of the door, sounding a bell inside. Almost instantly a young maid answered the door and smiled a greeting.

'Good evening, sir. The family are expecting you and asked me to show you to the drawing room. Would you like me to take your hat and coat first?'

'Yes, thank you.' He handed the girl his garments and followed her along the hallway, admiring the many works of art that hung on the walls on his way.

The girl stopped at a door and opened it before announcing, 'Your visitor, sir.'

'Thank you, Polly, and, Charlie, do come in, lad. It's so good to see you. Unfortunately Juliet isn't in – she'll be sorry she missed you.' Phineas Morgan strode across the room to shake Charlie's hand warmly, before saying, 'You're looking very well and making quite a name for yourself in the jewellery trade I hear.'

'I can't complain, sir. The shop is doing very well.' Charlie answered as he handed Isabella the flowers, which she thanked him for warmly. Finally, he allowed himself to look at Francesca, who was sitting beside her mother on a velvet, gilt-edged sofa, and his heart began to thump. She was as beautiful as he remembered, in fact probably more so.

'Don't I know it?' Phineas chuckled. 'My ladies here have spent a fortune there already; I'm surprised they've never run in to you there. Now, what would you like to drink?'

'A whisky, please,' he said distractedly, unable to tear his eyes away from Francesca, who was smiling at him, love shining in her eyes. He felt a surge of relief that it seemed her feelings for him had not changed.

Although they had exchanged letters, Charlie had forced himself to stay away from her since he had arrived back in England just over two years ago. It had been hard, and she had not been happy about it, but he had been determined to prove that he was worthy of her – to himself as well as to Francesca's father. But he was still an ex-convict, so he knew that even the success he had achieved might not be enough to convince Phineas Morgan that he was good enough for his daughter. Still, not many men in Phineas's position in society would even receive a man like him, so he was grateful for his warm welcome.

'Come along then, we're all dying to know what you've been up to since we last saw you,' Phineas encouraged as he topped up his glass.

'Well . . .' Charlie scratched his head and decided to start at the beginning. 'As you're aware when you first very kindly granted me a pardon, I went off gold prospecting. We had a measure of success but certainly not enough to make us rich. Then we met up with an Aborigine man, Nullah, and he suggested we should move to Lightning Ridge and try our hands at opal hunting. It was a risk as I didn't even know what I was looking for, and for the first few months we had no luck at all. In fact, I was all for throwing in the towel and heading for home – but then all of a sudden, we struck lucky, and from then on we did really well.'

He paused and smiled, feeling proud at the rapt expressions of the faces around him.

'Eventually I booked a cabin on a ship home and came back with bags of raw opals. When I arrived in London, I managed to sell half of them at a price far beyond what I had expected, and so I bought the shop and a small house in Knightsbridge. I employed a jeweller to cut and polish the remaining gems and set them into rings and pendants. I never dreamed they would be so popular, which is all thanks to Michael, my jeweller. I started to invest in other gems, mainly emeralds, diamonds, rubies and sapphires, and it's all gone on from there. In fact, I'm thinking of buying a second shop, so all in all I've been very lucky indeed.'

'From what you've told me, luck doesn't come into it,' Phineas said solemnly. 'It sounds like you've worked damned hard for everything you've got, so you deserve it.'

At that moment the young maid came to the door to inform them that dinner was ready, and Isabella took Phineas's arm, leaving Francesca to trail behind with Charlie.

They started with a thick lobster soup, followed by a slow-roasted shank of lamb and an assortment of potatoes and vegetables. For dessert there was a raspberry soufflé that melted in their mouths. Everything was delicious and the atmosphere was light as they chatted about Charlie's adventures. Phineas noticed that his beautiful daughter hung on every word Charlie said, and he exchanged a knowing glance with his wife.

During the years they had been back in London Francesca had had more than her fair share of would-be suitors, but she had shown no interest in any of them, and now it became obvious why. She and Charlie had grown close during their time in Australia, but they had been little more than children then. Now Charlie had grown from a misguided youth into a handsome, successful young man, and Francesca into a very lovely young woman, and it was clear they could hardly keep their eyes off each other. This left Phineas in something of a dilemma. Francesca had been brought up as a lady, whereas Charlie was from working stock and an ex-convict into the bargain.

The meal was followed by coffee after which Phineas suggested, 'Why don't we go and enjoy a glass of port and a cigar in my study and leave the ladies to chat, Charlie?'

Charlie inclined his head. 'Thank you, sir. That would be most pleasant.'

He's good-mannered, I'll give him that, Phineas thought as they left the room, and soon they were seated in the comfortable old leather wing chairs set either side of the fireplace in his study, with glasses of port in their hands.

They chatted of this and that for a moment until Phineas asked, 'So, have you done anything about tracking down the sisters you used to talk about since you got back, Charlie?'

Charlie's face clouded as he stared into the flames. 'I've been back to Nuneaton on a number of occasions to look for them, but with no success as yet, sir. It's as if they've

417

vanished off the face of the earth. But I'll keep trying. They're bound to be there somewhere.'

'Hm.' Phineas swirled the amber-coloured liquid round his glass, as he eyed the young man thoughtfully. 'Actually, I was surprised when Francesca told me you had chosen to stay in London when you first came back. I thought you were planning to return to your hometown.'

Charlie looked decidedly uncomfortable and in that moment, Phineas knew that his suspicions had been correct. His mind raced. Both he and his wife had always hoped for a good marriage for both their daughters. Could he really countenance Francesca marrying an ex-convict?

But then, his eldest daughter was much like her mother, in that she had a mind of her own. Who knew what she might do if he prevented her from seeing Charlie? And after all, Charlie was decent and hard-working, and who else apart from him and his family would ever know that he was an ex-convict? And so he decided to put him out of his misery.

'Would I be right in thinking that you have feelings for my daughter, Charlie?'

Charlie flushed. 'Yes, sir . . . you would. I always have, since the first moment I set eyes on her. Oh, I know I don't have a past to be proud of but I am trying hard now. My house is modest and nowhere near as big as this, but I own it and once I've acquired the new shop, I hope to buy a bigger and better one. All I can tell you is if you would allow me to marry your daughter, I would work my fingers to the bone to ensure that she never wanted for anything! Because you see . . . I love Francesca, with all my heart, and if I can't have her I doubt very much that I will ever wed!'

418

It was such an impassioned speech that Phineas blinked as he stared down into his glass. He believed every word the young man had said and it was clear Francesca felt the same about him.

Eventually he took a deep breath and said quietly, 'In that case, you have my permission to court her.'

'I have?' Charlie's face was incredulous as a wide grin spread from ear to ear, and the next minute, he had taken Phineas's hand and was shaking it up and down so hard that he feared it might drop off. Charlie fished in his pocket then and producing a small box he snapped the lid to show the contents to Phineas.

'Do I have your permission to give her this? It's one of the best I brought back from Lightning Ridge.'

Phineas stared down at a beautiful pendant suspended on a delicate gold chain; the centre of the pendant boasted a black opal the like of which he had never seen before. The stone was set in an ornate filigree gold mount and was a fine example of just how clever the jeweller Charlie employed really was. Although the stone was black, it caught and reflected the light in all the colours of the rainbow and Phineas could have stared at it for hours; it was mesmerising.

'It's quite beautiful,' he breathed truthfully. 'She'll love it. What woman wouldn't?'

'I had three commissioned,' Charlie told him. 'One for Francesca and one each for Opal and Susie . . . when I find them again. Thank you, sir.'

Phineas clapped him on the shoulder. 'Come on, let's put the women out of their misery. I'm sure they're both aware that something is afoot, and I want to hear Francesca's opinion on the opal.'

With a spring in his step, Charlie followed him back to the drawing room where the women were enjoying a glass of sherry, and the minute the door opened Francesca's eyes went anxiously to Charlie. Seeing his smile, her face relaxed into a beaming grin.

'Isabella, I have just given this young man permission to court our daughter,' he informed his wife. 'I hope that meets with your approval?'

'Very much so,' Isabella replied with a smile, as Francesca skipped across the room to slip her arm through Charlie's. 'And now I know why all my matchmaking has been in vain. You were waiting for Charlie all the time, my love, were you not?'

'I'm afraid I was.' Francesca blushed prettily.

Charlie handed her her gift, and as her eyes fell on the black opal, she cried out with delight. 'Oh Charlie, it's just *wonderful*. Did you dig this one out yourself?'

'I certainly did,' he told her, as he fastened the chain about her neck. 'Although of course they look nothing like this when they come out of the earth. It takes the skill of a good jeweller to cut and polish them and bring them to life.'

'I shall treasure it for always,' she promised him as she gazed adoringly up into his eyes.

At that moment, Isabella rose and taking her husband's arm she suggested, 'Why don't we give these two lovebirds a little privacy, my love?'

And then they were alone at last, and it was as if they were the only two left in the world.

'Your father has given me permission to court you, but I also intimated that, when the time was right, I could ask you to marry me, and he didn't object.'

'So, what are you waiting for?' Her eyes were sparkling and he felt like the luckiest man on earth.

'I'm waiting because I don't wish to appear disrespectful.'

'I see – but don't wait too long, will you?' she teased and as their lips joined they lost track of time.

From that moment on, Charlie became a regular visitor to the house, and as Christmas rushed towards them, he was delighted when he was asked to join the family for Christmas Day. But first he decided to fit in yet another trip to his hometown, for surely someone somewhere would know what had become of Opal and Susie.

He left four days before Christmas Day, promising Francesca that he would only stay away for one night; but when he returned, she saw immediately by his face that his trip had been unsuccessful yet again, and her tender heart went out to him. It was clear that Charlie and his sisters had been very close. He had spoken about them and his family often back in Australia and she knew how much he missed and worried about them.

'Never mind, darling.' She hugged him to her. 'You can try again in the New Year and hopefully next time you'll be successful. For now, you must try to look forward to us spending out first Christmas together.'

Charlie nodded. Deep inside, his hopes of ever finding Opal or Susie were fading but even so Francesca's words warmed him. For the first time since being transported, he would be spending Christmas with a family again. And this would be a very special Christmas. He smiled as he thought of the emerald and diamond ring that he had commissioned his jeweller to make especially for Francesca. On Christmas Day he was going to ask her to marry him.

Chapter Forty-Five

'All ready, are you, dear?' Opal's friend Emma Dawson-Myres asked, as she breezed into the Kings' drawing room early in the New Year. Seeing Opal sitting with her head bowed she sighed before crossing to her and lifting her chin.

'Not *another* shiner? Let me guess, you walked into a door again,' she said drily.

Opal gulped. There would be no point in lying. She and Emma had become close friends, and Emma could read her like a book.

'So what did you do . . . or not do this time?'

'He was drunk again,' Opal said sheepishly. 'When he came in late, I tried to help him up to his room and he lashed out.' She had arranged to go with Emma to decorate the church with flowers for a wedding that was taking place there the following day, but there was no way she wanted to be seen out in public now.

'Oh Opal, why don't you just leave him?' Emma scowled at her.

'And where would I go?' Opal smiled at her, a sad smile that tore at her friend's heart.

Seeing her friend's pitying expression, Opal had to blink back the tears. She had had to endure so much humiliation over the long, lonely years since her terrible accident; sometimes she wished that she had died that day, because surely it would be better than living with a man who despised her and who seemed to delight in punishing her.

Soon after she left the hospital, gossip had spread about the town about Henry being the father to his ex-housekeeper's unborn baby; and if the times he was seen visiting her in Weddington were anything to go by, it was true. Sometimes he would not come home for two and three days at a time. But then Blanche gave birth to a baby girl, and Henry's interest in her seemed to wane.

Since then, Henry had been disappearing to Birmingham on business, again. Opal was quite certain he had another woman – or women – tucked away there. She knew, too, that he had started gambling and drinking heavily, but while he left her alone, she could bear it.

In fact, it was much better for her when he didn't come home.

For almost a year after the accident she had lived reclusively, until Emma had put her foot down and started to encourage her to go out and about again. Now Opal helped Emma to raise money for the poor and was involved with a number of charities.

Surprisingly, Mrs King had also been very supportive. Secretly she felt guilty for allowing Opal to marry her son in the first place, because as much as she loved him, she was painfully aware of his faults and felt that Opal deserved better.

Now Emma scowled at her. 'Oh well, I suppose I shall have to do the flowers on my own,' she said quietly. She reached out and took her hand. 'But you must realise you can't go on like this? You're still young and have your whole life ahead of you, and I hate to see you this way.'

Opal gave a wry smile. 'Don't worry about me. I can hold my own with him. He doesn't get all his own way, and thanks to you I get out of the house often enough. If it were left up to Henry, I would never be seen outside again. Although . . .' She faltered, wondering if she should tell Emma her concerns, but then it all came pouring out. 'I wonder if Henry isn't having financial problems. Cook has been getting demands from all over the place for payment from the butcher, the coalman and his tailor, to name but a few. But every time I mention it to him, he flies into a rage.'

'Really?' Emma frowned, but after glancing at the clock she told her, 'I'm sorry but I really should get on – but don't worry, I'll pop in again tomorrow, and in the meantime get some raw steak on that eye.'

Opal gave a weak smile and saw her to the door, just as Eve appeared from the kitchen with a tea tray. She and Will Green had married the year before, much to Opal's delight, and they were now happily living in the rooms above the stables. Their marriage had coincided with the retirement of Henry's groom, and Will had taken his place and loved his new job. It was so much nicer than working down the pit. Eve had blossomed too and marriage clearly suited her.

Opal's only regret was that Henry had forbidden her from attending the wedding. Still, Opal loved to hear Eve chatter on about her parents and her younger brother, and she envied them their closeness. They reminded her of the family she had once had.

Now Eve placed the tray down on a small table in the dining room, and frowned as she examined Opal's eye.

'That husband o' yours is nowt but a bully,' she stated emphatically. 'Only a coward hits a woman an' he'll come to a sticky end the way he's carryin' on, you just mark my words.'

Opal shrugged as she poured the tea. She and Eve had a good relationship, and having someone there who was close to her own age gave Opal comfort. They were friends now rather than mistress and maid – apart from when Henry was there, and then they had to make sure that they were not overly familiar with each other; if he knew just how friendly she and Eve were, he would no doubt dismiss her.

'So why don't yer go fer a walk an' see Will's mum an' Charlie the dog?' Eve suggested. 'A bit o' fresh air would do yer good.'

'I might do that after lunch.'

Opal visited Mrs Green often. Charlie was getting old now and was not as nimble as he used to be, but Opal still loved him dearly and never went without a juicy bone and some treats for him. Mrs Green had given him a loving home and Opal would never be able to thank her enough for that, but she still felt resentful towards Henry for blaming the dog for the accident. The glimpse of the green cloak she had seen before the fall still haunted her. She had never tried to follow it up, but she still firmly believed that it was Esther Partridge who had pushed her. Luckily, though, as she no longer went to any social gatherings, she had not seen her since before her accident.

Later that afternoon, she set off for a walk armed with a basketful of treats for Charlie and some from Cook for Mrs Green and they spent a pleasant afternoon together. More than once, Opal noticed Will's mother glancing at her bruised eye, but she tactfully didn't mention it. It was only as she made her way home in the darkening afternoon that the loneliness set in again as she faced yet another solitary night.

Henry was home for dinner that evening, but clearly not in the mood to talk, and as soon as the meal was over, he left the table telling Opal abruptly that he would be out for the night.

After he had gone, Opal read for a while and then decided on an early night. The walk in the fresh air had tired her and almost before her head hit the pillow she was fast asleep.

A pounding on the front door in the early hours of the morning startled her awake. It occurred to her that there was no one to hear it apart from herself. Eve now slept in the rooms above the stable with her husband, and Cook was going deaf. Wondering who it might be at such an hour, Opal struggled into her dressing robe and, after hastily lighting an oil lamp, she groggily made her way downstairs.

When she opened the door, she was shocked to find two policemen standing on the step.

'We would like to speak with Mrs King,' the taller of the two said, obviously mistaking her for a maid.

'Oh, that's me. Won't you come in?' Opal stood aside for them to enter, and once they had both removed their helmets, they glanced at each other uncomfortably.

The taller one cleared his throat and told her, 'I'm afraid we have very bad news for you, Mrs King. Might we go somewhere where you may sit down?'

Opal blinked in confusion as she nodded, and led them into the drawing room where he went on, 'Are you the wife of Mr Henry King?'

'Yes, yes I am. Why? What has happened?'

'I'm afraid there was an incident some hours ago involving your husband.'

'An incident? What sort of an incident? Is Henry hurt?'

'Not exactly . . . I'm afraid it's worse than that.' The constable rolled his helmet in his hands nervously. 'He, er . . . was visiting a house of ill repute in Birmingham and there was a stabbing. I'm sorry, Mrs King, but I'm afraid your husband has died.'

Opal paled to the colour of lint and slammed the oil lamp down on the console table. 'A . . . a house of *ill repute* you say? . . . A stabbing? . . . But, there must be some mistake.'

He shook his head. 'I'm afraid there's no mistake. Your husband has been clearly identified by documents about his person and a number of people.'

'You mean . . . he was at a *brothel*!'

'I'm afraid so. I'm sorry, ma'am, but it appears that your husband was a regular visitor there.'

Opal's head wagged from side to side in disbelief. She had always suspected that Henry had other women, but *paying for them*!

Her legs suddenly started to fold, and the young constable took her elbow and guided her to the nearest chair, asking, 'Is there anyone we can get to be with you?'

She croakily told him about Eve in the rooms above the stables, and while the other officer stayed with her, he shot off to fetch her.

'Oh Opal, I can't *believe* it. But how did Henry get stabbed?' Eve said, when she appeared in her dressing robe with Will close behind her. He had pulled his shirt and trousers on, but his braces were dangling about his backside and his hair was on end.

'We don't know the details yet, but it looks like a fight broke out and Mr King was stabbed.'

'Well, all I can say is good riddance to bad rubbish, the cruel old bastard!' Eve said heatedly, as she placed a comforting arm about Opal's shaking shoulders. All Opal could do was sit there as if she had been turned to stone as she tried to take it in.

'So, what will happen now?' Eve asked.

The constable shrugged. 'His body is at a morgue in Birmingham, but you will be able to have it brought home for burial.'

'Huh! If it were up to me it could stay where it is to rot!' Eve exploded – but then remembering Opal, she gave her shoulders a reassuring squeeze and, as her mistress was in no state to talk, she addressed the two officers. 'Anyway, thank you for letting us know. We'll be in touch presently with arrangements . . .'

The policemen took their leave and Eve led Opal into the drawing room, while Will bolted off to put the kettle on.

His mother was a great believer in hot, sweet tea being good for shock, and poor Opal certainly looked like she could do with some at the minute.

Opal sat rocking backwards and forwards for some time as Eve raked the fire back into life and threw on some more coal.

Finally, as Will came into the room with a loaded tea tray, Opal said quietly, 'We must let his mother know. But not until the morning. I don't want to distress her any more than I have to. She's going to be heartbroken and this is going to be hard for her.'

'I'll set off first thing and bring her back here,' Will volunteered, and Opal nodded numbly. The news had shaken her to the core, but she knew it would affect Mrs King even more badly. 'But what shall I tell her?'

'The truth. There is no way we'll be able to keep this quiet; I've no doubt it will be splashed all across the newspapers in no time.'

'You're probably right.' Will clumsily poured the tea, splashing almost as much into the saucers as went into the cups, and they sat staring at the window until the dawn broke.

Poor Mrs King took the news as badly as Opal had feared she would, and for the first time in all the years since she had known her, Opal watched her weep brokenly. It was all the harder for Opal to witness because Mrs King was not a woman who showed her feelings easily.

'I'm so sorry I ever allowed you to marry him,' she said brokenly as she stared in horror at Opal's bruised face.

'You weren't to know that we wouldn't suit,' Opal told her kindly. She felt that she was just as much to blame, for she had not loved Henry when she married him. She had hoped that love would grow in time, but it hadn't happened – and when Henry had begun to show his true colours, any respect or fondness she had felt for him had withered and died. So she couldn't be a hypocrite and pretend that she would miss him now. Even so, Opal felt guilty for not shedding a tear. But now she was faced with a funeral to arrange – she owed him that much at least.

And so a few days later, Henry's body was brought back to his hometown and placed in a chapel of rest at the local undertaker – Opal couldn't face having him in the house again. She just wanted to lay him to rest and put this whole sorry chapter of her life far behind her.

Chapter Forty-Six

The funeral was arranged as quickly as possible. It was to be a very small service as they were not expecting anyone else to attend – even Esther Partridge had not bothered to send her sympathies to his mother – because only days before, the news of Henry's death and how it had come about had been splashed across the newspapers.

The morning dawned dismal and drizzly. It had briefly snowed the day before, and now the rain had turned what had settled to slush and it was dangerously slippery underfoot. Henry's coffin was taken straight to the church from the undertaker, and there was to be no gathering afterwards. As the cook had pointed out, 'Why go to the bother? There's not many as'll bother comin' anyway, now that they know how 'e died.'

And so Mrs King, Opal, Cook, Will and Eve set off for the service, which at Opal's request was as short as the vicar could make it. It seemed they had barely entered the church before they were on their way back out again, following the pall-bearers to the grave.

The only wreath was from his mother. Opal had not been able to bring herself to order one, and as they stood at the side of the gaping hole, watching Henry being lowered into it, there was nothing to be heard save the sound of the rain driving on the coffin lid. The vicar performed the rest of the service as quickly as possible, and soon they turned and made for the carriage that was waiting outside the lychgate for them.

'I . . . I'm so sorry the service was so poorly attended,' Opal faltered to Mrs King. Henry had been her only child, and for all his faults, she was aware that his mother had loved him.

The old woman shook her head. 'Don't be; he deserved nothing more.' Her face was set, and Opal could only imagine how heartbroken she must be feeling.

They headed back to the house with Henry's solicitor, who had been one of the few present at the service, following on behind to read Henry's will to his widow.

'At least he will have left you well provided for,' Mrs King commented as they rattled through the streets. 'That's something, I suppose, after all the humiliation he has caused you.'

On entering the house, Cook shot off to the kitchen to put the kettle on, as Mrs King hovered in the hallway, saying, 'I suppose I should be getting home now.'

'Oh no, please stay for the reading of the will,' Opal urged, feeling that she needed someone with her. The old woman nodded obligingly, and headed for the drawing room as Eve admitted Mr Cane the solicitor.

Presently, as Mr Cane took the documents he needed from his bag, they sat sipping hot tea and slowly life returned to their frozen limbs.

'Mrs King . . .' The man looked decidedly uncomfortable as he glanced at Opal. 'May I offer my condolences on your loss before we begin?'

The older Mrs King waved her hand at him. 'Oh, just get on with it, man. In this case, there are no condolences necessary. He got what he deserved, so let's get this over with. My daughter-in-law has gone through quite enough as it is! I have no doubt my son will be warming his backside in hell by now!'

'Er . . . yes, quite.' He coughed and began. 'This is the last will and testimony of Henry . . .' His voice droned on, although Opal barely took in a word of what he was saying, until she heard Mrs King gasp.

'*What* did you just say? Could you kindly repeat it!'

'I said that unfortunately I have discovered that Mr King had been taking equity out of the house for some time. In fact, there is nothing left in the house whatsoever. Of course, the furniture, pictures and silverware will have some value, but I'm afraid once they are sold, they will barely cover his debts.'

'*What debts?*' Mrs King demanded, as Opal's mouth fell open.

'It seems that Mr King had run up quite considerable gambling debts which will need to be paid . . .' The man's voice trailed away miserably, as Mrs King and Opal looked at each other in horror.

The old lady found her voice first and she ground out, 'You mean to tell me he has left Opal with no home?'

'I'm afraid so,' he mumbled, keeping his eyes downcast.

'But what will happen to the staff?' Opal said worriedly.

Mrs King was so angry she looked as if she was about to explode. 'The three of them can come and live with me,' she said, solving one problem at least. 'And as the horses and carriages were once mine anyway, we shall take them back to my house. And of course, you shall have a home with me for as long as you wish,' she ended.

Tears sprung to Opal's eyes, temporarily blinding her. 'B-but I can't do that. How shall I pay my way?'

'Pah!' The old lady snorted. 'You're family and have no need to. Truth be told, I've missed you and we'll be good company for each other.' Then, turning her attention to the solicitor again, she told him, 'Arrange an auction or whatever you have to do to sell the contents of the house and if they don't cover the cost of his debts, I shall settle the rest in full and that will be an end to it.'

'As you wish, ma'am. And again, I'm so sorry to have to tell you such bad news.'

Once the solicitor had left, Mrs King took control of the situation – which was just as well because Opal was in deep shock – and rang the bell pull to call for Eve.

'Yes, ma'am?' Eve said as she entered the room.

'I would like you to ask the staff to join us.'

'Yes, ma'am. Although I believe Will is in the stables rubbing the horses down until you are ready to leave.'

'Very well, you and Cook will do.'

Eve disappeared the way she had come and was back in minutes, with Cook beside her.

'For reasons that we won't go into at the minute, we shall be closing the house and Mrs King will be coming to live with me,' the old woman told them without preamble.

Eve gasped with dismay and opened her mouth to speak, but the old lady got in before her. 'However, my maid will be getting married shortly and will be leaving me, so, Eve, I am happy to offer you her position. There will also be a job for your husband as the horse and carriage will be coming with your mistress, and I will require a groom. And Cook—'

Here the cook held her hand up and smiled sadly. 'You have no need to worry about me, Mrs King,' she assured her. 'I've been wantin' to retire fer some time now, but didn't like to leave the young mistress 'ere.' She smiled fondly at Opal before going on, 'Me daughter's little 'uns are a bit older now an' she'd like me to go an' live wi' her an' look after 'em so she can go to work, so I reckon I'll do that, but thank yer kindly fer the offer, ma'am.'

'And what about your husband, Eve?' Mrs King asked, after nodding at the cook. 'Do you think he will be happy with my offer?'

'Oh, I'm sure he will, thank you,' Eve gushed, vastly relieved that she wasn't going to be put out of a job and a home.

'Then that is settled. You will probably find that I will be paying you slightly more than my son was. Henry would never spend a penny where a ha'penny would do, and although I am a firm mistress, I think you will find I am fair. Eve, over the next few days, I would like you to pack up anything that yourselves and your mistress wish to bring with you, and then you will all leave this house for good.' She looked around sadly for a moment. 'It has never been a happy home,' she mused, 'at least not while my son

436

resided here – but hopefully the next people who buy it will change that.'

Once they were alone again, Mrs King said in a gentle voice, 'I am sickened by what my son has done and the dire straits he has left you in. But all is not lost, my dear. You are a beautiful young woman with your whole life still before you, and hopefully in the not too distant future you will meet a man who will treat you as you deserve to be treated.'

Opal shook her head. 'I shall *never* get married again,' she said vehemently.

Her mother-in-law smiled. 'Never is a very long time, and who knows what the future has in store for you.' She rose stiffly, leaning heavily on her stick. 'But I should be going now. Would you ask Will to bring the carriage round to the front?'

Once the old lady had left, Opal dropped into the nearest chair, trying to take in the latest developments. Henry had used her, abused her, humiliated her and left her homeless, and yet as she looked around the familiar room, she was surprised to find that she would not be sorry to leave this grand house. As Mrs King has said, she had never known happiness here, so she would walk away without looking back.

When Emma called in the next morning and Opal told her of the solicitor's findings, she was horrified.

'Oh, my dear!' She was clearly as shocked as Opal had been. 'I thought you at least would have been well provided for. That *dreadful* man!'

Opal shrugged. 'He didn't force me to marry him and I didn't even love him, so I suppose I brought it on myself,' she remarked dully.

'Don't talk such rot!' Emma was enraged. 'Everyone knows how hard you tried to be a good wife, but the man was sick in the head. He must have been. Still, at least now you can start again.'

Opal gave a wry smile. 'Start again? I don't think so, Emma. I'm so ashamed I daren't even step out of the door at present. I must be the talk of the town and I can guess what they're all saying – "Serves her right! A girl from Rapper's Hole trying to be a lady!"'

'Rubbish! If people are talking, it will be about Henry and not you! And don't forget it will be a nine-day wonder. But when will you be moving?'

'I shall be gone by this weekend. Eve is packing our things even as we speak and then Henry's solicitor will arrange to have an auction house come in to value the house and contents.'

'Well, it's probably better to do it sooner rather than later.' Emma glanced around the room, suspecting that Opal would probably just be glad to get away from the place. She certainly would if she were in her shoes, after all that had happened. She decided to change the subject then. 'Peter stayed in London for a couple of nights last week at Matthew's house and it seems he has troubles too.'

'Oh?' Opal tried not to sound too interested.

'Yes, it's Alicia. She's been ill for some time, as you know, but it appears that she doesn't have much longer now.'

'What?' Opal was horrified to hear it. 'But what's wrong with her?'

'A tumour ... well, actually a number of them.' Emma shook her head. 'Matthew was telling Peter that their daughter, Suzanne, has been an absolute little angel. She's barely left her mother's side for months, apparently, bless her. Peter said that after seeing Alicia he thinks it will be a blessed relief for the poor soul when she does go. He said she looks absolutely dreadful and is as weak as a kitten. The staff or Matthew have to carry her downstairs – when she's well enough to get out of bed that is – and it seems that isn't often now.'

'How awful.' Opal thought of how Alicia had looked at the balls she had attended and how beautiful she had been. It was hard to imagine her as Emma was describing her. 'Poor Mr Darby-Jones.'

Eve brought the tea in then, distracting them, and Emma decided it was time to steer the conversation away from anything sad.

'Would you like me to come and help you with the move?' she offered after a time, but Opal shook her head.

'It's very kind of you, but everything appears to be in hand. Will has already almost emptied the stables and prepared the ones at Mrs King's for the horses, and Eve won't allow me to help her pack so I feel at a bit of a loose end at the moment.'

'In that case I won't interfere, but just remember I'm here if there's anything at all I can do. And don't think you're going to turn into a recluse because of what has happened. I won't allow it, and next week I shall be calling to see you at Mrs King's – you'll not be getting rid of me too easily.'

'I wouldn't wish to,' Opal said truthfully. Emma had been her rock and her confidante for some time, and she knew she would never be able to thank her enough for her support. At least in these times of trouble, she knew she still had friends she could turn to.

Chapter Forty-Seven

Over the next few days, Opal fell into a deep depression and refused to leave the house even to go and see her beloved Charlie. Life held no meaning or hope for her anymore, and she felt very much as she had in the year after her accident. Her thoughts returned to that terrible day often. Her little boy would be five if he'd lived, and in her mind he looked just like Jack: cheeky, smiling and full of mischief. But she would never have a family to call her own now, and sometimes when she lay in bed she prayed that she wouldn't wake up. When she did manage to sleep, her dreams were plagued with nightmares about Henry, and she would wake in a cold sweat convinced that she would find him standing at the end of the bed.

Eventually the weekend rolled around, and on the morning she was due to move back in with her mother-in-law, Cook said a tearful goodbye.

'Now you just take care o' yourself,' she ordered Opal sternly. 'An' remember that none o' what's happened is your fault. You get out there an' hold yer head high, do yer hear me? You have *nothin'* to be ashamed of!'

Opal nodded tearfully, as the older woman wrapped her in a warm embrace. 'And you take care of yourself too.'

'Oh, don't yer get worryin' about me. I shall be as happy as Larry staying wi' our Kathy an' her family. But now I should be off. It's enough to freeze the hairs off a brass monkey out there an' I don't want to keep Will an' Eve's young brother waitin'. Christopher 'as come along to help wi' the move, bless 'im. Goodbye fer now, pet.'

Will had the carriage waiting outside to take Cook and her belongings to her daughter's home in Willington Street, and curiosity drew Opal to the window where she twitched the lace curtain to one side. She had met Eve's parents but not the young brother she spoke of so lovingly, and she was curious. However, all she could see of him was his back as he sat next to Will on the driving seat, swaddled up to the eyebrows.

Once Cook was comfortably seated in the carriage, it rattled away and Opal wearily went upstairs to see if she could help Eve with the last-minute packing.

Two hours later, she left Henry's home for the last time and she did not look back once, although she did fleetingly think of the nursery she had so lovingly prepared. Hopefully the next family that lived there would have a baby to put in it one day.

Mrs King gave her a royal welcome when she arrived at Hollow's House. 'There's a nice fire burning in your old bedroom,' she told her. 'But you come into the drawing room and have a cup of tea with me while Eve is putting your clothes away. Eve and Will shall have a bedroom in the servants' quarters. They'll be a lot more comfortable up there than they were in the rooms above the stables at the other house. In fact, I've told them they can use another empty room as a little sitting room if they wish.'

'That's very kind of you,' Opal answered, as she removed her bonnet and followed the old lady into the drawing room where a cheery fire was burning in the grate. But nothing could lift her depression, and as she sat silently staring into the flames, her life stretched out before her with nothing to look forward to.

Her sleep was still plagued by nightmares; sometimes they would be about Henry, at other times she dreamed of falling into the quarry again and the pain she had suffered. Over and over she saw flashes of the dark-green cloak and felt the hand on her back as it pushed her over the edge of the quarry. The worst of it was, though, she had no one to talk to about it. Who would believe it? Her hand rose uncon-sciously to the scar on her face. Although it had faded to a white line, it still made her shudder every time she looked at herself in the mirror. Still, she consoled herself. She would never marry again after what had happened with Henry, so what did it matter what she looked like?

Two days after arriving back at Hollow's House, Eve went to find Opal in the day room. 'You have a visitor, ma'am.'

'A visitor . . . for *me*?' Opal looked surprised.

'It is Mrs Wood, ma'am. Would you like me to send her away?'

Opal blinked with surprise. Why would Mrs Wood be visiting her? 'No . . . show her in, would you, please?'

Soon Mrs Wood appeared, clutching a young girl of about five tightly by the hand. Her face was cold and she looked gravely ill as she stared at Opal with disdain.

'I've come for what is rightfully mine,' she said without preamble, and Opal looked confused.

'I have no idea what you're talking about, Mrs Wood,' she answered calmly.

The child began to whimper, but the woman ignored her as she continued to stare at Opal. 'I'm sure you're aware that this is your late husband's child,' Mrs Wood said cruelly. 'And had you not come on the scene when you did, he would have been *my* husband. What he saw in a girl from Rapper's Hole, I'll never know! Anyway, what's done is done, but I think I deserve at least *some* of his estate. I have his child to bring up and educate, so I trust you will do the right thing.'

Opal's face hardened, making the scar that ran down her cheek stand out. 'Had I any money to give you I would, if only for the sake of the child,' she said heatedly. 'But as it is, Henry left me without a penny to my name.'

'*What?*' Mrs Wood looked shocked. 'But how . . .'

'Gambling!' Opal told her curtly. 'And I'm afraid I cannot give what I haven't got.'

The woman's face turned red with rage as she leaned towards Opal. 'You should have *died* when you went over the edge of the quarry, then everything would have been all right and Henry would have made an honest woman of me!'

Then she turned on her heel and stormed from the room, dragging her child behind her. Shaken, Opal crossed to the window and watched as Mrs Wood strode down the drive, her long, dark-green cloak flapping about her legs like ravens' wings. *Long green cloak!* Suddenly in her mind's eye Opal was standing on the edge of the quarry again and it hit her like a blow.

It hadn't been Esther Partridge she had glimpsed that day – it had been Mrs Wood. She must have been carrying Henry's child at that time, and no doubt she had hoped that with Opal out of the way, he would do the right thing by her and his child. The more she thought about it, the more Opal knew she was right – not that the knowing would do her much good. If she went to the police with her suspicions, she would never be able to prove it and so she decided that she would keep it to herself. What else could she do? It would be another dark secret that she would have to bear alone.

At the end of that week, Mrs King received a letter from Mrs Wood demanding enough money to support the old lady's grandchild until she was grown.

It had come as a great shock to her to find that she had a grandchild. Somehow this piece of gossip had never reached her ears, but now that she did know about it her conscience was pricked.

'I suppose I should give her *something*, if only for the sake of the child,' she told Opal uncertainly. Opal secretly hoped that she would; it wasn't the little girl's fault, after all, but she didn't feel able to say it. But before Mrs King had the chance to make arrangements, word reached them that both Mrs Wood and the child had died after catching the influenza that was sweeping through the town.

On hearing the news, Opal wept for the little girl. What chance did the poor thing have with a callous woman like Mrs Wood for a mother, and a gambling drunk for a father? The child had been her own little boy's half-sister and she hadn't deserved her fate. But then, neither had her beautiful boy. And her heart broke anew at yet another senseless death of an innocent child. But it was the grief for her own child that made her weep the longest; the pain of losing her baby had never lessened, and she wondered whether she would ever be able to feel happiness again.

Within no time at all, Eve and Will had settled into their new home and Eve looked happier than Opal had ever seen her.

'Mrs King is a rare 'un,' she told Opal, as she helped her put her hair up one morning. Emma was due to visit that day, so Opal supposed she should make an effort to look nice. 'She's a crusty old bird on the outside but soft as butter inside, ain't she? Me an' Will love it 'ere, an' she's already told Will that she'll find our Christopher a job an' all when he leaves school.'

'Why is there such an age gap between you and your brother?' Opal asked, thinking of Jack, he would have been about the same age as Christopher, and the thought made her heart ache.

'Sadly me mam lost one baby after another till Christopher came along. She adopted him after one of her friends died and he was left an orphan, so I dare say that's why we all spoil 'im. I'd given up all hope of ever havin' a brother or sister by the time he made an appearance. But there, that's the best I can do, what do yer think?'

She stood back while Opal examined her hair in the mirror. Eve had styled it into a neat roll on the back of her head and it made her look like a schoolteacher. Even so she smiled. She didn't much care how she looked and she wouldn't have hurt Eve's feelings for the world.

'Very neat and tidy, thank you.'

'Right, I'd best be off an' set the table if Mrs Dawson-Myers is join in' you an' the mistress fer lunch,' she said, hurrying out of the room.

Opal rose and stared sightlessly out of the window. The days just seemed to be rolling aimlessly into each other, and sometimes she was so bored she could have screamed. Yet still, she couldn't force herself to set foot out of the door.

Chapter Forty-Eight

Matthew was feeling very low. Suzanne had been a tower of strength throughout his wife's illness, barely leaving her side for the last few months of her life, but now that Alicia was gone Matthew was keen to introduce Susie into society. She would be seventeen that year and was turning into a beautiful young woman, and he felt it was unfair that she had sacrificed so much to care for her adoptive mother.

'Here,' he told her one morning over breakfast as he handed her a generous wad of notes. 'You haven't been shopping for ages. Go and spoil yourself.'

She frowned as she stared at him doubtfully. 'But I don't need anything.'

Matthew laughed. 'Since when have women ever had to need anything before treating themselves? Why, when your mother was well, she could shop whether she needed anything or not, as I found out to my cost. Now go on, I insist. You've spent far too long cooped up in the house and it's time you got out and about with people your own age again.'

He was painfully aware that once the novelty of adopting a child had worn off, Alicia had had little time for her daughter; and yet as her health failed, Susie had nursed her lovingly with rarely a word of complaint. Matthew had pointed out on more than one occasion that he was willing to employ a full-time nurse, but Susie wouldn't hear of it. And now he was determined to make it up to her.

'Very well, thank you,' Susie told him. 'I might go into the city this morning, but I won't go in the carriage. I'll walk; it'll do me good.'

And so, an hour later, warmly wrapped in a thick coat and a pretty bonnet, she set off. It was nice to be out and about again and eventually she reached the main street and started to window-shop. Some of the displays were beautiful and she wandered along enjoying the fact that she didn't have to rush home. Eventually she stopped in front of a jewellers' to admire the display in the window. They were black opals and she was sure she had never seen anything so beautiful. As she wandered on, she became aware of an old lady shuffling towards her. She had nothing but a thin shawl wrapped about her shoulders and her sparse grey hair stood out like a wispy halo about her bare head. Her shoes, or what was left of them, were flapping off her feet and her clothes were threadbare and dirty.

Poor old thing, Susie thought as she fumbled in her purse for some coins. The old dear looked like a hearty meal would do her the world of good. Then, when the woman was almost abreast of her, she raised her head, and Susie gasped.

Even now, after all the time that had elapsed since she had last seen her, she would have recognised her anywhere.

'Miss Deverell!' The words had left Susie's lips before she could stop them, and the woman paused in her shuffling to peer at her through bleary eyes. As recognition dawned in them, her lips curled back from her rotten teeth in a sneer.

Susie noticed she was clutching a half-empty bottle of cheap gin in her claw-like hand and she shuddered as she caught a whiff of her. She smelled as if she hadn't bathed in months.

How had the woman been reduced to such a state? she wondered. But then, she thought, if she had treated any other children as cruelly as she had once treated her, she would not have lasted long as a nanny to anyone's offspring. How the mighty were fallen.

'So, it's Miss High-an-Mighty Suzanne all grown up, is it?' The woman took a swig from the bottle, swaying unsteadily on her feet. 'It were your father brought me to this state, kicking me out as he did!'

Susie bit her lip as the woman continued to glare at her, but instead of feeling that she had got her comeuppance, a wave of pity swept through her.

'Do you have somewhere to live?' she asked tentatively.

'Oh yes, indeed I do; in a freezing, filthy garret with *rats* for company,' Agatha Deverell sneered. 'But what would *you* care?' At odds with her appearance her voice was still cultured, which to Susie made it all the sadder.

Susie took a deep breath, then extracting a large number of the bank notes Matthew had given her from her bag she pressed them into Agatha's cold hand. 'Go and get yourself a hot meal and some warm clothes,' she said quietly and, turning about, she left the woman staring after her open-mouthed.

Agatha blinked down at the notes gleefully then with a chuckle she headed for the nearest gin house. *Some folks never learn*, she thought to herself, as she tucked the money down the front of her grimy gown, and without a word of thanks she went on her way. The way she saw it, she had no need to thank the little bitch. It was her fault she had lost her cosy position in her father's house in the first place. And what chance had she had of gaining another position when her snooty father had refused to give her a reference?

Seeing her old nanny had brought back painful memories of Susie's childhood and her adopted mother, and suddenly she didn't feel like shopping anymore; so she entered the first tea shop she came to, ordered a pot of tea and took a seat in the corner. Over the years, she had often wondered what had become of Miss Deverell and now she knew. She supposed she shouldn't feel any pity for the woman after the way she had treated her, and yet she did.

But it was thoughts of Alicia that had her blinking back the tears. She had never been able to think of her as her mother, but for all that she had tended her in her final days and the woman had finally softened towards her. It was sad, but Susie was very aware that Alicia had soon tired of being a mother and that she had been little more than a doll for the woman to parade in front of her visitors.

But she had grown very fond of Matthew, who had never shown her anything but kindness since the day she had entered his house. She suspected that in the final years, her adopted parents' marriage had not been quite as close as Alicia had tried to make out. She had been very beautiful but thoroughly spoiled by both her parents and her husband, and in the end, she sensed that Matthew had grown tired of pandering to her every whim. Even so, he had made sure that she had the best medical care, and between them she hoped they had made Alicia's final days as happy as they could be.

As they so often did, her thoughts turned to her real family – as she always thought of them. Not a day went by when she didn't miss them and wonder what had become of them. Where were they all now? Opal and Charlie would be all grown up, and little Jack would be soon too. She supposed she would never know what had happened to them. Too much time had gone by to begin a search for them, but she would hold each of them in her heart until the day she died.

When she arrived home less than an hour later, Matthew was just coming out of his study and he raised an eyebrow in surprise. 'That was quick. When your mother went shopping, it was rare to see her for the rest of the day.'

Susie smiled as she removed her gloves and bonnet and handed them to the maid. 'I saw Miss Deverell, my old nanny. She looks like she lives on the streets now and after that I didn't feel much like shopping.'

Matthew pursed his lips. The woman didn't deserve any better, but he knew how soft-hearted Susie was. She had barely stepped out of the house since Alicia had died, and he sensed that now she no longer had her to care for she was finding that she had a lot of spare time on her hands.

'I tell you what, why don't I arrange a little holiday at the coast for us both? It would do us both the power of good to get away for a time.'

Susie smiled, really smiled for the first time in ages. 'That would be nice, but are you sure you don't have to work? And we are supposed to be in mourning.'

'I can rearrange my work schedule, and as for the mourning period, no one is going to know we've had a bereavement if we don't tell them, are they?' he assured her, taking her arm and leading her into the drawing room to discuss where they might want to go.

Chapter Forty-Nine

'Please, ma'am, could you spare me a minute? I'd like a private word.'

Mrs King laid aside the book she was reading – *The Tenant of Wildfell Hall*. 'Of course, Eve, come in.' She was sitting in her favourite chair by the window where she could enjoy the late autumn sunshine streaming through the window.

Eve softly closed the door behind her and, licking her lips nervously, she walked towards her mistress. 'Forgive me if it seems that I'm interferin',' she began hesitantly. 'But I'm gettin' gravely concerned about the young mistress. She's barely set foot out o' the house since she came back to live here, an' she seems so low, but I reckon I've come up with an idea that might cheer her up a bit.'

'Oh yes, go on.' Mrs King narrowed her eyes.

'Well, it's like this . . .' Eve told the older woman of her plan and when she was done Mrs King frowned. 'Hm, this could be just the tonic she needs. I quite agree with you; she does seem very down and she's so thin I'm sure that one good puff of wind would blow her away. I have no idea why she should be so ashamed and hide herself away as she does. It wasn't her that did wrong, it was my son.' She chewed on her lip thoughtfully for a moment and finally nodded. 'Go ahead with your idea. I can't say as it's something I particularly look forward to but if it cheers her up, I dare say I shall be able to bear it.'

'Oh, thank you, ma'am.' Eve looked delighted. 'I'll go and speak to Will about it straightaway.' And with that she bobbed her knee and fairly skipped from the room.

Later that evening, as the two women were having dinner, Mrs King told Opal, 'You might like to visit the kitchen when you've finished your meal. I believe there's a surprise waiting for you in there.'

'A surprise . . . for *me*?' Opal looked shocked. 'What sort of surprise? It isn't my birthday.'

Mrs King smiled. 'If I told you what it was it wouldn't be a surprise, would it? Now go on, get off and find out for yourself.'

Curious, Opal dabbed her lips with the fine lawn napkin and headed for the door. She could hear laughter coming from the kitchen but nothing could have prepared her for what happened when she opened the door. A large bundle of fluff with his tail wagging furiously suddenly came bounding towards her and leaped at her so enthusiastically that he almost knocked her off her feet.

'Oh, *Charlie!*' She was delighted to see him and laughed as he licked every inch of her he could reach. 'Have you brought him to see me, Will?' she asked as she dropped to her knees to give him a hug.

Will and Eve were grinning from ear to ear. 'Actually, we've done better than that,' Eve said. 'Charlie has come here to live . . . if you still want him, that is? An' don't look so worried. The mistress knows all about it an' has given her permission for him to stay. We thought it might cheer you up.' And judging by her young mistress's smiling face it clearly had.

'Oh . . . I can't believe it!' Happy tears were rolling down Opal's pale cheeks. 'And my mother-in-law really doesn't mind?'

Eve giggled. 'To be honest, I don't think she'd have chose to 'ave a dog in the house, but she agreed you needed somethin' to get you out an' about again an' now Charlie boy's here you'll have to take him for his walks. The rest of us have got enough to do as it is.'

'Oh, I'll do that, all right, won't we, boy?'

'Yes, an' you can see to the feedin' of 'im an' all,' the cook told her with a sniff, although Opal noticed she had already provided him with a juicy bone.

Opal felt happy for the first time in months and soon after she wrapped up warmly, put Charlie on his lead and set off for a walk.

Mrs King was watching from the window as Eve served her coffee and she smiled. 'It seems your idea was a good one,' she commented. 'She might get a bit of colour back in her cheeks now she'll be getting out and about again. I dare say it will be worth having a few dog hairs about the place if it cheers her up.'

Eve beamed and nodded in agreement, feeling very pleased with herself.

Just as Eve had hoped, with Charlie's arrival, Opal began to come out of her dark depression. Now she had a reason to get up each day and soon Charlie had everyone in the household wrapped around his paw. Even Mrs King seemed to quite like him, although she would never openly have admitted it.

'Just be sure and keep him off the furniture,' she would grumble, which proved to be easier said than done as Charlie made himself at home.

Before they knew it, December had rolled around and when Emma visited one day, she told Opal, 'We're going to have a ball on New Year's Eve this year. You will come, won't you?' Seeing that Opal was about to refuse, she rushed on, 'You have no excuse not to. Your mourning period is almost over – not that that vile man deserved anyone to mourn for him – and your mother-in-law is coming, so it would look strange if you weren't with her. And Matthew is coming from London and quite a few people you know will be there. Oh, *please* say you will – for *me*?'

Opal looked undecided. She still found it hard to face people, but she realised that she couldn't lock herself away forever. She even got out of the way when Mrs King had visitors, although thankfully they had seen neither hide nor hair of Esther Partridge since the news of Henry's shame had been plastered all across the newspapers, which was one blessing at least. No doubt she was thinking herself lucky that he hadn't married her after all.

'I suppose I *could* do,' she said uncertainly, and Emma beamed.

'That's decided then. I'm going to the dressmaker next week to be fitted for a new gown so you can come with me and get a new one for yourself too. I called in to make the appointment earlier on and she's got the most gorgeous pale-gold satin that would look absolutely beautiful with your hair and eyes. I've got my eye on a lovely lilac colour.'

Opal smiled, knowing when she was beaten – but for all that, she suddenly found herself looking forward to it. She tried to tell herself that it had nothing to do with the fact that Emma had told her a certain gentleman would be there, but deep inside she knew she was lying. But then – her hand rose to the scar on her cheek and she frowned – would she really want Matthew to see her as she was now? With a sigh, she resigned herself to the fact that she had already given her word to go. She couldn't back out of it now, and it was highly unlikely Matthew would remember her anyway.

Opal and Mrs King planned to spend Christmas quietly together that year, although Mrs King instructed Eve to order a Christmas tree and decorate it. To Eve's excitement, the old lady had also given her permission to have her family for Christmas tea in the kitchen, insisting that after their Christmas lunch she and Opal could manage with a few sandwiches. And when it started to snow on Christmas Eve, Mrs King even gave Will permission to fetch the family in her carriage.

'Why don't you come through an' join us?' Eve encouraged Opal when Will set off to fetch them, but Opal shook her head.

'Thank you, but I'd feel like I was intruding, and anyway I'm looking forward to curling up in bed with a book.'

In truth she felt neither one thing nor the other now; she wasn't a servant, but she had nothing of her own to speak of and was living on Mrs King's charity, a fact that went sorely against the grain. So much so, in fact, that she was thinking of suggesting to the old lady that she should look for a job. But not until the New Year; she didn't want to spoil the holidays.

So, after taking a light tea, she retired to her room and stood gazing through the window at the snowy landscape. Although the scar on her face was the only outward sign of how close she had come to death, mentally she was still scarred and shuddered every time she thought of what Mrs Wood had tried to do to her. Her hand dropped to stroke Charlie, and as he licked her hand, she found herself thinking of his namesake. How she still missed him and wondered what had become of little Susie? Then she realised with a jolt that Susie would be sixteen now, almost a woman.

'Come on, boy,' she sighed, and leading the dog to the bed, they cuddled up together on the quilted bedspread. He was all she had left in the world now and it was a daunting thought.

Chapter Fifty

At last it was New Year's Eve and Opal was alternately looking forward to the ball and dreading it, for it would be the first time she had attended such an event since before Henry's death, almost a year before.

'You just hold your head high and remember you have done nothing to be ashamed of,' Emma had scolded her, when Opal had told her how nervous she felt when they'd picked up their gowns from the dressmaker the day before. The woman had done a wonderful job and Opal could hardly wait to wear hers.

In the afternoon she took a long, leisurely bath and washed her hair before sitting in front of the fire and brushing it until it gleamed. After an early tea, Eve went upstairs with her to help her get ready. She was almost as excited as Opal, and stared at the gown hanging on the wardrobe door admiringly.

'Eeh, this is goin' to set your hair an' eyes off a treat,' she breathed as she stroked the pale-golden skirts. 'I don't think I've ever seen a more beautiful gown. But come on, let's get yer hair done.'

Opal obediently sat down, while Eve piled her long hair on top of her head before teasing it into ringlets. Next came the job of clambering into the many petticoats and under-garments and finally the gown.

'You look like a princess,' Eve assured her with a catch in her voice when she was finally ready and Opal sighed.

'Hardly, with this scar on my face.'

Eve frowned at her. 'Don't talk so daft. You can hardly notice it now. But come along.' She snatched up Opal's cloak, and ushered her towards the door. 'The mistress said she wanted a word with you in the drawin' room before you left, so you'd best not keep her waiting. Will is round at the stables gettin' the carriage ready so you just have a wonder-ful time, do yer hear me?'

'I hear you.' Opal grinned as she followed her from the room, wondering what Mrs King wanted to see her about. She hoped she hadn't done anything wrong.

The old lady raised her eyebrow admiringly when she saw Opal. 'Goodness me, I'd forgotten how pretty you could look, my dear.' She smiled. 'That gown suits you perfectly. But come and sit here a minute. I've something I want to tell you.' She patted the seat beside her and Opal obediently sat down. 'The thing is . . .' Mrs King began. 'I had my solicitor visit me yesterday, as you may be aware. The reason being I wished to change my will.'

Opal frowned; she had grown fond of her mother-in-law and hated to think of her passing away, but the old woman held her hand up to silence her when Opal opened her mouth to speak. 'Hear me out, do. You see, it suddenly occurred to me that in my previous will I had left everything to Henry.' Opal saw a hint of sadness behind the old woman's eyes before she hurried on, 'And so I have now amended it.

I have no one left now apart from you, and so I wanted you to know that, when I go, you will be my sole beneficiary. The house, my money, my jewels – everything will be yours.'

'Oh no . . .' Opal was so shocked that tears sprang to her eyes. 'But I can't let you do that!'

Mrs King shrugged. 'And who else am I supposed to leave it all to? I'm only telling you because I know what an independent little soul you can be. And don't worry; there are no strings attached. It will all be yours to do with as you please. Sell it, live in it, whatever you like. If you should remarry you might not wish to stay here, but it will be up to you. It's the least I can do after the way my son treated you.'

Opal gulped. It was all so much to take in. 'I don't think there's any chance of me ever marrying again . . .' she said forcefully. She was about to say that Henry had turned her off men for life, but managed to stop herself in time. He had been Mrs King's only son after all.

Mrs King chuckled. 'There's far stranger things have happened,' she told her wisely. 'You're still young and beautiful, and it would be a sin for you to spend the rest of your life alone. But I wanted you to know what I'd done, so that you didn't feel I was having you here on sufferance. So, come along, I have a feeling you're going to be the belle of the ball.'

'You look very nice yourself,' Opal told her, as the old woman patted down the folds of the new mauve taffeta gown she was wearing. She looked very regal. 'And . . . Well, thank you hardly seems adequate for what you've just told me.'

Mrs King waved her hand. 'Huh! I don't want to hear it mentioned again after this evening, and be prepared because I have no intentions of popping off just yet.'

Opal grinned as she followed her from the room, and soon they were tucked up in the back of the carriage heading for Peter and Emma's grand house in Caldecote.

From the second the carriage turned into the drive, the night took on a magical quality for Opal. Lanterns had been strung in the trees lining the drive and with the snow softly falling it looked like a scene from one of the fairy tales she had been so fond of when she was a child. The lights were shining from the windows of the house making the snow sparkle like crushed diamonds and the instant the carriage pulled up footmen in scarlet and gold livery hurried down the steps to help the ladies alight and go into the house. Maids in tiny white aprons and lace-trimmed mop caps were dotted about with trays of champagne on silver trays, while others helped the ladies off with their cloaks.

Peter and Emma spotted them and hurried towards them.

'Oh Opal, you look *just* beautiful,' Emma told her, before pecking Mrs King on the cheek.

'You certainly do, my dear,' Peter chipped in and Opal blushed. But just then more guests arrived and Emma told them, 'Do get a drink and mingle with the guests. I'll catch up with you again just as soon as I can.' And she hurried away to greet the new arrivals, as Opal led Mrs King into the dining room where a buffet fit for a king was laid out on long tables along one wall.

'Do you want anything to eat yet?' Mrs King enquired.

Opal shook her head. 'Oh, not yet, thank you. I'm still full from dinner, but may I get you something?'

The old woman shook her head as she headed purposefully for the ballroom where they could hear the orchestra tuning up. 'I'd rather get a good seat where I've got a nice view of the dance floor. But I wouldn't mind a glass of that champagne.'

Opal took two glasses from a passing maid and, once Mrs King was settled on the chair of her choice, Opal glanced nervously around. Thankfully she saw no one she knew, so she sipped the champagne and began to relax as people milled about. A huge crystal chandelier lit by a myriad of tiny candles was suspended above the highly polished wooden dance floor and as Opal glanced out of the enormous floor-to-ceiling windows, which were draped with deep-red velvet curtains, to the snowy scene beyond, she felt butterflies flutter to life in her stomach as she wondered if Matthew had arrived. Emma had said he would be here, but would the snow have stopped him? And even if he did come, would he even remember her? She doubted it very much, but still she looked forward to seeing him.

At last all the visitors had arrived, and the house seemed to be bursting at the seams with people. The women in multi-coloured gowns and sparkling jewellery looked truly beautiful and the men in their dark evening suits and dickie bows looked handsome. Opal felt as if she could have watched them forever. Eventually, the orchestra began to play and couples took to the floor as Emma rushed up to them, her face alight.

'Opal, look who I found,' she said and Opal felt colour rush into her cheeks as she glanced up to see Matthew smiling down at her.

'Good evening, Mrs King.' Matthew gave a little bow and a cheeky smile. 'May I have the pleasure of this dance? From what I can remember, you were very good at the waltz.'

'Go on then, girl, don't just sit there,' the elderly Mrs King scolded in her usual forthright way, as she gave her a none too gentle nudge in the back – and before Opal had time to think about it, Matthew was leading her on to the dance floor.

'May I say you look absolutely beautiful this evening,' Matthew whispered in her ear and she flushed with pleasure. He hadn't even seemed to notice her scarred cheek, and if he had, it clearly didn't bother him. His face became serious then as he said softly, 'I was, er . . . sorry to hear of your, er . . . trouble.'

Opal sighed. 'I'm trying to put it all behind me now, but I was sorry to hear of your loss too.' They were gliding effortlessly around the floor and Opal felt as if she was floating on air.

'Alicia had been ill for many years,' he told her quietly. 'So it came as no surprise; in fact her death was a blessed release for her. She suffered terribly towards the end but my daughter, Susie, was marvellous with her. I don't know how we would have managed without her.'

He felt Opal stiffen in his arms. 'Susie? I thought your daughter's name was Suzanne.'

'Well, that was what Alicia insisted on calling her, she thought it was a bit grander than Susie, but her name was Susie when we adopted her, and that's what she prefers to be known as.'

He watched the colour drain from her face like water from a dam and, as her steps faltered, she almost tripped them up. 'My dear . . . are you all right?' His voice was full of concern as they came to a stop and she managed a weak smile.

'Y-yes, I'm sorry. It's just that . . . I once had a little sister called Susie. She was adopted when she was six years old without my permission and I've been trying to trace her ever since. Henry told me that he was trying to find her for me, but looking back, I don't think he was, and hearing her name . . . Sorry, it was just a shock.'

Matthew paused and frowned before taking her elbow. 'I think we need to talk,' he told her, and led her purposefully through the throng of dancers towards Peter's study. Hopefully, there would be no one else in there and they would be able to speak in private.

But before they reached the door, a young woman in a beautiful ivory gown suddenly grasped Matthew's arm, and as Opal looked at her, she felt her knees buckle. The girl's hair and eyes were exactly the same colour as her own, and although she was no longer the little girl that Opal remembered, she would have recognised her anywhere.

'*Susie . . .*' she choked, as tears sprang to her eyes.

The girl looked at her with a puzzled frown. The woman looked familiar, but she couldn't remember when . . . Then she looked into her eyes, beautiful brown eyes the same colour as her own – eyes she had never forgotten, despite the long years since she had seen them. She felt her stomach swoop with shock.

'Opal ... Oh, *Opal*, I thought I would never see you again!'

And then they were in each other's arms, sobbing as if their hearts would break. Against all the odds, they had found one another again.

Peter appeared at their side, alerted by the commotion – and, realising that something was going on, he ushered them all into his study. It was only when the door was closed behind them that he asked with concern, 'Is everything all right?'

Matthew looked completely bewildered as the two young women clung to each other.

'Sh-she is my sister!' Opal told him, and now it was Peter's turn to look shocked.

Slowly Opal told them all about the terrible circumstances that had led to what was left of their family being forced to find shelter in the dilapidated cottage in Rapper's Hole.

'Susie and Jack and I were all gravely ill with the fever that took our father,' she said in a croaky voice, 'and so our brother Charlie took the two of them to the work-house where he hoped they would be treated by a doctor. But by the time I was well enough to go there both of them had gone: Susie for adoption and Jack had died.' Tears coursed down her cheeks as she relived that terrible time. 'And then Charlie was charged with stealing from Henry and sent to a penal colony in Australia and the rest you know. Henry took me under his wing and I ended up marrying him.'

Matthew's face was grim. 'We did adopt Susie from the workhouse,' he admitted. 'And I knew that her name at the time was Sharp, but until now I didn't realise that had been your maiden name too. But tell me, was your brother called Charlie Sharp? Because if he was, I think I might just be able to find another piece of the missing jigsaw.'

'What do you mean?' Opal was still holding on to Susie as if she might never let her go.

'Just wait here,' Matthew said as he turned and strode from the room.

Opal and Susie sat down on a sofa, arms wrapped around each other, with tears of joy still pouring down their cheeks. They barely noticed the minutes ticking by, as they gazed at each other in disbelief. Susie reached her hand up to touch Opal's scar, murmuring, 'How?'

Opal shook her head. Now was not the time to talk of past sorrows. 'Another time. Soon, we will tell each other everything—'

She was interrupted by the door opening as Matthew returned, followed by a handsome young man with a beautiful young woman on his arm.

For a moment they all just stared at each other, then Opal let out a cry, half rising to her feet. Before she could stand, Charlie reached his sisters in two strides and threw his arms about them.

'I . . . I can't believe it.' He was sobbing unashamedly. 'I'd almost given up hope of ever seeing either of you again.'

The group around them watched the emotional reunion with tears in their eyes.

Finally, Matthew said, 'As soon as you said Charlie's name it rang a bell,' he told them. 'A good friend of mine and Peter's, Phineas Morgan, is here this evening and I had the very great honour of attending his daughter Francesca's wedding some time ago. I'll let Charlie tell you the rest himself, but for now I think we should all leave these three young people to themselves. They certainly have a lot of catching up to do.'

Nodding in agreement, Peter and Francesca hurriedly left the room, with broad smiles on their faces.

Chapter Fifty-One

On the morning after the ball, Opal, Susie, Matthew, Francesca and Charlie gathered in Mrs King's drawing room. She had insisted that they should all come for lunch and they were all in fine spirits.

'So, what do you intend to do now that you've found one another again?' Mrs King asked eventually, in her usual no-nonsense way.

They had not stopped talking since they got there, but now a silence settled on the room as the newly reunited brother and sisters stared at each other. They hadn't had time to think that far ahead yet but now they realised that they would have to.

'Well . . . I don't really want to leave my father,' Susie said falteringly, for over the years that was how she had come to regard Matthew.

'And obviously my home, businesses and Francesca's family are in London,' Charlie pointed out practically – he'd introduced them all to his new wife at the ball.

Opal could understand how they felt, but oh it was going to be so hard to see them leave now that she had found them again.

'But that doesn't mean you can't come and stay with us whenever you wish,' Charlie piped up and Susie nodded vigorously.

'And she can come and stay with us too, can't she?' she pleaded, looking towards Matthew.

'She may come as often as she wishes and stay for as long as she wishes,' he answered.

Mrs King smiled. She had a feeling he wasn't being completely unselfish. She'd seen the way he and Opal looked at each other. Opal had never looked at Henry that way, and she had the feeling that she might be witnessing the start of a true romance. She hoped so. She bitterly regretted letting Opal marry her son now and she deserved to be happy.

'And of course, any of you are welcome to come and stay here too whenever you like,' she chipped in. The house had never seen so much excitement or seemed so happy.

Opal gave her a grateful smile.

'Thank you,' Matthew said. 'As it happens, Susie and I have already decided to extend our stay for a couple of weeks before we return to London. There is still part of the family chain missing – little Jack. I want to find out where he is buried so that you can all at least visit his grave.'

'I've already tried to get that information from the workhouse but they wouldn't tell me,' Opal told him regretfully.

'Well, I think you'll find they'll tell me,' Matthew said, his expression grim. 'That's the very least they can do. Just leave it with me.'

'If that's the case, you and Susie must stay here,' Mrs King said firmly.

He gave her a grateful smile. 'That's very kind of you. I was going to book us both into the Bull Hotel in the town. Are you quite sure we wouldn't be imposing?'

'Of course you wouldn't!' Mrs King waved her hand in the air; she was enjoying all the excitement. 'And anyway, I reckon you'd have a job tearing these two apart just yet.' She smiled at Susie and Opal who were sitting as closely together on the sofa as they could possibly get, gripping each other's hands, while Charlie and Francesca looked on smiling. Both of the young women had really taken to Charlie's lovely young wife and they knew already that they were going to get along famously.

Eve came in with a tray of coffee and biscuits and she too was smiling broadly. Opal had told her what had happened early that morning and she couldn't have been more pleased for her.

'Cook says to tell you lunch will be ready in an hour, but this should keep you going till then.'

As Eve poured the coffee into tiny china cups, Matthew told Mrs King, 'Then if you're quite sure about us staying, I'll leave after lunch and have our luggage brought here from Peter's. I might even have time to call in at the workhouse and start my enquiries, and God help them if they try to fob me off about little Jack's resting place.'

'You can take my carriage,' Mrs King offered generously. 'I'm sure your Will won't mind driving him, will he, Eve?'

'Not at all,' Eve answered. Will was as thrilled about what had happened as the rest of them. It was so nice to see Opal smiling again.

Shortly after lunch, Matthew set off, leaving the family to make up for lost time. He returned briefly to bring his and Susie's luggage before leaving for the workhouse, and Eve, Susie and Opal spent the afternoon putting their clothes away in the rooms Eve had prepared for them, chattering non-stop while they worked. Francesca and Charlie had returned to Peter's with the promise that they would be back for dinner and suddenly the house seemed to have come alive again.

Matthew returned from the workhouse grim-faced. 'Your little brother's death is recorded in the book,' he told Opal and Susie. 'But the odd thing is no one seems to know where he is buried, which is strange because the rest of the inmates who pass away there are buried in a tiny cemetery out the back, and their resting places are all marked with simple crosses with their names on.'

'That's it then,' Opal said quietly, her lovely brown eyes awash with tears. 'We'll never know now.'

But Matthew wasn't to be put off so easily. 'I haven't finished yet. Someone must know. The master who was in charge then has long since retired, but I shan't rest until I've questioned every single person that worked there at the time. Don't give up just yet.'

And somehow Opal believed and trusted him.

Later that evening, they all dined together and, when Francesca and Charlie once again returned to Peter and Emma's house, Susie and Mrs King retired to bed, worn out with all that had happened, leaving Matthew and Opal alone by the cosy fire in the drawing room.

'You've done a wonderful job of bringing Susie up,' Opal told him sincerely. 'She's a credit to you.'

'Thank you.' He swirled the whisky in the glass he was holding and sighed. 'Truthfully, I was very disappointed with Alicia once we had adopted her. Susie was such a delightful little girl, but after the initial novelty of having a child wore off Alicia didn't seem to have much time for her.'

'Oh!' Opal didn't quite know what to say.

'Alicia was very beautiful, but I'm afraid she was also very spoiled,' he admitted. 'And for the last few years of her life, we weren't particularly close.'

'Oh!' Opal said again. She was shocked; she had thought they were so happy. But then she smiled in understanding and sighed. 'Henry and I weren't close either. I should never have married him,' she said sadly. 'I didn't love him, but I'd lost Charlie, Susie and Jack, and he was so kind to me. I hoped I would grow to love him in time.'

Before they knew it, they were telling each other their life stories and by the end of the evening Opal felt as if she had known him for years.

When they went to their bedrooms, they walked up the stairs together and he saw her to her door where he lifted her hand and kissed it gently.

'I've thought of you often since we first met,' he told her and she felt herself blush.

'I've thought of you too,' she admitted, her heart racing, but before he could say anything else, she turned and went into her room; she could hardly wait to see him again the next morning.

Straight after breakfast, Matthew set out for the workhouse again, leaving the sisters to spend time together. Francesca and Charlie were coming for dinner that evening along with Peter and Emma, and Opal was so excited she could hardly wait. Sadly, Charlie and Francesca would be leaving for London early the next morning. He now had a string of jewellery shops and needed to be there to oversee them but they would keep in regular contact from now on, which made the parting a little more bearable.

While they waited for Matthew to return, she and Susie spent the day talking non-stop as they caught up with each other's lives. There were many tears and also much laughter, and Opal felt happier than she had since her parents had died so many years before.

Matthew didn't arrive back until late in the afternoon, by which time Opal, Susie and Mrs King, along with Charlie and Francesca, who had just arrived, were in the drawing room.

As soon as Opal saw him she knew something had happened and she stood up. 'Have you found out where Jack is buried?' she asked expectantly.

'Not exactly, but I do have a surprise for you,' he told her, his eyes sparkling. 'You see . . . Jack isn't dead.'

Opal felt the floor rush up to meet her as she gripped the back of a chair, and she saw the colour drain from Charlie's face. He had lived with terrible guilt ever since placing Jack and Susie in the workhouse and now he could hardly dare to believe what he was hearing.

'What . . .? But I don't understand . . .' Opal said in a wobbly voice.

Taking her hand, he led her to the sofa and when they were both seated, he stroked her arm gently. 'As I told you yesterday, there was no record of where Jack might be buried, so I decided to speak to any of the staff that still worked there who were there when he and Susie were admitted, and early this afternoon, I struck lucky. I spoke to an old woman who'd worked in the nursery there. She remembered Jack well, and said that he was almost at death's door when he arrived. Anyway, it seemed that there was another lady who worked there who took a huge shine to him. She feared that the babies weren't given the care they needed when they were admitted – the poorly ones especially – so the long and the short of it is . . . she took him home to bring him up as her own. When the master discovered that the child was gone, he was worried about what the board of governors would say about a missing child, so he had him recorded as dead. The old lady was able to direct me to the boy's home and he's here right now if you'd like to meet him.'

Charlie, Susie and Opal were all as pale as ghosts as they stared at each other. Finally Opal nodded. 'Yes . . . we . . . we'd like that very much,' she said, her voice barely audible.

Matthew went out into the hallway and a moment later Opal was surprised to see Eve's parents, with Eve close beside them, enter the room.

'Mrs King.' Eve's mother inclined her head. 'I think I owe you an explanation, but I'll offer no apology for what I did all them years ago.' Her chin was high. 'I fell in love wi' your little brother the second I laid eyes on him, an' I knew if he stayed in that awful nursery in the workhouse he'd die. Most o' the babies that went in there never reached their third birthdays, an' the poor little souls soon learned to not even bother cryin' cos nobody went to tend 'em half the time. Anyway, me an' Eve's dad had lost so many babies, so I took him an' he became the son we could never have, although o' course I had no idea he were your little brother. I told everyone that a friend of mine had died and he had no one to care for him. I took him home an' nursed him back to health an' we called him Christopher.'

'I didn't know Opal . . . I swear it!' Eve told her, wringing her hands together – but she needn't have worried, as Opal was smiling again.

'You owe me no apology, Mrs Fellows,' she assured the woman. 'Only my sincere thanks because, as you say, had you not taken him, he probably would have died. But now . . . please, may we see him?'

Matthew crossed to the door and when he opened it a leggy twelve-year-old, who was the spitting image of his natural father, entered and went immediately to stand beside Mrs Fellows as he stared about, his eyes as big as saucers. There was no sign now of the sickly child they all remembered, and they saw immediately that he had been well loved and cared for. That was obvious from the way he shrank into his mother's side.

'When the gentleman turned up an' told us why he was there, I told Christopher everythin',' Mrs Fellows explained. 'But truthfully, he don't remember livin' wi' no one but me an' his dad here. It's a lot fer the little chap to take in so's you'll 'ave to be patient wi' him.'

'Oh . . . *Jack*.' Opal reached out to him but he shrank away from her and she gulped.

'Me name is Christopher,' he muttered sullenly.

Opal nodded quickly as she exchanged a glance with Charlie.

'Yes . . . yes of course it is, but it was Jack when you lived with us.' He frowned and glared at her, and Opal knew then that they would have to take things very carefully if they were ever to establish any sort of a relationship with him. 'So . . . you must be twelve now?'

Eyeing her suspiciously, he nodded, as Susie came to stand beside her sister. 'We're so glad to have found you,' she told him sincerely. 'And I do hope that we can all be friends?'

He sniffed but made no move towards her. 'S'pose so.' But he didn't sound at all certain.

Opal longed to hurry over to him and hug him, but she didn't dare, and Charlie was so shocked he looked as if he had been turned to stone.

It was Eve's mother who broke the awkward silence when she said, 'I reckon this little chap has a lot to come to terms wi' at the moment, so if it's all the same to you I'll be takin' him back off home now.'

'Of course.' It wasn't the reunion Opal would have wished for, but after all the years of believing him to be dead she was just profoundly grateful to the woman standing in front of her, for without her tender loving care she had no doubt that he might well have been. 'But . . . may we see him again . . . when he's ready?'

Mrs Fellows slowly nodded. 'Yes, I'll bring him back tomorrow afternoon, if that suits.'

Opal's beaming face was her answer, and she turned to leave.

Opal, one hand clutched tight in Susie's, and Charlie's strong arm about her waist, watched them go with tears in her eyes.

'I can't believe we're finally all reunited.' Susie's voice was choked as Opal placed her arm about her shoulders and glanced over at Matthew, who looked like the cat that had got the cream.

'And it's all thanks to you,' she told him. 'Somehow, against all the odds, you've found all the missing pieces of the jigsaw and put them back together again.'

Yet even as the words were spoken, it dawned on her that this wasn't entirely true. In her heart she had always dreamed that if ever she was reunited with Charlie and Susie again, they would all live together once more, but this would not be possible. Charlie was a married man with a home and businesses in London, Susie clearly had a deep allegiance to her adopted father and had no intention of leaving him, and Jack – or Christopher as he now preferred to be called – was quite obviously very close to the people he had believed were his birth family. Even so, she had never thought to see him again, so all she really cared about was growing close to him once more, even if it took a long time to win his trust.

'It's been a truly remarkable couple of days,' Opal commented, and they all nodded in agreement. 'And from now on things can only get better.'

And indeed, things did get better. Over the next four weeks, Susie and Opal grew close again, and after the initial shock of discovering his true roots, Christopher became a regular visitor. Charlie wrote to Opal each and every week and arranged for her to go and stay with them once Matthew and Susie had returned to London, and she was greatly looking forward to it.

But the best times for Opal were the evenings when everyone else had retired to bed and she and Matthew would sit and chat and really get to know each other. They soon found out that they had a lot in common, and the time they spent together seemed to pass in the blink of an eye.

'She's like a different woman,' Mrs King commented to Eve one morning when Matthew, Susie and Opal had gone for a walk.

'She certainly is, ma'am.' Eve grinned. 'She's got her old sparkle back, ain't she?'

'Hm, and I have a feeling a lot of that is due to a certain gentleman.'

Eve glanced at her, uncertain how to answer – Opal had been married to her son after all. But to her relief, she saw that the old lady's eyes were twinkling with mischief.

'It wouldn't surprise me if we didn't hear wedding bells again in the not too distant future,' Mrs King said optimistically and Eve hoped with all her heart that she was right. Opal deserved some happiness.

All too soon the day for Matthew and Susie to leave rolled around and Opal was tearful as she helped her sister to pack.

'I don't suppose I could persuade you to stay for just a *little* bit longer?' she wheedled. Susie shook her head. 'I have to go back to London. But you know you can come to stay with us as often as you like and for as long as you like. And don't worry, I shall be coming back here too. I don't intend to lose you again!'

Eventually all the bags were down in the hall and after saying a tearful farewell while Will loaded the luggage on to the carriage Susie discreetly went to sit inside it. Mrs King and Eve then said their goodbyes to Matthew too before quietly slipping away and suddenly there was just the two of them, and it would have been hard to say who looked the most miserable at the prospect of parting.

'This is it, then?' Matthew's brow was creased.

'For now.' Opal took his hand. 'But it won't be for long. You're not going to get rid of me that easily.'

He paused as if he were considering saying something and then throwing caution to the wind, he told her, 'I don't know if you're aware of this . . . but I . . . Well, the truth of it is, I think I'm falling in love with you, Opal. I felt something for you the very first time I met you and now . . . I suppose what I'm trying to say is, do you think you could ever look on me that way?'

Opal's eyes were gleaming as she looked up at him. 'I already do, my love,' she whispered and before she knew it, she was wrapped in his arms and as his soft lips came down on hers she felt as if she had finally come home after a very hard long journey.

Through the gap in the green baize door further along the hallway, Eve stifled a giggle as she spied unashamedly on them. 'It looks like I might have to hold on a while afore I go an' make the fire up in the drawin' room,' she whispered to Mrs King, who was sitting at the kitchen table enjoying a cup of tea with Cook. 'The young mistress an' Matthew are busy, if yer know what I mean!'

'And about time too,' Mrs King declared with a smug expression on her face. 'I wondered how long it'd take for them to get around to it! Now come away, girl and leave them to it.'

And Eve was only too happy to do just that. Suddenly, the future looked rosy for all of them.

Epilogue

'Come along now, m'dear. You're almost there – one more good push should do it,' the motherly little midwife encouraged, as she leaned over Opal. The poor young woman was exhausted.

Knowing that she was close to meeting her baby, as the next pain built, Opal gave an inhuman cry and, with her chin on her chest, she made one last mighty effort. At that moment the door burst open and Matthew charged in, his face grey with concern. He had been marching up and down the landing, beside himself with worry for hours, and he could stand it no more. The nurse he had employed to help the midwife looked at him disapprovingly. As far as she was concerned, the birthing room was no place for a man to be but seeing the look on his face, she knew better than to ask him to leave. He looked positively murderous.

'Oh, my poor sweet love.' His eyes were shining with unshed tears as he leaned over his wife and took her damp hand in his.

Just then the midwife gave a crow of approval. 'That's it . . . *that's it*! Keep it going – I can see the head.'

Matthew kept his eyes firmly fixed on Opal's face and seconds later a newborn's indignant cry echoed around the room.

'It's a boy, and a right bonnie one too,' the midwife cried triumphantly, as she deftly cut the cord connecting him to his mother and handed him to the waiting nurse. 'And would you just look at that shock of hair. I've never seen a newborn with such a thatch, and it's exactly the same colour as his mother's.'

The nurse meanwhile quickly dried the baby in the towel she had warmed ready and placed him on his mother's chest as Opal stared down at him in awe.

'Oh, Matthew . . . just *look* at him,' she breathed. 'He's so perfect!'

'He certainly is, just like his mother,' Matthew answered in a choked voice as he stared with pride at his brand-new son. He was indeed a handsome little chap and Opal could hardly believe that she and Matthew had made something so perfect.

Suddenly Opal gasped and tightened her grip on her new son, as a pain ripped through her. She groaned and stared at the midwife in alarm.

'What's happening?' she gasped.

The midwife hurried over and grunted in surprise as she examined Opal.

'Is everything all right?' Matthew asked anxiously.

'Well . . . it all depends what you mean by all right,' the woman answered, as she rolled her sleeves up again. 'But I think she'd better hand the baby back to the nurse, because if I'm not very much mistaken his lordship is going to have a brother or sister any minute now!'

'*What!*' Matthew's eyes had opened so wide with shock that they looked as if they were about to pop out of his head. 'You mean you think there's still another one to come?'

The midwife nodded. 'I've no doubt about it,' she agreed, as Opal let out a long moan of pain.

The second baby, a little girl who was the image of her father, was delivered fifteen minutes later, and Matthew looked as if he was about to burst with pride.

As Opal was to tell Matthew later that day, 'After having the first one it was like shelling peas – well almost,' she added with a little grimace as she sat up.

'*Twins!*' he kept saying disbelievingly as he stared at them tucked into their mother's arms.

Opal giggled weakly. 'It's a good job I bought plenty of baby clothes, isn't it?'

'It wouldn't have mattered if you hadn't, they'll never go without anything,' her proud husband assured her.

After the delivery, the nurse had had to almost crowbar him from the room while they saw to Opal and now that he was back beside her, he didn't intend to leave anytime soon. In fact, he felt as if he could have stared at his brand-new family all day long.

'Have you let Susie and Charlie know about the babies?' Opal asked after a time and he nodded.

'Oh yes, I sent notes to both of them immediately after the births, so I wouldn't be surprised if they descended on us any time now. But you don't have to see anyone, if you don't feel up to it yet. I don't want you tiring yourself any more than you already are.'

Opal grinned. There was a glow about her, and she knew that she would remember this special time for as long as she lived.

'I wonder what their cousin will make of them?' she mused, as she stared down at the tiny faces. Charlie and Francesca had had a little girl, Florence, the year before, and they doted on her. 'And what about names?' she asked. 'Have you any preferences?'

'I quite like Albert for a little boy; we could call him Bertie. What do you think?'

'I love it,' she assured him with all the love she felt for him shining from her eyes. 'And what about Beatrice for our little girl? It's Mrs King's middle name. They can be known as Bertie and Bea then?'

'Perfect!' He sighed with satisfaction, but there was no time to say more, for at that moment there was a commotion on the landing and a flush-faced maid appeared, saying, 'I'm so sorry, ma'am. They wouldn't give me time to announce them but insisted on seeing you right—' Her words were cut short as Charlie gently elbowed her out of the way and charged towards the bed, Francesca with little Florence in her arms close behind him.

'*Twins!* Well done, sis.' He laughed as he stared down at his brand-new niece and nephew. 'And I have to say they're a lot prettier than our little Flo here was when she first put in an appearance. She was a right wrinkled little screwed-up thing. Though she's a picture now,' he added hastily as Francesca glared at him. 'But where's our Susie?'

486

'She's at the bookshop,' Matthew told him and Charlie chuckled. Susie had started to work part-time at a book-shop in Oxford Street, because she said she got bored with nothing to do at home all day – but she hadn't fooled any of them. They had all suspected that her desire to work had everything to do with the young man who owned the shop, and they had not been surprised when he and Susie had announced their engagement only the month before.

They all billed and cooed over the babies for a time, but then Opal's face became sad as she muttered, 'Isn't it sad that Mrs King didn't live to see the babies? She would have loved them.'

'Ah, but wherever she is she *will* see them,' Francesca said stoutly.

Mrs King had died peacefully in her sleep the year before, and as promised she had left the house and everything she possessed to Opal. Eventually she and Matthew had decided to keep the house open, and they now spent a few months each year there so that Opal could spend time with Christopher, who was now apprenticed to a carpenter in the town and loving every minute of it. He and his parents had moved into the house at Opal's request as the old cook had wished to retire, and Eve's mother had been only too happy to take her place. Eve's mother had also proved to be a great help with Eve and Will's two mischievous little sons, so all in all everything had worked out well and Opal couldn't have felt more contented.

'Just think, when Susie gets married in November, we will have had a death, a birth and a marriage all within the year,' Opal said quietly and they all nodded in agreement.

'It is the circle of life, let's drink to it,' Francesca suggested and, lifting a glass of champagne each from the silver tray the maid had delivered to the room shortly before, they all solemnly raised their glasses.

'To the circle of life, and to little Bertie and Bea – may they grow in love and strength.' Matthew led the toast and, as they all solemnly sipped from their crystal glasses, Opal looked around at the beloved faces gathered about the bed, feeling truly blessed. Seconds later Susie burst into the room like a ray of sunshine, her face alight.

'I thought it was a joke when I got the message that you'd had *two* babies!' She laughed, staring from one to the other of them with a wide smile on her face. The nurse Matthew had employed stood patiently aside for a time to give the family time to bill and coo over the new arrivals, but then she told them sternly, 'That's enough for now, if you please. The new mother must have her rest.'

Everyone reluctantly trooped from the room with promises to be back very soon, leaving Matthew alone with his wife. He kissed her soundly as he told her, 'Well done, my darling. I think you've made me the happiest man on earth! And while you have a well-deserved sleep, I'm going to go out and buy another crib.'

Opal stared up at him adoringly, her face aglow. At present the twins were tucked into the one crib they had bought and they looked so perfect lying there that just looking at them brought a lump to her throat.

She nodded as the nurse swished the curtains tightly together and tucked the blankets about her. 'Now you have a little nap and get your strength back, and when you wake up, I'll have a nice cup of tea ready for you,' she promised as she too left the room.

Opal sighed contentedly as she stared at the twins, and her mind drifted back in time. She felt so at peace that she could even find it in her heart to finally forgive Henry – for after all, had she never met him, she would never have met Mrs King or her Matthew. And then she thought of her parents and Mrs King. How she wished they could be here to see the new arrivals . . . but, perhaps they were?

She smiled contentedly and reaching out she tenderly stroked the tiny faces of her babies as a feeling of pure love coursed through her. She certainly hadn't done badly for herself for a girl from Rapper's Hole, she decided. In fact, she was sure she was the luckiest woman in the whole world, and from now on things would get even better, because she was where she was meant to be at last.

Acknowledgements

First as always I'd like to say a huge thank you to 'The Rosie Team' at Zaffre! To Sarah, Katie, Kate Parkin, Ellen, Felice and all the rest of the team who have worked with me on this the first of my brand-new series. I feel blessed to have you all.

Also special thanks to Gillian Holmes, my wonderful copy-editor, and to my lovely agent, the remarkable Sheila Crowley, for your all your support and encouragement.

Not forgetting my long-suffering family who are used to me disappearing off to the computer at the drop of a hat when a new idea occurs – and of course, my wonderful readers!

Welcome to the world of Rosie Goodwin!

Keep reading for more from Rosie Goodwin, to discover a recipe that features in this novel and to find out more about Rosie Goodwin's next book . . .

We'd also like to welcome you to Memory Lane, a place to discuss the very best saga stories from authors you know and love with other readers, plus get recommendations for new books we think you'll enjoy. Read on and join our club!

www.MemoryLane.Club

f /MemoryLaneClub

Dear Readers,

Here we are again with yet another Christmas behind us, and what a Christmas it's been, what with all the lockdowns and regulations due to this awful pandemic. Still we've all been in the same boat and I suppose like me you've all had to make the best of it and just be grateful that we're still here. I must admit I couldn't help but think of all the people who have been affected by the virus over the holidays. What a dreadful time it must have been for them and my heart goes out to each and every one who has lost family or friends.

Still, on a happier note, here we are in a brand-new year, let's hope it's better than the last one! And also, it's time for the release of the paperback of *The Winter Promise*. A lot of you have been in touch to say you were looking forward to it so I hope you'll enjoy it.

I must admit, after the huge success of my Days of the Week collection, I was a little nervous about how you would all find the first of my new Precious Stones series, but I needn't have worried. Thank you all so much for your support. The reviews you have left for it on Memory Lane and Amazon are amazing and I'm so relieved you are enjoying it! As usual I gave poor Opal a hard time but you all seemed to like the book.

Now I am looking forward to the release of *An Orphan's Journey*, which will be out next month. In this one you will meet Pearl, and like Opal she'll have a hard journey to travel. The book after that will centre on the character of Ruby (title yet to be decided!) and that one will be out later in the year.

So, as you'll see, I haven't been idle during lockdown – if anything I think I've spent even more time writing than I usually do as I haven't been able to get out in the garden as much. It can be very therapeutic because when you're writing you can't think of anything but the characters you're creating, and it takes your mind off what's happening in the world. None of us knows what will happen this year and all we can do is hope that the virus is brought under control.

I'd like to thank all my team at Zaffre for the hard work they've done keeping all the publications on track! It hasn't been easy for them as they're having to work from home. We've all had to adapt slightly to the way we normally work, but somehow they've done it, so a massive well done to them from me.

It's been lovely to see so many of you joining the Memory Lane Facebook page and newsletter, where you can see what myself and all the other authors are up to. There are some lovely prizes to be won, too, so if you haven't already joined up, please do. And of course,

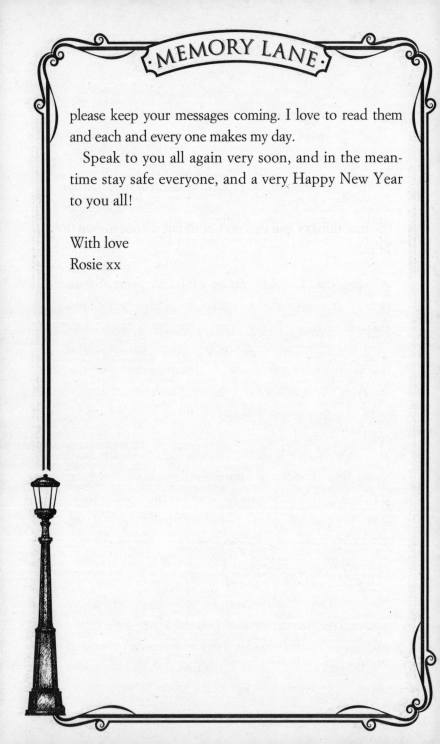

please keep your messages coming. I love to read them and each and every one makes my day.

Speak to you all again very soon, and in the meantime stay safe everyone, and a very Happy New Year to you all!

With love
Rosie xx

French Onion Soup

French onion soup is a traditional dish popular in France since at least the eighteenth century. It is one of the first things Opal eats on her ill-fated honeymoon in France.

You will need:
6 tbsp olive oil
6 large onions, peeled and thinly sliced in strips
50g butter
1 tsp of sugar
½ tsp salt
2 cloves garlic, chopped finely
2 tbsp plain flour
250ml white wine
1.3l beef stock
½ tsp thyme, or mixed herbs
½ tsp black pepper
8 slices baguette, cut into 2cm slices
150g Gruyere cheese, grated

Method:

1. Heat 4 tbsp of oil on a medium heat, then add in the onions. Fry them with the lid on, stirring regularly, for 15 minutes.

2. Increase the heat, add in the butter, and cook the onions for another 10 minutes, stirring regularly.

3. Sprinkle the onions with sugar and salt and cook for another 15 minutes, until the onions are browned.

4. Then add the garlic, and cook for another few minutes.

5. Sprinkle with the flour and stir in thoroughly.

6. Pour the wine into the pot and stir. Then, increasing the heat, add in the stock and seasoning

7. Put the lid on, and cook on a low heat for 20 minutes.

8. While the soup is cooking, line a baking tray with parchment and preheat the grill to 250°C.

9. Brush both sides of the slices of baguette with olive oil, then toast under the grill until lightly browned.

10. Turn the bread over and sprinkle with Gruyere cheese. Then grill until the cheese is bubbling.

11. To serve, ladle the soup into bowls, then place a slice of toasted baguette on the top of each.

12. Enjoy!

Read on to learn more about Rosie Goodwin's other
books, and for a sneak peek of her next novel,
An Orphan's Journey . . .

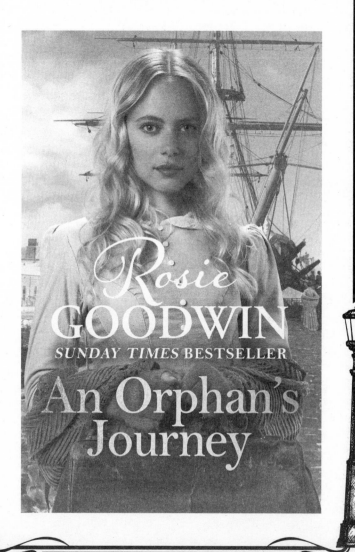

Prologue

December 1874

'Come on, girl, your dad will be home wi' no dinner on the table if yer don't get a shifty on, an' yer know what that means!'

'Yes, Ma.' Pearl renewed her efforts as she struggled to fill the pan of potatoes she was peeling, daring to glance across her shoulder just once at her mother, who was sitting at the side of the dying fire with a glass of cheap gin in her hand.

At twelve years old, Pearl was small for her age, as were all her brothers and sisters. It was no wonder really; both their mother and father spent most of the small amount of money that came into the house on drink. They often all went without food. But at least today they would eat. When the potatoes were softened, Pearl would mash them and smear the stale loaf she had managed to get from the bakers with dripping. It would be a feast, and her mouth watered at the thought of it.

At that moment, Matthew, Pearl's youngest sibling, a baby lying in the drawer on the floor next to her mother's chair, began to whimper. Sighing resignedly, Molly Parker lifted the infant none too gently, roughly yanking aside the dirty blouse she was wearing to allow him to suckle.

He must be practically drinking neat gin, Pearl thought to herself, *it's no wonder he's so sickly* – but she wouldn't dare voice her thoughts. Her mother might be small, but she could certainly pack a punch, which accounted for the many bruises that covered poor Pearl's arms and legs.

Molly Parker was only twenty-eight years old, and while she had once been pretty, the hard life she had led, lack of good food and the countless beatings she had received from her husband, meant that now she could easily have been taken for a woman in her fifties. She had married her husband, Fred, just over twelve years ago and Pearl had been born shortly after. Fred had promised her the world, but all she had to show for their marriage were the two downstairs rooms in a slum terrace house in a courtyard in Whitechapel that led down to the docks, which they shared with two other families, cockroaches and a legion of rats. From then on, the children had come one a year with frightening regularity – although not all of them had survived – and now, with all her dreams knocked out of her, Molly found her only solace lay in the bottom of a bottle of gin.

Ten minutes later, the potatoes were peeled and, after adding salt to the water, Pearl crossed the room to place them in over the dying fire, hoping they would cook through before it went out altogether. Yet again the coal store was empty, and if her father hadn't got work on the docks today, they would all face yet another cold night.

As she crossed to the fire, she stumbled and some of the water in the pan sloshed across the hard-packed earth floor, causing her mother to growl.

'Mind what yer doin', you useless little sod. Yer neither use nor ornament, why did I have to 'ave a cripple, eh?'

Thankfully the infant in her arms stopped her from being able to lash out, but even so it didn't stop the flood of colour that poured into Pearl's cheeks. With her shock of blonde curls and her striking blue eyes she was a pretty little thing, or so people said, but she had been born with one leg slightly shorter than the other which made her walk ungainly – and her mother never let her forget it.

'Right, now get this place tidied up a bit,' her mother barked, once the potatoes were safely hanging above the flames.

Pearl nodded, although as she looked about the tiny room, she didn't quite know where to start. Her brothers and sisters sat lethargically about on the bare floor, propped up against the walls, scratching at the lice in their hair, looking pale and wan. Pearl gave them an affectionate smile as she lifted a broom to start sweeping the floor.

But then, her mother remembered something and started, she said, somewhat fearfully, 'Oh Lordie, I just remembered. It's rent day. You'll 'ave to get 'em all out o' the way till the rent man's been an' gone. I can't pay him, so we'll have to pretend no one's home. That won't work if he hears any o' this lot. Go on, away wi' yer, an' pull the curtains to afore yer go!'

'But Ma, it's freezing out there. Davey an' Maggie have got a hackin' cough already an' they ain't got any shoes,' Pearl said worriedly, as she stared towards the grimy window.

'Wrap a bit o' that sackin' about their feet,' Molly ordered, pointing to the old sack that had held the last of the potatoes.

'But where can I take 'em in this weather?'

Molly's face hardened. 'Can't you think of anything for yerself? Take 'em up town an' let 'em look in the shop winders,' she ordered. 'They'll like that. They'll be all decked out fer Christmas now. Now get a move on and less o' your backchat or you'll be feelin' me foot up yer arse!'

Pearl quickly wrapped the children in anything she could lay her hands on, including tying some torn sacking around their feet; then she herded them all towards the door.

As usual, there was no sign of her other sister, Eliza. Once again, she had gone on one of her many walkabouts, so all Pearl could do was hope that she didn't turn up at the house at the same time as the rent man. Once they were outside, Pearl quickly shepherded her siblings through the twisting alleys that led to the docks, telling them encouragingly, 'We'll take a look at the ships first, shall we? You'll like that.'

None of her siblings looked very enthusiastic and Pearl couldn't blame them, but she fixed a smile to her face and urged them along until they came eventually to the docks. There were ships of all shapes and sizes bobbing at anchor. Some were being unloaded of their cargo, others were being loaded, and burly seamen darted about everywhere they looked. There were also a number of ladies with pockmarked, painted faces wearing revealing, low-cut dresses, standing against the walls, hoping to entice the seamen who had just returned from long journeys to part with some of their hard-earned wages.

Three-year-old Davey was whimpering with the cold by then, so after a time Pearl led them towards the city centre.

'I's 'ungry, Pearl,' nine-year-old Amy told her sister gravely, and Pearl squeezed her hand reassuringly.

'Never mind, pet. Mr Grimley will have been an' gone soon an' then we can go home an' get you all some dinner,' Pearl told her sister, trying to ignore her own rumbling stomach.

Mr Grimley was the rent man and much dreaded by his tenants. As Lil, the woman who lived in the floor above them, had once commented to Molly, 'I reckon that man 'as got a swingin' brick fer a heart. He chucked the Freemans out on the bloody street in the snow last year 'cos they couldn't pay the rent, but how were they supposed to when Bill Freeman had broke his leg unpackin' cargo at the docks? The poor sods promised him they'd catch up just as soon as ever Bill got back to work, but he wouldn't have a bar of it an' out they went, wi' her ready to drop her babby any minute an' another two little 'uns not even out o' bindin's.'

Pearl shuddered as she remembered, and prayed that the same fate would not befall their family.

Minutes later, they came to a main road, and as they all strolled along, the children gazed in awe at the smartly dressed people walking to and fro. The women wore fur stoles or thick capes and pretty bonnets, while the men sported top hats and heavy great coats.

'Is they rich, our Pearl?' eight-year-old Tom asked, and Pearl smiled dreamily, trying to imagine how it would feel to be dressed in such fine clothes.

'I suppose they must be – but look at this window 'ere.'

They all stopped as one to stare at a display of toys. There were wind-up train sets, dolls with pretty china faces and all manner of things to catch the young ones' attention.

'It must be nice to be rich,' Tom commented enviously, and the little sea of pale faces crowded about Pearl's dull brown skirt all nodded in agreement.

They were still standing there gazing into the window when a smartly dressed lady carrying a number of loaded shopping bags paused to smile at them. She was wearing a thick navy woollen cape that had a collar trimmed with fur and a beautiful bonnet with feathers that bobbed and danced in the breeze.

'Are you hoping for Father Christmas to bring some of them to you?' she asked kindly, but they all shook their heads in unison.

'Nah! Christmas Day is just anuvver day to us, we won't get nowt,' Tom told her sadly.

The smile slid from the woman's face and seconds later she rummaged in her purse and produced a shiny silver sixpence which she held out to them.

Pearl frowned. They might be poor, but she still had her pride and would have refused it – but before she could utter a word, Tom's hand had snaked out and grabbed it.

'Fanks, missus!'

'You're very welcome. Why don't you go to the cart at the end of the road and get yourselves a nice plate of hot faggots and peas? It'll warm you all up.'

And then, without another word, she hurried on her way, feeling that she had done her good deed for the day.

'Can we?' the children piped up, as the kind lady was swallowed up by the crowd. Their mouths were watering in anticipation and Pearl didn't have the heart to refuse them.

'Well … it is nearly Christmas, so I s'ppose we could,' she answered uncertainly. Usually when their mother sent them out begging they had to tip anything they were given up to her, but then it was only spent on drink, as Pearl knew only too well, and the children had precious few treats.

Ten minutes later, they all sat on the wall surrounding a frozen fountain, tucking into their feast, and Pearl couldn't help but smile to see them all looking so happy. But all too soon they had licked the plates clean and it was time to move on.

As they continued along the street, admiring the displays in the shop window, feather-soft flakes of snow began to fall, and Amy started to whimper again. 'I can't feel me 'ands, Pearl. They've all gone blue. Can we go 'ome now?'

'Nor me,' Davey piped up.

Taking her thin shawl from about her shoulders, Pearl wrapped it about him. The snow was coming down thicker now and within seconds Pearl's thin shoulders were soaked to the skin and her teeth were chattering as she led the children back the way they had come.

Whether Mr Grimley had called or not, she couldn't keep them out in such weather any longer.

They had only just turned into the grim courtyard that led to their home when their mother's raised voice came to them.

'So, where the bleedin' 'ell 'ave yer been all day if yer didn't get taken on to work?'

'In The Mermaid!' they heard her father's voice sullenly answer her.

'Oh ar! An' what did yer use fer money then? It's funny that yer can find money fer drink yet I have to 'ide from the bleedin' rent man!'

'The landlord put it on the slate fer me, so now stop naggin' woman, else you'll feel the back o' me 'and!'

'That's it, yer cowardly bastard, 'it a woman,' their mother screeched. 'But think on afore yer do, 'cos I may as well tell yer there'll be another bleedin' mouth to feed in a few months' time!'

As they tentatively approached the door, they heard their father groan. 'Oh *no*! You are kiddin' me, ain' yer? That one there is only five months old, fer God's sake. The way yer turnin' 'em out, we won't be able to move in 'ere soon. An' there's only Pearl who's old enough to work as yet – not that anyone 'ud want 'er wi' that gammy leg of 'er's.'

'Well if yer didn't keep demandin' yer rights when yer come in pissed up of a night, there wouldn't *be* another on the way would there?' they heard their mother scream back. 'An' it's 'ardly my fault that Pearl's a cripple, is it?'

They heard a dull thud then and the sound of something overturning followed by a sob from their mother.

'Dad's hittin' Ma again,' Tom whispered fearfully, and he shrank into Pearl's side.

She was already smarting from what she had just overheard, but some of the smaller children were crying now and she urged them ahead of her, keen to get them out of the biting cold.

'Don't worry. He'll fall asleep in a minute. He allus does when he's had a drink,' she soothed.

Sure enough, when they entered the kitchen seconds later, they saw that their father had stormed off into the other room that served as a bedroom, and their mother sat crying on the floor.

'Lousy swine. He'll 'it me once too often an' I'll swing fer 'im one o' these days, you just see if I don't,' she muttered, as Pearl helped her up.

The children had all huddled together on the floor in one corner for warmth, and after flashing them a reassuring smile, Pearl went and lifted the pan of potatoes from the fire and carried it across to the large wooden draining board that stood next to the deep stone sink. Unfortunately, their mother had let them boil dry and some of them had stuck to the bottom of the pan, but thankfully she was able to salvage most of them. Not that the children were hungry for once, but she wouldn't tell her mother that.

It was six o' clock before their father emerged from the bedroom to ask blearily, 'What's fer dinner then? I'm starvin'!'

Molly glared at him, but remained silent as Pearl carried a plate of cold mash and bread with dripping across to him at the old rickety table. 'I'm sorry it's cold but the fire's gone out an' we're out o' coal, so I had no way o' keepin' it warm fer you.'

Some of the younger children had already drifted off to sleep on the itchy hay mattresses that were spread along one wall, but the older ones sat silently, afraid of drawing attention to themselves.

He fell on the food like a man who hadn't eaten for a month, before he rose and snatched his coat from the back of the door. The only light in the room now was from a cheap tallow candle on the table, and they stared back at him fearfully.

'You lots is goin' to 'ave to pull yer socks up if yer wanna eat,' he growled. 'So, first thing in the mornin' I want yer out on the main streets beggin'. All the toffs will be doin' their Christmas shoppin' this week an' they'll no doubt dig deep in their pockets . . . Do you 'ear me?'

'Yes, Dad!' they all said together and, satisfied, he stormed from the room, slamming the door behind him.

Eventually they all fell asleep, until there was only Molly and Pearl left awake and it was then that Pearl dared to ask, 'Did I hear yer aright, Ma? That yer goin' to 'ave another baby?'

Molly hugged herself as she rocked back and forth and nodded dejectedly. Pearl felt a stab of pity for her. The gin bottle was empty now, and the thump she had received from their father had caused a large purple bruise to form across her chin and right cheek.

'Don't worry, we'll manage some'ow.' She reached out to stroke her mother's arm and, in a rare affection-ate gesture, Molly patted her hand.

It was only when Pearl had gone to bed and Molly sat alone, listening to the tick of the tin clock on the mantelpiece that she considered a suggestion Lil from upstairs had put to her the week before. At the time it had seemed so preposterous that Molly had waved it aside, but now she was at the end of her tether and she knew that she must give it some serios consideration. She knew she couldn't go on like this.

The very next morning, just as their father had insisted, the younger children were sent begging and once they had gone Molly told Pearl, 'Go an' collect yer things together, girl. Yer goin' on a little holiday.'

'What?' Pearl's mouth gaped with surprise as Molly gulped and squirmed uncomfortably.

'Well, the thing is, as yer already know there's gonna be another mouth 'ere to feed soon, so . . .' She patted her flabby stomach and forced herself to go on. 'Lil told me about a scheme they've got goin' wi' the work'ouse an' the orphanages. See, it seems that some o' the older kids in them places are bein' transported abroad. Just think o' that, a life in the sunshine. No more cold or snow.'

Secretly, Molly very much doubted that Pearl would be chosen to go with her lame leg, but even if she wasn't, she would at least be assured of a good meal each day and it would be one less mouth to feed and worry about.

It was usual for the people thereabouts to send the younger children away to such places if things got too desperate, for the older ones could normally be sent out to earn a wage, but there was little chance of Pearl doing that and the younger ones could earn more by begging. People had more sympathy for smaller children. She was only sorry that Eliza, the girl next to Pearl in age, who was simple in the head, wasn't there too, she could have gone with her, but as usual she had wandered off early this morning.

Pearl was so shocked that she couldn't even answer for a moment, but eventually she found her voice to ask, 'An' what happens to the kids when they get there?'

'Apparently the settlers take 'em into their homes to help wi' the chores. I'm sure you'd soon find a place 'cos you can cook an' clean along wi' the best o' them. An' they have schools there an' all. Yer could learn to read an' write. You've always wanted to, ain't yer?'

Pearl was so stunned when she realised that her mother meant it that she was rendered temporarily speechless. This had come like a bolt from the blue, but eventually she blurted out, 'But I don't *want* to go away . . . this is my 'ome an' yer all me family!' Tears started to roll down her cheeks. It might not have ever been the best of homes, but it was the only one she had ever known and the thought of leaving it was terrifying.

But Molly's mind was made up. 'It'll be fer the best,' she said gravely, guiltily looking away from the stricken

look on her daughter's face. 'You'll get the start there that yer'd never get 'ere, an' one day yer can come back an' see us all again, so go an' get your stuff together an' I'll have no more arguin'.'

Somehow Pearl managed to do as she was told, despite the fact that she was blinded by tears. In truth there was very little to collect, and soon after she carried her small bundle to her mother, who had wrapped a shawl around her shoulders, ready to leave. Lil upstairs had taken the baby for now.

'B-but surely you ain't takin' me there *now*?' Pearl was panicking. 'I ain't even 'ad time to say goodbye to everyone, an' it'll be Christmas in a few days' time. *Surely* it can wait till after then?'

'It's better this way.' Molly stroked a tear from her first-born daughter's cheek with her thumb. 'Come on, let's get it over wi'.'

And before Pearl knew it, they were striding through the fast-falling snow towards the workhouse and Pearl's new life.

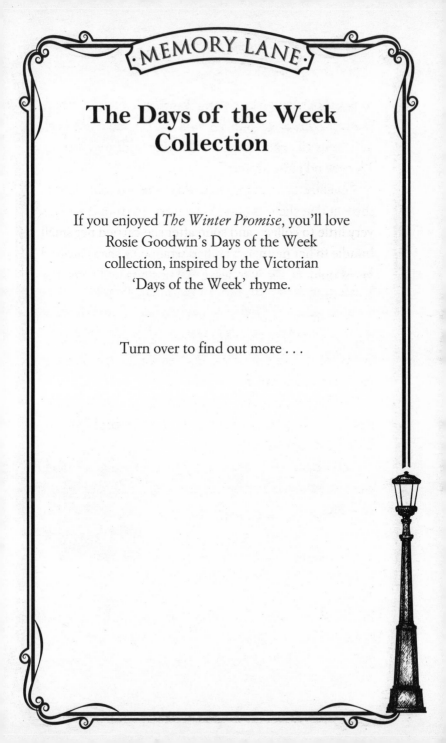

·MEMORY LANE·

The Days of the Week Collection

If you enjoyed *The Winter Promise*, you'll love
Rosie Goodwin's Days of the Week
collection, inspired by the Victorian
'Days of the Week' rhyme.

Turn over to find out more . . .

Mothering Sunday

The child born on the Sabbath Day,
Is bonny and blithe, and good and gay.

1884, Nuneaton.

Fourteen-year-old Sunday has grown up in the cruelty of the Nuneaton workhouse. When she finally strikes out on her own, she is determined to return for those she left behind, and to find the long-lost mother who gave her away. But she's about to discover that the brutal world of the workhouse will not let her go without a fight.

The Little Angel

Monday's child is fair of face.

1896, Nuneaton.

Left on the doorstep of Treetops Children's Home, young Kitty captures the heart of her guardian, Sunday Branning, and grows into a beguiling and favoured young girl – until she is summoned to live with her birth mother. In London, nothing is what it seems, and her old home begins to feel very far away. If Kitty is to have any chance of happiness, this little angel must protect herself from devils in disguise . . . and before it's too late.

A Mother's Grace

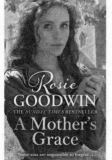

Tuesday's child is full of grace.

1910, Nuneaton.

When her father's threatening behaviour grows worse, pious young Grace Kettle escapes her home to train to be a nun. But when she meets the dashing and devout Father Luke, her world is turned upside down. She is driven to make a scandalous choice – one she may well spend the rest of her days seeking forgiveness for.

The Blessed Child

Wednesday's child is full of woe.

1864, Nuneaton.

After Nessie Carson's mother is brutally murdered and her father abandons them, Nessie knows she will do anything to keep her family safe. As her fragile young brother's health deteriorates and she attracts the attention of her lecherous landlord, soon Nessie finds herself in the darkest of times. But there is light and the promise of happiness if only she is brave enough to fight for it.

A Maiden's Voyage

Thursday's child has far to go.

1912, London.

Eighteen-year-old maid Flora Butler has her life turned upside-down when her mistress's father dies in a tragic accident. Her mistress is forced to move to New York to live with her aunt until she comes of age, and begs Flora to go with her. Flora has never left the country before, and now faces a difficult decision – give up her position, or leave her family behind. Soon, Flora and her mistress head for Southampton to board the RMS *Titanic*.

A Precious Gift

Friday's child is loving and giving.

1911, Nuneaton.

When Holly Farthing's overbearing grandfather tries to force her to marry a widower twice her age, she flees to London, bringing her best friend and maid, Ivy, with her. In the big smoke, Holly begins nurse training in the local hospital. There she meets the dashing Doctor Parkin, everything Holly has ever dreamt of. But soon, she discovers some shocking news that means they can never be together, and her life is suddenly thrown into turmoil. Supporting the war effort, she heads to France and throws herself into volunteering on the front line . . .

Time to Say Goodbye

Saturday's child works hard for their living.

1935, Nuneaton.

Kathy has grown up at Treetops home for children, where Sunday and Tom Branning have always cared for her as one of their own. With her foster sister Livvy at her side, and a future as a nurse ahead of her, she could wish for nothing more. But when Tom dies suddenly in a riding accident, life at Treetops will never be the same again. As their financial difficulties mount, will the women of Treetops be forced to leave their home?

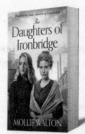

Rosie Goodwin
Britain's best-loved saga author

'Rosie's books take you to the heart of her stories. Every chapter is
like talking to an old friend'
Nuala

'A wonderful story of loss, hardship, love and hope [that] once again
brings all the emotions imaginable . . . Another beautiful,
heartrending and, at the same time, heartwarming tale'
Nona

'Rosie's characters are so lifelike, it feels as if we're right there
beside them as they live their lives'
Bryony

'I have read every single one of Rosie's books. She never disappoints'
Jean

'I absolutely loved the Days of the Week series and *The Blessed
Child* was one of my all-time favourites'
Heather

'So emotional and heartfelt. I truly adored it'

'I haven't enjoyed reading a book this much in a long, long time'

'Rosie is such a clever, talented writer'

'I was gripped from page one to the end'

'Rosie Goodwin is a great storyteller who pulls you into the lives
of her characters, sharing their trials and tribulations'

'I'd give this book ten stars if I could'

Reader reviews of Rosie Goodwin's novels

·MEMORY LANE·

Introducing the place for story lovers – a welcoming home for all readers who love heartwarming tales of wartime, family and romance. Join us to discuss your favourite stories with other readers, plus get book recommendations, book giveaways and behind-the-scenes writing moments from your favourite authors.

·MEMORY LANE·

Newport Community
Learning & Libraries

www.MemoryLane.Club

f /MemoryLaneClub